The Girl Who Talked With Trees

Julie Martinmaas

Photographs courtesy of Steven Jaccard Photography

First Edition

ISBN: 978-1-7340232-0-6

Acknowledgements

I've been blessed with copious amounts of support from my friends and family while writing The Girl Who Talked With Trees, and I am forever grateful. I thank each one of you. The list is long, so know I hold you in my heart, with gratitude.

Cancer is a big subject to tackle. It's life-altering for the one diagnosed as well as the friends and family who love the one receiving the diagnosis. I was processing my personal denial, anger, grief, belief systems, and God, not to mention my ego as I wrote this. A fictional story was not the book I set out to write, and not one I intended to share. It started as a way to journal my conflicting emotions during a time my husband was deployed in Afghanistan (for the second time), and I was already feeling fragile and alone. Then one day, as I sat with my mom in an emergency room, hearing the word cancer firsthand with her, I went into "mode" as they say. I was purely analytical—a taskmaster. During this time, I negotiated my way through a tumultuous relationship with my mother, as she made her peace with cancer and her life.

Cancer reared its ugly head once again the day my sister heard her diagnosis. Ours is not a tumultuous relationship that she and I share. This was my person who always had my back—I often would feel quite helpless to do anything but watch her fight her fight. I witnessed her persevere and rise like a phoenix from the flame, victorious, as she claimed her new power. Watching her grace, determination, and clear vision was a miracle to behold.

One day during all of these jumbled events, I was challenged to write a book as a way to vent and heal. I laughed at the thought. I've only written flowery sentiments in birthday cards, after all. Then I sat down at the computer. Long story short (forgive the pun), this story demanded to be released into the world, and I agreed to be its muse. Perhaps this experience is for further healing of my own soul, or to soothe and walk the path with someone else experiencing cancer—or both. Maybe I will never know.

With that in mind—first, last, and always, this book would absolutely not be a reality without my husband and my son.

Dave, you've gone above and beyond with your endless and tireless edits, formative feedback, tough love, cheerleading, and space for me to do what I was called to do. Your enthusiasm coaxed me through this crazy learning processes. The entire time, I felt loved, supported, and encouraged, even when I doubted my work. Your willingness to read, reread and then reread again, never showing anything other than curiosity and desire to see a proper story told through the eyes of the characters, buoyed my heart and confidence. What an amazing time I've had collaborating with you! I spent many hours in my office, and you never once complained. I treasure our long walks through the park amongst the trees brainstorming. Thank you for dreaming and exploring life with me.

Steven, Holy Moly! Where do I start with you? The moment you heard I was going to try my hand at this writing thing, you jumped on my bandwagon, supporting my lofty bucket-list dream. Not only did you accept this wild new phase I surprised everyone with, but you also gifted me a beautiful leather journal with a tree embossed on its cover. It was my inspiration then, and again during the middle of this story. You set me up with a computer program to make my journey more manageable and streamlined, and when I wanted to quit, you reminded me why that was not an option. You were the technical, creative, and logical human handling all the behind the scenes drama for me, right down to photographing and creating the book cover I envisioned. Thank you does not come close to the love, gratitude, and appreciation I have for you and your support. Continue to dream big and cultivate the creativity in your soul that lives up to your destiny. You are an extraordinary human.

Kathleen, my soul sister, a partner in crime, friend, reader of my first few jumbled drafts! Thank you for everything. Thank you for sharing your thoughts, insights, never-ending support, and feedback in the early stages of my manuscript, and coming to my rescue at the end. I won't put into words here what you already know to be true, but you inspire me to stay curious, joyful, and willing to surrender fully to this crazy journey.

Tom, reader of my second, nails on the chalkboard, manuscript. I am grateful for all your kind and sage counsel. Our interaction taught me so much early on and challenged me to grow. Thank you, Maureen, for your friendship and paving the way for new understanding to develop.

Amber, my third manuscript reader. Thank you for sharing your creative talents with me, sweet one! I value and treasure the time, thoughtfulness, earnest input you generously gave me. You are forever a gift in my heart and life. I cannot wait to read what you write in the coming years! You inspire me.

Chris, my sounding board, and friend. Thank you. From day one, you have graciously taken me under your wing when it comes to this complex writing gig. It's interesting and quite serendipitous that we met on the night of my sister's very last chemotherapy treatment. Life is crazy.

Margaret, thank you for sharing your intuitive insights with me. It was you who suggested I consider writing a fictional story. Years earlier, you predicted I'd reunite and play a role in my mother's life. I thought it insane at the time, but boy did you prove me wrong. Blessings, dear light.

Louisa, my mentor on many levels, during this life and beyond. Thank you for your medical input, your encouragement, and taking time to meet with me while you journeyed through cancer. Although you aren't physically here to read the final draft, I felt your presence as I wrote and edited. You once asked me, years before I ever decide to write The Girl Who Talked With Trees, "Julie, what kind of tree would you be?" I replied I'd like to be an oak. When I asked you the same question, you replied you would like to be an apple tree, because of the fruit it gives back. Ahh, dear one, you were and are an apple tree, and you continue to give back to the world and those whose lives you've touched!

Kait, you old soul! Another unexpected surprise in life. Thank you for your friendship and encouragement along this long road.

Sue and Judith, thank you for your professional insights, directions, and feedback. I gained a lot from working with you both.

To those of you who are in the deep rivers of this cancer journey, I am in awe of your strength, courage, and humanity. I am painfully aware of how cancer is a part of your lives every moment of every day. I hope you do not feel my story minimizes you or your personal journey.

×

For Karen, my big, bold, brave, larger than life super hero of a cancer thriver, kick ass sister!

To Mom—I understand now.

"Someday you will be old enough to start reading fairy tales again."

-C. S.Lewis

Prologue

The Ancient Ones

Through the ages, the trees and those with open hearts have shared a strong, sacred bond. This is their story.

The Priestess and Ferax

The High Priestess walked barefoot in her sapphire tunic, down a familiar path. A bright amber torch glowed in her left hand, a red ribbon with a single gold strand down the center fluttered in her right. Pillowy clouds drifted across the moon. A white calf, her faithful companion, a beast with soulful dark eyes, ambled quietly by her side. The Priestess walked in two worlds at the same time—the seen and the unseen. She was many wondrous things to the people of her tribe. She was their physician, the keeper of the sacred mysteries, and a gifted way-seer.

As the Priestess traveled through the quiet village in the Kingdom of Eire, she repeated a lilting chant-like prayer, then paused momentarily as she reached her destination. Raising her face to the sky, she whispered into the wind as her silver belt sparkled around her hips. An older woman opened the door to a thatched roof home and welcomed the Priestess into the small dwelling. The Priestess nodded her head in greeting, and after warming herself by the stone hearth, she walked to the birthing bed.

"My daughter, your time has come," The Priestess said as she gently wiped the brow of the woman about to give birth.

Taking her daughter's hand in hers, the Priestess placed the red ribbon gently in her open palm. Staring at it for the briefest of moments, the younger woman nodded, accepted the token of great importance and closed her hand around the simple strand of material. The strip of fabric was said to be as old as the Moon Goddess and to carry enormous power. By receiving the symbolic ribbon, the Priestess's daughter understood she would raise the new-born to assume great power, privilege, and responsibility. The child, named Ferax, would be trained by the noble Priestess and commit to memory the guarded secrets shared only with a few born of her nobility.

From the Priestess, Ferax would gain the knowledge of how to conduct rituals and blessings, assist those coming into the world as well as those preparing to leave their earthly bodies behind. The Priestess would impress upon Ferax the importance of the seasons and the proper ways and times to harvest crops to ensure their tribe's longevity. Young Ferax would be known to communicate with all things in nature—the wind, the elementals, and spirit guides. It would be the trees Ferax shared her closest bonds with—the trees and the mighty crane who brought messages from near and far as he landed upon the welcoming branches of the oaks, yews, and rowan trees.

Ferax and Ana

Dressed in her ceremonial clothes, Ferax stood in the middle of an ancient oak grove. She burrowed her bare feet into the welcoming ground still damp with fresh morning dew, as if anchoring her roots. She chanted softly while the branches of the yew tree above her swayed in the sun. Ferax appeared ethereal as she leaned down to pet the velvet-like fur of the white calf by her side. Young Ana sat a few feet away, watching in awe as the older woman she cherished most in the world communicated with the beloved animal.

Ana lived on the Isle of Éire and was the sole grandchild of the Priestess, Ferax. Ana's mischievous sea-green eyes perpetually danced with merriment, while her known compassion and good nature made Ana a favorite in her village. The young child was doted upon by Ferax, and Ana loved her grandmother with all her heart.

Priestess Ferax ruled with a gentle and quiet strength in her village—yet was respected by chiefs, tribes, and clans across the land. Sovereigns from far and wide of clashing tribes, would often seek Ferax out to tend to their sick, to look into the fire that would tell their future, as well as to counsel them as they sought out either peace or battle, for her sage counsel was known to be fair and just.

Ana spent her days learning and practicing the customs of their people. "Grandmother, of course, I can remember why we eat this purple berry. It keeps our people healthy. But, sometimes I forget if it is the nettle or the burdock that stops bleeding." Ana worried her lower lip waiting for her grandmother's reply.

"Dear child, there is much to remember, which is why we practice like we do today. The burdock has purple flowers, see?" Ferax said as she bent to pick the plant, digging carefully to make sure she pulled the roots with it.

"Oh yes, I remember this one. We gave some to old Arden just last week. Now his fever is gone, and his hands work better," Ana said.

"Excellent, Ana. Do you remember what we use the roots for?"

Ana reached out her hand, taking the plant with long wood-like roots that Ferax offered. After studying the plant for several moments, Ana shook her head. "No. See, Grandmother, I will never learn all that you know. Promise you will never leave me," the child pleaded.

"Ana, I once said the same words to my grandmother, but she was patient as I learned. You shall learn, just as I did, as time goes on, child."

Ferax continued their walk in silence until Ana stopped and, reached down scooping a handful of fertile brown soil from a nearby tree.

"Grandmother, do you think I will remember about the dirt?"

"Yes, Ana, you will remember. We will practice many times over the years until you have the steps committed to your memory. This will be one of the most important lessons you learn, child. You must carry out every detail I instruct you on, or the ground in the New World will be worthless."

"Grandmother, why is it you will not tell the future priestesses and healers yourself?"

"It is not how it is meant to be, child. The ways in which we live, our customs, our communication, will one day be very different. There are those who wish to extinguish our knowledge. Very dark times will reign for generations. There will be those who think themselves superior, and victorious in suppressing our ways. For some time they will retain power, and all will seem lost. Many will lose hope. This is why you must commit to memory our people's traditions and practices. You know the truth, Ana. You see and work with the reality of all that is. It will be your duty to communicate our ways to future healers and priestesses alike."

"Grandmother, how will the sacred knowledge reach the New World?"

"Oh, that's the fun part Ana! Our friend, the great white messenger crane, Turlough, will travel through time and space to assist in the transfer of knowledge from the unseen to the seen with the help of one his friends—and into the New World Healers hands."

"I don't understand Grandmother," Ana said, biting her lower lip.

"Dear child, there are significant discoveries yet to unfold, but the chosen one in the New World has an open heart. Just as you and I communicate with all of nature, so will she. What she does not understand, the trees and Turlough will explain."

"What if she doesn't hear the oaks and the yews? What if she doesn't believe Turlough, Grandmother?"

"Oh, Ana darling, she shall be very wise and know it in her heart to be true—for just like you, she is a girl who talks with trees."

Ana and Conlaoch

Ana spent many happy years in her grandmother's company, but there were times she thought it impossible to recall all Ferax had taught her.

"Grandmother, I know I've learned much since my childhood, but I admit, I still worry I'll mistakenly give someone hemlock."

Ferax laughed, knowing Ana would never give a member of their tribe the poisonous plant. In a show of affection, Ana reached over to kiss Ferax on the cheek. "I don't know what I would do without you, Grandmother," Ana said with a wry smile.

Ferax took both of Ana's hands in hers, as she gathered her thoughts.

"Those who have passed to the otherworld are still present. You will always have the ability to call upon us child, but seek the counsel of the trees and Turlough, when in doubt. They will speak for those of us who have traveled on past the veil," Ferax told Ana.

Three days later, Ferax passed away peacefully in her sleep.

Even knowing and understanding all she did, Ana was sad. Her world drastically changed, and the young woman was left unprepared for the grief that swept over her. She could never physically hug her grandmother again, or follow her down to the stream to fetch water. The sudden death of Ferax shook the land, but to Ana, it was a cruel and unjust blow to her heart. They would never again hold hands and sit by the hearth sharing stories. Ana had to find a way to accept that things had changed, and she did not want to do this.

Today marked a shift for Ana and her people. On the first day of the winter solstice, they would honor her grandmother's passing to the otherworld, and Ana wrestled with the seeming finality of death. No one in her immediate family had crossed over the veil besides Ferax.

Ana questioned her mother, Nemetona, why the rituals and herbs did not heal her grandmother. Her mother explained that Ferax's journey on this land was complete.

"My daughter, for your grandmother to fulfill her purpose, she understood she must move past the veil to the otherworld, where her soul and her life's work will continue."

"But on to *where* Mother?" Ana pleaded.

"Some things we are not yet to know, my daughter, but it is a place supported by peace and much joy," Nemetona quietly said.

Ana bit her lip and pondered her mother's words. She tried to comprehend this thing called death, and the mystery of not walking the earth but not being gone either. She recalled over the years Ferax aiding those about to pass or saving the lives of others. Ana realized she had not been ready to accept passing as part of life and must have somehow pushed it out of her mind. She did not allow death to touch her happy existence.

"If we know that Ferax is not truly gone, why is it we all cried?" Ana challenged her mother's words.

"It is for ourselves that we cry and mourn. It is not for our beloved Ferax who has crossed over. We long for something familiar, something solid, something that once was. Often, we can no longer physically see, touch, or hear those who have gone to the otherworld, and it appears so final. Daughter, the opportunity never slips away, communication simply changes."

Nemetona continued after the briefest of moments, "In our humanness, we must allow ourselves time to mourn the change in life, but also to celebrate it. Do you understand?"

"I think so, Mother."

"You must now pass this knowledge, and all that Ferax has taught you, to our people.

One day, I too will pass through the veil to the otherworld my daughter, but you are not to fear this. Be sad and mourn if you wish, but do not fear this cycle of life."

Ana's eyes filled with tears. "I understand Mother."

"My daughter, it is time for you to own your power. Trust that you can heal those you are called to heal. Claim the greatness that is your destiny."

Nemetona continued, "It will not always be that you heal every illness you come upon. People are not intended to walk in this world a moment longer than their assigned time. You will offer to heal those whose journey is not yet complete, and one day you will teach others to do the same."

"I understand. Grandmother would often tell me it was important to remember that one day, I would take her place in our community. I just never thought she would be taken from us so soon."

"In time daughter, when your heart has had a chance to heal, perhaps you will smile knowing that Ferax is busy continuing the work she loved and that she is assisting you in your destiny, as much if not more, than she has always lovingly done."

Nemetona took Ana's hand in hers. "You now take the place of Ferax as the Healer of our people."

"I fear I am not ready," Ana replied in a shaky voice, as she worried her lower lip.

The older woman removed a red strip of fabric from her pocket and gently pressed the strand into Ana's waiting hand.

"Ferax will guide you. Surely, she would not have had me give you the ribbon traditionally presented to the woman in a birthing bed. Handing it to you now breaks tradition. It signifies we are shifting closer to the new world prophecy," Nemetoma reassured her daughter, who quietly closed her hand around the simple yet powerful symbolic gesture.

Feeling overwhelmed, Ana called to the ageless white calf who was now to be her companion. As the calf reached the two women, he stood leaning against Ana's side. She gave a gentle pet to his soft coat.

"I think I wish to be alone unless you would like me to stay with you. After all, Ferax was your mother," Ana said as a tear slid down her cheek.

Nemetoma wiped Ana's tear. "My heart is full, for I still feel Ferax right here. I know she is present, even now. Go, child. Seek the counsel and solace of the trees. With them, you shall find the answers your heart seeks."

Ana hugged her mother, then wandered off to the sacred grove of oaks where she often went to think. She craved the company of the majestic trees and the serenity that came from being in their presence. She needed her beloved friends today more than ever.

Ana came to rest in the shade, under the strong branches of her dear friend Conlaoch, the wise oak, whose rough scales of bark made him appear every bit his age. She knew that many of the priestesses who passed long before her often sought Conlaoch's counsel. Ana could not remember a time that the tree did not welcome her, comfort her, and offer his gentle wisdom.

It was not long before he spoke.

"Your heart is troubled today, little one."

Ana leaned her head back on the thick, stable base of the oak, dug her bare feet into the soft earth, closed her eyes, and sighed. She was grateful he knew her so well.

"Oh Conlaoch, I am so confused and sad. I know I should be able to hear Grandmother, but she is silent. It frightens me. Am I to never see, hear, or feel her again?"

The burly oak was quiet. The soft swaying of his branches filled the silence, as both he and Ana thought about the magnitude of the question. A butterfly with gloriously large wings came into sight. It was sturdy but elegant and vibrant in color. The velvety appendages had what appeared to be two bluish-green eyes, one on each tip of its delicate wings. As it fluttered, she noticed the creamy, warm earth-colored belly of the elusive creature.

"Ana?" Conlaoch spoke as Ana watched the butterfly hover even more closely to her.

"Yes, my friend," she whispered so as not to scare off the elusive creature.

"Do you know what happens after the spirit has left the body?"

"I understand that the soul never actually dies, but right now, all I *know* is Grandmother is gone. I cannot hug her, prepare salves and cures with her, or see her in her beautiful colorful dresses."

As Ana spoke, she felt the butterfly brush against her cheek. She took a slow deep breath, as tears spilled from her eyes. She quietly spoke, while the butterfly continued to dance around her, eventually making her smile.

"The butterfly smells like Grandmother, Conlaoch," she whispered.

"Could it be Ferax in a new form? Perhaps she has come to you like a butterfly today, to tell you she is still with you and well?"

"Do you think it is possible?"

"It does not matter what I think little one. All that matters is what you know to be true in your heart."

Ana held out her finger, willing the butterfly to land. Without hesitation, the butterfly accepted the slender perch.

"Hello, Grandmother. You're beautiful in your dress of many colors."

The butterfly remained still. Ana's hand tingled with a welcome warmth that soon spread throughout her body like a hug. Ever so gently, the colorful butterfly released Ana's finger, floating effortlessly to the young woman's face. It brushed the tip of her nose as it flew away. It felt like a gentle kiss, Ana thought to herself,

She watched for a moment longer, as the colorful winged creature disappeared, then suddenly feeling exhausted, Ana lay down at the base of Conlaoch on the soft grass. She cried herself to sleep under the watchful eye of the calf, who came to rest beside her.

While Ana slept, the old tree sang an ancient lullaby, as he had when she was a child. In her dream state, Ferax came to Ana. "Child, I am still with you, and always will be."

Ana hugged her grandmother tightly. "Listen to me Ana, and I shall tell you how you are destined to live and die for what you believe in, just as I chose to do, of my own free will, in this life."

Ana's eyes widened as a sparkling shimmer of light surrounded her grandmother. The air about them became more fragrant, and the flowers beneath their feet appeared more vibrant. Ana could feel her heart flutter softy as if in time with the beat of a drum.

"Some of what I tell you now, you will not remember after you awake. This is so you are not tempted to alter the course of our legacy. My child, your path moving forward, is not an easy one. A great darkness is about to descend on the people of our land. If you so choose, you will go on to be a great leader for our people. You will meet an equal from a rival clan and fall in love with him. Your union will anger many people from many tribes, but he, like you, is bold, noble, and just. He will search for the cure to the great darkness, and in your love for each other and your joined desire to save the people of every tribe, you will ignore the danger that surrounds you both. You will follow your heart, which leads you to your intended, but this is not the lifetime you both are destined to be united and live in peace."

"What are you saying, Grandmother?"

"You, Ana, are part of our long legacy, and through generations of oral tradition and prophecy, the healer in the new world will hear your whispers. During that lifetime, you and your beloved will be a part of the reawakening after the long darkness. Ana, I will now impress upon your heart and mind all that we need you to do. Are you ready to step into your power, Granddaughter?"

"I am Grandmother. I choose this life willingly."

The white calf nudged closer as Ana stirred and murmured in her sleep.

As Conloach's rich baritone voice echoed his song throughout the land, he knew Ana would rise up and accept her new role in leading her people. He knew her heart would ache for the woman she loved most, but Ana would also come to make peace with her grandmother's passing as she learned a new form of communication with her.

As foretold, Ana did indeed become a beloved Priestess just as Ferax had been. She handed down the red ribbon and the secrets of healing the body and the soul, just as the Priestess with the white calf predicted. In her lifetime, Ana would fall in love with the rival clansman chief from the Kingdom of Dalriada. His knowledge of healing modalities would match Ana's, and together, they would vow to rid the country of the great darkness.

The Chief and Priestess of rivaling clans would sacrifice much to be together. Tragically, in lifetime after lifetime, they would be torn from each other's arms, until finally one day, when the humans of earth were ready to be awakened, they would meet again and unite their knowledge of the ancient healing modalities. However, for the prophecies of great healing and even greater love to come to fruition, bloodshed was inevitable.

Ana would meet her death fearlessly, with a great and undying love in her heart, and just as predicted, her legacy and journey would continue into the New World where at long last love would reign.

1

Ashling Rafferty stood in her cozy kitchen and sank her bare feet into the handmade rug, which was a gift from her parents in Ireland. The old house was quiet except for the soft crackle and pop of pine needles coming from the hundred and fifty-year-old river rock fireplace. She began to fill the kettle with water for her morning tea while looking out her kitchen window. Catching sight of her husband, Ethan, walking towards the barn where he was finishing his morning chores left Ashling time to appreciate all she had in life.

She loved everything about the home she and Ethan shared with their young daughter, Brigid, and often marveled at the history of the old structure. It was familiar and welcoming. It reminded her of what life was like growing up in Ireland. She smiled, thinking about how it took someone like Ethan Rafferty to make her consider leaving her beloved County Cork. However, for Ethan, she eventually did.

As a young couple dating, Ashling loved hearing Ethan talk about the cabin his great-great-grandfather constructed by hand, and that had remained in the Rafferty family of ranchers and foresters ever since. The Raffertys were a tenacious bunch, and with luck, determination, and a bit of audacity, they not only survived the harsh Pacific Northwest winters but they thrived. Eventually, their ranch became one of the largest working cattle farms in Oregon. It was a legacy Ethan was proud to share with Ashling and Brigid.

As Ashling waited for the kettle to boil, she looked around, thinking about how their home had changed over the years. The log cabin with extraordinarily tall vaulted ceilings, expanded and modernized, but one thing remained unchanged—a live oak tree in the center of the family home. It was, of course, the first topic of conversation when new guests visited. In-depth discussions ensued about the stability and ingenuity of raising the frame of the house so the roots would never interfere with the structure of the cabin.

The height of the home was an architectural masterpiece that Ethan loved to share with guests. The newly remodeled playroom in the loft, called the treehouse, showcased the oak, while still allowing the space to feel roomy and comfortable. The design purposefully brought the feel of nature indoors. Ashling marveled at Ethan's ancestors who loved trees as much as she did and recalled the story of how Ethan's great-great-grandfather, Redmond, standing on Oregon soil for the first time, informed his wife they would build in the exact spot the oak grew so they could witness both sunrise and sunset for many years to come.

Redmond's new bride instantly refused to let her husband kill the beautiful tree. Seeing his wife's determination, and secretly loving her all the more for her convictions, he compromised and built the house around it.

As the years passed, it became more and more a task to maintain the well-being of the old tree. The yearly pruning was something Ashling never looked forward to, in part because of the reverence she had for oaks. She worried about harming them, but in truth, it was a messy business trimming an oversized tree in one's home.

Staring out into the living room, she thought back to a conversation early on in her relationship with Ethan.

"Trees are sacred, and have always been a central thread in my life and the lives of my ancestors. I love thinking of how people would gather around them as part of their ceremonies—like people today gather in churches. They hold great knowledge and most are quite insightful if you take the time to get to know them. Of course, they don't need humans to hear them, but they have much wisdom they want to share."

Ethan smiled at Ashling and the apparent joy that talking about trees brought out in her. She remembered Ethan urging her to continue, so she did.

"Yew trees are associated with longevity and resurrection, whereas the rowan tree is believed to protect those who have passed over. It was common to bury a piece of the rowan tree with the deceased. In my family, we still honor this tradition," Ashling stated.

Ethan listened as Ashling told him how her Celtic ancestors believed the birch tree had the power to protect them from evil fairies and spirits, and how a Celtic celebration would likely take place beneath the oaks.

"Oaks and yews are my favorites," Ashling whispered in a conspiratorial tone as if she thought the other trees might hear her.

Ethan tried not to laugh.

When she heard Ethan talk about a tree in the center of his family home, Ashling knew she had discovered a mysterious link she was waiting for in her life—one Ashling's ancestors had whispered in her ear. She knew at that moment, Ethan was her future, and her home would be wherever Ethan was.

The whistling kettle made Ashling jump, bringing her out of her memories. Pouring the hot liquid into her mug, and leaving it to steep with the loose aromatics, she found herself wandering around the center of the home where the tree flourished.

Part of the old oak's charm came from her being able to explore all the Rafferty names carved in the massive trunk. Here, one could discover a rich history nestled for well over a hundred years. Ashling felt nostalgic as she remembered engraving her initials into the tree as she lovingly touched the initials of grandparents, siblings, cousins, and those who had long since passed to the next realm. The tree was an existing account of its ancestry, a testament of dreams and hopes. It reflected the past and the present, and it was their tree of life.

Wandering back to the kitchen, Ashling caught sight of Ethan carrying medium-sized plant containers from the barn. Sensing he was being watched, Ethan glanced towards the house, tipping his ball cap up slightly. The man still turned Ashling's head in his faded blue jeans, flannel shirt, and dusty old ball cap. He was ruggedly handsome, with his unruly waves of dark hair.

It was something about his eyes though, that crinkled at the corners when he smiled, that mesmerized Ashling, even after all these years. Ethan's eyes were wise and thoughtful. When he spoke or was listening to someone talk, the person always knew they had Ethan's full

3

attention. He had a way of making people feel important. Ashling saw many a woman gawk at her husband as the years went by and yet it never bothered her. She knew Ethan Rafferty had eyes only for her.

She hummed a whimsical tune as she watched her husband methodically place tree saplings in the bed of his 1955 Chevy pickup they called Old Blue. It was a lazy morning, one made for daydreaming, and Ashling did just that as she poured milk into her tea. She sipped it while staring out the window as her husband happily went about loading the truck. She knew by the way his mouth moved he was singing. Ethan loved to sing.

Music, it was what brought Ethan and Ashling together in the first place. They first met in Cork, Ireland, at a local pub where she was a waitress and Ethan a tourist on vacation. Ethan once told her, he fell instantly in love with the spirited redhead who barely gave him and his friends the time of day. It wasn't as if Ashling purposefully ignored the Americans. She was pleasant enough to all the customers, although the locals would regularly tease her about being in a world of her own.

Ethan was genuinely intrigued, and a bit surprised to find he wanted to know what was going on in the waitress's mind as she looked off into the distance, lost in her thoughts, scrubbing at an invisible spot on the counter.

It didn't bother Ethan if she didn't talk, as long as she continued to hum or sing as she moved lightly around the quaint establishment. Her pure voice held him spellbound. He tried once to describe to his friends how hauntingly beautiful the Irish girl's voice was.

"I swear she sings like an angel," he argued when they teased him mercilessly.

"Come listen for yourselves," Ethan challenged his buddies.

The teasing stopped the night the young men gathered at the pub where the woman in question was a waitress by day and enchantress by night. The regulars, having settled in with their pints, began to lightly pound their hands on the bar or tables while they chanted, "Ashling... Ashling..."

Not needing much encouragement, she tossed the towel she was using to the side as she walked from behind the bar. Someone offered her a mug filled with a dark amber ale, and she took a long sip. Then, Ashling began to sing with a voice like soft velvet. The once noisy room fell silent as her hypnotic ballad rose and fell. The teasing Ethan got from his friends also came to an abrupt end that night. Simon, Ethan's best friend, was equally taken with Ashling.

"Find someone else," Ethan replied tersely, seeing the wolfish gleam in Simon's eye. Simon, already having had a pint too many, decided it would be wise to challenge Ethan to a fight.

"Winner gets the girl," Simon slurred as he tried several times to stand.

Ethan pushed Simon back down on his bar stool, fighting feelings of jealousy he'd never experienced before. "Go find someone else, not this girl."

A barrel-chested bartender stood nearby, listening as he wiped a glass, then hung it above the bar on a wire rack.

"You got it bad, my friend. For the sake of our friendship, I shall be the bigger man, and bow out gracefully," Simon slurred.

Then laughing at his joke, he tried to stand and give a deep bow to Ethan in a show of mock surrender. Instead, Simon promptly fell to the floor, cutting his chin on the bar stool as he lurched unceremoniously to the ground.

Simon's fall brought Ashling running around the counter with a towel in hand. The surly-looking bartender who had been filling a pitcher of water during the last exchange of barbs between the two young men quietly walked around as well, assessing the damage. Having determined it wasn't severe, he calmly poured the pitcher of water on Simon's head.

Simon, instantly sobered enough to stand, but Ashling, getting doused with a significant portion of the water, yelped, "Dad!"

Ethan did the only thing he could think to do after realizing the bartender overheard every word Ethan and Simon uttered about his daughter—sheepishly, he shoved out his hand to shake the older man's as he blurted out, "Sir, I'm Ethan Rafferty. One day I intend to marry your daughter."

Ashling giggled and graced Ethan with an approving grin. Two minutes later, Ethan and Simon found themselves promptly thrown out of the bar with strict instructions never to come back.

Smiling at the memory, Ashling sipped her tea and walked to the refrigerator, saying absently to herself, "Seems like only yesterday."

"What seems like only yesterday?" asked a tiny child who was the spitting image of Ashling, but with lighter hair.

The little girl came into the kitchen and hugged her mother.

"Oh, I was just thinkin' to way back when, and how I met your dad."

"Oh, I love that story. Will you tell it to me again, *pleeease*," Brigid asked between yawns.

"You could probably tell the story as well as I, by this point my girl."

She reached down to pick up her daughter and set her on a tall barstool across the island from where she started Brigid's favorite morning meal of oatmeal. Brigid loved everything oatmeal. The young girl sat quietly watching her mom stir the steaming copper pot filled with oats using her favorite wooden spoon. Ashling would tease, it was the spoon that made the food taste just right.

"What has you smiling so?"

"Oh, nothing, I just remembered I don't have to go to school today."

"That's right. Do you want to help me pick some herbs after breakfast? I can tell you some of the stories you like about the Wee Folk from my childhood along the way."

Ashling spoke in a confidential tone, "You know I swear I saw one by the yews just yesterday." She was surprised that this news did not make her daughter happy. Instead, Brigid bit her lower lip and was quiet for a few moments.

"Darlin', you're biting that lip of yours. Out with it," Ashling urged.

There was another long pause. In a small voice, Brigid confessed to her mother, "The kids at school laughed at me when I told 'em we have Wee Folk that live with us on the ranch."

Ethan stood at the kitchen door listening to Brigid retell the story about her first-grade classmates who teased her, calling her a baby, for believing in little people who hid in the grass and played in the tiny flowers. Exchanging knowing glances with Ashling, Ethan silently entered the kitchen and planted a kiss on Brigid's head.

Brigid turned to hug her father then quickly devoted her attention to the bowl being placed before her, counting out ten plump raisins and making a smiley face in her cereal as she always did.

"So, it's starting already, huh?" Ethan said, whispering in Ashling's ear. She looked from Ethan to Brigid, as she contemplated them both.

With a mouth full of oatmeal, Brigid exclaimed, "Mom is going to tell the story of your first ... *anna, anna* ..."

"Anniversary." Ashling supplied when Brigid looked at her questioningly.

"You going to listen too, Dad?" Brigid asked, placing her small hand on his, as he sat down beside her.

"Couldn't keep me from it, my little woodland sprite. It's one of the best stories of all."

"I thought I was the best story of all?"

"Ah, true. You are, but your story comes later. First, your mom must tell the story of how she fell madly and deeply in love with a handsome rogue from Oregon, and how she chased him across the ocean to be at his side."

2

"What's got you in such a hurry all of a sudden, Sprite?" Ethan asked as Brigid rushed past him.

"No school today! I wanna go say hi to Malachi. It's okay, isn't it?" Brigid asked with the slightest of pleas.

Smiling, Ethan nodded his approval, knowing how much Brigid enjoyed the whimsical stories their trusted old family friend could weave.

Brigid looked sheepishly at her mother. "Malachi was going to finish a story about a girl and her pet deer that traveled to a magical village and all the fun they have, but I can go get herbs with you instead."

"No, no, we'll do that another time darlin'. I know this story Malachi is telling. You won't want to miss it! Now be off with you then, and tell Malachi hello for me."

Brigid however, was already out the door skipping and singing as she scurried off.

"I'm concerned about her Ash. Things won't get any easier on her, you know. Kids can be so cruel at this age."

Ashling was quiet for a moment. "It's only right that she remains true to herself, Ethan. Think about our lives—our choices. Look at what you've got in store for today alone at the university. There are those who will laugh, but is it enough to stop you?" Ashling challenged.

"You know it won't. If anything good comes from this study, we might be able to save lives. It's a big risk and a big *if* at that, but it's worth looking into," Ethan replied.

"I don't want to squash her intuition, besides, Brigid's gonna bump up against those who think differently regardless of what she believes. That's part of life. The more we help her grow in self-worth and confidence now, the less other people's opinions will matter to her."

"I know you're right, Ash. It's just hard—Brigid's still so young."

"Promise me, husband, you will always be there for our baby girl. A daughter will always need her father to help her navigate life. You must stay strong."

The look on Ashling's face made Ethan uneasy as he grabbed her around the waist, kissing her swiftly on her forehead. "Of course, *together*, you and I will be there for our daughter. We'll watch her grow into an amazingly strong woman, just like her mother."

"What will be, has already been set in motion," Ashling replied, as she handed Ethan a plate with two perfectly fried eggs on it.

"I'm starving," she said, turning her attention to a piece of toast, hoping to end the conversation.

"Every time you talk like that Ash, it makes me wonder what you know that I don't," Ethan said, somewhat agitated.

"Aye, and a mystery I will always be," she said, biting her lower lip before giving Ethan a sassy glance, attempting to lighten the mood.

"Of course, we give Brigid our guidance, and you can give her your years of wisdom."

Ethan chuckled at the way Ashling wiggled her eyebrows up and down at him.

"And you, wife, will continue to encourage her freedom to think her own thoughts."

Ethan and Ashling continued their meal in comfortable silence, although Ashling knew by the creases on Ethan's forehead, he was deep in thought.

"You know Ash, you and I were raised in such different ways. The adults in my life would tell me what to think and what to do when I was a boy. That was just our way. When you were a child, there was no single right way. You were encouraged to explore options, break the rules, think for yourself. I envy that. Maybe that's why I can be so *boxed-in* with my thinking sometimes."

"Ah love, you of all people, boxed-in? Not only did you throw caution to the wind when you came back to Ireland to claim my hand, but you also took heed of our ancient family lore by planting even more magical trees all those years ago. Now, would a boxed-in thinker have gone and done that?" She challenged.

"I don't know about magical trees, but Ash, coming after you made me the smartest man in the world. That just made sense. As for the yews, you trust your instinct, and that's always been good enough for me."

"You're a good man Ethan Rafferty."

Having finished breakfast, Ashling shooed Ethan from the kitchen so she could finish her chores, but as was common with Ashling, she gave in to nostalgic memories. Casually, she ran her finger over the top of a dusty framed photo on the kitchen wall. Staring back at her was Ethan, maybe eleven or twelve years of age, standing next to his father, Eric. The photo showed father and son beaming proudly, pointing at yew trees, indicating how tall they had grown.

Looking at the picture, she remembered when Ethan told her about the grove he planted as a boy with his father, and how their trees had grown beyond all reason.

"Best we could figure, it was the soil-blend he and I developed. The trees are really quite unusual. You should come to Oregon to see them," Ethan added hopefully, knowing Ashling's love of trees matched his own.

Ten years had passed since that day when they both sat on the open tailgate of her father's truck, bantering over which trees were their favorite, and which were the most useful or the most beautiful.

Ashling hung onto every word, as her new beau explained the process he and his father used to create the nutrient-rich soil in which their Oregon yews thrived. In turn, she shared how her family fully believed in the healing properties of trees. Ashling explained how her ancestors would use the bark, leaves, and berries from different trees, shrubs, and herbs in holistic ways, always passing the knowledge down from generation to generation.

Seeing Ethan close the tailgate, filled Ashling with anticipation for the day's event. She believed the trees loaded in the back of Ethan's truck were even more remarkable than her husband yet knew.

"So, my love, are you excited or nervous?"

Ethan shrugged his shoulders as Ashling came to stand beside him. "I guess I'm a bit of both. Nothing should have grown as these trees have out here. Scientifically it doesn't make sense. Even with our proprietary soil," Ethan remarked—and not for the first time.

"It's as I've said, husband, you've got the Wee Folk taking care of those trees."

"Well, if the yews keep up this healthy growth rate, I might just start to believe it myself, wife!"

Ethan rounded the truck to face Ashling. "Well, here goes nothing. Wish me luck."

She winked. "You have me, husband. How much more luck do you need?"

Giving her a wry grin, he climbed behind the wheel of Old Blue. After waving goodbye, Ashling walked over to the large wrap-around porch. Leaning against the freshly painted railing, she watched her husband drive out of sight while she stroked the chin of the tabby beside her.

"Miss Cuddles, Ethan looks just as excited as he did the first time he saw the Hawthorne tree at Saint Mary's Well. Ah, the wonder on his face as he stood staring at the old tree."

The tabby purred in response. "I suppose I had the same look when I first saw the tree in the middle of our living room here."

Ashling continued. "You know what Ethan told me just the other day? He said it was easy to believe that the Wee Folk had a hand in the beauty of the old trees, and even admitted he felt the special energy around them. That was a first."

With a final stroke across the now sleeping cat's back, Ashling stepped away from the railing, unaware that her husband watched her as she wandered back into the house.

Catching sight of Ashling in his rearview mirror as he drove down their long gravel road, Ethan knew that far-away look in her eyes she often had meant she was daydreaming once again. Grinning, he wondered where his spirited wife drifted off to this time.

Ethan spotted Brigid and Malachi. She was looking up at him intently. Old Malachi was likely weaving a magical adventure that captivated the child. Waving hello, Ethan shook his head, not the least bit surprised his daughter didn't see or hear him drive past. Brigid became lost in the stories Malachi told as quickly as Ashling would.

It wasn't that he minded Malachi telling old folk tales that entertained Brigid, it was that Ethan sometimes worried about his daughter and her vivid imagination. As much as he nurtured her free spirit, he was old enough to know that such a carefree life was a fleeting moment in time.

Eventually, like Santa Claus, the Easter Bunny, and the Tooth Fairy, one had to grow up, put lofty ideas away, and live in the real world. Ethan envied Ashling and Brigid in their unfettered, childlike view of the world, but he also admired their ability to maintain it. Brigid would only be a child for a short time. Soon enough, the realities of life would replace the innocence he wanted to preserve for his little girl.

Moments later, after pushing buttons on a coded gate system, the chain linked fence rolled open, allowing him to exit. Ethan watched to make sure it closed securely behind him, then turned onto the street that shielded his property from traffic. He headed towards the main highway leading into town. Once on the road, Ethan cranked up the volume on the radio and strummed his hands on the steering wheel to the rhythm of a song from his youth. He knew Ashling would laugh and roll her eyes at him. The thought of it made him sing even louder and served as a distraction from over-analyzing his and Ashling's decision to partner with the university.

It had taken some time before agreements were reached that paved the way for a collaboration with the school that wanted unlimited access to the yew trees for research in cancer treatment. The Raffertys required privacy clauses and controlling interest in all discoveries involving the yews from their property, and refused the demands seeking the unlimited use of their trees. Eventually, the university and their legal team conceded, intrigued by the possibilities, and contracts were signed.

"The summer session will be the perfect time to launch the new program. I'll set up a meeting between you and Albert Jones. He's as excited as I am to see how we can use these particular trees," The Dean, and a personal friend of Eric Rafferty, told Ethan over the phone.

Sitting in a line of stalled traffic made Ethan realize he'd been playing the last year over in his head while he drove. "Damn train."

As the Southern Pacific crawled past the intersection with tortoise-like speed, Ethan concluded he'd be at least fifteen minutes late for the meeting at the school. After shooting a quick text and receiving a thumbs up emoji from the grad student waiting for him, Ethan settled in for the long wait, which left plenty of time for him to think about how today came to be.

In the years since Ethan and Ashling had worked their land together, unexplainable changes had occurred at their yew grove.

"The answer is in the bark of these trees and the magic of the soil in which they are rooted. Over time, as my ancestors predicted, the sacred knowledge of how to extract the properties without harming the trees was lost. The legend says that one day, a Healer in the New World would re-discover the ancient and divine secret modalities that will cure the world of a devastating disease. If modern-day researchers can replicate the forgotten technique of my ancestors, and put it in the proper sequence, we will once again be able to end all the devastating side-effects cancer protocols today have," Ashling once told Ethan.

"Ash, you can't deny though that millions of lives have been saved thanks to the advancements in cancer research and treatments," Ethan countered.

"Darlin', modern technology and the diligence of brilliant and dedicated minds isn't in question at all. We are still an evolving society.

I'm just sayin' in time I believe our talented scientists, doctors, and dreamers will solve the mysteries of the human ailments. That's all."

"No small feat, wife. It more than borders on the *woo-woo*, even for you, Ash," Ethan concluded.

Looking up, Ethan saw the train slow to a stop. "You gotta be kidding me," he said as he dialed his phone.

"Rafferty here. So, the freight train decided now was the time to stop on the tracks. I'm sandwiched in and gonna have to wait it out. I'll be there as soon as I can, Greg," he said after being assured there was no hurry.

In truth, Ethan welcomed the longer reprieve, and admitted to himself he was behaving more like Ashling as he allowed his thoughts to meander back to the time he brought her to the yew tree grove upon her first visit to his home they called the Double R. The memory instantly calmed him.

Ethan wasn't sure what he expected when he brought Ashling there. He allowed only a handful of people to visit this particular spot on his property as he considered it sacred ground. Ethan, however, was not prepared for Ashling to toss her head back in laughter, and to wrap her arms around his neck in a way that made him feel like he gave his beautiful wife the world! She began to run like a child without a care, weaving and twirling through the magnificent yews.

"The Wee Folk have smiled upon you Ethan Rafferty," she said as she slipped off her shoes, wandering through the grove barefoot, murmuring to herself as she lovingly touched the trees.

Ashling turned, looking up at Ethan with her dazzling turquoise eyes. He was lost to her forever in that glance, her smile taking his breath away. It was then he realized he would do anything to see her smile like that for the rest of their lives.

Finally, the train began to move, and the caboose was soon to follow. Reaching the university, Ethan pulled Old Blue into a spot closest to the research laboratory. He got out, stretching his long legs. He turned as he heard someone call out his name. Greg offered a friendly greeting. The two men proceeded to unload the truck, and not long after, Ethan was back on the road with his trees safely delivered. He turned the radio up once again and began to sing.

3

Brigid watched a silky butterfly with iridescent wings float past her. It reminded her of the tiny fairies that flitted from blades of grass or moss near solitary trees on their property. She watched closely while the delicate weightless dancer with colorful appendages swished past her as she sat beside Malachi.

Slowly, she stretched her arms out wide like the painted creature. Malachi never questioned why a pillow and small suitcase sat by Brigid's side. He knew the child would tell him in her own time.

"I wish I could fly away like that butterfly," Brigid told her friend.

"Child, where would you fly to?"

"Oh, I don't know, to a place where there isn't a school, I guess."

"I thought you'd like school, Brigid. You are inquisitive, and there are many things to learn and children your own age to meet."

Brigid bit her lip and twisted her hands in her lap while looking at Malachi with a worried face.

"Kids at school say I'm a freak."

"Brigid, why do you hang your head? I do not know what the term freak conveys these days. I'm an old, old man, but if it means to be different, then this is a good thing. A splendid thing. It means you are special, and you should hold your head high."

Brigid shook her head slowly, not convinced that what he said was true.

"Why does it matter right now if you are different or the same as someone else?"

"Don't you see? The kids at school would like me if I was more like them." Brigid, unlaced her little sneakers, freeing her feet from their confinement, then squished her toes in the soft ground.

"I don't think I understand," Malachi replied.

"They make fun of me . . . and my friends here at the ranch."

Again, Brigid bit her lower lip.

"They say I'm a baby because I talk to the cows and birds, and if I'm going to act like a baby, I should stay home and wear diapers."

"Oh."

They both sat, quietly listening to the breeze rustling the massive tree branches all around them. Brigid told Malachi she thought the way the leaves fluttered looked like a million butterflies dancing in the wind. Malachi loved the way Brigid saw everything with fresh eyes. He told her he agreed.

Brigid changed the subject. "Malachi, do you ever wish you could fly?"

"Never given it much thought before." He paused, thinking for a moment as Malachi often did. "I am me. I wasn't born to fly like the butterfly there. If I could take flight, I would no longer be me, but someone or something other than myself. That would change me."

Malachi paused, "I like me. So—no."

Brigid wasn't sure why, but she giggled at that. Sometimes she didn't understand all the things Malachi said, but the way he spoke always made her feel better.

"I like you, Malachi."

"Thank you. I like you, too, Brigid."

Brigid knew the kids at school didn't like her, only she didn't understand why talking to the animals was so strange.

Sitting next to Malachi, Brigid thought about being different. She never gave it much thought before her parents informed her she was old enough to attend school. The trouble was, Brigid didn't want to leave her home, even though her mom and dad made starting first grade seem like an adventure.

Life on the ranch was simple and fun. In Brigid's young mind, things were just fine the way they were. She sighed, thinking about how first grade wasn't for her, and the plan she crafted to escape the world into which she felt unfairly thrust.

After the first day of school, life felt like a puzzle with too many pieces. She felt like the piece that never fit as she watched the other kids laugh and play together. Once, during recess, Brigid tried to join a small group of kids playing tag. One girl laughed at her unusual eyes and hair. The other children, sensing the need to follow suit, giggled as well. One by one, they all ran off, leaving Brigid standing alone. This was the first time Brigid experienced the cruelty of life.

On another occasion, as Brigid sat on the swings, two girls came and joined her. Brigid's heart soared with the possibility of making new friends. As the girls swished back and forth, going higher and higher, Brigid remembered how her parents would encourage her to try new things, so she asked if the girls would like to come to her house and play on the farm. Both girls laughed as they jumped from their swings without a backward glance at Brigid. As they ran off hand in hand, Brigid stared at the girls and held back her tears.

After the first few weeks, Brigid withdrew into herself, no longer caring if she fit in and all but gave up on the idea of making friends. Instead, at recess, Brigid would walk around the playground, picking up roly-polies and caterpillars. She would go to a secret place inside her mind that was safe as she talked to the tiny creatures, making the other children roar with laughter. Brigid refused to cry, however.

At home, no one laughed at Brigid or thought she was different. She was always just Brigid or Sprite. Once, Brigid asked her dad why he called her Sprite. Ethan explained it was because she reminded him of the elusive magical creatures Ashling told him about when they were in Ireland.

"They're said to be very quick, seldom seen, and impossible to catch," Ethan told Brigid.

Brigid looked bewildered.

"They aren't that fast Dad! You just have to look for them, and they have to trust you. Most of them like to talk. It's just people don't take the time to listen or see them," Brigid told Ethan.

Ruffling her hair, Ethan smiled indulgently.

All that Brigid knew was she felt happiest outdoors or visiting Malachi and her other friends around her home. They never teased her or made her feel left out or different. They talked kindly to her, made her laugh, and asked questions that made her curious about the world. Brigid was disappointed that school and the kids there were not the same.

That is how Brigid came to be sitting with her friend, tapping her fingers on her suitcase, wondering why her perfect idea hadn't worked out the way she thought. Brigid stared miserably at her pillow, now tucked under her lightly freckled arm, playing over her plan and the morning events.

Earlier In The Day

Brigid woke with focused determination. Walking into the kitchen, knowing full well both her parents would be there, she grabbed some cookies from the kitchen table, and marched right past both her mom and dad towards the back door—all as planned! Brigid needed to make sure both parents understood the importance of letting her stay home at the ranch, forever! She knew they wouldn't make her go to school when they saw how serious she was.

"Where are you off to Sprite?"

"I'm going to stay with Malachi."

"Why?" her mother asked.

"Cuz I'm not going to school again—ever, and you can't make me!" Brigid announced feeling immensely grown up.

Brigid stopped, realizing her hands were full. She couldn't open the door to make a grand exit like her parents knew she was trying to do. Ashling sought to hide her smile while Ethan, dumbfounded, merely stared. Ashling walked over to Brigid and turned the knob on the door and opened it for her daughter. Brigid only hesitated a moment when she bit her lower lip.

19

"You're not going to stop me?" she looked up at her mother.

"No, darlin', you seem to have your mind made up. Did you remember your toothbrush?" Ashling asked with motherly concern.

"Yes," Brigid replied.

Brigid was so sure after her big announcement, her mom would cry, and her dad would scoop her up and ruffle her hair like he always did. Brigid expected him to tell her it was okay, and that she didn't have to go to that terrible place called school. Somehow, the conversation was not going how Brigid thought it would. Not at all.

Ethan followed his wife's lead. "We're going to miss you something awful Sprite. The door will be unlocked if you ever want to come back home."

Both parents echoed their love for their daughter, but neither one tried to stop her. Brigid stood rooted in place, trying to think of why this was not going according to the plan. She told Miss Cuddles about her plan while practicing what she would say in a mirror. Miss Cuddles seemed to agree, but then the tabby thought every idea Brigid had was a good one. The cat would typically purr, stretch and plop contently down at Brigid's feet. The meows of agreement as Brigid laid out her plan to her beloved cat told her all she needed to know.

Faced with a choice, she said goodbye to her parents and with only the smallest trace of a tremor in her voice, told them they knew where they could find her when they came to their senses.

Brigid stormed off with her long curls bouncing down her back. Kicking up dust along the gravel drive, Brigid eventually cut through a path of old trees and was soon out of sight. Ethan and Ashling, ever vigilant, remained in place, watching Brigid until she was on the familiar path on their secure property. They knew Malachi would see her coming and welcome her with open arms. Both parents never doubted that their daughter would be safe. They knew Malachi would listen and help her reason things out.

It was Ethan who gave in to a moment of doubt and started to go after his little girl who walked alone down the drive with a pillow tucked under her small arm. Ashling gently stopped her husband, loving him all the more for wanting to protect Brigid. He gave her a wary look. She wrapped her arms tightly around Ethan's waist. There, they both stood. And waited.

"You're testing my resolve, wife," Ethan tried for a light-hearted tone, falling just short.

"Trust me. She'll be back for lunch."

"I guess this is where all those things you've told me about your upbringing come into play, huh?"

Ashling merely nodded, having grown up free to explore all beliefs and expressions of herself. Thinking all kids grew up the way she did, it was quite a surprise to learn how Ethan, although raised by loving parents, had a different experience.

Ethan attended a private school for twelve years, wearing the same uniform as every other boy. As expected, they all had the same haircut, short and cropped an inch above their collars, and they diligently polished their black shoes at the first sign of a scuff—as required. It was during his years of attending a parochial school that Ethan learned how he was expected to think, how to reason things out logically, as well as what to believe.

Maintaining a structured life was comfortable for Ethan. He liked knowing each step before it happened, but Ashling hadn't a clue what she wanted to do in life as a young girl. Ethan knew early on that he would go to the same university both his parents attended, then work in the family business. The latter seemed a natural fit since Ethan loved the outdoors, working with the earth, and protecting the environment.

Where Ethan was book smart, Ashling was intuitive and used to following her gut. Ethan's parents were kind, loving people who wanted the best for their son, just as Ashling's parents did for her. Sometimes, they all just went about life a bit differently.

Knowing Brigid would one day test her wings was why her parents now stood at the kitchen door, watching their only child stepping into her independence, making her own choices. Ashling and Ethan were thankful they could stand side by side to support Brigid as she grew into the strong, self-reliant woman they knew she would become one day.

"I know she's going to see Malachi. Everything will be okay," Ethan added as if trying to convince himself.

As suspected, Brigid came back through the same door she walked out of earlier that day. The little girl knew it was lunchtime, her stomach told her so. It took restraint for Brigid to hide the urge to run to the table her mom had set with her favorite foods. Brigid could smell the rich aroma of soup from the door. She was confident a perfectly grilled cheese sandwich would be sitting next to the bowl with its edges neatly cut off. But first things first.

"Mom, Dad, I changed my mind. I'm gonna try out school again, for one week, maybe two," Brigid announced, using her most grown-up voice as she thrust two tiny fingers into the air, to make her point clear.

"Oh? What made you decide that, darlin'?" Ashling asked.

"Well, when I told Malachi I didn't wanna go to school anymore, he said, I didn't seem like someone who would quit so easily. He said there were way better things I could learn about there, and then he said there must be a reason for school if you guys thought it was important. He was sayin' I might miss out on something fun because I was too afraid to try. I got mad, and I told him I wasn't afraid! I just didn't want to leave home. He said I should *compro-prize*."

"Compromise?" Ethan supplied.

"Yes, that's what he said I should do," Brigid replied, nodding her head up and down.

"I didn't know what it meant, so he *esplainded* it to me," Brigid confided, and then continued.

"I was still kinda mad he said I was afraid, so I said I'd show him, and I left." Brigid forgot to mention she'd also left her pillow behind.

Ashling knew Malachi would quietly listen to Brigid, allowing her to work out the struggle in her own way, just as he had done the same for Ashling many times over the years. Their old friend understood that Brigid was adventurous. Any hint of her being afraid of

22

school would send the spirited child flying straight back to the classroom. His approach worked well, but even so, Ashling made up her mind to wander out later and chat with Malachi—and collect the forgotten pillow her daughter left behind.

With things now settled in Brigid's mind, she finally told the story of her first days at school. Ethan listened intently to his daughter, ignoring that his fears were starting to come true.

4

The following week started much like the first. Brigid found little joy in her days at school, but she made a promise, and Brigid always kept her word. After telling Malachi she would give it one more try, he taught her something called the gratitude game to help her make a fresh start.

"Brigid, my girl, it's easy and fun, if you wish it to be! When you become sad or discouraged at school, try to find at least one thing to be happy about. Start with something small."

So when Brigid entered the classroom, she was grateful it wasn't as hot as usual. Next, Brigid decided she was thankful that her eyes could see the whiteboard. Hard as she tried to find the things Malachi asked her to look for, the one thing that made Brigid truly grateful, was when the school day was over and she could be back on the ranch with Malachi and her family where everything was normal.

Brigid tried to remember what Malachi told her, but really, Brigid just wanted a friend.

And so it went each day, she would try to find one thing new for which to be grateful. Just this morning someone smiled at her, and Brigid smiled back. She felt very thankful for that! Malachi said, "Counting one's blessings while feeling gratitude was the way to have more people, places and things to be grateful for." Brigid trusted Malachi, so she continued to play his game. Then, something big happened that made Brigid know Malachi was very wise indeed.

It was the middle of the week when the teacher had the students pair up for an outdoor exercise. Mrs. Blair assigned Brigid to a girl named Emma Daily. Brigid knew exactly who Emma was. All the kids talked to Emma, and they all laughed and played together at recess. Everyone wanted to be around Em, as the kids called her.

Standing as the teacher called their names, the two girls could not look more opposite. Brigid was tall and lanky for her age, while

Emma was petite. Brigid had long strawberry blond hair. Emma wore her hair in a perfectly bobbed cut, showing off her shiny ebony locks. Brigid knew the girl beside her never had to blow unruly bangs out of her eyes like she sometimes had to. Brigid marveled at how Emma stood perfectly straight in the beautiful dress she wore.

"I like your dress," Brigid said.

"Thank you. It's new," Emma replied kindly.

Emma seemed just as intrigued by Brigid.

The girl standing beside Emma had sparkling eyes and a dusting of freckles barely noticeable on her perfect nose. The two girls quietly observed each other with curious expressions on their faces. In contrast to Brigid's fair skin and easy-going appearance, Emma's warm olive skin, and chocolate brown eyes made her appear thoughtful. Emma suddenly became shy when she and Brigid were told to pair up in line together, but Brigid, seemingly having made a decision, took her new friend by the hand and quickly guided them to the front of the line. Others soon followed. The two girls smiled at each other. Somehow Brigid began to feel that this school thing just might work out.

"I didn't know we'd get to go to school outside. I can't wait!" Brigid said brightly to Emma, who was staring down at her feet, looking concerned.

"My shoes," Emma said.

"They are very pretty," Brigid supplied and meant it.

Most of Brigid's shoes, when she wore them, were dusty from life on the ranch but she didn't think Emma's shoes ever got dirty.

"My mother told me I couldn't get my new school shoes dirty. I begged her to let me wear them today! What if there's mud?" Emma's voice trembled.

Brigid didn't think that was such a bad thing but bit her lower lip instead. "Oh I'm real good at cleaning shoes, I'll help you if they get dirty, okay?" Brigid offered and hoped this would make Emma smile again.

Emma's relief was evident.

All was suddenly right in Brigid's world as the teacher led them outside to the playground. Trees and play equipment mingled together to create an inviting scene. Brigid felt like she was seeing her surroundings for the first time.

"Look Emma, no mud in sight, just lots of grass, so that's something to be grateful for!" Emma nodded her head, looking a little more relaxed.

Mrs. Blair began explaining the task to her students standing in pairs. They were to work together, finding the items on their sheets of paper, consisting of various specimens of nuts, flowers, and leaves that would be used later in a class experiment.

"It's a scavenger hunt of sorts. You will have thirty minutes students. Meet me back here when you hear the bell!"

Clapping her hands in rapid succession, Mrs. Blair called out, "Ready, set, go!"

Students ran off, scattering in various directions with screeches of laughter, lists, and bags in which to hold their treasures. Spying the acorns nearby, both girls ran towards their first find. Brigid held the bag open while Emma placed the nuts inside.

"Well, there's one thing we can cross off our list," Emma said, concentrating on the paper in her hand.

When it looked like the ground might dirty Emma's shoes, Brigid happily ran ahead and gathered up the objects.

"Thank you, Brigid," Emma would say politely.

One mean-spirited boy teased Emma about getting stuck with the freak. Emma took Brigid's hand, raised her pert little nose a bit higher, and led Brigid away from the bad-tempered boy.

"Thank you, Emma," Brigid said quietly, making a mental note to tell Malachi how grateful she felt at that moment.

As the thirty minutes came to an end, Emma found a flower from the list and Brigid found the Maple leaf from a tree. They were not the first to complete their task, but it no longer mattered. Brigid was grateful that finally, something about school was fun. Later that day, hopping off the school bus at her usual time, Brigid carefully pushed the numbers on the box that opened their security gate. She couldn't wait to see Malachi and tell him her great news.

"Malachi, I made a friend today! Her name is Emma."

Winded, she ran towards him, stopping once to catch her breath.

"I want to hear all about your new friend Brigid," Malachi said in his welcoming voice.

Brigid began to tell him how she and Emma pinky swore always to be the best of friends.

"Emma's kinda quiet. She doesn't say much, but she says smart stuff when she does talk. She already has lots of friends, though. I wish I were as smart as Emma."

Brigid told Malachi how Emma's parents were even smarter. "Emma's parents are both lawyers. Doesn't that sound important Mal? That's why I think Em is so smart too."

"You're very bright and clever Brigid. You must never compare yourself to anyone but you. You'll remember that won't you?" Malachi asked Brigid, who promptly bit her lip, nodding.

"Many adults never learn this valuable lesson. You must try never to imitate another in the future, my little friend," Malachi gently reminded Brigid.

Brigid nodded her head.

"Brigid," Ashling called out from up the trail.

"Coming Mom."

After giving Malachi a quick hug, she confided, "I try to remember the stuff you tell me. It's kinda confusing, but I know it matters, or you wouldn't talk about it. See you tomorrow!"

Malachi

Malachi was tired.

"Perhaps I'll rest just a bit," he said to no one in particular.

It was natural for a young one like Brigid to wear him out from time to time with her exuberance, he thought to himself.

His attention wandered, as an older man's mind is apt to do, back to when Ashling was a new mother. She brought Brigid to meet him soon after she was born. Malachi fell in love instantly as he whispered hello to the baby girl, who quickly cooed and smiled in response.

"Malachi I hope one day Brigid will have the same kind of friendship that you and I share. You know I think of you as part of my family now too?"

"I feel the same. The Raffertys have made me feel like family, all the years I've lived here. This is a good place to live and grow old."

He thought about the time when Ashling, new to being a mother, came running down the trail in search of him. Sobbing, she called out his name, holding the infant who cried inconsolably. When Ashling reached Malachi, she stared up at him with worried eyes.

"Brigid won't stop crying, Malachi. I've tried everything. I'm so scared. I don't know what to do, Ethan won't be home for hours!"

"Come closer dear one and quiet yourself. Worry and panic will not solve your problem now, will it? Let me see the child," Malachi said in a tone that immediately calmed Ashling.

Taking several deep breaths, Ashling slowly stopped shaking as she did what Malachi asked.

"Fever?" He asked.

"No, she's just been fussing all day. Ethan has been out doing field work since dawn, and I don't know what to do!"

The baby started to wail loudly once more. The more Brigid cried, the more Ashling became anxious, knowing something was seriously wrong.

"Sit down, dear one. You're upsetting the baby. Your worry and fear do not help you or Brigid! Behavior like this is not like you," he scolded gently.

"You know she is sensitive to the energy around her, and Brigid feeds off your emotions, so close your eyes and breathe."

Malachi patiently waited while Ashling did as he asked.

"What do you hear?" Malachi asked after a short time.

Taking another deep breath to collect herself, she replied, "I hear the birds, the river, and the leaves rustling in the trees."

"What else?" her friend asked.

"I hear my heartbeat," she slowly smiled.

"Dear one, what is it you don't hear anymore?"

Ashling opened one eye, peeking at the serene face of her daughter, staring expectantly at her. Brigid was a bit red around the eyes, but her heart melted when little Brigid reached up, touching Ashling's cheek as if trying to comfort her mother. The three sat in silence for some time.

Malachi cleared his throat. "When we think about things that might happen, that have not happened, and that may never happen, it robs us and others of the joy in that moment."

"I know you're right, Mal, but my head sometimes screams something different."

Ashling then began to tell Malachi of a dream. In it, Brigid disappeared. When she woke, it still felt very real. Ashling admitted she let her mind run wild with horrible thoughts.

"Mal, I've spent the day hovering over Brigid. The dream did not feel at all like a dream. When it came time for Brigid's nap, I couldn't bring myself to put her down. What if she didn't wake up?"

It didn't take much for Malachi to realize the new mother conjured up some unlikely and dark scenarios as she kept Brigid up past her regular nap time. Understandably, the tired infant started to cry and became inconsolable, then grew worse as Ashling's anxiety heightened, fearing the worst was going to happen. Still, she knew Malachi spoke the truth. Brigid fell asleep in her mother's arms, and Ashling, seeing her daughter at peace, was in no hurry to leave her friend.

"I've done this kind of thing before Mal, in high school. I had this boyfriend who seemed to be getting way too close to my—then best friend. I'd catch them walking down the hall with their heads close together. I was sure he was cheating on me. I confronted them one day after about a week of it going on."

"What did they say?"

"Nothing. They both just stared at me and walked away. I didn't see or hear from either of them again until later that night—at the surprise birthday party they had planned for me."

"Oh, I see."

"Ya, neither of them ever spoke to me again after that. I thought I learned my lesson, but look at what I did today with poor Brigid here."

"You're only human and allowed to make mistakes."

Ashling tucked the soft blanket under Brigid's chubby chin.

Malachi remembered telling Ashling she was too hard on herself. "You're a parent now. It is natural to worry, but you will learn to trust your instincts more as time goes on."

Malachi had an excellent memory for stories like this, but people such as Ashling and Brigid Rafferty were rare. He figured it was natural for him to remember so many details of their lives—sometimes feeling like he knew them over many lifetimes.

Old Malachi would do and give anything for the Rafferty family. He would gladly give his life for this family, but he knew, he could do nothing more but stand firmly rooted in his friendship, comfort, and hospitality when they came to visit.

Malachi knew his place in this young family's life, and it was on rare days like this, that he wished he didn't feel so alone.

5

Ethan navigated Old Blue to the side of the road, where his property line began. After parking, he honked once, then waved to get his foreman's attention. Tomas Elmer turned, nodded his head in greeting, and waited for Ethan to approach.

Tomas had been a part of the Double R as long as Ethan could remember. After Jim Elmer, the Rafferty's friend and neighbor was struck and killed by a drunk driver, his son Tomas was left alone in the world and unprepared with how to move forward in life. Eric and Cara Rafferty opened their home to Ethan's childhood friend, Tomas.

"We want you to stay with us at least until you and Ethan graduate, and we'd like you to think of this as your home," Eric told Tomas.

Tomas gratefully accepted the Rafferty's offer and was glad for Eric's help when shortly after Jim's funeral, he received an offer to buy his father's ranch. The proposal was generous and would easily secure the young man's future.

"I feel disloyal if I sell the ranch. It's all I have left of him," Tomas stated.

"I knew your father well. He knew being a rancher was his dream, not yours. There's a big difference between working the land and being a business owner. It's not for everyone. He'd be proud of you either way. Take your time deciding," Eric said, grasping Tomas' shoulder in a fatherly way.

Tomas eventually did accept the offer—but not before selling Eric a parcel of the Elmer land that connected with the Double R.

"I know Dad planned to sell you the back forty before he died. I found the contracts he'd drawn up, and I want to honor that deal if you are still interested," Tomas told Eric, who did purchase the acres where he intended to plant yews and test a new soil.

After Tomas and Ethan graduated high school, Tomas stayed on the ranch working side by side with Eric and the crew and finding a new purpose as he slowly began to heal thanks in part to Sally, his high school sweetheart. They were both eager to marry and start a family of their own—but tragedy struck again. Weeks before they were to be married she died in a freak accident. No one was with Sally as she fell two flights of stairs.

After his fiancé's death, Tomas became a shell of the man he once was. If it weren't for the Raffertys, Tomas knew he would not be alive today. Over the years, he once again began to rebuild his life, finding moments of peace and contentment. The Double R became his home, a refuge, and his lifeline.

Today, Tomas had brought supplies out to the ranch hands who were replacing a section of loose fencing.

"Can't have the cows headed to town on their own, now can we?" Tomas called out, wiping his brow with the back of his hand, waiting for Ethan to reach him.

"Don't know how we'd get by without you Tomas. Sorry I haven't had a chance to talk to you since last week. Thanks for picking up the slack for me. That meeting with the university was somewhat more intensive than I thought it'd be," Ethan confided.

"No problem. You got the saplings dropped off okay though?"

"Yep. Just getting back. Now we wait," Ethan replied.

Tomas nodded then gave a loud whistle. A shaggy dog sprinted to his side. He opened the passenger door of his work truck, and the dog jumped in, happily wagging his tail.

Tomas called out instructions to the workers, then brought his attention back to Ethan.

"Well, congratulations on sealing the deal with the university. You and the missus have worked hard. I know how important it—the yew research, is to you both," he said.

"Thanks, man. Although I wouldn't be surprised if Dad put in a call to his old alma mater, and opened a few doors," Ethan shrugged.

Reaching over, Ethan began to pet the dog through the open window of the truck.

"Eric's a good man, Ethan. He believes there's something to those trees and soil as much as you and Ashling do," Tomas said getting in his Ford and starting the engine.

"Sometimes it seems like only yesterday you and your old man planted all those trees."

"Over a thousand of them. Just me and Dad. When we came up with that fertilizer idea back then, we had no idea what was in store for us," Ethan laughed.

"You, remember how old Hanson down the road, bombarded your family that summer trying to get even a truckload of that dirt after seeing how tall your corn grew? He wanted to have it analyzed so he could copy what you guys were doing."

"Dad was on to him. He refused, of course. I remember it as a game. I was pretty secretive about it too."

"You were kind of a pain in the ass that year. You'd go on about ratios, fertilizer, and natural supplements the rest of us kids couldn't pronounce," Tomas chuckled.

"I was kind of a geek about it wasn't I?"

"Well, while everyone else was talking about football season and fishing, all your talk seemed a bit over our heads as fourth graders," Tomas added.

Ethan shook his head and gave his friend a lopsided grin.

"It was a crazy year. Dad and I have spoken of it since. It's like we were driven that year, like mad scientists."

"Still crazy thinking how rapidly the saplings grew into such spectacular trees," Tomas concluded.

The two men talked a minute longer, then proceeded in opposite directions on the Rafferty property.

Watching Tomas drive away, Ethan thought how merely getting a meeting with the university was years in the making.

Ethan had been just a young boy when he began helping his father plant saplings as part of a soil experiment. Today he delivered a sample of their yews to the university in hopes of finding a non-invasive cure for cancer, unlike what was used currently in chemotherapies. One Ashling was sure *once* existed. After all, her ancestors whispered the reality of a cancer-free world into her ear. They had yet to fail her, and Ethan trusted Ashling.

Feeling a bit nostalgic, Ethan drove the short distance to the yew grove, where he parked Old Blue and began walking among his trees. Hearing what sounded like a moan or cry, he stopped and listened intently, but heard nothing more. "Just the wind," he said, but then saw something move beneath one of the trees in the near distance.

He began to walk towards what appeared to be a small mound on the ground not far from him. Catching sight of long, auburn hair, Ethan started to run. He came upon his wife, crying out in her sleep. Reaching down with hands that trembled, Ethan spoke to her in a ragged voice that sounded foreign to his ears. "Ashling!"

Ethan knew he sounded harsh. Being overcome with fear and concern at the sight of his fragile looking wife, who was curled up in a ball and crying like a small child, was more than he could take. Slowly Ashling began to stir and stretch. She rubbed her eyes and saw the anxiety on Ethan's face, which left her feeling confused. She instantly pulled herself into a sitting position and reached for him, fear etching her pale face.

"Ethan, what's wrong? You look a sight! There's not an ounce of color in that handsome face."

Staring blankly at each other, Ashling finally realized how this must look to Ethan.

"Oh, I fell asleep," she said, giving a shaky laugh.

"I got dizzy. I only meant to sit a moment and rest. I must have fallen asleep feeling so content amongst the trees."

"You were crying in your sleep again, Ash. Did you have another one of those nightmares?"

Sighing, she nodded as Ethan came to sit beside her.

"This time in the dream, I started out being very happy. I was with Malachi. We were laughing, but then the dream turned dark. He disappeared. I started hearing voices that taunted me. I was calling out for them to stop."

She continued, wanting to rid herself of the memory.

"The voices claimed that you and Brigid were gone and never coming back again. It felt so real," Ashling said trembling.

"It was not like the other dreams or visits," she said adamantly looking into Ethan's eyes.

"It was a *bad dream*, Ash. That's all."

"Tell me somethin' happy, husband," she said, determined to turn the day around.

Ethan pulled her closer as he began to recall details of the meeting at the university. Every once in a while, she would comment or ask a question as they both sat and pondered the events that led to this week.

"Ashling, the actuality of your vision for the yew trees may be years out still, but the early feedback sounds very promising with what the school is planning."

They sat hand in hand under the trees, reminiscing of years ago when Ashling laughed and ran through their magical grove cared for by the Wee Folk.

"I can still see your face the first time I brought you here to the yews. You were so damned captivating—*ethereal* even!" Ethan stated with the conviction of a lovesick boy.

"Ethereal, huh?" Ashling chuckled.

"You hypnotized me then, barefoot and in full abandonment running through the grove. I'm still under your spell, wife!"

She tossed her head back, laughing.

"I was lost to your powers when you grabbed my hand and pulled me down on the grass," Ethan affirmed.

"I remember it like it was just yesterday too," she said quietly.

That day, years ago, Ashling had turned suddenly pensive. It was then she told Ethan about a different dream vision—a message passed down from generation to generation.

"We've always just called it the *Legend*. I don't know why. I've told you a little bit over the years Ethan, but some truly unusual occurrences have transpired over the generations. It's quite hard to ignore completely."

Ashling stared at Ethan, gauging his reaction. When she found no trace of doubt, she continued.

"We come from a long line of healers, but I think it skipped me," she said with a shrug.

"Well, the day I met you Ashling, you saved my life. So, I believe that makes you the most magical healer of them all."

"Oh, Ethan," Ashling sighed, contentedly.

"I truly think *we* might be a part of the Legend," Ashling continued.

"How so?"

"Well, call it my intuition or my gut feelings, but my dream-state has been more vivid these days. I trust my guides and ancestors. I feel like whatever is going on is powerful."

"If that's so, why do these dreams make you cry, and why are they so disturbing? I have a bad feeling about all of it."

"Ethan, I'm not quite sure just yet what to make of this either. I have been kind of resisting. I think that's why they are trying so hard to get my attention. Something definitely feels sad about whatever they are tryin' to convey. Sad and scary."

"Then can't you just tell them to stop and leave you alone or something?"

Hearing the frustration in Ethan's voice, she wanted to reassure him.

"My *knowings*, or my gut feelings, as you call them, have never let me down. I trust that they are here now to help in the highest good. It just feels big, and maybe I am not ready to hear the rest," she said, worrying her lip.

"Ethan, remember how my dream-state led you to me, and me to Oregon? What about the dream where I saw you driving Old Blue with the saplings to the university years ago? Then there's Brigid. They told me I would have a daughter whose skills would match that of the Priestess from the Legend." Ashling's smile brightened the somber mood.

"That part I like. Hey, what was that one story I heard you telling Brigid about the other night?"

"Oh, the one about little Ana and her grandmother Ferax? Well, Ferax was a highly respected Healer—a guardian of the earth. She had a vast knowledge of all things, plants, trees, and herbs. The wise woman had a special kinship with animals and nature elementals. Ferax would also communicate with the Wee Folk, Fairies, Elves, as well as the Spirits from the other side of the veil."

"The *veil*, Ash? What's that mean?"

"Some people call it heaven, others the afterlife," Ashling told him.

"I get that. Tell me more about Ferax."

"Well, it was Ferax who knew how to cure her people of a terrible sickness. Although, as predicted, the knowledge became lost after a plague or something. The Legend said after many centuries two people with considerable power from opposing clans would meet. Each would hold a piece of the sacred elixir code and once reunited the couple would do as Ferax had done lifetimes ago to cure the deadly illness for all time to come."

Having finished her story of Ana and Ferax, Ashling and Ethan sat together in comfortable silence.

"Hey, maybe that story is about you and me. Our life is like a fairy tale. You have a way of making me believe in them, you know?"

"It's easy to do in this magical place among the yews and the Wee Folk."

"Ya, there's something special about being right here," Ethan added.

"It's amazing what these trees have the capacity to give us. The soil you and your father created will change the world, Ethan. Just look at how many yews are on the property."

"I think you're getting ahead of yourself Ash. It's just a theory at this point," Ethan cautioned.

"Sure, scientifically, we know the importance of yews in current cancer protocols, but Ethan, thanks to you and your dad—what you have recreated is beyond logical reason."

"Still, Ash, the challenge is, how do we extract the bark and sap without depleting the grove? I won't sacrifice them in the name of science," Ethan stated-matter-of factly.

"Which is why we are lucky the university decided to take a second look at the trees you brought out today. I'm glad you insisted on the separate blind test and side by side test of our yews versus a typical Oregon Yew."

Finally feeling more like herself, Ashling gave Ethan a reassuring smile as she stood up and dusted herself off. "I must look a fright."

She reached out a hand to pull her husband up beside her; Ethan accepted it. He reached over in an intimate gesture to free a tangled leaf from her hair, and wipe a smudge from her face as they laughed.

"Well, at least I feel much better now."

"Good because I'm hungry! Let's get home so you can feed me, wife," Ethan teased as they turned to walk the half mile to their home, hand in hand.

"It's always food with you, husband! I'm surprised you don't weigh as much as old Quinn there," she teased, pointing towards the calf who munched on a blade of grass nearby.

Ethan stopped abruptly.

"Ashling, where are your shoes woman? What have you done with them this time?"

She shrugged her shoulders.

"Um, worried about my feet, are you? However, did you forget about your beloved truck?" she said, playfully pointing toward Old Blue parked nearby.

"Good point! It's such a beautiful day, let's walk. I'll come back later for it."

Ashling was grateful for the fresh air, the walk, and her husband by her side. Spying Malachi from the corner of her eye, she waved a friendly hello.

"Hello, Malachi. A glorious day to be alive, isn't it?" Ashling said in passing.

"Every day for an old guy like me is glorious," Malachi chuckled.

6

The school year settled into a comfortable routine for Brigid. Most of the children accepted her, even though some kids, like her classmate Billy, still thought she talked and behaved strangely. Once, at recess, Billy was poking at a small insect on the ground. Seeing the boy torture the tiny creature, Brigid yelled from across the schoolyard.

"Stop that!"

Billy froze in his tracks, not understanding the warning he heard in Brigid's voice. With a singular focus, Brigid stopped abruptly in front of the wide-eyed student who could not have known young Brigid's attachment to the slinky critter. Paying him no heed, Brigid carefully bent down towards the ground. She held out her hand to a plump orange and black caterpillar. As the long, furry insect meandered onto her tiny finger, she spoke to it in a reassuring tone. Slowly standing, Brigid placed it on a nearby tree leaf. Once she was sure the creature was safe, she waved goodbye—quietly walking away from the boy she had all but forgotten.

Toward the end of the school year, Emma's parents finally allowed the girls to have a playdate. Brigid found it hard to contain her excitement, hardly sleeping the night before. She was out of bed before Joe, their dutiful rooster, who signaled his decree of the new day. She quickly made her way to the kitchen where Ethan, who always woke first, stood leaning against the counter, drinking his coffee.

"Sprite, the sun's barely up yet. What are you doing out of bed already?"

"Emma comes today, don't you remember?" Brigid asked.

She shifted her weight, hands on her hips, as she reminded her dad with an anguished expression—as if it was apparent why she stood there.

"The chickens aren't even awake yet. You should still be asleep, snuggled up with Miss Cuddles."

"Oh, she's still sleepin'. I didn't wake her. It's way too early," Brigid told her father, rolling her eyes at him, as she spoke.

"It's still a few hours before we get to meet your friend, why don't you try to go back to sleep?"

"Sleep? Seriously Dad? I can't sleep. I'm too excited!" Brigid added, raising her hands above her head for emphasis.

"We still get to ride Sir Prance A Lot, right?"

"Of course," Ethan replied.

Ashling was next to arrive in the kitchen, trying to stifle a yawn.

"What on earth do we have going on so early in the mornin'?" she asked the pair standing before her.

Ethan explained as Ashling stood before the lit fireplace, warming her hands.

"Oh, a wee bit excited, are you? Well, an early morning breakfast it'll be. Did you get the eggs yet darlin'?" Ashling asked Ethan as she put the water on for her morning tea.

"I'm on it," Ethan threw a coat over his shoulders as he made his way to the door.

The morning moved much too slowly for Brigid, but finally, she saw the sleek black Mercedes drive up the lane, stopping in front of their roundabout driveway. The Rafferty's screen door flew opened just as quickly as the Mercedes back door did. Both girls bounded towards each other at lightning speed and threw themselves into each other's arms laughing.

Ashling met Emma's mother halfway. They exchanged pleasantries and similar stories of how their day started before the sun had come up, thanks to two incredibly excited girls.

"Emma and I were discussing how neither of us had been on a working ranch before today. This should be quite the educational experience for her," Evelyn Daily, told Ashling.

"Oh, the girls won't get bored, that's for sure. Do you have time for tea, Evelyn?"

"Thanks, but I'm already late for a meeting across town."

"Well, thank you for dropping Emma off, and I'll make sure I have her home at four-thirty so that she'll be on time for her piano lesson," Ashling assured Evelyn who was already checking her watch, giving Ashling a quick affirmative nod.

"Yes, her teacher does not tolerate tardiness. Thank you, Ashling."

With a quick wave to her daughter, Evelyn closed her car door, and drove quickly back down the lane.

Brigid And Emma

"What's your plan for the day Brigid, my girl? You've been working on that list all week," Ashling asked.

"Well, we're gonna go down to the stream to toss stones in the water, and Emma has never seen a goat. She'll love the goats. I want her to meet Mal and the others if we have time before Dad takes us to ride Sir Prance A Lot," Brigid paused, looking at her list.

"Darlin', why don't you save a visit to Malachi for another day? There's plenty to see and do today."

Brigid merely shrugged her shoulders, while Emma politely followed the conversation between Ashling and Brigid.

"Maybe Emma would like to see the house, while I get you two something to eat? Then you can head out on your adventures," Ashling suggested.

"Sure. Come on, Emma," Brigid said, taking Emma's hand.

Brigid began first by showing Emma her room, filled with stuffed animals and dolls. Then Brigid introduced her to Miss Cuddles, whom Emma instantly took a liking to.

"Mother said I am allergic, but I'm not sneezing Brig. I can't wait to tell her. Maybe I can get a cat too," Emma said hopefully.

By the way, the tabby was purring when Emma kissed the felines head Miss Cuddles quite liked Emma as well.

Next was the tree. Brigid giggled at the way Emma's mouth dropped open as she silently walked around the base of the live oak in the center of their living room.

"Brigid, you have a tree—a huge tree in your living room!"

Brigid giggled again, nodding her head.

"Girls, your snacks are ready," Ashling called from the kitchen.

Taking Emma's hand, Brigid led her to the kitchen.

Emma stared once again at the oak growing inside the Rafferty's home. She did not speak for quite some time until Brigid finally started laughing.

"Mom, it's just like I said. Emma couldn't believe we have a tree in the living room."

"Can we climb it?" Emma asked.

"Naw, we just look after it. But my dad made a playroom upstairs. We call it the treehouse. Wanna play there later?"

"Oh, yes! I've always wanted a tree house," Emma added.

Having finished their treats, Brigid hugged her mom, and soon the two girls were out the door, promising to check in later.

"Thank you, Mrs. Rafferty," Emma said.

"Can we see the goats first Brig?" Emma asked, sounding hopeful.

"Sure, let's go!"

Reaching the goat's pen, Brigid carefully unlatched the gate to where the noisy animals greeted them. Suddenly becoming shy, Emma stepped behind her friend. That changed as soon as one of the baby goats came around the corner, bumping into Emma. The surprised goat plopped down on its rump, staring up at Emma in bewilderment.

"Aww, it's okay," Emma said, sinking to her knees whispering to the large round eyes looking questioningly back at her. Emma began to pet then hug the adorable grey and white creature who doled out kisses in her direction, making Emma giggle. Both girls made a game out of letting the goats chase them. Tired out from running, Brigid suggested it was time to go.

"I don't ever want to leave," Emma declared.

"We'll stay longer next time you come over. I have so many things I want to show you today."

With one final hug for the small goat, the girls ambled down toward the creek where they skipped stones and floated leaves down the lazy stream of water.

"Today is already so much fun, I know I'll never forget it," Emma assured her friend.

"What do you wanna do next?" asked Brigid.

"Can we ride the pony yet?"

"We have to wait for my dad. He has to work for a while, and then he'll come to get us."

"My father works all the time. You're lucky your dad can take time to play with you," Emma replied.

"You wanna go meet Malachi?"

"Oh, is that your grandfather?"

"No, but my mom says Mal is like her second dad. I don't know what that means, but mom always smiles when she says it. You and me wouldn't be friends now if I hadn't listened to him. He's funny and a real good listener, and he wants to meet you. I've told him all about you already," Brigid confided.

"Okay, let's go," Emma said, jumping to her feet and tossing one last pebble in the stream.

The two girls began to walk, stopping every now and again to watch an eagle fly overhead or to stare at a squirrel who scrambled by, flicking its thick bushy tail.

Not long after starting down the well-worn path, Brigid spied Malachi near an open pasture. She waved a cheery hello.

"Hey Mal, I brought my friend Emma to meet you. She got to come here today to play. We want to tell you about our day."

As the girls took a few more steps, Brigid slipped out of her little sneakers, still rambling on to Malachi as she squished her toes into the soft ground.

Emma tilted her head, staring at her friend who sat down on a lush green patch of grass as if she'd done this a million times.

Emma decided to sit too.

Brigid laughed.

"Oh but Malachi, I haven't even gotten to the funny part."

Emma stared at Brigid, who continued to talk and answer questions.

Emma listened with a quizzical expression on her face. After a few moments of listening to her friend, Emma stood, looking left, and then to the right. With deliberate steps, she made a loop around a massive oak tree beneath which Brigid sat. Emma, having made a complete turn around the tree, looked everywhere. Finally, she stood with her hands on her hips in front of Brigid, who now held her stomach from giggling so hard at some unknown joke.

With a stern expression, Emma raised her hands in the air in a dramatic and exasperated manner.

"Who are you talking to Brigid Rafferty?" Emma demanded.

Brigid stopped laughing instantly. Emma glared back, only now Brigid could tell that her friend was angry as she tapped her toe—kind of like Ashling did when she was unhappy.

"Why Emma, I'm talking to Malachi, of course. Don't you think what he said about the goats was funny?"

Emma turned around, stomping off in the direction they had recently come. Her arms angrily swished back and forth at her side. Panicked and confused, Brigid jumped up and began running after her. Quickly catching up with Emma, Brigid gave a gentle tug on her friend's arm in a silent plea to stop. When Emma finally did, Brigid's sad face looked into Emma's dark eyes, wondering what could have happened to make Emma so angry.

"What's wrong, Emma, why are you mad? Where you goin'?"

Once again, Emma tapped her toe. This time her arms were folded tightly in front of her tiny body, standing as tall as she possibly could, while trying to look Brigid in the eyes.

"Brigid Rafferty, there isn't anyone out here but you and me! You being out here laughing and talking to yourself is dumb—and mean! I'm leaving!" Emma scolded.

Emma turned again away from Brigid. With purposeful steps, she began to walk towards the Rafferty home, which was now in sight.

"Wait. Stop! Please, Emma," Brigid pleaded.

"I'm not trying to be mean. Did me and Malachi say something wrong? We didn't mean to leave you out. Mom says never to do that, and so does Malachi. Come back. We'll talk to him about it."

Brigid's voice cracked with emotion, as her eyes welled with tears. Stopping, Emma tilted her head once again, carefully considering her friend. Emma was no longer tapping her toe, which Brigid was grateful for, but she thought Emma looked like she held her breath, as her face turned red.

Brigid held her breath too, wishing her friend would say something soon.

"Brigid, tell me the truth. Who do you think you were you talking to over there? No one was there, but you and me. Stuff like this is why the kids at school say you're weird, you know. You say and do strange things."

Brigid hung her head, but she refused to let one tear fall.

"But Malachi is right there Emma, didn't you hear him say hello to you? He said your hair was a pretty color, and you had a kind smile."

"Brigid Rafferty, I may be only seven years old, but I'm not stupid," she told Brigid, who quickly agreed.

"Oh Emma, you're probably smarter than most of the teachers at school!"

Brigid began rattling off all the things Emma could do that Brigid couldn't.

"You can play songs on the piano. You know French and Spanish words, and you're the only kid in class that always get the gold stars."

Emma's face began to soften as she listened to the sincerity in her friend's voice. Maybe, just maybe, Brigid wasn't making fun of or teasing her.

"Brigid, walk me over to Malachi and point to him," Emma cautiously said.

Dumbfounded, but willing to do anything to make Emma want to be her friend, Brigid stood beside Malachi and placed her hand on his trunk.

"This?" Emma asked as she waved her hands at Malachi.

"This your friend, Brigid?"

Emma waited for Brigid to respond.

"Well, of course, he is! Mal just told you so."

Now it was Brigid's turn to tap her toe and cross her arms. She also stuck her chin out to show Emma she didn't like how she was treating Malachi. "Why are you being so mean, Emma?"

"This is a tree, Brig. Just a big old tree! So, all the times you've talked about Malachi at school, this is what you were talking to? Brigid Rafferty, this is silly. I thought you had some cool grandfather, but no. You're telling me—this tree is Malachi?"

"He's not just an old tree. Say you're sorry!"

The two girls stared unblinkingly at each other. Emma was the first to break the silence.

"Geez Brig, you seriously want me to believe that you talk with *trees*?"

7

It was on this day, once filled with innocence, exploration, and laughter that two young girls found themselves standing next to a mammoth-sized oak tree, facing an unspoken and significant—crossroad.

Emma did not for one minute, believe Brigid's tree Malachi talked to her or anyone else. Brigid did not understand how Emma could not hear Malachi or why she was acting so mean. Even Brigid's dad, who admitted he didn't hear Mal so clearly, would at least say hello and be kind to him. Brigid remembered earlier in the day, Ashling had suggested she wait for another day to introduce Malachi to Emma, but Brigid wanted her two friends to meet.

Malachi, for his part, wisely remained silent while the friends worked out their dilemma. Neither girl wanted to fight but was unsure how to move forward. Brigid stood, staring at the ground, absently kicking at the dirt with her tiny toes. Her bare feet were stirring up dust that made her sneeze.

"Bless you," Emma said.

"Thank you," Brigid responded.

Brigid walked back to the oak, sat down with her back resting on Malachi's trunk. Emma followed Brigid, then sat down on a bench opposite of her and Malachi just a few feet away. Emma remained in quiet contemplation, admiring the tree swing and the shade the fullness of the old tree provided, trying to understand why this particular tree was so important to her friend who sat leaning against it.

Sitting in silence, Emma thought back to Christmas-time and the talk she had with her parents about Santa. Emma very much believed in a man in a red suit, as the other kids did. Weeks before Christmas, she handed her mother a handwritten letter in her best penmanship and asked her to help her mail it to the North Pole.

"What's this, darling?" Evelyn asked.

"It's my Christmas list to Santa. Don't worry, I remembered to say please and thank you. I kept the list small, not like Billy, who said his letter was four pages. I asked Mr. Claus to say hello to Mrs. Claus and his elves too."

Emma's parents sat her down that day, and calmly explained how irrational her request was.

"Emma, dear, your mother and I are truly sorry for deceiving you. We thought one small imaginary indulgence would do no harm," Emma's father said, patting her hand awkwardly.

"Darling, how could it be possible for one man to deliver toys to all the children around the world?" her mother reasoned.

"Well, if it's you and Father who put the presents under the tree, why do I usually just get a book or something like that, when other kids are getting fun toys?" Emma innocently asked.

"Look at our home, our clothes, all the extra activities you are involved in. We have more than enough. Don't you think it's selfish by wanting more when we have so much, while others go without?" Evelyn stated more than asked her daughter.

Feeling ashamed, Emma never dared speak of it again.

Still staring up at the oak tree named Malachi, slowly swaying in the breeze, Emma also remembered losing her first tooth. She asked her father to help her find a safe place to keep it until bedtime.

"Why would we do that, darling?" Her father asked frowning in confusion.

"So I can put it under my pillow tonight. That's where the Tooth Fairy gets it, right?"

It was still embarrassing to Emma, thinking about how her father laughed, picked up his briefcase then told her he'd see her later that night.

Emma's father left her, staring at the closed door. In need of answers, she went in search of her mother. Emma knew Evelyn would be sitting at her desk, fingers clicking furiously at the keyboard of the computer in front of her. Emma never interrupted her mother when she was working from home, but she needed answers. Taking a deep breath to gather the courage, Emma tapped on her mother's half-closed door and slowly entered.

Emma asked her mom the same question she had asked her father, then patiently waited—unsure if her mother had heard her. Moments later, Evelyn, a thin, dark haired woman with an olive complexion, removed the stylish glasses she was wearing, rubbed the bridge of her nose, then turned off the monitor.

"Come in darling," Evelyn said, motioning for Emma to sit down next to her. Emma always felt warm all over when her mother would smile at her the way she did that day. Small acts of affection were rare since her parents were often away from home, but Emma knew they loved her very much.

"Darling," her mother said.

Emma knew that tone all too well. This wasn't going to be something she particularly wanted to hear, but she waited for her mother to continue.

"Where did you get the idea that a winged *fairy* would come to take your tooth sweetheart?" Her mother asked gently.

"Tanner at school. He lost a tooth, and he said the Tooth Fairy left him ten dollars under his pillow, and in the morning, his tooth was gone," Emma replied, looking with earnest attention at the tooth in the palm of her hand.

"Emma, remember when we talked about Santa and how he isn't real?" Evelyn asked, placing her hand on her daughter's shoulder.

Emma nodded her head, wanting to cry.

"Well, I guess your father and I just assumed you would realize that of course, it isn't rational to think there is some type of fairy that flies into a child's room at night, and takes their tooth, then leaves money in its place. How would one even get past the security system?"

Evelyn continued, "You do see how silly that sounds, don't you, darling?"

Emma remembered feeling ashamed, yet she sat tall, trying to keep her voice from cracking, and a tear from falling. Emma knew what she must do. Lifting her chin, just like her mother did in the chair next to her, Emma tucked her perfectly white tooth in her pocket, feeling much older than her seven years of age.

"Of course I didn't *really* believe it, Mother. Maybe I just hoped for ten dollar's like Tanner's parents gave him so I could tell the kids at school."

Evelyn nodded, then having considered the subject closed, turned the monitor back on and began tapping away on the computer keys while Emma quietly left the office.

"So much for the Easter Bunny," Emma mumbled to the empty hall.

Brigid sneezed again bringing Emma out of her silent contemplation.

Emma realized what she had to do. If her friend needed to believe Malachi could talk, well that was perfectly fine with Emma. How many long lonely nights after her nanny tucked her into bed, did Emma wait for her parents to come home from a meeting or dinner party, leaving her with only an imaginary friend to talk to? Of course, Emma never told anyone this, but just maybe though, one day she would tell her secret to Brigid. She now knew her friend would understand.

Jumping to her feet and dusting herself off, Emma approached Brigid. Holding out her hand, Brigid accepted the gesture, and Emma quickly pulled Brigid to her feet.

"I'm sorry I got mad Brig," Emma said with her brightest smile.

Taking a long, slow look up the tree, Emma gently brushed her hand along the rough, craggy skin of the oak.

"Hello, Malachi! I'm very sorry I was rude to you. It's nice to meet you."

Brigid felt the wall of dread, slip away.

The girls turned their heads in unison when they heard Ethan honk the truck's horn while he slowly made his way up the drive.

"My dad's home. Let's go!"

Quickly slipping into her sneakers, Brigid took hold of Emma's hand. Both girls took off with squeals of delight to catch up with the truck—leaving their disagreement behind. As Ethan stepped out of Old Blue, Brigid flung herself into her father's waiting arms. Emma, having never witnessed such an act of affection, felt sad, yet did not know the reason why.

"Dad, this is Emma."

To Ethan's surprise, the small child next to his daughter was reaching out her hand to shake his much larger, calloused hand. He took her hand in his.

"Very nice to meet you, Mr. Rafferty."

"Call me Ethan, all our friends do." Ethan winked, and Emma instantly felt at ease.

"Well, I'm off to cut some firewood, you girls have fun," Ethan said, teasing the girls.

Brigid knew her father was joking, but Emma understood only too well, forgotten plans sometimes happened with grown-ups. So she merely stood stoically waiting for what would happen next.

To her surprise, both Brigid and Ethan began to laugh.

"*Dad*," Brigid said, joining in on the secret.

"Well, maybe the wood can be chopped later. What do you two ladies say we take the ponies out for a little ride?"

The cheers of approval made Ethan laugh even louder. Once inside the small arena, Ethan slowly introduced Emma to the horses, while the ranch hands saddled up the Shetland ponies for the girls. Sir Prance A Lot, a slow and easy-going brown miniature Shetland was the perfect choice for a small child not accustomed to the four-legged creatures, while Brigid rode a sassy pony named Isabelle.

"I'm for sure gonna remember this day for the rest of my life," Emma added sincerely.

"Me too, Emma," Brigid agreed.

Ethan kept a watchful eye on the two girls and marveled at how quickly Brigid was growing up. Ashling walked into the arena, waved to the girls and sank into the warmth of her husband's bear hug. Ethan and Ashling stood together for some time, watching the girls talk and giggle as they made slow circles about the indoor ring, lost in a world of their own.

Ashling had the unfortunate task of reminding the group of the promise to have Emma home in time for her piano lesson.

"No!" Both girls echoed their sentiment in accord.

"We'll get another play date together very soon girls," Ashling assured Emma and Brigid.

With one last gallop around the large loop, all was feeling normal in Brigid's world, but something was worrying her about Malachi. She wanted to check on him and hoped there would be enough daylight to visit after they took Emma home. She knew Malachi would want to know everything worked out just fine between her and Emma.

8

Malachi was old. If he remembered correctly, he was close to two hundred and fifty years now—give or take a few. Not too old though to understand what had transpired with young Brigid and Emma earlier in the day. Malachi knew that not everyone could hear him. Although he was content with that, little Brigid was heartbroken, and Emma was just as confused, yet they found a way to move forward, as children do.

Malachi saw and heard a great deal in all his years, having his roots anchored deep in the Rafferty land. Humans, animals, as well as spirits on this earth and the other side of the veil, admired the mighty oak. He had what some called an honest and fair reputation. Malachi supposed it was because he was a good listener, and chose not to cast judgment on others. The subject of judgment was complicated when it came to the humans of the earth, but not so much for other life forces. Souls who passed to the otherworld no longer quantified good or bad, right or wrong in the same way humans often did. They focused more on joy or suffering instead. He also knew humans judged themselves the hardest.

"Maybe it's just my nature, but I cannot find fault with a pine tree for having needles and cones, or a sunflower for not blooming like a rose," Malachi said as his branches drooped ever so slightly.

"I wonder why humans judge themselves by another's standards or beliefs? Young Brigid and Emma found a way to accept each other's differences easily enough," he said to no one in particular.

Malachi learned long ago, from those who sat beneath his branches, that humans merely desired to be accepted and loved. By listening more and talking less, he was able to gain much understanding of human nature.

Malachi witnessed this earlier with the little ones as they navigated their differences. He admired that while they could have got stuck in a battle of beliefs, they wisely chose to honor the unique part of their individuality and friendship.

"I wish more humans would sit under a tree and stare into each other's eyes and hearts. The earth would be more peaceful if they did."

Malachi became silent. His branches fluttered in the breeze like a slow rhythmic breath.

"Maybe my age is catching up with me—what was it I was thinking about?" Malachi muttered.

"Hello Malachi. Are you well, my friend? Did I wake you?" A soft whisper in the wind called out.

"Is that you Zara?" he asked the unseen voice in the sky.

"It is," replied the silvery female voice.

"I've been showing a new one around, and she mentioned loving the mountains and trees in her human experience, so I told her I had a magnificent, wise oak to introduce her to. She didn't understand what I meant, so I decided to show her. You don't mind, do you, friend?" Zara asked, kindly.

"Of course not, Zara."

"Who are you called?" Malachi asked the golf ball sized orb next to Zara.

It took some time for Malachi to hear her answer, but the tiny yellow-gold ball of swirling energy that faded in and out of view did eventually respond in a timid whisper of a voice. "Amelia."

"She's just learning to communicate," Zara explained.

"Well, you are most welcome here anytime, Amelia. Soon you will see how easy it is to be with those you love and in places you choose to be."

"Amelia always wanted to travel in her human experience, so I'm going to show her the trees of Oregon, the Highlands of Scotland, then the majestic animals in Africa. Oh and the Grand Canyon! She will love the bird's eye view!" Zara laughed at her joke.

Zara spoke like an enthusiastic tour guide. She appeared as a globe the size of a tennis ball, sizzling with bright, vivid hues bursting forth from an indigo core, and pulsing outward with colors of a faint rainbow. A noticeable halo of gold surrounded her.

"Well, then, Zara, Amelia, I shall expect to hear exciting stories about your adventures upon your return," Malachi told the two travelers.

In the blink of an eye, they disappeared.

Malachi turned his symmetrical leaves ever so slightly towards the bright sun just beginning to slip behind the Cascade Range. He was quite content to bask in the afternoon rays resting on his tufts of silky moss that clung to his branches.

Relaxing as the heat soaked deep into his core, it didn't take long before Malachi fell asleep, but soon a loud bugling sound coming from the southern sky woke him with a start. Gathering his wits, he knew who would soon be approaching long before he saw his old friend Turlough—thanks to his customary trumpet-like greeting.

Within seconds, seemingly from nowhere, a large, sleek, white bird with a scarlet feathered crown upon his head, dipped his long neck, while descending elegantly towards Malachi. A powerful pulsation whirred from the bird's flapping wings. *Tun-tun, tun-tun, tun-tun.*

Malachi instinctively knew his friend was in a hurry.

Turlough typically liked to make an entrance, like an actor taking a bow on stage. The giant bird could be ostentatious at times, but a more elegant bird in flight would be hard to find. Malachi stretched, lowering a branch, so his friend could land with ease. Without preamble, the Crane began to speak in a dignified yet loud nasally sing-song voice.

"Could hear you miles away Malachi, going on and on, probably rambling on to yourself again until you bore yourself to sleep. Am I right?"

Malachi jostled the branch his friend sat upon—simply to ruffle his feathers.

"Tell me, Crane, what brings you here today? Just wanted to weigh down my branches with your ill will?" Malachi asked grumpily.

Turlough stared, round eyes unblinking at the tree.

"You're not usually grumpy old fellow, what's got your roots all tangled up today?" the Crane asked with moderate concern.

"You just woke me from a little nap Turlough. I guess you startled me a bit," he told the bird.

"Zara was here today," Malachi added, sounding much more like himself.

"Was she with the new one?" Turlough asked with sincere interest.

"If you mean the one who called herself Amelia, then yes. Have you met her?"

"Hadn't had the pleasure yet, when she came through I was busy showing a couple who was married fifty-eight human years around. Went to sleep holding hands on this side, woke up giddy as can be on the other side. They're going to do great things those two!"

Turlough was proud of his many jobs, like greeting new souls, but he was best known as the one who carried messages of great importance, so Malachi knew his arrival marked a significant event.

"I have much to do today, but I've something you need to know," Turlough said in a solemn tone.

Malachi remained silent. The showy bird liked to create an air of importance with a drawn-out speech before he delivered news, but today, Turlough showed no arrogance.

"I knew you would want to hear this from me, and she will need to hear it from you so she can prepare," the Crane said matter of factly.

"She, who?" Malachi prompted.

"The girl," Turlough continued in his breathy timbre.

He bugled as his elongated neck quivered.

Malachi was instantly concerned. "Brigid? What could you possibly want with young Brigid?"

Turlough flapped his wings twice, leaving his perch with visible agitation. Gliding to the ground, he began to pace on long stick-like legs that seemed impossible to hold the weight of the bird.

"Not that one!" The Crane fixed his unblinking eyes once again on Malachi, bugling louder, to make his point.

"The mother," Turlough responded.

"Ashling?" Malachi inquired.

"Yes, Ashling Elizabeth."

9

Ethan entered the master bedroom, carefully avoiding the creaking floorboards in need of repair. The early morning sunlight peeked through the curtains and came to rest on the fireplace mantle, illuminating photos of the Rafferty Family. He made his way across the room to where Ashling slept. It was rare if ever that she slept late into the morning. Gently, Ethan ran his hand along her forehead, finding her cheeks flushed, and her forehead warm.

Ashling stirred, as her brow furrowed.

Ethan longed to wake her as she began to toss and turn. Her breathing became rapid, and she began to sweat. Ethan could take it no more. Sitting on the bed, he gathered his wife into his arms. Ashling, in her sleep, clung to Ethan and quickly calmed. Her breathing once again becoming smooth and rhythmic.

As the house became silent once again, Ethan was tempted to close his eyes and rest, but a slight tap on the bedroom door—and the tiny figure standing before him changed his mind.

Ethan smiled at Brigid, who wandered into the room. Holding a finger to his lips, Brigid nodded her understanding and tiptoed across the room and gently climbed into the bed. As she snuggled in-between her parents, Ethan tucked the blanket under the sleepy child's chin and marveled at how quickly his daughter drifted back to sleep. Ethan kept a vigil over his wife and daughter while they slept.

It was with an awkward smile and stretch that Ashling greeted the day. The movement awakened Brigid, and the faces staring back at Ashling slightly unnerved her. Brigid's expression was tender, but Ethan's unmistakable look of relief was evident to Ashling.

"Oh my! Did I oversleep?"

"You never sleep longer than me. Are you sick? We should take your temperature," Brigid informed her mother.

"No, darlin', I think I just stayed up a little too late last night. Thank you both for letting me sleep."

Ashling began to push the blankets aside to stand. Swaying ever so slightly, she closed her eyes. Quickly, Ethan was at her side, propping her pillows up and helping her settle back into bed.

"You're to stay put in bed. Brigid and I are going to fix you breakfast today," Ethan told his wife, who was already in mid-protest.

Seeing the excitement on her daughter's face silenced Ashling.

"And we're gonna make pancakes in funny shapes and toast and hot chocolate..." Brigid exclaimed as her bare feet pattered down the hall.

"What's wrong, Ash?"

"I guess I'm just feeling a wee bit light-headed again. I'd like to think I was pregnant, but more likely it's just the flu."

"I think you should see a doctor right away. After last time," he softened his voice, "I don't want you to take any chances with your health."

Seeing the worried look on her husband's face, Ashling would not deny him this request.

"Of course, my love. I'll call after breakfast."

Relieved the subject was settled, and with a small spark of hope in his heart, Ethan made his way to the kitchen to make the morning meal with his daughter.

Brigid was closing the refrigerator door as Ethan entered the room. Reaching over, he held the eggs for her, as she climbed onto the chair she had already pushed next to the island where they would often cook together. They chatted comfortably, both at ease in the kitchen and with each others company. Brigid carefully cracked eggs into the bowl as Ethan instructed her. Only after she climbed down, and turned away, did Ethan discreetly pick out the fragmented eggshells from the metal bowl.

"Whatcha lookin' for Sprite?"

"Mom's magic wooden spoon. It makes the food extra yummy."

Ethan handed Brigid the spoon that was just out of arms reach, and together they mixed the pancake batter and made silly creatures with the creamy mixture.

"It smells mighty good in there you two, I'm starving," Ashling playfully called out from the room down the hall.

In truth, she wasn't hungry. If Ashling was honest with herself, she hadn't had much of an appetite for days now.

"Pesky flu," she muttered, not allowing the hope of being pregnant to linger in her conscious thoughts.

Hearing Brigid's sweet voice brought Ashling out of her shrouded thoughts.

"We're coming," Brigid assured her mom excitedly, while carefully arranging plates and cups on a tray for Ethan to carry down the hall.

The Raffertys sat on the king-sized bed, eating and chatting about the new baby goats.

"We should do this every day." Brigid declared.

"Mmm, these eggs are delicious darlin'."

"I made em, and Dad helped," Brigid announced proudly, but she soon became distracted.

"Can I go out to play now?" Brigid asked after she finished her meal.

"You know the drill, sweater, and boots, and brush your teeth," Ethan instructed.

Kissing her parents on the cheek, Brigid scrambled down from the bed, running with pigtails flying, to start a new adventure.

"Talk to me," Ethan said after he was sure Brigid was out of earshot.

"It happened again, Ethan. This time, it was much more vivid," Ashling answered quietly, looking sad and tired—her face still pale.

"It wasn't a good message in your dream I take it?"

"No."

"I don't like the way you're looking at me, Ash."

"Maybe, you're wrong, or misunderstood it, perhaps…"

"Husband, it's me you're talking about. Ferax and the Priestess came to me last night. They showed me things I believe only a handful of people experience."

"What *things*, Ash?"

"Well, like what people who write those books about being in a coma or that have near-death experiences write about."

"What do you mean?"

"Well, I believe that those who don't *completely* pass over to the other side of the veil, after a trauma, or for whatever reason, have unfinished business. Like there's a choice to cross over or wake up. I've read stories about those who choose to awaken. What they say they witness in the *in-between* space—is life-altering even."

"You're talking in riddles, Ash."

"Ferax and the Priestess came and showed me two paths coming into my life, and I have a choice to make."

"What kind of choices?"

If Ethan's hand shook a bit as he took hers in his, neither one mentioned it.

"The Legend of my people is a powerful one, as you know. You've witnessed yourself the predicted events that have come to fruition."

"Okay. What's it got to do with you and choices?"

"Do you remember me telling you how in the Legend, a mother must make the ultimate sacrifice so that the new Healer could fulfill her role for humanity?" Ashling asked.

"Well, yes, but that's just an old wives tale, Ashling!"

Ashling slowly shook her head no.

"I'm destined to be part of the Legend. You and Brigid will be too. They showed me what life would be like if I stayed here and what it would be like if I chose to pass."

"Pass to *where*?"

He would later remember the moments that followed to be like an old-time silent movie, shot in slow motion as his wife continued with her revelation. Ethan stared, but Ashling's mouth and words were not in sync. She continued speaking much too calmly, Ethan decided.

"I, of course, have my free will, but in the years ahead I'll be presented with the decision to save my life or to pass beyond the veil to do more significant work that would help and heal many others to come."

Ethan scoffed.

"Well, you're staying *here* Ashling, with our daughter and me, just to be clear. I'm sure you would never consider the alternative. Let someone else do these good deeds. Legend be damned! There is no conversation to be had between you and me on this subject. Do you hear me?" Ethan barked harshly and a bit too loudly.

Pushing the chair roughly to the side, he stood, looking down as Ashling's eyes filled with tears. Silence hung in the air as they remained deadlocked in an anguished dance of denial and fear. Small drops of diamond-like tears slid down her face, but she was not about to let go of Ethan's hand. It was as if by mutual understanding, they clung to each other like a lifeline.

He sat back down.

"Ash, say it out loud. Say the words. Tell me you are choosing to stay here. In this world, no—*veil*, or whatever the hell you call it, but here with Brigid and me. Say it, dammit!"

Ashling slowly removed one hand from Ethan's to brush his cheek with gentle care.

Ethan sat staring past Ashling, finding it hard to breathe. Fear gripped his heart and tightened around his throat, making it impossible to voice the foreboding pain threatening to shatter their lives.

Ashling's predictions from her dream-state came true in the past, so whatever she said now, Ethan knew she believed. She often shared what Ethan called coincidences with him, and sure it was odd, and maybe a little creepy at times, but Ashling was highly aware of things about to happen.

"It's common. Many people have these experiences," she had explained.

"Once, when I was five, Ferax warned me not to touch a poisonous plant I was tempted to taste. It was so enticing with its cherry colored berries, but I waited. Instead, I took part of the plant to show my mom, and ask her if it was safe."

"Was it?"

"No. I remember Mom instantly grabbed a smelly, sticky ointment of herbs, and began rubbing it all over my hands as she brought me to the sink to wash them off. Then she made me drink this thick brown tea, while she gave a not so quiet thank you to Ferax."

"So, it was dangerous?" Ethan asked.

"Aye, highly poisonous to people and animals. I remember taking my dad to the plant. It was so vibrant and pretty. It was hard to imagine it being harmful, but Dad put on some heavy gloves and dug it up. I never knew what he did with it, but I know I felt safer after that day. I began trusting what Ferax or the Priestess would tell me."

"That's pretty cool, Ash," Ethan said at the time and meant it.

"Then there was the time I was still in high school, and the Priestess beckoned me not to get into a car with a boy who would be drunk at a party I had plans to go to the following night. I was awake when she came to me that time. I liked Randy, and I was more than a wee bit tempted to get in his new convertible. He was the only boy in town with one quite like it."

"What'd you do?"

"He was quite the catch, and I admit it was flattering that a popular boy asked me out," she confided to Ethan who feigned mock jealously over a high school crush Ashling once had.

"I just wanted to fit in with the other kids, but the Priestess was persistent. I ended up calling my mom for a ride home."

"Well, that was a good choice, Ash!"

"I learned the next day Randy died that night after he drove his car off a cliff."

"Ashling, you could have been with him," Ethan said, stating the obvious.

"His death shook me for a very long time. I vowed then always to trust when the Priestess or Ferax came to me. It's always for a good reason, and in my best interest."

Ethan remained silent, replaying the past conversations Ashling once shared about all the times her ancestors foretold of an important occurrence. He sat looking around the room where only moments earlier, he was sharing food and laughter with his wife and daughter. Something was drastically wrong, he mused, to now be participating in a horrific nightmare of his wife's making.

"I know you, husband. You're sitting there making arguments in your head as to why all of what I'm saying is irrelevant. I need you to remember all the times they have been right."

"I do not think those times haven't existed Ashling—I'm sitting here thinking some unseen force is playing God with you and our lives, and you're buying into it."

Ethan knew his words were biting. He could see it on Ashling's face they stung. She remained calm, nonetheless.

"What about the time at the ER, Ethan? We were certainly glad for the intervention then."

Ashling reminded her husband of the time early in their marriage when he had to rush her to the hospital. The doctor feared there was something drastically wrong with the baby she was carrying. The overworked emergency physician hastily reading another patients charts, counseled her to terminate the pregnancy to save her life that night.

A week prior, the white calf woke Ashling by nudging her arm. Ferax stood nearby, gently warning her a choice was coming, yet all would be well.

"There will come a dire scare soon Ashling, but do not panic. Do not heed the advice of the weary," Ferax warned.

Ferax had come through in the most crucial visit ever, assuring Ashling she would indeed live, as would the baby girl.

Ethan remembered all too well the night Ferax warned Ashling about the baby. He woke from a sound sleep. Startled, he jumped out of bed while charging at the air.

"Ethan Rafferty, what on earth are you doing?" Ashling whispered in a frantic voice.

"Didn't you hear it? The woman? I swear a woman was talking right above our heads. I couldn't understand her, but holy shit!"

"Come back to bed. I think you just heard Ferax talking to me in Gaelic," she told her husband softly.

Ashling was instantly comforted. She knew whatever was to come, Ferax had just confirmed that all would be well. And it was.

Ashling and Ethan insisted on more tests that night. After two days of bed rest in the hospital, a very pregnant Ashling received a clean bill of health. Three weeks later, little Brigid Ann Rafferty came into the world without a single complication.

It was also Ferax, who came to tell Ashling that her second pregnancy, two years back, would not produce the child they hoped for. Ferax gently explained to Ashling, some things didn't make sense in this world but that they would in the next. Ashling cried in her sleep as Ferax sang with an angelic voice, an old Gaelic lullaby.

In her sleep, Ashling saw the face of her unborn son. She dreamt of a white crane with a lovely red velvet crown of feathers on his head. His strong yet gentle wings fanned out about the tiny body as he held Ashling's infant son with great tenderness. When Ashling woke the next morning—she had already miscarried.

Knowing these dreams, premonitions or actual visits—whatever they were, often came true, frightened Ethan more than he had ever been in his life.

Husband and wife sat in silence. An occasional sniff or sob echoed around them.

Ethan tried to make sense of what started as an ordinary day, wondering how the bottom had just dropped out of his world? He struggled to gather his thoughts and focus on the facts.

"Start from the beginning, Ash. Maybe you are missing something. Let's go step by step through everything you remember. Maybe it's like the time with Brigid. Ferax told you all would be well, but you were still scared, right?"

In truth, Ashling was *sad*, but she was no longer afraid. "Remember when you found me under the tree crying a while back, Ethan?"

He nodded slowly.

"Yes, but you see Ash, you thought it was Brigid and I that was taken from you, so maybe you are confused."

She shook her head and continued.

"No, darlin', my heart, and head simply couldn't wrap itself around the thought of us all not being together. There have been two other visits from the Priestess and Ferax I haven't told you about. Yet, everything working out, depends on you, Ethan."

"Well, I'll be damned if I go along with this craziness. That's what this is—plain crazy if you think for one minute I'm going to let you go! I'll fight for both of us if I have to Ashling Rafferty," he croaked out in ragged despair.

Silence followed.

Ashling slowly nodded her head

"I love you, Ethan," she murmured.

"So there, it's settled then. You'll fight whatever this is. You're going to make a doctor's appointment like you said you would. You'll get a clean bill of health like I know you will. Then, we put all this behind us, Ash—Even *you* can be wrong," he said pointedly.

"These things are called legends for a reason," Ethan said in a more rational tone.

They were at a crossroads.

"All right darlin', I'll make the appointment."

With that, she gingerly got out of bed and ran her fingers through her hair. After wiping one last tear from her face, she told Ethan, "I think I'll get dressed and go clear my head. I feel like I'm needin' to sit with Malachi for a wee bit."

She sounded weak but determined.

"That's an excellent idea. Maybe he can put some perspective in that beautiful head of yours."

"They'll be waiting. I better get a move on," Ashling said, putting her hair up in a quick ponytail.

"*They*, who, Ash?" Ethan questioned.

"Oh, I meant Malachi."

Ashling gave him a passing glance from the mirror she used while tying her hair back. Ethan waited while Ashling tied her sneakers, then together they walked outside where Ethan finally felt the air return to his lungs.

An unexpected breeze picked up, giving Ashling a slight chill. She shook it off as Brigid ran towards them, kicking up a whirlwind of dust.

"Miss Cuddles had her kittens! They're in the barn, hurry!" Brigid said, reaching for her mother's hand.

Ashling was conflicted, but she knew what she had to do first.

"Oh my, how exciting!" she responded.

"Why don't you two go check on them, and I will be there shortly. We'll start to pick out names for them, yes?"

Brigid was only too happy to return to the barn.

"Come on, Dad. I'll show you where they are. I only found Miss Cuddles, cuz one of the babies was crying."

"Hurry up, okay, Mom? We have to count how many kittens there are, and I don't want you to miss all the fun."

At that, both Ethan and Ash exchanged bittersweet glances.

Ethan walked away, knowing his wife would be just fine, and Ashling walked the opposite direction, knowing nothing would ever be the same again.

10

Malachi and Turlough

"Turlough, what's taking you so long?" Malachi asked, hearing the approach of his friend.

Tun-tun, tun-tun, tun-tun. A whirring heartbeat signaled Turlough's arrival. Malachi lowered a sturdy branch for him to land upon.

"You ever tried pushing through the barrier, Malachi? It takes some time," Turlough grumbled in a nasally timbre. "I would have been here sooner, but the Priestess tasked me with a matter of grave importance. I'm here now. Where is Ashling Elizabeth?" Turlough asked, twisting his long neck from side to side in search of the woman in question.

"She is on her way. I see her from here."

"Ashling Elizabeth must be very excited for the next phase in her journey," Turlough stated brightly.

"I hardly think she is excited, as you say, old friend. You forget humans do not understand as we do," Malachi reminded the Crane.

"Pity. Human lives would be less dreary if they understood by embracing the—how would they say it? Ah, yes, the *bigger picture* and how it assists the elevation of their collective world..."

"Hush, Turlough, she might overhear you. Ashling is still coming to terms with so much overwhelming information."

Turlough bugled his displeasure at not being able to complete his verbal dissertation on humankind, then ruffled his feathers, yet said nothing more.

"I'm sorry, my friend, I suppose I am feeling overly concerned for Ashling and her young family."

"Yes, I forgot these particular humans have a special place in your heart. The Priestess is most benevolent and understands both you and the Raffertys require support. Which is of course why she thought to send *me* here today."

"I am glad for your company, Turlough. While we both know that much good will come from Ashling's life, we must show her compassion today. Now hush friend, I see her coming."

Ashling ignored the speckled wildflowers that called out their cheerful hellos to her as she slowly wandered up to the gravel path. On most days, she would stop and return their greetings and breathe in the pleasant sweet scent, as she and the nature around her spoke to one other. Ashling did not hear or notice the cedars trying their best to get her attention as they danced in a slow melodic motion that generally filled her with joy.

Usually, the fresh mountain air, so clean and untainted instantly revitalized her, but today Ashling found it to be a melancholy stroll. She was void of emotion and connection with all that typically brought her peace.

"Maybe Ethan was right. Perhaps I made a mistake or misunderstood some part of the message. Maybe it is all in my head. After all, who in their right mind takes advice from ancestors who died hundreds of years ago? Malachi will know what I should do," she said, seeing the wise oak come into sight.

"Good morning, child," he called out.

"Hey, Mal. How are you today?"

"I am well, child. We were just visiting with a new friend who asked to make a home in my branches," he replied.

She peered up to see a sparrow building her nest. Seeing Turlough a few branches away made Ashling nervous. Still, she greeted him politely. The elegant crane's presence was always a prelude to an essential piece of information. She forced herself to make eye contact with the unblinking black orbs.

"Greetings, Ashling Elizabeth. The Priestess sends her salutations," Turlough said, bowing his neck in homage.

"I told Ethan this morning about Ferax and the Priestess," Ashling stated, seeing no reason to drag out the visit.

"Did you also tell him that you have chosen to step into the role as your ancestors who came before you have done?" Turlough questioned.

"I tried. Ethan didn't take it well. Not that I expected him to. I basically told him I was going to leave him and Brigid alone in this world," she sighed.

"Some things you don't have control over child. Did you tell Ethan about your current illness?" Malachi gently asked.

"He wouldn't listen, Mal. He wants me to make a doctors appointment, and I told him I would. I tried to pass it off as something else. I wasn't ready to say the word out loud, but giving him false hope was wrong of me, and it doesn't change the outcome. I tried to talk about choices and following my heart on how to live out the rest of my life that honors what I believe. I couldn't quite get the words out Mal," Ashling sounded frustrated.

"You mean on your choice of treatments moving forward, as unconventional as they may sound to Ethan Eric?" Turlough pressed.

"Yes. At best, he hopes I'm pregnant. At worst, he thinks I'm telling him I'm not going to *fight it*, as he put it. I don't blame him. After all, believing as I do, is a wee bit challenging for others to understand. It's just I finally know what my purpose is. Ferax and the Priestess gave me a glimpse the other night. You know how you've told me if a person finds out what they're passionate about in life, then they've found their purpose?"

"Yes, child. Every human life has a purpose, no matter how big and grand, or quiet and simple. Remember that can change over time with the changing seasons," Malachi confirmed.

"What do you understand your purpose to be, Ashling Elizabeth?"

"I don't have all the pieces yet Turlough. I imagine, if what I've seen is true I will become a part of our Legend. I assume that is why you are here—to tell me about my future. All I know is Ferax showed me special herbs and teas that I am to use—but for how long, she did not say. All I know is that they can be found where the yews are growing. She told me how to create an ancient elixir that will somehow fuel my body. I'm hopeful," Ashling shrugged.

"Do you believe the visions, Ashling Elizabeth?" Turlough asked regarding her closely. The unblinking eyes peering through Ashling gave her chills.

"I do. I'm still scared, though. I don't truly know the outcome, and I don't want to leave my husband and daughter, but if I'm going to regardless because of this *illness*, I'm going to make it worth it—for them, you know?"

"Child, you must follow your intuition, and know that you are never alone."

"Mal, sometimes when I get anxious, I feel like I hear a heartbeat sound swishing near my head. I can't see anyone, but every time it happens, I calm instantly. Do you know why this is?"

"Ahhh, that is Turlough. You will know he is nearby by the sound of his heartbeat. It is a reminder that all is well and in perfect order," Malachi added.

Turlough blinked as he twisted his head from side to side as if listening for something. "Yes, you are correct, Ashling Elizabeth."

"Turlough, I have not spoken anything to you—to be correct about."

"You thought about the vibration my wings make," he replied.

"You can hear thoughts Turlough? Fascinating. Yes, your wings, they sound like a soothing heartbeat—whenever I hear the sound, I feel better."

"It is seldom humans are permitted to see me Ashling Elizabeth, but to alert the senses is entirely acceptable. Do not fear me. I will come to you and your family in times of need. For now, I shall leave you and our old friend, and report to the Priestess your willingness and desire to accept the mantle placed upon your shoulders. Be at peace Ashling Elizabeth. Great events will come to humanity, thanks to your bravery and willing heart."

With a thunderous swish of Turlough's massive wings, Ashling closed her eyes tightly, and covered her ears. When she opened them, Turlough was gone.

She sat quietly near Malachi for some time.

"Do you think I have long Mal?"

"Yes, child, I feel you have much left in this world to do. Focus on living and being present in each moment. After all, no human ever truly knows how much time they have on this side of the veil."

Ashling leaned back on the soft, warm scales of Malachi's trunk.

"What would I do without you, my dear friend?"

"You shall never have to find out," Malachi concluded.

11

Four Years Later

Ethan surveyed the new saplings that were growing in abundance on the property once belonging to Tomas Elmer. He clearly remembered the day Ashling suggested they plan for the future and expand the grove.

"The Wee Folk protect the earth around the trees and have assured me they will see that this sacred ground flourishes in the years to come," Ashling told Ethan.

And flourish it had.

The research at the university involving the Rafferty's yews, however, suddenly stalled thanks to new government regulations. The previous year the team celebrated a monumental breakthrough. Their data showed a viable, non-invasive, natural cancer protocol was possible—a cure without harmful side effects.

The team, however, reached the limits of their capabilities. It would take a benefactor with foresight, credentials, and funding to move it forward to clinical testing on a broader scale.

"How can this not bother you, Ash? We've sunk so many years, not to mention time and money into this," Ethan would confront Ashling when he became disheartened.

Ashling would remain unfazed.

"Oh husband, you have the patience of Angel when he doesn't get fed on time," she would calmly reply.

"You know I hate when you compare me to that rooster, Ash," Ethan would complain.

"Then stop gettin' your feathers so ruffled and just keep doin' what you can, it will all happen in the right time," Ashling would reply serenely.

Still, it wasn't uncommon for Ethan to become restless, hop in Old Blue and drive to the school to knock on Dean Roberts office door. Sometimes Ethan would present a new plan on how to advance the program funded by the Rafferty Foundation, and other times, Ethan would directly gift the university with a donation towards the research. In truth, the Rafferty grants had carried the program for the past year.

On Ethan's last visit, Dean Robert's opened up about his struggles, having lost his father, after a long battle with cancer.

"My dad was optimistic until the end that he'd beat it. It's been over three years, but it still feels like it was just yesterday. Most days, it's just a quiet companion, but there are times I still get overwhelmed by the grief. I'll be damned Rafferty if the pain doesn't still come crashing in on me like waves. You know what pisses me off though? We know this protocol works. It's got no side effects. Period. Yet we can't get it out there to the public," he stated with annoyance while fidgeting with his pen.

"But we can't be short-sighted in all this either. We only have so many trees, and we need further clinical testing on a larger scale before we can say that definitely. From what we know, the protocol is completely ineffective if we don't use the trees from the ranch. Why? Maybe it's the soil, but the tests are inconclusive. I don't know. However, I can't risk depleting all those trees on a crapshoot," Ethan added.

"I hear you. It's just if we could find someone with resources and connections to take a sniff at the research—they'd be compelled to invest," Dean Roberts said with more conviction than he felt.

"It always seems to come down to money. Speaking of which, *Clever Goats*, is starting to turn a profit," Ethan said.

"Not surprised. The wife keeps Ashling's cheeses stocked in the refrigerator for guests. It's always a hit. Heard she was branching out, that true?"

"Ashling has turned into quite a savvy businesswoman. Yes, she's got cheese and milk going into Smith's Mercantile starting next week, plus she's a got a yarn and clothing launch coming out in the winter. To that end, here's a donation she wanted to make. Maybe it'll be enough to hire that firm you were talking about last week," Ethan said as he placed a check of a sizable amount on the desk before his father's old friend.

"That will more than cover it. Maybe we should all get into the cheese business," Dean Roberts said raising his eyebrows.

"Okay. Well, let me know what happens," Ethan said, giving the older man a wry grin.

Parting ways, Ethan got back in Old Blue and headed home. After punching in the code for the secure access to their property, he waved to a ranch hand in passing. He continued down the well-worn path towards the back of their home where a smaller replica of their main barn came into sight that housed the chickens. He drove slowly, thinking back over the years to the day he surprised his new wife with the coop, chickens, and one angry rooster named Angel.

Surprising Ashling made Ethan happy. He was always conjuring up small ways to bring his wife joy. Knowing her love of goats, he secretly tasked a couple of his men to convert an unused shed, along with an acre of land, into something suitable for goats. Then having completed the work to Ethan's standards, with metal gates and pens that were sturdy enough to hold the small, curious creatures, Ethan was ready to show Ashling. He chuckled thinking back to how she could not contain her excitement that spring afternoon as she watched him drive up to the house. Tomas sat in the passenger seat singing to a song on the radio. The sweet faces of two kid goats wailing at the top of their lungs, as if singing along with the tune on the radio, peered over their cages from the truck bed of Old Blue. Ashling could feel her heart melt as she took in the sight.

"Darlin', what have you gone and done this time?"

"They needed a home. I hear they're sisters and inseparable," Ethan said.

"Hello, sweet girls," Ashling said as she warmly greeted the pair.

Tomas, having stepped out of the truck, tipped his hat at Ashling and walked to the back of Old Blue. Lowering the tailgate, Ashling was able to get her first look at the pair calling out to her.

"Let's get them to their stalls," Ethan said to Tomas, who was already lifting one of the metal cages gently to the ground.

The first goat off the truck was talkative, outgoing, and covered in splashes of black and white, and reminded Ashling instantly of a Dalmatian pup. "I think you are Perdita," Ashling said casually. The goat vocalized her agreement.

Next out, came a shy, light-colored runt with soft caramel colored fur that faded to white. Her four feet appeared to have black socks covering them. She was demure and petite.

"We'll call you Belle if that is okay. Do you like that name?" Ashling asked the reserved goat who licked her face in reply.

Tomas's faithful dog was ready for the command to herd the animals to their new home and with a series of three short whistles the exuberant canine got to work efficiently prodding the pair to their newly constructed home.

"Oh, Ethan. So this is what you've been so secretive about."

"Tomas deserves the credit. I never knew what escape artists these little critters can be until he told me. He's the one who made sure they'd be safe and sound here."

"Thanks, Tomas. It's perfect!"

Perdita and Belle took quickly to their new home and kept Ashling quite entertained.

A week later, Ethan came home unexpectedly with four milking goats. "Don't laugh Ash, but when I saw those ears, I'll be darned if they didn't remind me of a basset hound I had as a kid. Then, Carl made me a good deal, so I took all four," Ethan chuckled.

"There's plenty of space—and just wait until you taste the cheese I can make."

"You can make cheese from scratch, huh? Ash, your talents are never-ending," Ethan told her at the time.

Ashling was eager to test her memory by creating the recipes she helped with as a girl in her mother's kitchen. She labored lovingly, perfecting the texture and flavors. After many months, she was ready to unveil her samples for all the ranch hands to taste.

"I've got a brie here—it's got a lemony mellow taste, and over here is a gouda, if you like a wee more crunch. Oh, and this has a hint of bourbon, but don't give my secrets away guys! This one here is my favorite because it's creamy like butter but also has a hazelnut flavor to it," Ashling beamed, then waited as the once full plate was picked clean leaving just a single cracker.

"We've taken a vote out here Ashling, and we're in agreement these are the finest flavors we've ever tried," Tomas told her.

Word soon got out in the rural community, and requests began to pour in with people wanting to know where to purchase Ashling's cheeses.

"Ash, you've got quite a list of requests. Maybe it's time you made this into a full-fledged business," Ethan told her with admiration. It was not long after that, the *Clever Goats Co.* came into being.

Over the years, Ashling could often be found experimenting with new recipes to try out at the local farmers market and Co-Ops. Ethan wasn't surprised then or now at her entrepreneurial spirit, nor at the successful business she ran today. Ashling proved to be a naturally sharp businesswoman, knowing exactly when to turn on her Irish charm or fiery stubbornness.

"Has it really been over ten years that she started all this?" Ethan mused as he continued down their lane. "So much has changed," he said.

Ethan's concerns for Brigid and her ability to interact with nature as easily as Ashling did, subsided as well. Brigid was well-liked at school, proved to be an excellent student, and Emma became more like a sister to his daughter as the years passed.

Ethan parked Old Blue, catching sight of two particular goats, belonging to Brigid and her friend Emma. From an early age, Brigid took a particular liking to the goats, just as Emma did when she first saw them. The girls, now in fifth-grade, decided they wanted to join the local 4-H, each entering a goat of their own.

It took some persuading to get Robert and Evelyn Daily to agree, but eventually, they did. Emma blossomed the more time she spent with the Rafferty's. Ashling and Emma developed a particularly close bond that would grow over the years. They always seemed to be delighting and conspiring about something new involving the goats.

Ethan parked Old Blue and walked over to the goats calling out loudly to him, hoping for a special treat.

"Spoiled little buggers," Ethan said, tossing a few sliced apples in the pen, and patting the head of Perdita.

"It's a good thing we all got going here on the ranch. I guess I'm spoiled too. Can't imagine a better life," he said, walking towards the house where he spotted Evelyn's car pulling away.

"Mother, my cheeks hurt from laughing so much today. Do yours ever feel like that?" Emma asked as she climbed into the car, then rolled down the window to wave goodbye to Brigid and Ashling, yet again.

"No, Emma, I can't say that they do," Evelyn replied, giving her daughter a sideways glance in the rearview mirror then turned up the volume on the latest news broadcast.

Emma, left to her own thoughts of the day, recalled picking flowers near Malachi for their teacher when Brigid started to speak.

"Oh, yes, it is!" Brigid smiled brightly.

"Huh?" Emma said, bewildered, but seeing her friend staring at Malachi, she understood.

Walking over to the beautiful oak, Brigid patted the deep ridges of his trunk.

"What's he sayin' Brig?"

"He just said hello to you Em. Oh, and he said it's a beautiful day to be out in nature."

"Hi Malachi, you're looking... um, healthy today," Emma said shrugging her shoulders, knowing it wasn't much of a response. She sat down on the tree swing while she waited for Malachi and Brigid to continue their visit. She secretly longed to hear him too, as she had done many times. Once she even told Brigid, that Malachi did talk to her, but later confessed it was just wishful thinking.

"Well, maybe it's not trees you hear, might be birds, or the goats? You love the goats Em. Maybe it's cats, or maybe frogs you hear," Brigid suggested not wanting to hurt Emma's feelings by leaving her out.

"That would be my luck since my parents would never allow any of those creatures at our home."

Emma reminded Brigid about the flowers for their teacher. "Oh, and let's pick some yellow daisies for your mom. She kinda looked sad today, didn't she?"

"She did? I didn't notice. Well, let's go pick lots then Em."

"Hey Mal, we gotta get going, but can you see the closest patch of daisies from up there?"

Malachi's branches swayed more rapidly, then suddenly stoped.

"Cool. Thanks. We'll see you later, okay?"

Wrapping her arms as far as she could around Malachi's trunk, Brigid hugged her friend.

Turning to go, Brigid noticed Emma staring up at Malachi with a quizzical expression on her face.

"What is it, Em?"

"Brig, do you think Malachi would mind if I hugged him too?" She asked in a small voice.

"He said it would be his honor," Brigid smiled while giving Emma a little push towards Malachi.

With no more encouragement needed, Emma slowly walked to the tree and silently wrapped her arms around him with all her might.

Malachi rewarded little Emma with a fluttering of his leaves. Because there was no wind at that moment, Emma allowed herself to believe that was Malachi's way of communicating with her. Staying rooted in place a minute longer, she swiped at a tear running down her cheek, as she began to feel something close to love for this gnarled, and magical tree.

"Malachi just said to trust your heart, Em."

Yes, Emma thought she heard her heart say something to her. She'd need more time to reason this out of course. However, it was a start.

Back at home, the persistent tiredness Ashling began to experience increased. Years earlier, she had her physicians run all the tests just as she promised Ethan she would do.

"Just the flu," she later announced to Ethan.

Lately, though, Ashling had developed a slight cough, which she passed off as spring allergies, but spring turned to summer, and the cough remained.

"Ash, I think you need to go back and get a new doctor," Ethan told her.

"No, Ethan. This time I need to trust my own body. Right now, I feel better doing this my way—natures way. I want to drink my teas and eat the foods I am called to eat. You'll see, I'll be better in no time, or I won't. But try to understand Ethan, it goes against every fiber of my being not to do it this way," Ashling calmly but firmly replied.

Ethan didn't argue, even though he disagreed with his wife.

Ashling was also having disturbing dreams again, which she tried to keep from Ethan, but they were becoming more frequent, vibrant even. She understood that life soon would be changing drastically. She would need to start preparing her husband and daughter for what they would understandably resist.

No, Ethan and Brigid would not understand her choices in the beginning. While they might not support or embrace the path she chose, Ashling hoped that one day they would forgive her.

Her only regret was that for her to fulfill her part of the ancient Legend, she would not live to witness the New World Healer take her rightful place in history.

12

Seven years later

A rush of pride swept over Ashling as she stood in the doorway of Brigid's room, watching her daughter apply a light colored lip gloss. "Is this too pink?" Brigid asked, glancing back at her mother through the reflective glass.

"No darlin', it's perfect," Ashling replied approvingly.

"Well, what do you think?" Brigid asked as she twirled in her gown.

Just then Ethan happened down the hall and stopped in his tracks. A wave of emotion overcame him.

"You'll be the prettiest girl at the prom!" Ashling beamed.

From the doorway, Ethan cleared his throat.

"Hey, where'd my little Sprite go?" Ethan didn't mean for his voice to crack. Brigid walked over to her dad and kissed him on the cheek. "I'm still here, don't worry Dad. I love you," she said, wiping the smudge of gloss from his cheek.

"Well, we better get going. Your mom wants a few pictures of you with Malachi before the photos at the Fleming's begin," Ethan announced to cover the emotions threatening to betray him.

"We've got less than an hour," he said, looking at his watch.

After the brief drive to Malachi, the Rafferty family stood taking in the golden sunlight bouncing lightly through the oak, making him look even more spectacular than he usually did. Ethan grabbed a thin blanket from the back of their SUV and carefully laid it out on the ground for his daughter to stand on.

"Don't want your dress or shoes to get dirty," Ethan said, trying to remain aloof.

"You're getting all squishy, Dad, I kinda like it!"

Ethan ignored Brigid and began snapping pictures.

"My turn to take a few father-daughter photos," Ashling told the pair, reaching for the camera.

Ethan heard Ashling whisper to Malachi.

"Oh, that's a wonderful idea," Ashling announced.

Brigid nodded her approval.

"What's a good idea?" Ethan asked, bewildered.

"Malachi says we should get a picture of me, sitting on the swing, with you looking like you're about to push me. Just like when I was a kid," Brigid answered enthusiastically.

"Well, if that won't be my undoing, I don't know what will. Tell your friend there, I said so," Ethan announced, trying to sound gruff, but failed miserably. Nonetheless, he meandered over to the old tree swing, dusted off the wood seat, and held it steady for Brigid.

"Mal said to tell you, that you will thank him for this picture one day," Ashling told Ethan, with a tinge of melancholy.

"Come on, husband, smile."

It was a tender moment of Ethan and Brigid that Ashling captured as she took the picture.

"We'll frame this and put it on the wall next to the one of you pushing Brigid and me on this very swing as I held her all those years ago."

Ethan nodded, "We have many memories hung on that entry wall, Ash."

It was a bittersweet exchange for Ashling.

"We gotta get going. We're gonna be late," Brigid reminded to her parents.

Ashling quickly wrapped her arms around Malachi's thick trunk and said her goodbye as Ethan folded up the blanket. Brigid, already in the family car, was excited to join the others at her friend Brian Fleming's home just down the road.

Seemingly at once, cars began to arrive at the Fleming's house.

"Brian and Lauren are a shoo-in for this year's Prom King and Queen," Brigid said as Lauren waved excitedly. Brigid waved in return.

Brigid and Emma would accompany Matt and Dean, who were identical twins. Over the years, somehow the group became known as *The Crew* and rarely went on outings without each other in tow.

The last member of The Crew to arrive was Sam Bolden. Sam was average in height with blond hair and blue eyes, making him look like an all American kid. Not only was Sam well liked by his peers, but he was smart and funny.

"Oh look, there's Sam," Brigid said in a conspiratorial tone.

Tonight Sam was bringing Tiffany Ann Carlisle. No one in the group was especially thrilled to have Tiffy, as she liked to be called, along for the night, but Sam was their friend, so they accepted the fact without too much complaint.

"I think it's nice how you all are so supportive of Sam. I don't think he looks all that happy tonight though," Ashling said as the car pulled to a stop.

"It's hard for me to keep up with all the drama, but Sam is the guy Emma likes, right? Yet she's going to the dance with Matt?" Ethan asked.

"No, Dad, I'm going with Matt, Emma's going with Dean. But we're all just friends," Brigid clarified.

"Sam friend zoned Emma, Ethan. You heard about that, remember?" Ashling nudged Ethan playfully.

"Friend zoned? What—no, I don't want to know. Come on, your friends are waiting, and I've been looking forward to seeing that Porsche Ed's been talking about."

"How's our Emma really doing? It's gotta be difficult for her to see Sam with yet another girl," Ashling said.

"It's definitely hard for her Mom. I couldn't do it. Every time he breaks up with one of the girls, which we all know he doesn't care about, he goes to cry on Emma's shoulder. I think she's about had it, to be honest," Brigid said as she and Ashling went to greet the group.

"Sam just hasn't found his way yet," Ashling quietly added.

Neither Brigid nor Emma could see what there was about Tiffy that Sam liked so much. She was cruel to less popular girls and mean to Sam as well.

The photo shoot momentarily halted when Tiffy struggled to sit inside one of the convertibles thanks to her tight red mermaid pageant dress. To their credit, nobody laughed. Instead, they helped Tiffy sit gracefully. For Sam's sake, they all agreed to make the best of it.

Proud parents snapped pictures while the couples made a production getting into a waiting limo and were quickly whisked off to *Zane's*, a fancy steakhouse in town before heading to the dance.

Once at the dance, the excitement continued. Emma couldn't help but stare at Sam and Tiffy.

"He doesn't look like he's having a good time. He actually looks relieved that T.J. cut in to dance with her," Emma sighed.

Sam looked at Emma and caught a slight blush on her cheeks, even from across the room. Slowly he began weaving his way through the crowd of teenagers until he stood directly in front of Emma.

"Let's dance," he said in a tight voice.

If Emma had a gift of the English language, she did not possess it at that moment. Sam, not waiting for her reply, caught Emma around the waist, and slowly turned her onto the dance floor. Emma tried to tell herself it was just her imagination that her friend Sam held her a little too tight, a bit too familiarly, and all the while praying he didn't hear her heart pounding as loudly as she felt it in her chest. The song, having ended way too soon, left Sam and Emma both wanting something more.

"Em, do you ever…"

The question on Sam's lips was left unasked as Tiffy breathlessly stepped in front of Emma, taking Sam's hand in hers.

"I've been looking all over for you. Come on they're about to crown the king and queen. Let's go." Tiffy edged past Emma without a glance.

Sam allowed himself one brief look in Emma's direction. The look on her face was an unreadable mask.

After the dance, everyone, except Tiffy, agreed the highlight of the night was seeing Brian and Lauren crowned Prom King and Queen.

"I can't wait for the bonfire," Brigid said, trying to engage Emma who looked so forlorn.

The party down by the river was what everyone was looking forward to most after the dance. Brigid and Emma sat with their shoes by their side on a blanket surrounded by lit torches, watching a small group playing volleyball.

"It was a fun dance. I'm glad Matt and Dean aren't about the drama. They're so easy to hang out with, don't you think, Em?" Brigid asked.

Emma appeared not to hear her.

"Em!"

"Um...ya... uh-huh," Emma answered distractedly.

"Em, you are not listening at all! I asked what you really think of me becoming a doctor and studying overseas for the first year or two? I mean seriously? Do you think I have what it takes? Do you think I could be away from home a whole year? And is studying holistic medicine right for me?"

A long pause followed.

"Seriously," Emma groaned with an excessive hiss.

It was a tone Brigid never heard her friend use before.

"I think I am going to pull her extensions out and feed them to her through her nose..." Emma continued, ignoring Brigid.

The sudden hysterical laughter coming from Brigid garnered stares from several of their classmates.

"Seriously, I've had enough," proper, sweet, and logical Emma announced.

"Then, for Pete's sake, do something about it!"

Springing up like a cat ready to pounce on its prey, Emma felt ten feet tall as she silently closed in on Sam and Tiffy, while listening to the shrill teen currently in mid hysteria, berating Sam about the train of her dress that was torn and dirty. Reaching the unsuspecting couple, Emma wedged herself between the two, then bent down in the most unladylike manner, pulling the useless piece of material connected to the pouting girls dress off the ground. Emma handed the wadded up train to Tiffy.

"Problem solved," Emma railed.

Emma turned, looking at Sam.

"And you… you're… an idiot." She stated, pointing one delicate finger toward him.

Emma was feeling oddly empowered, but suddenly with nothing left to say, she turned her back, leaving the couple to stare at her disappearing into the night.

In the distance, everyone around could hear Tiffy on the phone.

"Get me out of here, *now*!"

Tiffy's dad merely nodded his head as Sam tried to explain the night's events. After several attempts to maneuver Tiffy into her parent's car, they spun off leaving Sam feeling relieved and determined as he made his way towards the river and his friends, who were sitting on a fallen log. Hands in his suit pockets, his head slightly bent, Sam gave a sheepish grin to the group. Emma looked oddly vindicated, although not quite ready to meet Sam's unreadable stare.

"Hey guys, can I talk to Em alone for a few?"

"Em?" Brigid asked her friend.

Without looking up, Emma nodded her head. Brigid whispered something in Emma's ear, and Dean gave a brotherly slug on Sam's arm as he left.

Taking a seat next to Emma, Sam nudged her shoulder playfully.

"So I'm an idiot, huh?"

"Major idiot," she mumbled.

"Care to tell me why?"

"Nope, not particularly."

"Hmm, well can I at least thank you for saving me from the worst night of my life?"

Slowly raising her face to meet Sam's boyish grin, Emma's heart began pounding in her ears. He was smiling. Why in the world would he be grinning like that when, literally, the world as she knew it came to a crashing halt?

"Excuse me?"

"Em, you look like an owl, staring at me like that," Sam said leaning in and tapping her leg with his.

If this were anyone other than Sam, the guy she thought about every day for years, Emma would swear he was flirting with her.

"I tried to break up with her last week, but she freaked out, going on about the cost of the dress, her shoes, and prom king and queen..." He mimicked Tiffy while rolling his eyes.

"Why were you going to break up with her?"

"Well, Em, if I have to explain this to you then maybe I was wrong about..." his voice trailed off.

"Why were you breaking up with her?"

"I was only dating her because I couldn't get the girl I've wanted for years now. It's why I've dated the string of dead-end relationships all along."

"Oh, great. Look, Sam, you are the nicest guy around, a good friend and any girl would want to be with you, so whoever she is, it's got to be better than Tiffany Ann."

Emma was trying to keep the frustration out of her voice and failing miserably.

"You think I should tell her? What if I go for it, and she shoots me down?"

Emma didn't try to hide her disdain.

"A girl would have to be crazy to turn you down, and I think you know that."

"Well, that's good to know. Thanks, Em, I feel better."

"Oh, great," Emma said again.

"So where should I take her if I ask her out? She's the smartest girl I know. She is also the cutest girl I have ever seen, kinda quiet but once you get to know her, she has the biggest heart ever. She's way outside my league though. It's why I've never told her how I feel."

At that moment, Emma wished the earth would open up and swallow her whole as Sam went on and on.

"You know, I've tried to ask her out before, but there is always another guy glued to her side." Emma stood, grabbing her shoes, glaring at Sam. He was smiling again.

"Sam, I could care less where you take her, just stop coming to me with your girlfriend problems anymore, okay?"

Turning her back on Sam, and spying their friends, Emma began making her escape towards the group of teenagers packing up their cars. Sam quickly caught up to Emma, whispering in her ear.*"You're an idiot."*

Sam ducked, barely missing Emma's shoe.

"I'm an idiot? Seriously?"

"For such a smart girl—the smartest girl I know by the way and the cutest girl I've ever seen. Did I mention the part of also having the biggest heart?"

Sam's dimples broadened in a way that made Emma want to trace them.

"And since neither Dean or Matt are currently aren't glued to your side…" Sam deliberately paused, letting the last part settle in.

Feeling the slightest bit of hope trickle into her heart, Emma dared to smile up at Sam.

He kissed her. Not a kiss you give a girl stuck in the friend zone, but a kiss that made her heart pound in her ears.

"You're an idiot," Sam murmured.

Emma laughed. "No, you're an idiot. You almost let me get away."

13

Brigid stood at her front door, waving goodnight to her friends. Once inside, she quickly freed her toes from the stylish pumps.

"I'm home!" Brigid called out, heading down the hall.

Finding her parents sitting comfortably in their favorite chairs reading by the lit fireplace, Brigid plopped down on the sofa and began to recall the evening. Finally, she animatedly recapped the escapades between Emma and Sam. Both parents listened intently and asked questions every now and again. Then suddenly, as if seeing her mother for the first time, Brigid's expression softened. Her forehead creased as she bit her lower lip.

"What is it, darlin'?" Her mother prompted.

Brigid began to study her mother more closely. Ashling was looking pale and thin. Why didn't Brigid remember seeing the dark circles under her eyes earlier? Was it the lighting that made Ashling look so frail to Brigid?

"Are you feeling okay Mom?" Brigid's voice filled with concern.

"Nothing a good night's sleep won't fix darlin'. I guess we all just had an exciting day is all." Ashling said by way of explanation.

"I think your mom spent a little too much time wandering around in the heat looking for some new herb, or root or something," Ethan supplied unconvincingly.

"Yes, Malachi reminded me of a particular tea my grandmother taught me to make. I was excited to brew a pot. I think the hours got away from me. It was warm today, wasn't it?"

Ashling purposefully left out the part of her coughing up blood earlier, and how scared she felt. No use borrowing trouble.

If it happened again, she'd have her tea ready.

Brigid, looking uncertain, only nodded.

"Those baby birds have left the nest finally, so I did get a bit distracted by them too. It was sweet watching them get used to their new wings."

"Oh Mom, that reminds me I've wanted to ask you about this. I've seen a stunning looking bird perched on Malachi lately. I've never seen one quite like it. It looks enormous, with a red patch on its head—might be a crane but it looks much bigger than any Oregon Crane I've ever noticed. At one point he stretched his wings, and I swear they were nine, maybe ten feet wide. It was crazy. I asked Mal about it, but he said he gets many visitors. Have you seen it?"

Ashling took a few moments before answering.

"Perhaps. Malachi attracts all kinds, doesn't he? Oh, darlin', there was a letter that came for you today. With all the excitement I forgot to give it to you."

"Who's it from?"

"The university in Dublin," Ashling said with sincere enthusiasm.

"I'll fetch it for you while you change outta your party clothes."

Once in the hallway, Ashling leaned against the wall to steady herself. Her loss of appetite was becoming physically evident on her slight frame. The fatigue seemed to be lasting longer and longer these days. Ashling knew she was squeezing precious days from life, and was at a place of tentative peace, having decided to embrace the journey and stay true to herself more fully.

Earlier in the day as Brigid and Emma were getting their nails done, Ashling had wandered the property looking for herbs. A coughing spell overcame her. The tiny speckles of blood in her handkerchief reminded her of the Legend. She intuitively knew at that moment, her life—or death—would somehow play a role in the curing or healing of some illness. She reasoned over the years it had to do with cancer treatments.

As if confirming this, out of the corner of her eye, Ashling briefly saw the Priestess with the white calf staring at her from under a nearby tree. The beautiful lady said something as she and the calf turned to go. Ashling was sure the Priestess dropped something as she vanished. Walking to where she last saw her standing, Ashling noticed a red ribbon fluttering on a nearby bush. She had been told to look for a sign that the time was near, and Ashling knew from the Legend, this red ribbon signified just that. She stared at the red ribbon, unwilling to yet grasp it in her hands.

Ashling knew she had done all she was asked to do. She ate the foods, drank the teas, and gathered the herbs that Ferax, or sometimes Turlough, would show her. She'd been drinking the elixir from their yews, prepared precisely as the Priestess told for years, knowing it was what had given her so much more time with Ethan and Brigid.

Ashling intuitively understood she was altering the cells in her body or bloodstream in some way but wasn't sure what would happen next. What difference would it make? And to whom? She left the details to fate. She quietly lifted the frayed ribbon, and tucked it in her pocket.

It had been easy to push all the what-ifs out of her mind until recently when she found a tab on her computer opened to a web page dealing with a highly controversial research project taking place in Scotland. She began reasoning to herself, "I shut the computer down last night. I know I did. Ethan and Brigid never use this one so it couldn't have been either of them."

Her heart began to pound wildly. Fear and understanding settled upon her like a heavy cloak. Sitting down, Ashling scanned the site and its extensive information. It became clear reading the pages what she needed to do. With shaking hands, Ashling found the contact page, quickly typed out what she must, then hit send before she could change her mind. Two months had passed since she posted the secret email.

Leaning against the wall in the hallway, the reality of her choices came rushing back to her. Ashling took a deep breath to steady herself. With purposeful steps, she regained her composure, making her way to the kitchen. Finding the envelope addressed to Brigid, Ashling tucked a much thicker envelope addressed to herself, into a drawer.

"That one can wait until morning," she said, giving the drawer a solid shove.

Pushing all but happy thoughts from her mind, she returned to her favorite place in their home, stopping briefly to listen to the laughter coming from the living room. Brigid animatedly chattered on, while Ethan chuckled in response. Instinctively Ashling knew she'd find them beside the family Oak.

As she reentered the room, Ashling memorized the river rock fireplace with the warm embers glowing, the tree with generations of initials carved into it making the house feel so alive, and the image of her husband and daughter sitting in deep conversation. Ashling purposefully embedded the scene in her heart and mind. She would need that in the coming days.

14

"Malachi, I'm afraid."

"Of what child?"

She paused a moment.

"I thought it was of dying, but it's more than that. Tell me how do I leave Ethan and Brigid? I physically ache when I think about it. It isn't the act of death. I know there's more after we pass. I become afraid when I think of life without us as a family. We still have so many dreams and plans. They need me, and I need them."

Ashling sat on the tree swing absently kicking her bare feet back and forth staring off into the fortress of trees shading her in the late afternoon sun. The branches were lingering with bursts of color, but soon they would fade and return to the earth.

"This will likely be the last autumn I witness this side of the veil," she said, resting her head on the rope of the swing that held her securely.

Ashling was feeling anything but secure or steady these days.

"It's time, Mal. I have to tell Ethan the cancer is back—but, I can't help but think he's going to be resentful."

"What makes you think that child? Why would he be resentful of something you have no control over?" Malachi asked.

"He never did understand that I wanted to try this my way. He wanted me to undergo chemo, and I didn't. I thought it would end my chances to ever get pregnant again. Maybe I should have. As it turned out, I never could conceive again. I understand Ethan's concerns, and maybe I'd feel the same way if it were him. I don't know. You and I have talked about it before. It's just that I know my body, and while I know the odds were much better if I chose treatment, I couldn't do it. In my heart I still feel it's the best way for me to handle this journey," Ashling said with more conviction than she felt.

"You made a compromise with Ethan—one he accepted years ago. You would use the remedies passed down in your dream-state from the Priestess and Ferax while still under your physician's care—without chemotherapy. It was a decision both you and Ethan agreed to," Malachi reminded Ashling.

"I know. It's just I see it in Ethan's eyes. He doesn't think I fought hard enough. Maybe he's right."

"It's human to have doubts. Tell me what you told me last year when you chose to use the bounty of the earth's resources to heal your body."

Ashling took a few deep breaths as she calmed her mind. "I promised you and myself that I would stay present, that I'd honor what I was brought up to believe. The earth has provided everything I needed for all these years to keep me healthy. It's just my time, I believe. I can accept that, but Mal, look at what this will cost Ethan and Brigid."

"Dear child," Malachi called to her in a gentle breeze. "Hear my words and know them to be true. You are facing a time that perhaps would have come regardless of what treatment you chose. No one knows. You do not know that you would have had more or less time during this earthly journey by making another choice. Ethan could not guarantee one more day, nor could your doctors, am I correct?"

Ashling merely nodded her head. "The statistics though..."

"You are not a statistic child. Life is precious, and you have given Brigid and Ethan wonderful memories all these years. Memories they will cherish."

"I'm greedy. I want more! I want to have it both ways. I want to fulfill a long-ago promise I made to the Legend and to stay here with Brigid and Ethan."

"You're human, not greedy. Your life, no matter what you choose or have chosen, makes a difference."

"That's the problem Mal. What if I didn't or don't make a difference? What if this is all a waste? What if the Legend is wrong?"

Malachi was quiet.

Everything around Ashling looked normal—the birds chirping, a frog croaking loudly in the background, the sound of a cow mooing in the distance. Ashling sat with her head once again resting on the corded rope as Malachi waited for his most favorite human, to process this thing called life.

"Nothing about this is normal," Ashling sighed.

"I got a letter from that man I was telling you about who owns the lab in Scotland. They'll take my body—you know after I've passed. I've officially donated my body to science. It doesn't get more real than that does it?" It pained Ashling to say the words out loud.

Malachi, old as he was, focused all his strength to sway the branch that held the swing. Rocking it gently back and forth, in his most fatherly way, he pushed the swing for the girl he dearly loved, just as he had watched Ashling do so many times over the years with young Brigid. Malachi was glad she did not know he was withering up inside at the thought of her not sitting here in physical form. Yes, he was wise to what came next, and it would be a glorious celebration indeed. However, for now, his Ashling was in pain, and so was he.

"I haven't told Ethan. Not sure how to tell Brigid. How do I even start the conversation? How do I tell him I signed papers with an innovative research team, without his knowledge? How do I say I'm sorry for leaving him and Brigid without a body to mourn? I got scared. I should have told him first. It was a selfish act. I know it."

A small part of Ashling remained hopeful Ethan and Brigid would forgive her and one day he'd come to understand why she made the choices that would affect them all.

"Ashling, it was wrong of you not to take this to your husband first. You denied both him and yourself of each other's counsel, comfort, and partnership. You must not make any more decisions in haste or fear," Malachi said, sounding very fatherly indeed.

"Ethan's going to be confused and rightfully angry. I just knew in his despair that he would try to bargain and sway me by any means possible, just like he had years earlier. I was persuaded then, and couldn't take the chance this time. I truly believe the Legend, and soon enough Brigid and Ethan will too," Ashling said a little too brightly.

"You've chosen not to reveal to Brigid the role she plays in this?" Malachi asked.

"I can't. I've already told Ethan too much. I won't do any more than I already have to disrupt their lives if that makes any sense. I trust they will find their way and if it works out how I think it does, I'll still be by their side—just in a different way. Brigid and Ethan will grieve and be justifiably angry no matter how or when I pass," Ashling barely managed to say.

She swayed slowly back and forth on the wooden seat, staring at her fragile hands. Her veins showed through her paper-thin skin like the veins of a leaf. Gently grasping the rope which held her safely, Ashling mused that it felt more like she was holding on by a frayed thread.

She sat in a silent storm of thoughts, knowing she was still just a woman who loved her life and family with all she had—and all Ashling had was what she was soon to leave behind.

"Legend or not Mal, I have cancer. It's not going to be long. I can feel it. Some things in life make us feel so helpless. I guess I've felt like I've had so little control over this, that the parts of my life that I knew I could control, I grabbed onto. Yet, in doing so, I neglected to think how *out of control* this must feel for Ethan. All this time I've felt like I've been doing the right thing for the right reasons, but I'm beginning to see how wrong I've been."

"Ashling, you are far too hard on yourself. There is no one right way to experience this life."

"I actually think I'd do it all over again the same way, even donating my body to science or as an organ donor, if they'd have me. I have lived this life as authentically as I know how to. I admire people who choose chemo, radiation, or whatever surgeries a physician might deem necessary. Maybe I'm a wee bit weak, but I just followed my gut on this. The only thing I would do differently is I would have talked with Ethan *before* I signed my name on that contract."

"You can still make this right between you and Ethan. You need to tell him what you've told me. He loves you, Ashling. Just give him time to process the information. It is a lot, after all," Malachi suggested.

"I'm gonna tell him tonight. He'll need to prepare himself, and I need him to be there for Brigid. There's still much to do. What if I run out of time before I make sure my husband and daughter are taken care of? Ethan doesn't know how to tend to my goats and chickens properly, and I have to help him get Brigid settled at the university. And, what will become of my company? The profits going to charity will cease. I guess I thought I'd have more time."

"My dear Ashling," Malachi said in a heartbreaking—soothing voice. "I wish I could take this burden from you, but I cannot. All I have is my trunk for you to rest your back upon, and my branches to shade you."

The wise tree was feeling quite old and sad. His roots seemed to ache with the weight of what was yet to come.

"It's more than enough, my dear friend. You being you, is more than enough. Thank you."

Ashling knew she was postponing the inevitable.

"I'm tired Mal, maybe I'll just rest here a bit before I head home," she said climbing off the swing, spreading her jacket on the ground at Malachi's trunk.

"Will you sing me a song?" she asked, sounding more like young Brigid than herself.

"Close your eyes, dear one. A song I can give you."

Ashling lay on the soft grass beside Malachi, fading into a gentle sleep. The loving tree, her friend and protector sang her an ancient lullaby.

Malachi made sure Ashling was sound asleep before he allowed his own voice to break.

15

Ethan stood with his back to Ashling, gripping the fireplace mantle in the room he shared with his wife of twenty years. He stared at the blue and amber flame that mocked him as it danced merrily in the fireplace. It was quiet—too quiet, Ashling thought, watching as Ethan fixated on the fire. Then, as if coming out of a trance, Ethan's deep voice shook the room.

"No, this can't be how it goes down. I sure as hell won't let you go without a fight." The veins in Ethan's neck were visibly protruding from the strain of his emotions.

"Dammit Ash, I expect you to fight as well," he barked out his demand in pain as Ashling sat in a worn leather chair that dwarfed her thinning frame.

One look at his wife, her head cast down like a small scolded child, crushed Ethan. Suddenly feeling very tired and old beyond his years, he came to stand before her with trembling legs. Utterly powerless, Ethan collapsed upon the ottoman in front of Ashling. They sat in silence—the crackling fire filling the void. Occasionally Ashling could hear Ethan's ragged breaths as he tried to calm himself. As much as she wanted to throw herself into his arms, telling him she'd do anything he asked—Ashling knew she must remain strong.

"Ethan, there isn't nor was there, a guarantee I'd have any more time if I would have undergone the chemo treatments. None."

"I know."

"There is no denying the cancer has advanced, and I won't have our last memories of my life with you and Brigid spent at a doctor's office being poked, prodded and experimented on. I will not watch Brigid drop out of school, which we both know she'll do if she understood the situation to the extent that you and I do. I can't bear the thought of you two watching me—die and be helpless to do anything. Don't you understand even a wee bit?"

Ethan cut her off, rattling off statistics, possibilities, and even miracles.

"Husband, I love you and our daughter with all my heart, but as I told you, in the beginning, I have to do this my way and honor what I believe is right for my body, and what goes on with it. I do believe I bought us more time this way. There is so little control as it is darlin', please try to understand."

What remaining color Ethan had drained from his face, and his hands visibly shook. Still, Ashling needed him to hear her.

"I never once asked for this cancer to be in my body, Ethan. The only thing I've had control over all these years was, and is, how I chose to spend the days that have been gifted to me. We've made beautiful memories, and until recently without having to burden Brigid."

"Am I wrong to want more?" Ethan said, sounding like a confused child.

Ashling slowly shook her head no.

"I'm the selfish one, Ethan. I want to have every last minute I live during this lifetime to be by your side as well."

Ashling prayed that Ethan understood. She needed him to understand, maybe even tell her it was okay.

It was a lot to hope for.

"I will always wonder what we might have had Ash if you took a different route and tried the chemo. What if you short changed us all?" Ethan verbally charged at Ashling like a caged animal.

Ashling knew this moment would come. She told Malachi just that earlier in the day. Still, she felt the full force of his truth in her heart, knowing it took a lot out of her husband to confront her like this.

"It's okay if you're angry at me, husband. I don't know how I'd be feeling if the shoe were on the other foot. I've made my choices, and they affect us all. Some due to the Legend at first, I admit, but honestly, I had to follow my path. I still believe, for me, the quality of life outweighs the quantity of time."

Ethan sat motionless, staring into the fire.

"Legend or no Legend, I would likely do it this way again. I've thought a lot about it over the years. I know it's not the right choice for everyone, and I can imagine what people might think of me. I'm selfish, a coward, and perhaps now, even deserve what I get. I know my choices have consequences."

Ethan shook his head. "I may forever struggle with your logic, Ash, but I'm not in your shoes," he interjected quietly.

Ashling gingerly kissed his forehead, then taking his face in her frail hands, gently wiped his tears away.

Stroking Ashling's hair, Ethan whispered in her ear, "I love you," as she cried unashamedly.

The two shadowed silhouettes dimly lit by the fading fire held on to each other as they came to terms with what lay ahead.

"With Brigid and Emma leaving for Ireland in the morning, we need to be on the same page, darlin', whatever it is we choose to tell Brigid or not to tell her," Ashling said wearily.

Ultimately, they decided not to tell Brigid how sick Ashling was. Ethan was against this approach, just as he opposed the original idea of Ashling seeking alternative treatment. In the end, he agreed.

"If, or when, the time comes, we'll call Brigid home," Ethan stated, although, he silently wondered if he was now just as guilty of taking a choice from Brigid—one she had a voice in.

Ethan dared not look too closely at what his choice implied.

Drained physically and emotionally, he finally stood and helped Ashling to her feet as they went about their nightly routine since taking their vows. How many of those nights did they take it for granted, Ethan thought to himself, standing next to his wife and brushing his teeth. Such an ordinary, yet personal ritual. What would he do when she was gone? He wasn't sure he could go on.

Ashling could read Ethan's expressions. They were not unlike her own.

"You will continue Ethan Rafferty. I need you to. Brigid *needs* you to, and those whom you'll never meet, need you to." With that, she left their bathroom with new resolve, pulled down the quilted comforter and climbed into bed. Ethan soon joined her, drawing her close to his side. Each pretended to sleep.

Down the hall, Brigid packed the last of her clothes into a small carry-on bag. After showering, she slipped into her favorite pajamas, grabbed her laptop, and plopped unceremoniously onto her bed.

Her fingers quickly flew over the keyboard to message Emma.

Are you packed? Ready? As excited as me?

Seconds later, Emma's response lit up the screen.

Ready as I can be, but I don't know how I will be able to stay away from Sam. LOL. It's a whole year, you know? Mother said I should be open to meeting someone new. I think that's why they ultimately agreed to a year of school in Ireland Brig, but I don't want someone new... I love him.

Brigid swiftly replied.

I know you do. You two will find a way to make it work. Maybe he can come visit you? Maybe a little distance will help you both see what you really want. You know?

Brigid continued to type her response.

It's like my parents always say, there's a reason for everything, and you never know what miracles are around the next corner.

She hit send and waited for Emma to respond.

I hope you're right. I am excited to go, you know. Night Brig, see you tomorrow.

Brigid closed the computer, taking a long look around the only bedroom she had ever known. So much was about to change. Still, Brigid couldn't push the gnawing voice out of her head, that told her she was being selfish.

Brigid knew Emma wanted to to be with Sam, and Brigid knew she had the power to release her best friend from the pinky swear promise they made years ago to travel and begin their studies in Ireland after high school.

Still, there was something in Brigid that kept her from typing the words that it was okay for Emma to change her mind and make a choice that was best for her and Sam.

As Brigid flipped off the light switch, she hoped one day Emma wouldn't resent her for not giving her a choice.

16

Brigid scooted closer to Emma as the plane floated effortlessly through the silvery cotton candy clouds. She grasped Emma's arm as they pushed through the last of the turbulence to reveal the lush tapestry of Ireland.

"Oh my. Look Em. It's more beautiful than I imagined."

"You've been here before Brig," Emma said, sounding slightly irritable.

"I was like *six*. The city is much larger than I remember."

Emma continued to stare out the window, but Brigid was confused by Emma's sudden change of moods.

"You okay Em? Does landing make you nervous?"

"Not at all, it's just been a long flight, and that kid has been kicking my seat the past three hours. I didn't mean to sound cranky."

"I get it. This plane wasn't built for my long legs. I can't wait to get out and stretch," Brigid said as she once again grasped Emma's arm as the plane landed with a small bounce.

Soon passengers were standing and reaching for their overhead luggage and shuffling off the plane.

Emma flipped her phone off airplane mode as did Brigid while they both searched for their passports.

"Let's take a couple of pictures to send back home. We should let everyone know we got here okay," Emma added, looking around at the new surroundings.

"You sure you don't want to check in on Sam? Your phone is blowing up," Brigid's laughed.

"Ya, I know, but I'll answer him once we're in the car. Come on, smile."

The girls made silly poses, and goofy faces then put their phones away to follow the line of travelers to the customs line. Once through they retrieved their waiting luggage and set off in search of

Brigid's grandparents, who would undoubtedly be nearby. The older couple saw the girls first and began waving happily. Maddie and Connor Mahoney took turns wrapping Brigid in their open arms as Emma watched the scene unfold.

Maddie reminded Emma of an elegant older Ashling with her long and unruly hair, although, where Ashling still retained her fiery locks, Maddie's hair shimmered with graying streaks. She had a naturally youthful face, belying her age, and Emma felt an instant bond, loving the way her bright green eyes seemed to smile as quickly as her lips did.

The couple seemed an odd pair to Emma. The large, heavily built man with curly tufts on his balding head, looked slightly out of place standing next to the graceful woman. He intimidated her at first, but once Connor welcomed Emma in his thick Irish brogue and wrapped her in a grandfatherly hug, she instantly forgot about the contrasts in the two older adults or her initial apprehension.

Connor loaded his Land Rover with the girls luggage, and the foursome was off.

"Do you remember anything about Ireland, lass?" Connor asked.

"Mostly just making cookies with Grandma, and ones of you letting me help feed the cows. Remember the white one that followed me everywhere?"

"I certainly do. You two had quite the bond. We still have the old girl. She never seems to age," Maddie's tone held a warm note.

"You two must be hungry. We thought we'd head over to the pub, if you're both up to it that is," Connor waited for the girls answer, as he peeked through the rearview mirror.

"I'm starving!" they answered in unison.

"The pub it is. Everyone is looking forward to meeting you both," Maddie said, turning to smile at the girls.

Brigid heard many stories over the years about her grandparents' well-known establishment. She knew it was where her parents met and fell in love.

Only for the briefest of moments did Brigid allow herself to daydream about falling in love in Ireland just like her parents. Quickly squelching the thought, Brigid reminded herself there wasn't time to get involved with anyone right now. There were too many things she wanted and needed to do. Brigid already noticed Emma losing some of her focus because of missing Sam—and they'd only said goodbye twenty hours earlier, but Brigid refused to take a detour when it came to her purpose in life.

From early on, Brigid knew what path she wanted to take when she grew up. The stories her mom would tell her of their ancestors opened the doors of her imagination.

"I'm gonna be a doctor one day Miss Cuddles. Mom and Dad said I could be whatever I want, and so that is what I'm gonna do," Brigid once confided to her tabby as they sat on the front porch swing.

Her fascination with helping others grew over the years. It was no surprise when Brigid presented her parents with her plan to fast track her education.

"That's my Sprite. Everything in life happens so quick with you," Ethan said, looking over the accelerated courses she and her guidance counselor managed to procure after much negotiation.

"School's never been my thing, you guys know that. I just want to get it over with, and I know I can do this," Brigid said, looking from one parent to the other.

"It's a wee ambitious, but our Brigid here is perfectly capable of handling this schedule. If this is what you truly want, I'm okay with it," Ashling said.

By the time Brigid walked with her high school class at graduation, both she and Emma had completed their first year of college courses. Nowhere in the plan was there time for distractions, especially when looking at the class load she would be taking on in the fall. School seemed all but effortless to Emma, but Brigid found she needed to be more focused. A guy would definitely be a hindrance. Having it once again settled in her mind, Brigid sat back to observe the scenery.

"It's amazing how much the countryside looks like Oregon," Brigid remarked casually, becoming silent once again, as she took in the sights along the way.

Staring out the window, Brigid thought about how Emma was just as committed to her own career plans, up until the last few months. The relationship between her and Sam became serious, fast, and Brigid feared Emma might ultimately back out of going to Ireland. Would Brigid alter her plans if Emma backed out? She was conflicted. The gnawing voice in her head was back, but Brigid clung to the last things Emma said. *"Brig, we've dreamt about this. I'm going."*

After a short drive from the airport, Connor parked the car across the street from the Mahoney's family business that sat nestled in-between two other equally quaint commercial properties. "It's exactly what I imagined a real Irish pub would look like," Emma commented as she stepped from the car and looked out over the gray stone cut exterior walls accented with red and black trim with MAHONEY'S spelled out in large gold letters above the entrance.

The establishment was a favorite to the locals who had been frequenting Mahoney's for decades, making them all feel like family. Tourists in the know were often seen mingling with the old-timers who were more than happy to share a story over a pint or two, especially if the visitors bought the first round.

The interior was warm and inviting, and Brigid instantly loved the energy of the people turning to greet them as they entered. Unobtrusive Edison lights hung in single strands above a long mahogany bar, wrapping around the small, crowded space. Patrons on bar stools were enthusiastically enjoying their meals—and their Guinness. Connor warmly greeted the patrons as he shook random hands, exchanged pleasantries or patted some on the back while kissing the cheeks of a few others as he led the three ladies to a corner table. It was evident to both girls that the Mahoney's were a very well-liked couple.

Brigid and Emma sat first, sharing a cushioned bench seat, while Connor pulled out a chair for Maddie. The warm yellow walls and the green patterned runner on the floor created a traditional setting, making it feel more like a home than a restaurant. While the pub wasn't overly large, it was nicely laid out for maximum use.

In one corner off to the side, a small room housed a well-used pool table. Brigid absently stared at two men bantering back and forth as one man racked the balls scattered about the green felt. The taller one had a nice laugh, Brigid thought to herself.

Continuing to take in the sights and smells of her grandparents' world, Brigid noticed the well-appointed bar and shelves stretching from floor to ceiling filled with every type of alcohol imaginable. Connor was very proud of the local drinks he poured. Offering the girls samples, they politely tasted a few, then wisely decided to stick with hot tea for their meal. Brigid found herself glancing towards the two men shooting pool as she sipped her warm drink, looking away quickly when the one with the contagious laugh caught her eye. Brigid was all too grateful for the distraction of the food's arrival.

"This smells amazing," Brigid declared.

"Looks delicious," Emma added, admiring the plates filled with generous portions presented before the group.

Emma decided on fish and chips, while Brigid opted for the Irish stew, secretly hoping it was as good as the one her mom would often make them at home. Neither girl was disappointed as they munched earnestly on their lunch, occasionally stopping to chat with the regulars whom Connor and Maddie proudly introduced them to.

Once again, Brigid found herself drawn to the men in the next room. "I wonder if they're related," Brigid said to no one in particular.

Glancing over at the young men, then back at Brigid, Emma grinned broadly. Suddenly, Brigid's cheeks flamed.

"Brig, what the heck is wrong with you?" Emma demanded in a low voice, grateful Maddie and Conner were deep in conversation with an acquaintance so that the girl's interaction went unnoticed.

"That guy just winked at me," Brigid answered quietly, staring at her food.

"Brig, which one?" Emma whispered.

"The cute one," Brigid said a bit too quickly.

Thinking them both equally attractive, a tad too old maybe, and not as cute as Sam, Emma nudged her friend.

"Let's walk over there so you can get a closer look," Emma challenged, knowing the answer would be an emphatic, no.

"A closer look at what darlin'?" Maddie asked Emma.

Having been caught teasing her friend, Emma was momentarily flustered but recovered quickly.

"Oh, at the rest of the pub, Mrs. Mahoney."

"Call me Maddie, dear, and of course after lunch, we'll give you both a tour, right, Connor?" Maddie looked at her husband.

"Takes all of about five minutes, but sure lasses, be happy to show you around," Connor responded with a good-natured laugh.

Intent on tackling her stew, Brigid bent her head to scoop a large spoonful of lamb and vegetables, not seeing the two men from the poolroom approach their table. Looking up in surprise, Brigid promptly dropped her utensil, splattering a large dollop of gravy squarely on the tip of her nose. Emma tried to suppress a laugh that danced on her lips as she watched a clearly shaken Brigid.

For some reason, seeing Brigid flustered, was funny to Emma, who knew her friend to be unflappable. The elder couple's confused glances toward their granddaughter's peculiar behavior caused Emma to sober. Time froze in Brigid's world. Her head began to spin wildly, and a chill ran down her spine as the tall young man with indeterminable eye color did it again—he winked at her—this time in front of everyone. His unabashed, spontaneous grin did nothing to comfort Brigid, nor did his deep-set dimples, now gracing his chiseled face. She was bewildered as to why he then merely touched the tip of his nose twice.

Brigid became painfully aware of the food on her face. She dearly wanted to slink down under the table and disappear, but her Rafferty pride forbade it. Instead, Brigid forced herself to hold his mirthful gaze while she gracefully lifted a crisp white napkin, raised her eyebrows and dabbed at her nose, then purposefully spooned another juicy bite from her bowl.

Brigid was proud of herself for maintaining eye contact with the rogue before her. A look of admiration flashed across the young man's face but was gone instantly. He chuckled then turned his attention to Maddie.

An unnamed emotion passed through Brigid. Sadness? Loss? She dipped her spoon once again, although no longer hungry.

"Maddie, you're looking lovely," the tall one said as he leaned over to plant a kiss on her cheek.

"Better be on the lookout Mahoney, someone better might scoop this lass right out from under you if you aren't careful," the stranger said as he hooked a finger towards Connor's wife, flashing his dimpled smile once again in Maddie direction.

"Someone better? Maybe Michael, but not a Scotsman to be sure," Connor tossed back, pleased at his own joke.

The one called Michael burst out laughing as he good-naturedly smacked the older man on the back. There was an apparent friendship between the two.

"Pull up a chair. I was just telling Maddie we haven't heard much from your grandparents lately. Are they well?"

"Where are your manners, husband," Maddie broke in, swatting at Connor's arm.

"Yes, my manners. I seem to forget there are people not familiar with this sharp-tongued lad. This one here is Michael, and the one with better manners is his friend, Ewan."

"These two lovely ladies are Brigid, our granddaughter, and her friend Emma. Came here from the United States, just today," Maddie added happily.

"Pleased to meet you both," Emma politely responded, holding out her hand. Both men took their turn to greet her. Brigid merely stared unblinking, back and forth at the exchange.

"Your accent is quite charming, where in the States are you from?" Ewan inquired.

Brigid, apparently not intimidated by Ewan, found her voice.

"We're from Oregon."

Then, daring a glance in Michael's direction, forgetting what she had just said, repeated herself.

"We're from Oregon."

"Um, Brig, they heard you the first time," Emma nudged her friend with her elbow.

"Brig is still jet lagged I'm afraid. Typically she knows how to eat and speak like a proper human, don't you Brig?" Emma said while kicking her friend under the table.

Brigid set her spoon down, casually placing her hands on her lap.

"Ha, jet lag, for sure. The flight was what, fourteen and a half hours?"

Emma nodded, relieved her friend was regaining her composure.

"You are all friends I take it?" Emma asked no one in particular.

"Michael's grandparents own the shop next door. Finest books and antiques in Ireland. It was a shame to see the shop close. Everything's just the way they left it since Helen and Alistair closed the doors," Conner commented.

"Sounds mysterious," Emma added.

"My grandparents have decided, life's too short not to travel the world," Michael offered, never once looking Brigid's way.

"Old Alastair likes to say he still works, but he's just out galavanting and collecting trinkets. Took your Helen away from us, didn't he Maddie," Connor said.

"She's happy traveling, although I miss her."

Then to the girls, Maddie added, "They collect and sell rare books."

"They just landed in Rome last week, didn't they?" Maddie asked.

"No, change of plans. Gramps got a tip on an original book by *Audubon*. The old fox thinks he can get it for a steal," Michael supplied.

"Alistair's last great steal cost him over 11 Million U.S dollars, lasses," Connor replied lightly, calculating the American conversion in his head.

"Connor!" Maddie reprimanded her husband.

Ewan laughed while Michael shook his head.

The conversation carried on as the girls learned Helen and Maddie grew up together, and much like Emma and Brigid, they were best friends.

"You know, I remember the day your grandparents met like it was only yesterday," Maddie said.

"Alistair was older, more worldly then Helen, but it was love at first sight. Right, dear?" Maddie asked Connor.

"How she fell for a Scot, I'll never know," Connor said winking in good fun at the girls while letting them in on his little joke.

Brigid thought to herself, maybe winking was a thing in Ireland.

Maddie swatted yet again at Connor's arm. Ready for the scolding, he deftly moved away.

"Aw, Maddie, can't an old guy like me have any fun?"

"Not at the boys expense."

"They know it's a running thing with me and Ol' Alistair. Right boys?"

"Joke as old as time," Ewan replied drolly.

Brigid quietly listened to the exchange going on around her and was painfully aware that Michael no longer even seemed to notice she was there. She was oddly disappointed. His phone pinged with a text message. After reading the brief news, Michael's face became an unreadable mask. He politely excused himself as he left without even a backward glance. Brigid did not expect to feel the pang of regret that she did as she watched him walk away. It was an odd sensation. One she did not want to look too close at.

Ewan remained, chatting a while longer as he explained to Brigid and Emma that he and Michael were in Cork on business.

"Sorry to interrupt, but we need you in the kitchen," a ruddy-faced young man said to Connor.

"Don't tell me. Jack's set fire to the kitchen again?" Connor sighed, pushing his chair away from the table.

"Worse, he fell asleep peeling potatoes. Guess what he used for his pillow?" The server asked with mild sarcasm as he turned to go.

"Excuse me, ladies, can't be having any of that going on in my kitchen. Ewan, good to see you again." With that, Connor made his way towards the kitchen.

"I should be on my way. No telling about that mate of mine, but I'll stop in to say goodbye before we head back to Glasgow," Ewan said, kissing Maddie's cheek and shaking each of the girls hands.

"Nice meeting you. Enjoy your visit," Ewan added pleasantly.

After finishing up their lunch, Connor rejoined them, making the girls laugh with his animated retelling of the young cook with potatoes stuck on his cheek!

"We should get you girls home, you're both probably exhausted," Maddie said, looking at Emma who was stifling a yawn.

"I'm dreaming of a long sleep, to be honest. I think the trip is catching up with me. What about you, Brig?"

"Now that you mention it, I could use a nap too."

Brigid wasn't sure why she felt a sense of loss. She couldn't put her finger on it, but she was suddenly sad. The gnawing voice in her head told her to think of how Emma must feel.

Jet lag, she told herself. Nothing more than jet lag.

17

The week the girls spent in Ireland flew by with activities Maddie and Connor planned. Brigid recalled one such outing to her mom during a late night video chat. Ethan's face came into view on Brigid's laptop as he sat down next to Ashling. Giving a brief wave, Ethan listened to his daughter talk of her adventures.

"Grandma and Grandpa never seem to run outta energy. We spent hours at the Ballycotton Cliff Walk, and Em and I got worn out way before they did."

"Sounds like they haven't changed," Ethan added.

"They act just like they did when I was little."

The conversation continued as Brigid shared her day. Now and then one of her parents would jump in, peppering her with questions or asking for more details. Brigid was happy to fill in the blanks as she ticked off the numerous perks to her home away from home.

"Em, and I took pictures of everything and everyone, like typical tourists," she laughingly told her parents.

"Grandpa said he loves our American enthusiasm, even though Em doesn't seem quite herself."

"Probably just the new environment. She can be a little overwhelmed with familys like ours," Ashling reminded Brigid as she tried to stifle a yawn.

With a final round of, *I love yous* echoing out—computers clicked off.

Brigid found Emma asleep in the room they shared, so she quietly climbed into her own bed with sheets that smelled of lavender.

Brigid ignored the fact that the last thought before she fell asleep was of a tall dark-haired man winking at her.

Finally, the day before Ethan and Ashling were to arrive, Connor and Maddie brought the girls to see Saint Anne's Church. Laced with a rich history, it sat proudly on top of a hill overlooking the River Lee. There was something familiar about this church to Brigid, or more so, the ground on which she was walking. It was as if it whispered her name, beckoning her to stay.

"Talk about deja vu. It feels like you're welcoming me home. I swear I have stood here before," she said to herself. Then sneaking a look around, Brigid slipped off her boots and began slowly walking forward, hearing what appeared to be a steady heartbeat.

Tun-tun, tun-tun, tun-tun.

"This feels so familiar," she said, shaking her head as if to clear the cobwebs fogging her mind. Looking to the left, Brigid intuitively knew she would see three trees clumped together with a small area in the center. The space, Brigid also knew, would be just the right size for a child to sit and daydream in. Chills ran down her arms and spine. Her mother always told her to pay attention to the angel chills, as she would lovingly call them.

"We're here, child."

Brigid looked around and saw no one.

Tun-tun, tun-tun, tun-tun.

She began to walk toward the trees, then stopped short as Emma and Maddie called out to her. Brigid became disoriented. She looked about as if unsure of where she was, but walked toward her grandmother and friend all the same.

"I just had the weirdest experience, you guys."

"What do you mean Brig? Why aren't you wearing shoes?" Emma asked.

"Oh, I took them off. I sat them down over there, I guess. I feel like I've been here before. Have I Grandma?"

"No dear. However, I'm not surprised you feel that way. Our family history runs deep in these parts. Perhaps you were connecting with our ancestors. They can be pretty vocal sometimes."

"Maddie, you too?" The words slipped out as Emma stared at Maddie and Brigid as if they were speaking a foreign language.

Maddie chuckled.

Emma merely shook her head.

"Would you both like to go ring the bells or light a candle in the church?" Maddie asked as they rejoined Connor, who was sitting on a nearby bench.

Emma was eager to do both things having read up on the Shandon Bells and Tower.

"I'm so glad we are here. I once wrote a paper in junior high on Saint Anne's Church," Brigid told the group.

"Your mom sent us the paper. I still have it. She was so proud of you and all the research you did," Maddie added sweetly.

"It was one of the first places your grandmother said we should take you both to. Seeing it first hand is special indeed," Connor added as he rejoined the women.

Once inside the church, Brigid confessed in a low voice she was worried about her mom, who as hard as she tried to pretend, just wasn't herself.

"Grandma, I don't want to concern either of you, but lately, mom seems exhausted all the time—she looks thinner and not in a healthy way."

"Yes, she's not looking like the Ashling I know. She stops a lot to catch her breath too. I've seen it when she's outside walking and doesn't think anyone sees her. At first, I figured she just had the flu or was tired. You know how Ashling likes to stay busy, but it's been going on a long time now," Emma said, her voice matching the uneasy tone of Brigid's.

Maddie listened intently as an unreadable expression played over both hers and Connor's faces.

"Let's light some candles, shall we? One for each of your parents. That means your parents too, Emma, dear. They have such a load on their shoulders, it seems."

Brigid pretended not to notice her grandmother pull out a handkerchief to wipe her nose as she lit her candle, or her grandfather as he gently squeezed Maddie's shoulder. It was the first time Brigid thought her grandparents looked their age.

"It's getting late dear. I think we should head for home," Connor said patting Maddie's back affectionately.

Back at the Mahoney's, their dinner passed in quiet conversation. As the evening wound down, Emma excused herself to go catch up on Sam's day over a video chat they had scheduled.

"It's a challenge with the time difference. I hope I don't seem rude," Emma said with a questioning look.

"No, not at all dear, plus it's getting late. Getting a wee bit tired myself," Maddie said stifling a yawn.

"Grandpa, I hope you and Grandma aren't too surprised when you see mom."

"Ah, we're all gettin' older, I'm afraid. Our Ashling is probably just slowing down like the rest of us," Connor said with a forced chuckle.

"Time for bed my love," Connor softly beckoned to his wife of fifty-eight years.

To Brigid, both her grandparents were so full of life, having seemingly boundless energy. It was easy to forget they were getting on in age. The pace she and Emma were keeping them at over the past week must have finally caught up with them both. Standing, Brigid hugged her grandfather.

"Thank you for everything you and Grandma have done to make me and Emma feel so at home," Brigid told the pair.

Maddie hugged Brigid in return.

As Brigid watched her grandparents walk down the hall hand in hand, she caught herself hoping she would one day have a forever love as strong as her parents and grandparents had found.

"There must be something in the air," Brigid mumbled to no one in particular as she padded to the room she and Emma shared. Opening the door she found Emma openly sobbing.

"Em, what's wrong?" Brigid was by her friend's side in the quickest of moments.

Sitting at a small table overlooking the night sky, Emma quickly wiped her tears.

"Em talk to me. Are you okay? Is Sam okay? What happened?" Brigid pressed.

"I'm sorry, Brig—guess I'm just a little homesick. I'll be okay tomorrow." She tried to smile at her worried friend.

"I know you like the back of my hand, Emma Daily. You are not just homesick. You're heartsick!"

Emma dropped her head into her hands, hopelessly failing to stifle her misery.

"I don't know what to do! I just miss him Brig. I feel so empty when we say goodbye. I'm so happy when I see him, talk to him, think about him, but I feel lost right now."

"Em, do you feel lost or torn?" Brigid's voice broke ever so slightly, but Emma heard it.

"It's okay Brig I'll get over it. We'll start school just like we planned, you know?"

Brigid instantly knew what she needed to do. She was sad but resolute. "Emma," Brigid started out in a soft, kind, reassuring voice.

"Go home."

Putting on a practiced smile, Emma grabbed a nearby tissue and quickly blew her nose.

"Never! Toss all our adventures out the window? Over a silly boy? Are you insane? It's going to be okay. It's just a year and Sam is saving up money to visit me, and I'll be home for Thanksgiving or Christmas—if my parents are there, that is. I'm just acting like a baby," she finished as her voice trailed off.

"Go home, Emma. Things change. It's okay. You've been in love with Sam since the first time you laid eyes on him. This isn't some passing thing. Besides, it took you two *forever* to get it together. You can't throw your chance away. Life's too short as it is." Brigid was feeling much stronger and sure now. Her heart hurt, but she would cry later.

"I feel like I'd be letting you down Brig. I think I have to try this out, you know?" The statement hung like a question in the air as Brigid remained thoughtful.

"Well Em, I feel like I'm holding you back."

The moment of truth had arrived. They both knew it, looking into each other's eyes.

"You and I will be friends forever. I won't be mad if you go Em. Sad? Of course. However, I will be angry and hurt if you stay for the wrong reasons. It's time to allow someone into your life that builds you up and loves you. Sam is that guy. Besides, you owe this to yourself. Do life your way, and not the way you think I want, or your parents or anyone else expects you to," Brigid said and meant it.

"But I made all these plans, and oh God, my parents will be mortified!" Emma started crying again.

"Em, you have options. Plus, you know that your dad just has to make one phone call and come September you'll be at the school both your parents graduated from, with Sam by your side, as it's meant to be."

Emma was feeling torn between fear and relief.

"Look, let's get some sleep. Tomorrow when my parents get here we'll tell them first. It will make it seem real, you know? Maybe it will be easier with all of us around, to tell your parents on Sunday when they get here," Brigid said.

"Oh Brig, you know how my parents hate weakness and indecisive people. They warned me I'd regret this. I can't think about it. What a nightmare."

"Look, your parents are going to give you grief, but they wanted you in Oregon anyway, so ultimately they are getting their way, right? Maybe spin it that way. You know, say something like, '*Hey Mom and*

Dad, you were right. I'm going to take your advice and come back home.' You know, something like that."

"Ugh, I'm going to bed. My head is pounding," Emma groaned in a strained whisper.

"We'll figure this out, my friend. Things always work out when you follow your heart and listen to your gut..."

"You sound like your mom," Emma replied, clicking off the light.

18

Brigid woke early the following day and quietly dressed in a pair of leggings and a baggy sweatshirt. After pulling her hair up into a loose bun, she navigated her way down the hallway to the front door—grateful she didn't wake Emma, who tossed most of the night on the bed next to her. Rest however eluded Brigid's troubled mind.

Once outside, the fresh smell of damp earth in the quiet hours of the morning reminded Brigid of home.

As if compelled, she slipped off her shoes. Even though she loved to go barefoot, it was a bit too chilly to deprive her feet of the warmth they now enjoyed. Brigid did it anyway, loving how the soft cushions of moss and cold cobblestones felt under her feet as she thoughtfully walked along the worn path, talking with nature and avoiding the spots the Wee Folk might be. Feeling homesick and conflicted made Brigid miss Malachi.

"Oh Mal, I wish I could talk to you, you'd know just what to say to me about Emma leaving, and me staying," Brigid said as she continued following the trail to a flat grassy field where an oak tree, almost as magnificent as Malachi stood. Suddenly Brigid felt small and alone. Doubt found an opening in her troubled thoughts.

Tun-tun, tun-tun, tun-tun.

Brigid swatted at the invisible thumping near her ear.

"That tree reminds me of everything I'm missing. Maybe this is a sign that I'm to go home with Emma. I'm worried about Mom anyway and maybe seeing this tree is the push I need," Brigid said out loud.

"You must not go," Brigid would have sworn she heard someone say. Looking around all she saw was the old white cow Brigid immediately recognized from her youth.

The watchful animal bent its head and lazily bit off the vegetation before her. Brigid continued her approach to the tree as if it were a magnet drawing her closer. The cow followed at a distance.

"What was I thinking, coming all the way here to go to school?"

"You must have come for a reason," a voice called out.

Startled, Brigid turned abruptly to see a crane, almost as tall as her with unblinking onyx eyes that seemed to transform to a burnt orange shade the more Brigid peered back at them. She studied the crimson tufted feathers atop his otherwise white and gray head. On closer inspection, she noticed faint ruby-red feathers which laid gently across his eyes like a mask.

"I've seen you before."

The crane cocked his head to the side but said nothing.

"You're the bird who was hanging around Malachi aren't you?"

The crane bobbed his sleek neck.

"Who are you?" Brigid asked softly.

The crane flapped his wings in reply. The sound thundered in Brigid's ears like a drum.

The *tun-tun, tun-tun, tun-tun* lasted only a moment.

Brigid would later recall that his whirring feathered wings, now fluttering softly at his side sounded like—no felt like, a heartbeat—a strong, healthy heartbeat. At that moment, Brigid felt as if their hearts beat as one.

"I am called Turlough, Brigid Ann," he stated in his nasally voice.

Brigid took a cautious step forward. He remained still and again cocked his head to the side.

"You are not afraid of me, this is good."

"*Turla*," Brigid slowly tested out his name on her tongue.

"I've heard that name before. Malachi has spoken of his friend Turlough, but, I don't understand..." Brigid's voice trailed off as she tried to decide which question to pose first.

"Why am I here? Is that your question Brigid Ann?"

"How do you know my name? Is Malachi all right?"

"Malachi is fine Brigid Ann. Have no doubt he is still firmly rooted in the ground where he has been growing for many years."

"How did you know what I was thinking? I didn't speak out loud."

"It's a gift! One of many I might add... however, I'm too modest to list them all. Entirely too humble."

"Why are you here Turlough, if Malachi is all right? Do you live here?"

"I have come to speak with you, Brigid Ann. It is of grave importance that you heed my warning," the crane continued.

"What kind of warning, Turlough?"

"I heard you speak of the foolish notion to return to Oregon. I could stay quiet no longer!" He bugled loudly—as if insulted.

"We have worked for too many centuries to have you come here and then leave without fulfilling your destiny. You must understand that this matter is of great importance."

Brigid's mind raced with unasked questions. Reading her thoughts, Turlough made a show of ruffling his feathers.

"To answer your question, Brigid Ann, I assure you I am of sound mind and body," he bugled somewhat more softly.

"Turlough, while I do believe you are a friend of Malachi's, and I do find this conversation quite... interesting, I'm afraid you must be confused."

"It is not I who is confused, Brigid Ann. You must realize the important role you have chosen to play at this time of your life. It is vital for you to remain in Ireland and attend to your education—at least for now," Turlough said cryptically.

"Why?"

"You must remain here, to once again bring light and healing to your people."

"I can study to be a doctor in the states just as easily. Actually, I'll have to finish my degree there at some point," Brigid replied.

"No, no, not just any physician! While the profession is a highly regarded one, Brigid Ann, there is more. You are the Chosen One. Don't you remember? You stood before the Priestess and accepted the role you would play in your ancestor's lineage."

Brigid became frightened. She did not like the way Turlough was staring, as if, through her. Suddenly, she did not feel comfortable at all with talk of being a chosen one by some made up Priestess from her mother's bedtime stories.

Brigid tried to look away, but she could not.

"You must stay and fulfill your destiny, Brigid Ann. So much depends on you and the choices you make from here on out."

Agitated, Turlough huffed as his neck feathers ruffled. He twisted his head from side to side, listening for what Brigid might be thinking.

"You heard the whispers, and you came," Turlough said quietly.

"What whispers?" Brigid forced herself to ask.

"Stop harassing the child, Turlough," a grandmotherly voice laced in old Irish chided.

The crane bowed his long neck in a respectful reply. Turning to see who spoke, Brigid expected to see one of her grandmother's friends arriving for an early visit, but quickly realized it was not just any woman's voice, but the oak tree Brigid stood beneath.

"Oh my, this is turning out to be quite the day," Brigid breathed, looking up at the tree.

"Sorry, my dear, we didn't mean to frighten you. My name is Deru. Turlough here can be quite intimidating when he's trying to make a point. Shame on you Turlough," the soft-spoken tree admonished.

The crane slowly stretched from his sitting position, standing to his full height, facing the tree trunk, his burnt orange eyes once again turning onyx. Turlough began to let out another loud bugle. Quickly, Brigid covered her ears, waiting, but the oak shook her branches with such force, Turlough sat back down, bowing his head once again.

"You know as well as I that Brigid Ann must remain!"

"Hush Turlough. It is not the time or place. You know the rules."

Then the oak addressed Brigid in a calm and reassuring voice.

"I said hello as you approached, but I fear now, you simply had your thoughts elsewhere."

Brigid gave a short laugh.

"Oh, it's all right—Deru, it's nice to meet you. I am so missing my friend Malachi, who is a majestic oak, just like you. I heard of a tree my parents were married beneath. It was many years ago, but I wonder if it was you? Ashling Mahoney and Ethan Rafferty—do you remember them?" Brigid asked, hopefully.

The old tree took her time, slowly swaying in the morning breeze. "I've witnessed many commitment ceremonies child, but I have a special bond with Ashling, and her mother, Madeline. Many of your ancestors have sat beneath my branches throughout the centuries, and each woman dear to me as a child could be," Deru replied warmly.

"Yes, I remember well the marriage of young Ethan to our beloved Ashling. Your parents were very much in love that day."

"You should see them now," Brigid supplied happily.

Turlough bugled loudly.

"Deru, Ashling Elizabeth arrives today—it has begun."

Brigid was afraid but not sure why.

"Enough Turlough. You have given the girl her message, and now you have other work to do. I think it is time for you to take your leave," Deru said in a kinder tone.

The crane's wings began flapping, once again creating a *tun-tun, tun-tun, tun-tun* sensation in Brigid's ear as he flew out of sight.

"His wings sounded like an angry drum at first, but as he was leaving, I felt like a part of my heart was leaving with him," Brigid confessed to Deru in a quiet voice.

"I know child. It is because he carries the essence of those who once were. You see, we are all connected, through all time and space. It is a bond that is not easily broken," Deru said kindly, even though her words seemed somewhat ominous.

Brigid stared up at the tree which seemed to speak in riddles.

"I have to go. My parents will be here soon. Goodbye Deru."

Brigid was feeling overwhelmed, yet hoping she didn't sound as panicked as she was feeling. As she turned to go, Deru softly began to sing an old Gaelic song, one that Brigid sometimes heard Ashling sing. For some unknown reason, this made Brigid want to run, far and fast from the tune and the tree. Deep in her heart, Brigid knew everything she relied on was about to change.

She forced herself to pace her steps, sorely wishing to be seven years old again, at home, where she could run to Malachi, and where a bowl of steaming soup and a melted cheese sandwich awaited her. Mostly though, Brigid needed the comfort of her parents waiting and open arms.

Step by step, Brigid felt the once steady earth betray her, falling away beneath her feet. The world around her tilted and swayed. Brigid could take it no longer as her breath came in ragged sobs. She began running as fast as her legs would carry her, weeping openly, although she did not know why.

Out of breath and feeling quite fragile, Brigid paused as her grandparent's car pulled slowly up the drive, coming to a stop in front of her. Instantly Ashling and Ethan were at their daughter's side, concern written on their faces at the sight of Brigid's tear-stained face. Brigid threw herself into their open arms, clinging to them as if her life depended on it.

19

"Brigid, darlin', what happened? Why are you crying?" Ashling asked frantically while gently tucking a loose strand of hair behind her daughter's ear. Ethan held Brigid at arm's length, inspecting her head to toe, to ensure no physical harm was evident, then wrapped her tightly in a fierce hug. Slowly regaining her composure, Brigid produced a shaky smile.

"Mom, Dad, I'm so happy to see you both. I didn't realize how late it had gotten and time slipped away this morning. I'm sorry I scared you."

"Sprite, what were you running from? Has someone hurt you?"

Brigid's cheeks flamed with embarrassment.

"Dad, I'm okay. It was just an odd sort of morning. You see, there was this bird, and..." Brigid shrugged her shoulders. An awkward silence followed as Brigid tried to find a way to change the subject.

"What bird darlin'?" Ashling asked in a high pitched tone, catching everyone's attention.

"A crane. Remember I told you a while back about a huge bird I saw hanging around Malachi?" Brigid looked at her mother, who barely nodded in return.

"Go on," Ashling encouraged.

"Well, I saw him by Deru..."

"Who's Deru?" Ethan broke in.

"Our oak tree," Ashling replied.

"Oh, the tree we got married underneath on the hill," Ethan replied with an understanding nod.

Brigid continued.

"I decided to take a walk early this morning to clear my head... about stuff. When I looked up, the crane was standing by Deru, so, I approached him and said hello. Turlough—that's his name, said some weird things."

Maddie leaned against Connor, who absently patted his wife's shoulder.

"Mom, the part that got me though was as I walked away, Deru started to sing that song, you know the one I think sounds sad? The Gaelic one."

"Yes, I know the one," Ashling said void of emotion.

"Well, it freaked me out. I don't know. I just had to get away. Something wasn't right." Looking at the faces surrounding her, Brigid didn't feel comforted.

She began to shift her weight nervously on bare feet, suddenly feeling the need to run off again. Ethan gently took hold of Brigid's hand, as if sensing her dilemma, staring only at Ashling.

"We tell her now," Ethan said in a deceptively soft tone.

Ashling merely nodded her head as she looked towards her father. Her resolve began to crumble. It was Connor's turn to take control of what would be the deconstruction of all their lives. Wrapping his arm protectively around Ashling's shoulder, she began to shake.

"Not here. Let's talk inside," Connor said, sounding every bit his age. Tenderly placing his free arm around Maddie's waist, he headed toward the house with his wife and his daughter.

Brigid allowed Ethan to lead her as well. Afraid to speak, she forced one wobbly leg to move and then the other. Intuitively, Brigid knew that what was to come would be something she was in no hurry to be a part of.

Entering the warmth of her childhood home, Ashling saw Emma, who was on the couch painting her nails. Emma popped out of her seat with palpable excitement, as she rushed in an uncustomary exuberance to hug Ashling. She stopped when she saw the subdued expressions on the faces around her.

"Jeez, you all look like someone just died. What happened, the airport lose your luggage?" Emma asked, looking down briefly at the nail polish cap she was tightening.

Silence filled the air.

Emma's stomach twisted nervously. She knew this feeling. She waited for the other shoe to drop. It always dropped.

"It's been an off day Em, and I have a feeling it's about to get worse. Sit with me. I don't want to hear this without you."

"Hear what, Brig? What on earth is going on?" Emma whispered.

Brigid shrugged her slender shoulders.

Emma took Brigid's hand, as both girls sank down on a small sofa, like Siamese twins.

"I'll be the one to tell her," Ashling said without preamble, testing out her confidence while trying to smile bravely at her parents and husband.

"You're scaring me, Mom. What is it? Tell me. You're sick, aren't you? Like, really sick, aren't you? You hardly eat, you've lost even more weight since I last saw you, and the circles under your eyes tell me you're not sleeping." It was now Brigid's turn to shiver and shake.

Emma once again grabbed onto Brigid's hand, sensing her friend's tenuous raw nerves. The two young women, more like sisters than friends, perched on the couch and were both anchor and buoy for each other.

"I have cancer girls. It's been with me quite a few years now actually." Ashling tried to sound confident as she went on.

"I've managed beautifully, keeping it at bay for well over five-plus years now, thanks to our yews, and a few of our ancestor's remedies. I believed it was gone. Truly I did. But, the remedies have ceased working," she said, not knowing what else to say.

Ethan sat by Ashling's side, clenching his jaw, wanting to scream at an unseen God, helpless to do anything as the color drained from his daughter's face, and the actual life—from his wife. It wasn't fair. They were good people, honest, caring, decent. He would never be able to make sense out of why this tragedy was striking his family. Ethan, shook his head, once again feeling helpless to protect his family.

Emma noticed Ethan's hands, tightly closed in defensive balls at his side and his knuckles turning an unnatural shade of white. An old grandfather clock in the corner of the room ticked steadily. Maddie sniffed loudly while Emma and Brigid leaned on each other, struggling to gather their thoughts. Ashling gently, yet matter-of-factly, continued explaining the details. Brigid was numb, unable to speak and grateful for Emma's calm presence as they sat side by side.

"Chemo? Radiation? Have you exhausted all your options Ashling?" Emma ticked off the questions Brigid could not.

Again, the loud ticking of the clock across the room pulsated. A chill ran down Brigid's spine, the truth settling on her, like a heavy cloak.

"Mom, you've refused traditional medical treatments haven't you?" Brigid's question came out part acceptance and part accusation.

Ashling gave a slow nod of her head.

"After much thought and consideration, and yes, against your father's initial pleas, I chose the path that felt right in my heart, darlin'. I never said anything to you because I was sure the cancer was gone. So, I didn't see why I should worry you unnecessarily. I asked your father not to tell you. Be angry with me, but not him, okay? I didn't even tell your dad until, well, I had to," Ashling finished.

An unnatural guttural sound escaped Brigid's lips as she felt herself snap inside. Desperate to avoid the reality unfolding before her, she saw herself separate from her body, as if in a movie. Floating now above her physical self, Brigid safely witnessed her family's conversation.

"I know this may sound selfish of me, but I just know my body, and in my heart and soul I knew I had to make the choices that would give me the quality of time and life, in a way I felt right about doing it," Ashling said, not trying to soften her answer.

"Ashling, there's so much available these days and so many options. What about combining Western and Eastern medicine along with your approach? I wrote a term paper last semester on how successful the combination of different philosophies and modalities are for people diagnosed with cancer. I cited several cases whereby utilizing the cumulative techniques it reversed and eliminated their cancer altogether," Emma blurted out, overcome with emotion.

Ashling, wisely remained silent, knowing Emma needed to have her say as well. Of course, even Emma was falling apart with such devastating news. It was easier for Brigid to let her mind wander to her friend sitting next to her, instead of wrapping her head around her mom's diagnosis, or her own feelings. Emma's upbringing was so different from her own in many ways.

Brigid knew Emma's parents would have been direct and forthcoming from the start with Emma if either of them received a cancer diagnosis. It might not be the news Emma would want to hear, but at least she would know the facts—the truth. Brigid admitted to herself, there were times over the years, she thought Mr. and Mrs. Daily were cold and uncaring, but at least Emma wasn't kept in the dark over events that affected her life.

Brigid was angry. She prayed she could remain above the scene unfolding below her.

Studying her friend's sad profile, Brigid understood something crucial about Emma's parents. They prepared Emma for life. In their line of work, it made sense now. Both the Dailys chose career paths where logic and facts saved lives, helping others who could not help themselves. Brigid's perception began to shift. What she observed as cold, Emma's parents viewed as empowering. Brigid, however, was feeling every bit the victim, and in no way empowered. Her parents should have told her about her mom's cancer. She had a right to know. Brigid struggled as she never had before. She felt the peaceful lightness of disassociation slip away as she reluctantly entered back into her own body.

It could have been hours or minutes that were passing by, but Brigid refused to glance at the clock she once loved clacking away. It was now a pessimistic metaphorical reminder as both girls slumped on the sofa in quiet contemplation. As much as Brigid wanted to beg, guilt, and plead with her mom to fight, she innately understood her mom truly lived the way she believed to be right. Of course, her mother would actively address the cancer in her body, but she did it in a way that honored her beliefs.

Ashling always followed her gut and taught Brigid to do the same. It certainly would not be a choice Brigid would make, but she understood, sadly, it was one her mom would. It couldn't have been an easy choice for Ashling, and Brigid's heart softened—if only in the slightest of ways. Giving herself a chance to think it through, Brigid came to realize, of course, her mom would not have taken a western medical route, even for her husband and daughter. It was not in her nature. It would be as if denying all she was raised to believe.

Brigid looked briefly at her dad. She saw grief and anger, but mostly sadness etched on his face. Brigid's once steady world disintegrated before her with every passing moment. She needed Malachi's counsel. She wanted to go home where he would calmly help her figure out this mess.

Brigid looked to Maddie and Connor sitting off to the left in the overstuffed chairs they sat in every night, suddenly comprehending that even her grandparents knew. Brigid felt betrayed. She thought about her grandparent's reaction inside Saint Anne's Church. It was pure grief Brigid witnessed as her grandmother lit her candle.

Brigid stared at her sweet grandmother, absently rubbing her hands together nervously, looking frail, and her cheeks pale, not rosy like Brigid always thought of them. Her grandfather, undoubtedly the strongest man she knew next to her father, was pulling out a worn handkerchief, dabbing his eyes and wiping his nose, then, haphazardly stuffing it back into his shirt pocket.

Brigid began taking in every last detail of the room. She made mental notes—pale yellow walls, natural stone fireplace, an antique clock ticking in mocking cadence. Brigid wished she could cry, but the tears would not come. Instead, she stared at a large oval rug her mother and grandmother made many years earlier—much like the oval rug in her childhood home. Oregon. Malachi. Safety. Brigid rubbed her temples, feeling queasy.

Suddenly, something began to buzz loudly in Brigid's ears. It wasn't the clock she surmised. She swatted at it aimlessly, thinking it a fly. Looking around to see where it came from, Brigid realized no one else appeared to notice, yet it was now so loud, how could they not, she silently wondered, wanting to cover her ears. She opened her mouth to ask if anyone else heard the annoying intrusion that compounded her already growing headache, but her voice caught in her throat, sounding more like an echo.

She began to experience a sense of tunnel vision as a diaphanous cloud started seeping through the walls of her grandparents living room. Why was it no one else was noticing the hazy, sweet-smelling mist? Brigid's mind was feeling fully present, yet blank at the same time.

Tun-tun, tun-tun, tun-tun.

A gentle wave of peace began settling over her, washing away the ache between her temples as the sensation of butterfly kisses fluttering over her cheeks and nose eased her mind. With each breath, she relaxed into the tranquility that came from inhaling the fragrant air, aware now—that only Ashling was recognizable to her. No longer did mother and daughter sit across the room from each other. Instead, they stood together in a light-filled space, each experiencing their peace-filled moments, while united in a private bubble.

Brigid sensed Ashling's essence, or her soul, as she would remember it later.

From a corner of the room, a glowing bluish-white orb began to hover and grow. Soon it was so bright both Ashling and Brigid turned to see what it was.

From out of the translucent orb, an ethereal looking woman dressed in a blue velvet gown stood before them, with a white calf by her side. The Priestess raised her hand in a friendly salutation. Ashling and Brigid did the same.

There were no actual words spoken by the woman with fiery red locks that hung loose and wild around her like a cape. It was as if thoughts and ideas forming sentences simply dropped into Brigid and Ashling's consciousness.

"You do not have to do this thing we, your ancestors present to you. You maintain your free will. You know this? Do you wish to move forward knowing what you know?"

Ashling looked from the Priestess to Brigid with a glistening tear in her eye.

"I understand everything. I do this out of love, and I have come to trust the Legend. So, yes."

Brigid watched in fascination, the exchange between her mother and the Priestess.

The calf with the deep brown eyes watched Brigid closely. Brigid was aware of what the calf would do next. It was as if she and the furry creature knew each other and had done this dance before. Slowly approaching Brigid then standing by her side, the calf bowed its head. Sensing his energy being one with her own, Brigid reached down to stroke the animal's neck. She knew intuitively that her hand would tingle, just like she understood she would be at total peace, and instantly comforted when her hand reached the warm fur.

While staring in awe at what Brigid thought looked like a hologram filled with pictures and words, flashing rapidly before her eyes, then oddly transposed on her mother, she tried to process blurry images of DNA strands, codes, letters, and strange mathematical equations. When she felt anxious, the white calf would lean closer to her, and once again, a calmness would envelop her.

Ashling appeared alert yet serene with a slight smile playing on her lips as the Priestess worked with her.

After a few moments, the Priestess handed Ashling a long red ribbon. Ashling accepted the strand and held it to her chest lovingly. Brigid struggled with her memory. She knew this was symbolic, but why? *The story.* What was the Legend her mother told her? The calf leaned in, and Brigid sighed a quiet exhalation. "I remember."

The calf mooed softly as he returned to the Priestess's side.

"Yes, friend, they both remember and accept their roles," she said softly in a foreign dialect.

Just as quickly as they appeared, they withdrew once again into the cloudy sapphire bubble, fading into a speck. Ashling reached for Brigid's hand, and Brigid willingly accepted the embrace her mother offered. The buzzing in Brigid's ear faded, and the old grandfather clock once again sounded calm, constant, reliable, and soothing. The room around Brigid became clear, in focus and stable.

Mother and daughter would never speak of the exchange. Brigid's memory would become cloudy, just like the misty bubble in the vision. She would occasionally wonder if the dialogue happened at all, believing she imagined the whole event out of some instinctual survival escapism.

Some things just felt too much, and this was one of those times, but as the cloud cleared and the bubble vanished, both Ashling and Brigid appeared outwardly calm. In those moments of clarity with the Priestess, Ashling understood what her purpose on this earth was, no matter how altruistic it may seem to others.

She saw the lives of her strong female ancestors who paved the way for this moment in life. Ashling was feeling empowered, all the while understanding that her husband and daughter did not. Still, she did not waver. Ashling knew Brigid would fulfill her destiny as well, and she felt a new sense of peace and comfort she hadn't known in many months.

Brigid also knew what she would do in the months and years to come. How she knew it, was a bit blurry, but somehow, Brigid knew she would one day become a skilled doctor in her own right, and that everything would be okay.

Looking at Ethan, Ashling physically hurt though, comprehending her husband's journey would be the hardest, and at that thought, another piece of her heart broke.

20

Emma sat drumming her fingers on the glass top of a round table made from broken teacups and plaster. The intricate design combined delicate blues and greens mixed with pink and yellow flower pieces and arranged in a way that wove a story of generations of Maddie's family heritage.

Many years back during a fierce storm with record-breaking winds that shook the county, a tree had fallen mercilessly onto the Mahoney's home, crashing into the wall that Maddie's great-grandmother's china hutch leaned against. The jolt toppled the antique structure, shattering all of Maddie's treasured teacups and saucers. The porcelain set had been in her family for as long as anyone could remember. Seeing her priceless possessions in fragments on the floor, was one of the few times Connor had seen his wife cry, and at that, it was for the briefest of moments.

Connor was in awe of his wife as she stood up and gave a shaky smile and through her tears added tenderly, "Thank the heavens we were not passing by as it toppled. The Wee Folk were looking after us for sure."

Disappearing briefly into the kitchen, she returned with a broom and bucket. Connor quickly relieved Maddie of her supplies then shooed her away, promising to clean up the mess that tore at his wife's heart.

"I don't want you cutting yourself," Connor said feeling helpless, knowing what the collection meant to his wife.

"Thank you, dear. I admit I can't bear to see such a legacy shattered like it is." Maddie did her best to steady her voice.

After giving his wife a gentle hug as she left the room, Connor began to carefully place the larger pieces of the teacups and saucers in one bucket and the smaller shards in another. Later that day he carefully arranged the beautiful porcelain in a sturdy plaster goop, mixing in the fragments of china others would have cast aside.

After completing the puzzle-like circular mold, he gently laid a thick piece of perfectly cut glass with beveled edges on top of the dry surface.

Connor was pleased with his effort. "Well, it's not the same, but at least it isn't in with the rubbish."

It was on their anniversary that Connor gave Maddie the table he made by hand, which made his wife cry tears of joy.

"That you would do this for me, makes it all the more of a treasure my dear," Maddie exclaimed.

It was at that table Emma now sat at drumming her fingertips.

It was appropriately cloudy and cold outside to suit her gray mood, but the sun porch was warmed by a small potbelly stove that sat in the corner challenging her to feel—*something* more.

"You know your place and purpose. Easy for you to judge, sitting over there all fat and happy and warm!" Emma lashed out at the undeserving cast iron heater.

"Great now I'm talking to inanimate objects, not even anything alive like trees," Emma mused.

Safe and cocooned in the charmingly decorated corner of Maddie and Connor's home allowed Emma a space to think, and Brigid time to be alone with her parents. There were so many changes over the past six months that Emma needed time to sift and sort it all out. She treasured her friendship with Brigid and didn't want to disappoint her, but she was entirely in love with Sam. She owed it to them both to see where it would go, yet felt torn by her bonds of friendship with Brigid that ran deep.

As much as she wanted to be out on an adventure for her first year of college with her best friend, Emma couldn't see her life without Sam. She wanted to go home. She emailed her parents earlier in the morning about her decision to return to Oregon, and was relieved that her mother was supportive and encouraging—much to Emma's surprise.

Opening her laptop and hitting the icon which instantly produced Sam's name, left Emma wondering what to say. For well over thirteen years, Ashling had been there for Emma. She knew Brigid was angry with her mom, but all Emma knew was that Ashling had always been there for her. What would happen now? She was feeling small and selfish, but she didn't care. Emma was tired of continually having to keep it together and typed the first thing that came into her mind.

Her fingers flew over the keyboard as she wrote:

Cancer.
A six letter word that alters lives forever.
Just found out Ashling has friggin' cancer!
Late stage.
Don't know what to think, or feel.
I'm scared.
I need you, Sam.

She hit send without thinking.

Twenty seconds passed. Sam's response came through:

I'm sorry to hear about Mrs. R. That's horrible news. I know how much she means to you. Em, just come home. I should have never let you leave. Let me take care of you. I'll be waiting. I love you.

Before she could tell Sam about her email to her parents, Brigid walked into the room, looking a mess and rubbing her eyes as she pushed a strand of unbrushed hair from her face. She saw the guilty look pass over Emma's face as she quickly snapped closed her laptop.

"Hey Em," Brigid said, placing a steaming cup of tea on the table top, and gingerly sitting across from her friend.

"Hey, Brig," Emma responded, "You get any sleep?"

Brigid shook her head in response.

"You?" Brigid asked, hopefully.

"No. I doubt anyone but the cat slept well last night, the way it was snoring, you know?"

Both girls sat in silence, looking out at the fading lavender hill as the sun tried to peek through. Although it didn't look like it gave much of an effort, Emma thought.

Without looking at her friend, Brigid said quietly, but firmly, "Em, nothing's changed. I want you to go home. You want to go home, and that's okay. We are all going to have to find our best way to live with this, you know, our new normal, and every other obstacle life throws at us. We can't constantly be worried about hurting each others feelings or not being there for each other."

Emma said nothing. Only Brigid knew the way her friend's nose would turn bright red when she tried her best not to cry or show emotion. Again silence filled the warm sun porch.

"I'm letting you down." Emma stared at a piece of the porcelain on the table, gently tracing its shape with her finger.

Brigid, searching for the right words, watched Emma's perfectly manicured nail outline the painted blue flower once belonging to her grandmother's tea set.

"There's a lot of history in this old table Em. You ever hear the story?"

"Yes, your grandmother told me the story the other day."

"It's not just a table, it's a testament of love, commitment and putting others needs above their own, you know? Grandpa, loving Grandma as he does, wanted to fix her broken heart. He did what he could. This table represents, to me anyway, how our life can be and will be marred by accidents, mistakes, broken pieces of our heart—but a simple act of love can make all the difference. You know, you want the other person to be happy, so you put their needs ahead of your own. I want you to be happy, Em."

"It's a beautiful testament to their love. However, Brig, leave the flowery sentiments to me, after all, I'm the writer."

Brigid gave a lopsided grin.

"True, but you get my point, right?"

"Yes. I understand you."

Silence.

"If it helps to make this easier, I want you to know I'll feel better knowing you are there, in Oregon, to check in on them, you know

—Mom, my dad, the animals... but I'm gonna stay. Maybe that makes me selfish," Brigid's voice trailed off.

Taking a few deep breaths, Brigid continued, "I had a long talk with my parents after everyone went to bed last night. I told them I wanted to come home too. Only they said they think I should stay, for at least a semester or two. They think it will be better for me if I stick with the plan! The truth is, my mom doesn't want me to see her..."

Brigid could not hide her frustration or heavy heart, as the tears rolled down her face.

"Brig, your parents are probably right. Your mom is proud and loves you so much. I can see why she wants you to remember her how she has always been... Active, full of life. I bet she feels, since this was her choice, she should give you that at least. I think it will be harder for you both if you go back right now, especially because no one knows what's going to happen. She can still get better—you know, go into remission."

"But, it's my mom, and I have the right to do this my way too! Em, I know it sounds selfish, but I'm really angry with them," she said like a petulant child.

Emma squeezed her friend's hand.

"What about your dad, Brig? He still has the ranch to run, and you know how he dotes on you. If you go back now, don't you think he'll feel torn? You know he'll be so worried about you and Ashling. Then you'll worry about them—and there isn't anything you can do. Your mom just wants to keep living life."

"I could be there to help her and make some memories." The last word came out more like a whisper.

"I feel guilty for staying and acting as if this isn't happening. But Em, can I tell you something?"

"Tell me," Emma encouraged her.

"The other night after Mom told us her news when we were all sitting around in the living room, I had the strangest experience. Like an out of body experience or more like I was in a dream but not."

"You were in shock, Brig."

"I thought so too until my mom told me she experienced the same thing."

"Well, you guys are very bonded. What happened?"

Brigid began to retell how the Priestess told them things about the past, the future, and how all the events and their lives were lining up to make the future events possible.

"What events?"

"That's the crazy part. I don't remember. It's fuzzy, but I feel like I'm supposed to stay here, in Ireland. At least for now. Mom said she thinks so too. I mean, maybe the crazy vision thing is about Mom actually being in remission. I don't want to mess any of that up, you know?"

Emma believed that her friend was in denial, but also understood Brigid was clinging to hope and a lifeline, just as Emma was when she reached out to Sam. Emma would not take this away from Brigid.

They both sat in silence, Brigid staring out the window, Emma continuing to trace the shapes of the delicate pieces of china inlaid on the tabletop. Brigid sipped her tea, and Emma tried not to look over at her computer. Finally, Brigid having come to a decision gave her friend a crooked smile. Pointing at the laptop next to Emma, Brigid nudged it a little closer to Emma.

"Go on. You've kept Sam waiting long enough. Answer the poor guy! Life's short, don't waste any chances Em. Promise me? You know, go make something beautiful out of the broken pieces. Maybe, just maybe we are all a piece of our own porcelain table, you know?"

Returning Brigid's grin, Emma nodded her head, opening up her computer, she clicked away at the keys, then looking satisfied, she closed it. It was a confident, clear-minded, rational Emma that Brigid saw sitting before her, with hands clasped in front of her on top of the laptop.

"Brigid, you are the one I am worried about. You have the chance to live a great and full life, but sometimes you bury your head and forget about the outside world." She held up her hands when Brigid began to interrupt her.

"I think it's great you find peace and comfort in nature, talking to your trees, birds, and Wee Folk, as you call them, but sometimes I think that's not enough. Please promise me you won't close your heart off to—um, real people after I go. Find a cute doctor, settle down or don't, but experience life. That is how you can honor your mother, Brig, no matter what comes next. None of us know how long we have. I think that is really what your mom is trying to get you to see. What I'm about to say, might sound harsh, so forgive me. You know how you told me to go home?"

Brigid nodded her head.

"Brigid, don't think twice about going home! Stay here, for now. You're making the right choice not to leave and wait for the other shoe to drop. Take it from me, nothing good will ever come from living life that way. You and your family taught me that. So, I think what your mom would say is, there are no promises or guarantees in this life. I think she would tell you to follow your heart and listen to your intuition."

Emma patiently waited for the rebuttal she felt sure was to come.

Instead, Brigid took a slow drink from her cup, holding Emma's tentative gaze.

"That's *exactly* what Mom said."

21

Four weeks had come and gone since Ethan and Ashling said goodbye to Brigid, Maddie, Connor, and Emma.

"Did your mom tell you she just booked your ticket home for Christmas?" Ethan asked Brigid before they departed.

"Ya, a few minutes ago. It helps. I know, we agreed to take it a day at a time, and try to live as normal a life as we can," Brigid added having resigned herself to the fact that was all they could do moving forward. It was none the less a tearful goodbye at the airport watching Ethan, and Ashling leave, and Brigid knew it would be just as hard when Emma left.

"Since tomorrow's my last day Brig, what do you say we head over to the campus and take a look around? I think it'll help ease your nerves, you know?" Emma suggested.

"Ya, I was going to ask you if you wanted to go by there with me. Thanks, Em."

Once on campus, both girls were taken with the architectural charm of the modern looking university. Instantly Brigid was relieved Emma had suggested they tour the school together. While the girls meandered up and down corridors, they overheard several students discussing a guest lecturer scheduled for the first day of the semester. After walking past yet another group who openly spoke of the reverence they had for the *prodigy* doctor, Brigid's interest was piqued.

"I wonder what's so great about this physician. I've never heard of him… or her, have you Brig?"

"I don't think so, but sounds like this person is a big deal around here," Brigid replied casually.

As the day progressed, the girls continued hearing whispers and comments, praising the physician with a long list of accomplishments.

"Look Brig, the student lounge. Let's check it out. Maybe we can find out more about this doctor," Emma said, pulling Brigid along with her.

The airy room was spacious with a casual feel and brightly colored armchairs placed strategically for group conversations. Long work tables with charging stations ran the length of one side, and on the opposite side, there were several round tables and chairs. Walking over to a bulletin board near the entrance, Emma and Brigid perused the already growing list of students in need of last-minute roommates, groups that were organizing, and upcoming events throughout the school year.

Brigid overheard yet another group making plans to come early for the lecture of the controversial physician.

"Did you hear just last year he was responsible for curing that four-year-old boy of lymphoma using a new type of immunotherapy?" a tall girl with a thick accent asked the young man beside her.

"What is more curious is the talk that he used some black market experimental drug therapy on the kid," her companion replied in a low voice.

Brigid and Emma listened while pretending to read the bulletin board until Emma, who was always on the lookout for a good story to write, broke in. "Excuse me. My friend here and I have been hearing a lot about this lecture. Is it open to anyone?"

"It is, but it's geared towards med students. If you're going, you best get there early to get a seat. Most likely be standing room only."

For some reason, Brigid felt compelled to hear the lecture but said nothing more.

"It's getting late Em, and I'm starving. Wanna go to the pub and get some dinner?"

"Let's go, my stomachs growling." Emma laughed.

A short time later the girls entered Mahoney's and were greeted warmly by the regulars who Brigid and Emma now knew by name. After taking a seat at their favorite table, the girls quickly ordered food.

Soon the waiter returned and placed a bowl before each girl. Emma immediately began to dunk warm bread into the hearty stew.

Once again, Brigid caught sight of the man called Michael.

Her heart sank, although she wasn't sure why when she noticed him at the corner of the bar with a petite porcelain-skinned woman, only a few years older than herself, Brigid assumed. The woman was exotically striking with curly ebony hair that glistened in the dim lighting, making it appear midnight blue. Sighing, Brigid looked away.

"You okay, Brig?"

"Um, ya, the day's just catching up with me I guess," Brigid lied.

"I know what will take care of that. Carbs! I think I'll go over and ask for some more bread. You want any?"

Brigid nodded her head.

"Sure, thanks."

Emma walked toward the bar, leaving Brigid time to discreetly observe Michael and the porcelain doll.

The conversation appeared very intense between the two, whose eyes remained locked on each other. The woman didn't look happy as an older man, a friend of Brigid's grandparents approached the pair. The trim, well-dressed man was one of the wealthiest men in Ireland according to Maddie, but his name Brigid could not recall. The porcelain doll put a hand over Michael's as if to calm him. A brief exchange took place, then after shaking hands and a good-natured laugh, Michael and the porcelain doll turned to leave.

Pausing, Michael fished through his wallet. Then after paying the tab, he nodded his thanks. It was then that Michael began scanning the room as if looking for someone. His hawk-like sweep of the bar stopped on Brigid, giving her the briefest of acknowledgment. Brigid could only stare with eyes locked on the man across the room. Whatever Brigid thought she read in his eyes disappeared as quickly as it came. Then, with a lopsided grin, he did what she knew he would do —he winked.

Without as much as a backward glance, Michael followed his companion out the door.

"Best to lock that far-far away for now," Brigid said to herself.

Perhaps tomorrow when she was alone, she'd analyze this strange encounter. "Maybe the guy has a twitch or something," she wondered out loud. Her fluttering stomach told her otherwise.

Finally, the day had come to an end, and both girls sat cross-legged on one of the twin beds in the Mahoney home talking about the year ahead. Brigid made a point of sharing her excitement for Sam and Emma's relationship.

"You'll be engaged by Christmas, New Years at the latest!"

"I can only hope," Emma said in a dreamy voice, so unlike her usual practical tone.

Tired as they were, the girls chatted, giggled and shed a few tears way into the early morning. When the rooster sounded his alarm bright and early the next morning, two exhausted girls staggered into the kitchen in search of caffeine.

Soon, Emma was packed and off to the airport. Brigid didn't think her heart could handle another goodbye, but somehow she and Emma both got through it. It was a melancholy drive home, and Brigid was grateful neither of her grandparents tried to engage her in conversation as they returned to a quiet house.

"Tomorrow's a big day, and I think we're all done in for the day," Connor stated with a yawn.

"I agree. Time for bed my love," Maddie said, taking Connor by the hand.

"Grandma, Grandpa, I don't know what I'd do without you both. I hope you know how much I appreciate everything."

Conner patted Brigid's shoulder. "We're equally grateful for our time with you little one." Coming as near to emotion as he'd let himself, the big old bear of a man laughed self-consciously. "Making a fool outta myself," he mumbled, scooping Brigid into a brief hug.

"Come on you old softy," Maddie said, placing her hand on Conner's.

"Goodnight Brigid dear," Maddie yawned.

"Night, love you both," Brigid said softly.

Once in her room, Brigid quickly showered, threw on her softest flannel nightshirt, then tumbled into bed. As she drifted off to sleep, she dreamt of the handsome man, who like in a fairytale woke her with a kiss. Only, it wasn't a kiss that woke her, but the ringtone from her alarm she set on her phone ushering in the new day.

Excited to start her school year, Brigid pushed the dream to the back of her mind and practically bounced out of bed. She dressed in a long green V-neck tunic, with dark leggings and her favorite pair of black boots. Quickly brushing her hair back into a neat ponytail, Brigid wrapped a cream-colored cashmere scarf loosely around her neck. Satisfied with the results, she headed to the front door, ready to attend her first lecture at the university.

"Plenty of time to grab a quick bite," Brigid said to the mirror, just as her phone began to ring.

"Mom, what time is it—like one in the morning there? Are you okay?" Brigid asked breathlessly, the words rushing together as Ashling gave a sweet laugh on the other end.

"It's your first day of school darlin'. You don't think I was about to let this day start without a good morning and hearing your voice did ya?"

"Oh Mom," was all Brigid could manage before her dad chimed in, "Good luck, Sprite, you'll do great. We love you!"

"Great. Now I'm going to start crying you two," Brigid said into her phone with a short laugh.

"Well we can't be having any of that, so we are going to say goodbye for now, but we want details later," Ashling said.

Hearing her mom's soothing voice over the phone made Brigid feel better. Goodbyes were said, and with a renewed confidence, Brigid once again headed for the door, tucking her phone into her overloaded purse with its frayed shoulder strap.

"Stupid zipper always sticks. I should have bought a new one like Emma said," Brigid said absently.

Getting the zipper back on track, Brigid closed her purse, thinking about how she was getting her life back on track too.

Having forgotten about breakfast after her parents touching phone call, Brigid decided to stop at the student lounge to grab a cup of coffee. Taking a sip of the flavorless liquid, she made a sour face.

"Ugh," she said cringing at the rather cold paper cup while heading down a long hall. As Brigid turned the corner, the long strap of her purse snapped, falling to the ground, leaving Brigid nothing to do but watch as the contents spilled out about her. Cursing the zipper, Brigid bent to pick up the scattered items. A man and woman turned the corner at the same inconvenient time. The man, not seeing Brigid leaning forward towards the floor in a rather unladylike way, walked directly into her, pushing her to the ground.

Brigid's coffee popped from her hand, splashing all over her new outfit. Mortified, and staring at the spilled contents sprawled all about the ground, Brigid quickly tried to scoop up the few items drenched in sticky coffee. The woman dared to laugh but stopped as the man next to her, rebuked her sternly.

"You okay, Lass?" He leaned down, asking with genuine concern.

Brigid, too embarrassed to look up, kept her head low, trying to compose herself. Mumbling her thanks and apologies at the same time, she scrambled to explain.

"My purse broke…"

Brigid tried hard to ignore the man and his undeniable masculine scent. It was not of a heavy cologne, masking unpleasantness, it was clean like cedar-wood, fresh like mountain air, and for some reason, she wanted to tell the man that he smelled like trees. To Brigid, it was high praise. She kept her compliment to herself, seeing the woman standing off to the side, tapping her small black pump, which from Brigid's view was quite expensive.

"Here, let me help you up, Lass," the man with the soothing voice, whose gaze she was not yet ready to meet said.

"We're late, and the girl is obviously fine," said the toe-tapping female with designer shoes.

"Yes, of course, I'm perfectly fine. Don't let me keep you," Brigid replied in a clipped tone, finding it more comfortable to address the woman than the man.

Brigid, typically very confident, felt anything but that as she once again began to pick up the rest of her belongings.

"Shame about your outfit, the scarf at least might be worth salvaging," the man's companion smirked, as she brushed her hand over her perfectly manicured nails.

"Fi," he admonished the churlish woman who instantly quieted down.

Brigid looked at her now ruined clothes covered in brown liquid stains, then at her watch. "Great, now I'm gonna be late," she lamented more to herself as she tried to drape her scarf to cover the coffee stains, finally retrieving the last of her scattered belongings.

"Sorry again, but I gotta run, I'm late for a lecture. It's gonna be packed, and the topic is personal for me," Brigid stammered, rattling on, knowing how inept she sounded.

She raised her head to look at the man for the first time since the exchange.

A look of recognition crossed her face as he presented her with a lopsided grin. At least this time he didn't wink.

Before she had the chance to say another word, the door to her right opened. Out breezed a smartly dressed woman with thick horn-rimmed glasses wearing a plaid skirt and crisp white blouse, looking entirely beside herself.

She called out to the couple, "There you are. You had me worried. Come on, dear, let's go."

The older woman didn't wait for a response, while the glacier porcelain doll, Brigid now fully recognized, all but pushed Michael through the door.

"You know how I despise being tardy for these things Michael."

The door closed quickly, and Brigid was left staring at a small but legible sign. STAFF ONLY.

With her bruised ego and disheveled appearance, Brigid had no time to make sense of what business the friend of her grandparents had at the university, but she made a mental note to ask her grandmother more about this—Michael when she got home. Rushing around the corner, Brigid opened the door to the lecture hall as quietly as she could, desperately hoping the speaker wasn't already halfway through his talk.

To her surprise, the hall was silent, disturbed only by the ringing of a student's phone. Silencing his phone, the young man stood to leave, allowing Brigid the only vacant seat, even though it meant she would have to take the walk of shame with coffee stains, a broken purse and hair now falling from its tie, for all to see.

She did it anyway, feeling lucky she was able to get to the empty chair, right in front of the podium with little notice.

Taking advantage of the reprieve, Brigid did her best to compose herself. Pulling a mirror from her purse, she dabbed on a small amount of light pink lip gloss, used a tissue to wipe the sticky splashes of coffee from her cheek, then quickly pulled on the tie that released her wild mane of hair. She ran her fingers through its length in the hope of covering the dark coffee stain on her shoulder.

"Students at this time we ask you to turn off your cell phones and laptops," a woman's voice called out over the microphone.

Instantly the lights changed, focusing on the podium, and the applause revved up. Brigid quickly deposited her mirror back into her purse, looking up with eager and smiling eyes, right into those of the one and only Doctor Michael MacShane, whose focus was solely on her.

She'd be damned if he didn't wink!

22

At the ripe age of twenty-five, Doctor Michael MacShane was familiar with the term *prodigy*. God, how he hated that label when the inevitable question of, "How does it feel?" would be asked.

"I'm driven, I guess," he would say lackadaisically, when confronted with the tired old subject, feeling no need to explain it was sheer hard work that got him where he was today. That, and years of burying any and every emotion he felt, leaving in place only absolute determination to achieve his goals.

Few people, besides Ewan and Fiona, his friends and business partners, knew Michael to be a kind, compassionate, and highly misunderstood individual—and that was fine with him. He kept most people at arm's length. It was a coping mechanism Michael learned soon after his parent's death when he was a young boy.

The loss of his parents, Gavin and Doctor Faith MacShane was senseless, starting with the moment of Gavin's tragic choice—one that hundreds of people regularly make after drinking too much. He willingly put the key into the ignition of his brand new BMW.

"Gavin, maybe I should drive," Faith suggested.

"So now I'm not even qualified to drive? Both of our names were published in that journal you know. But there wasn't even one single mention of me when they announced your name. Not one!"

"Gavin, I knew nothing about this. I only found out when they called my name."

False confidence and a bruised ego over his wife's recognition fueled Gavin as he sped off down the winding road. It was the last— sweet, burning swallow of scotch from the expensive crystal glass that had impaired his judgment. He missed the sharp curve, sending their vehicle cascading down the unforgiving mountain as they were both mercifully thrown from the car that continued its descent, crashing into the water below. Sometime later, as Gavin lay bandaged and bruised in his hospital bed, he learned Faith was in a coma.

"We don't expect your wife to recover," a stone-faced physician told Gavin.

Young Michael, their only child, spent every moment after the crash by his mother's side, talking to her as he usually would, reading her the daily newspaper knowing she would want to keep up on current events. Michael never once went to see his father, even after Helen and Alistair MacShane, Michael's grandparents, flew in to be by their son and daughter-in-law's side.

"I'm sorry, Mom needs me so she can wake up. She'll hear my voice, just like I hear her when she has to wake me up in the mornings for school. Besides, Dad shouldn't have been drinking and driving," Michael told his grandfather in his most grown-up voice.

"We understand. Take all the time you need, son," Alistair told his grandson.

The staff at the hospital came to expect to see Michael curled up in a ball in the chair next to his mother come nighttime. One of the nurses would gently place a blanket over the boy as to not wake him and assure Gavin's parents, who alternated between the two hospital rooms that Michael was safe.

Six weeks after the accident, Faith opened her eyes. She grasped Michael's hand in her own, and after giving him a weak smile—she took her last breath. Two days after Faith's funeral, Gavin took his own life—the grief, shame, and guilt being too much to bear. He left his son all but alone in the world.

"Michael, we want you to come home and live with us, dear. I know we can never replace your parents, but we love you and will continue to love you with all our hearts," Helen told Michael as his shoulders shook and he sobbed openly.

"But what if I hate my dad forever? Maybe you won't love me so much," Michael said, looking his grandfather in the eyes.

"Michael, we are all grieving. We will grieve together—as a family. There is nothing you can do to change our love for you. Come home with us," Alistair said hugging young Michael.

The first year after his parent's death, Michael fell into a relatively isolated life. It was common for him to grab his backpack filled with snacks his grandmother packed and his rustic leather bound journal his mother had given him, and walk the mile to his favorite place in all of Scotland—a spot he found quite by accident one day when he stopped to pick up a shiny coin.

A small opening in the brush caught his attention. It was just large enough for a curious boy to climb through. His reward was an open area surrounded by shrubs reminding Michael of a fortress that protected a massive ancient yew tree. The neglected, overgrown garden became Michael's refuge, a hideout from the cruel and unjust world.

The stocky reddish-brown tree trunk with shades of dark purple became his base. His tower became the gnarled swooping branches, protruding out like tentacles and holding off a vicious enemy. Only Michael knew the tree was more than it appeared. The yew—*his yew*, was unique. Here, Michael felt safe, untouchable, as if he entered another world where he was immune to the pain and grief that had become his constant companions.

Sitting on the tree's thick branches, Michael would feel his mother's presence. With childlike confidence, he would await the floral scent that preceded the knowledge that Faith was by his side. One day after one such encounter, Michael began to intuitively write out precise calculations and formulas in his journal that he somehow understood outlined the cure for various strains of cancer. The journal was the last gift Faith gave Michael before her death and in his mind made the journal magical. When he ran his fingers over the leather indentations that formed the tree on the book's cover, he remembered the day she gave it to him.

"Mikey dear, I chose this one with the yew tree on the front for you because I know you love them as much as I do."

Michael still kept the journal by his bedside.

Along with the written messages, Michael began hearing his mother, not physically talking to him, but dropping or downloading thoughts, her thoughts, into his consciousness. He never told a living soul how she would guide and instruct him, like in a daydream. He would clearly hear her by his side, saying, "Mikey dear, you need to consider this." Or things like, "That's right my smart boy, you have to factor that into the equation."

Michael was a clever student, and intuitively realized he was somehow channeling his mother and her work. Once he confided to Ewan that it was his mother who saved him from following his parents to their final resting place and that he once believed it was his only hope of finding peace.

"Bloody tragic," Ewan replied as the pair downed another drink.

Before the channeling of his mother began, Michael experienced feelings of grief too overwhelming for such a small boy to make sense of. The idea of free falling off a cliff seemed logical. After all, if his father could do it—so could he, Michael reasoned as one day his little feet slowly inched towards the edge of a jagged cliff. Before Michael could take the fatal step, a hand pulled him back, knocking him to the solid ground.

"No Michael James MacShane, this is not the answer!"

"Mother!" he called out.

However, Faith was not there. She would never be physically there again.

Michael wept openly.

"I miss you," his raspy voice cried out in pain.

"I'm here," his mother gently whispered in his ear.

"You are never alone, and what you were about to do is not the answer. Mikey, I need you to stay here and live," Faith told her son.

Exhausted from holding in the pain and sadness of the past year, Michael sat cradling his knees with his tightly wrapped arms, rocking back and forth. It was this sight Alistair came upon so near the cliff's edge that looked out towards Ireland.

Alistair bent down to help his grandson stand. After wiping his tears and hugging him fiercely, they began walking towards Helen, who stood nearby, wringing her hands as she waited for the pair to approach. A silent understanding of shared grief was their unspoken companion as they drove home. The day on the cliff was a turning point in Michael's life. He became a shell of the once lively young boy he had been—caring only for the company of his grandparents.

Kids at school began bullying him the more he withdrew. Michael responded by using his powerful fists, much to his grandparent's dismay. The fighting became more serious, and the students mistook his aloofness as cocky and arrogant. Eventually, Michael no longer cared. He was all too aware that letting people close to him proved costly.

"Alistair, we need to make a change for Michael. Traditional education is not challenging him academically, and the fighting is getting worse. I just got a call from the school's headmaster. If he gets into one more fight, they'll expel him," Helen told her husband.

"Then a change we'll make. We'll hire tutors or whatever it takes dear. I've been thinking more and more about an entirely different change. Perhaps it's time for a new beginning. I know how you miss your home in Ireland and your friend, Maddie. I think a break from Scotland will give Michael and us the fresh start we're all in need of," Alistair stated.

"I wouldn't mind being near Maddie again. She and Connor have been after us to move closer to them for a long time."

Eventually, Helen, Alistair, and Michael returned to Ireland where Helen grew up and purchased a quaint bookstore next to the Mahoney's pub.

The years that followed were happy ones for the MacShane's, supported by the Mahoney's and their community. Michael began to thrive once again, exceeding every expectation set before him. He graduated high school, then college, years ahead of his classmates, making Michael one of the youngest physicians in Ireland or Scotland, garnering grudging respect from his colleagues.

Eventually, Michael returned to Scotland where he met back up with his childhood friend, Ewan Brodie, a gregarious entrepreneur and financier. Over drinks one night, Michael and Ewan quickly discovered a shared drive to rid the world of cancer.

"Mate, with my money and resources and your brains and degrees, we could bloodily-well find a way to beat this thing," Ewan quickly assessed.

"I have discovered something pretty remarkable, Ewan, but I admit what I'm lacking is someone with deep pockets and a true desire to see that a holistic approach is taken in solving such a devastating reality for far too many people."

"Do you remember Fiona?" Ewan asked offhandedly.

"Of course, she was your foster sister who tagged along with us everywhere we went. I remember that summer she came to stay with you and your family. I always thought it was endearing how she pushed us around and told us what to do—and we'd do it!" Michael chuckled.

"What you call endearing, I called a bloody nuisance," Ewan grumbled.

"I remember right before I left Scotland you and Fi were being pitted between your parents."

"Ya, after my parents split, Mum took Fi and Dad claimed me. Quite the brutal tug-war with kids I might add. Anyway, Fi is still around."

"Poor kid. She had it tough before she came to you guys. It must have been brutal for you and her to be caught in the crosshairs of a divorce. Is she well?"

"Still a pain in me arse! But yes, even though there were years we went without speaking because of the split. I brought her up because I think we could utilize her talents if you're serious about us joining forces," Ewan tossed out, wondering if Michael was as invested in his plan as he was.

"Fi's a chemist, isn't she? I ran into a colleague of hers last year who sang her praises," Michael commented.

"I'm afraid if we bring her into the loop she'll ramrod us the way she did when we were kids."

"Ewan, she was spunky and quick on her feet, and if she's as efficient as she used to be, she might just be a pivotal piece to this jigsaw puzzle we're forming."

"Or, she'll turn out being an irritating headache and pain in me arse once again!"

Michael smiled at the memory.

"Darling, focus," Fiona hissed as the door to the auditorium closed behind her and Michael.

Hearing Fiona's shrill order forced the memory of the past from his head. They both watched as the silver-haired woman walked to the podium.

"Focus? I only learned you railroaded me into this lecture three days ago. And, Fi, you could have been kinder to the poor lass in the hallway," Michael chided.

"Michael, darling, all you should be thinking about right now is your speech to these aspiring physicians and thanking your lucky stars, the only thing our new investor required was ninety minutes of your time here today."

"Ninety minutes I can't get back, and that was set up without my knowledge, I might add. You tricked me into going to the pub the other night. If I didn't know any better I'd swear you have no conscience," Michael teased.

"Now you're starting to sound like that buffoon," Fiona pouted.

"You need to come up with a better name for Ewan. Buffoon is getting old," Michael told Fiona, who was shuffling papers in her hand.

"Here, darling. Make sure you mention this case study and the data. We've spent years proving the immunotherapy is safe," Fiona said as if talking to a child. Michael appeared unfazed to Fiona's tone.

"Fi, we know through our controlled study that patients taking the protocol experienced a complete reversal of certain types of cancer with zero side effects, but I just don't know if these kids will buy..."

Fiona quickly cut him off, not liking the turn the conversation was taking.

"That's why we chose this university. I've done the research. The philosophy of this school is in complete alignment with ours."

"I'm sure it helped to know our new benefactor all but owns this school, and to get his money, you sold me off like cattle," Michael added dryly.

"Since he's putting in millions, I think a little inconvenience on your part, is a small price to pay. Besides, these young adults are the best of the best. Almost every student here would *pay* to intern for you. You must keep that in mind."

"Hmm," Michael murmured, looking over the notes Fiona handed him.

"Can you imagine the recognition they'll receive apprenticing with the man who cures cancer? Trust me. These sharp minds are already three steps ahead of you there. Now you simply have to go out there and sell our vision, get the conversation going and be thankful all that was required of us was a bit of the great Doctor Michael MacShane's time."

"Fi, I could save sixty minutes by going out there and putting the results up on the screen that proves we have the cure that will eradicate most types of cancer and without any negative side effects," Michael stated hopefully.

"Funny. Come now, darling, quit behaving like a petulant child."

"Fi, I admit, I was bloody pissed you went behind our backs and contacted the Mahoney's friend, but I see why you did it. I know you are just as invested as Ewan and me."

"Pissed? Michael, darling, you should be thanking me. Now you not only have the four years of funding you need, but now you have the money to hire quality professionals to assist you."

"Fi, you knew it was Ewan's job to handle the financials."

"When isn't he bothered by something I say or do?" Fiona quipped.

Michael knew by her furrowed brow he'd hurt Fiona's feelings. "I'll admit, it takes someone special to get a meeting with one of Ireland's most well-known philanthropists," he whispered as his introduction went on and on by the overly animated woman at the podium.

"Michael darling, how can anyone resist me? I just had to find the right person with endless resources looking for offshore investments," Fiona said confidently.

Michael couldn't deny whatever Fiona said had worked. Earlier in the week, all it had taken was a simple introduction, and a gentleman's handshake for the elder Irishman and younger Scot to come to an understanding. Wisely, Michael put his pride aside for the sake of the project, but only had moments to process their great fortune the night at the pub before Fiona dropped the news of his required presence at the university to receive the generous financial backing.

"Michael, you're brooding over how we got here, I can tell by the look on your face. There will be time enough later to rake me over the coals."

Fiona was mistaken. Glancing out into the audience, Michael caught sight of a woman's hair falling loose from its constraint, and his heart began to race. He would know the Mahoney's granddaughter anywhere. She didn't look as young as he remembered at the pub but admonished himself none the less.

"She just called your name." Fiona gave Michael a slight push in the direction of the stage as the silver-haired woman smiled broadly in his direction.

Michael succeeded in intriguing the audience with his background in cancer research and data. Even Fiona was impressed with his amusing anecdotes and the way he related to the adults sitting before him. She was inspired just listening to Michael share his thoughts, experiences, and pitfalls along his journey.

"You are the generation to make the next big holistic discoveries and push the new ideas out into the world where big pharmaceutical and insurance companies will have to pay attention. There are those who will laugh and try to put you in your so-called place, but do not fall prey to these tactics. I was teased mercilessly during my residency, being so young. It just made me bloody mad and I worked harder. The worst was when my elder colleagues wouldn't take me seriously because of my age. I had to fight twice as hard for credibility. I quickly grew a thick skin, because I understood what possibilities lay before me, and what stakes I was fighting for," Michael told the students, knowing he had their full attention as he surveyed the crowd.

Michael concluded his speech with a joke that made the audience laugh, and with a lopsided grin, he scanned the crowd, stopping on Brigid, who was staring up at him with her shaded eyes. The face staring back at him was a sad one. Michael had a sudden need to know what caused her suffering. He coughed to cover his urge to blurt out he understood sadness all too well—or worse, ask what he could do to heal her pain? Only a moment passed as they stared at each other.

He winked so quickly, Brigid wondered if she imagined or wished it to happen.

As the audience clapped and whistled their approval, Michael knew one thing for sure—he had to get off the stage and fast. The Mahoney's eighteen-year-old granddaughter was too young, and off limits. He couldn't risk another chance encounter with her. There was something about the tilt of her head, the way she looked at him that felt hauntingly familiar. A feeling of panic washed over him. It was the kind of fear that woke him from his dreams in a cold sweat.

23

Glancing up, Brigid saw Michael being escorted out of the lecture hall by the silver-haired woman and the porcelain doll who had a possessive grip on his right arm. Sitting back down, she watched the three shadows fade around the corner. The heavy auditorium door latched closed with a loud thud, making Brigid feel as if something valuable had quietly slipped away.

"I wonder just how old he is? Can't be too old," Brigid speculated absently. Glancing at the large clock on the wall, Brigid realized she would soon be late for her first class. "I have to stick to the plan," she repeated her mantra out loud.

Once again, Brigid's mind began to wander as she slipped in and out of the mass of students making their way through the noisy halls.

What was it he said? *"Life is precious, and time valuable?"* Today confirmed what Brigid had been thinking all month. Time was indeed fragile, and somehow, she viewed time as a brutal nemesis.

Brigid wanted more time with her mom, and needed time to learn all she could, so she could go back to Oregon and bring with her the knowledge that would breathe new life into the cancer treatment program utilizing her family's yews. It was a lofty goal, but her parents taught her to reach for the stars. Besides, the necessary technology and the studies would be ready, most likely, in the next few years, according to Doctor MacShane.

Brigid knew his knowledge was cutting edge and today proved what she and her parents already understood about the power and potential of the unique trees growing on their property. Brigid needed time to be qualified so she could take over the program at the university in Oregon. Once she became a doctor, she intended to dedicate her life and career to furthering her family's dream. Brigid decided long ago that no one could ever match her motivation—until today when she listened to Doctor Michael MacShane speak.

"Stay focused!" Brigid quietly instructed her wandering mind, which instantly disobeyed her by reminding her of the man whose heart-stopping wink and lopsided grin had the power to threaten her resolve. No man was going to get in the way of her dreams. Sure, Emma would say she was running or fooling herself, Malachi would ask her what her heart was telling her, but Brigid knew now was the time to—how did Doctor MacShane say it in his lecture? *Follow her passion and purpose.*

"Geez, I sound more like the old Emma every day," she mumbled then blushed at the odd look yet another fellow student gave her. Feeling a renewed sense of conviction take shape as she neared the classroom, Brigid rearranged the cashmere scarf to camouflage the sweater speckled with coffee. She was ready to dive into this new chapter in her life.

Brigid was looking forward to her full schedule, and since she was currently years ahead of most entry-level students, she could anticipate entering med school almost two years, maybe three ahead of the typical progression.

"Stay focused Brig," she reminded herself again as she stepped into the classroom. Two writing assignments with a short deadline later, Brigid was humming her way back to her grandparents home.

Once inside, she was greeted with delightful aromatics of cinnamon, nutmeg, and tempting sweetness, reminding Brigid of home as her eyes filled with tears. She instantly became overwhelmed with a deep feeling of longing for home. She gave herself a moment to collect her emotions as she set her backpack down by the front door before cheerfully calling out to her grandmother. "Hi Grandma, I'm home!"

"In here, Brigid dear," Maddie's responded, beckoning her to the kitchen.

Soon Brigid was wrapping her arms around the next best thing to her own mother, and feeling more than a twinge of guilt for the thought. As if reading her mind, Maddie kissed Brigid's temple.

"Your mom emailed me a few days ago, asking me if I would do her a favor. Well, of course, I said yes."

Maddie walked to the small refrigerator, pulling out a pitcher of milk, as Brigid often watched her mother do over the years. Maddie handed the container to her granddaughter, motioning for her to grab glasses from the open-faced cupboard.

Maddie continued. "Ashling said that when you were growing up, you always wanted oatmeal on your first day of school. She told me you'd wake early and tiptoe into the kitchen and watch her make and dish up the homemade oats, sprinkling just the right amount of cinnamon on top."

Brigid added softly, "I got to add the raisins. Mom has a magic wooden spoon. Did you know that Grandma? It always makes everything taste so much better," Brigid's smile never reached her eyes.

Maddie walked over to the O'Keefe stove, so much like the one back home in Oregon. Upon opening the oven door, the kitchen filled with love. It was a corny thought, but Brigid had no other words to describe it.

It wasn't just the comfort and warmth the sweet aroma invoked —because it did. It had to do with the memories. It was then that Brigid knew what she was about to hear, and her heart felt ready to burst.

"So, your mom asked me to make you something with oatmeal since she couldn't today. Ashling knew that having this come from me would be the next best thing."

Maddie waited a full minute before turning around with the hot baking sheet filled with oatmeal and cinnamon cookies. She set them down on the butcher block in front of Brigid, who didn't trust herself to speak. Instead, she rounded the short distance between them, gently placing a feathery kiss on the side of Maddie's cheek. The older woman hugged the younger one, drawing from it, much comfort as well.

At that moment, Brigid understood that her grandmother was also missing Ashling. A silent understanding seemed to emerge between the two women. Brigid took the two glasses, filling them halfway with milk as Maddie placed a small plate in front of each of them. Without bothering to sit, they each took a cookie. Maddie seemed pleased with the look of sheer indulgence on her granddaughter's face as she plunged the first half of her cookie into the milk, taking one satisfying bite after another. For whatever reason, both women began to laugh uncontrollably.

That is how Connor found his wife and granddaughter as he wandered into the cozy kitchen with the crackling fire burning in the nearby stove.

"Well, what do we have here? Dessert before supper, and no one called me?" Connor gently squeezed his granddaughter's shoulder.

"What are we celebrating? The first day of school, perhaps?"

"Oh Grandpa, wait until you hear about it!" Brigid exclaimed.

"Well, why don't we all have one more cookie and head down to the pub for supper. I came home to gather you two up, but looks like someone beat me to the punch," He said light-heartedly.

"I worked up quite the appetite today, just let me go change."

Finally noticing their granddaughter's disheveled appearance, Maddie and Connor both gave Brigid a shocked once over.

Before they could ask Brigid said, "Oh, it's a story all right, but I want to save it for over dinner. It's a good one."

Brigid gulped the last of the milk, giving a backhanded swipe at the crumb on her lips. Thanking her grandmother once again, Brigid headed swiftly down the hall to her room.

A short half hour later, the Mahoney's sat with Brigid, caught up between laughter and sympathy hearing her tale. Neither could decide on the best course, so they settled mostly for nodding attentively. Brigid was able to find the humor, once she understood she had not offended her grandparents.

When the mention of the porcelain doll came up, Brigid, chose her words cautiously. Too carefully, her grandmother thought. With a sideways glance at Connor, Maddie knew her husband picked up on it as well. Brigid, trying her best to keep her voice neutral, told her story between bites of lamb, carrots, and potatoes, as her grandfather enjoyed his scotch, nodding his head in a non-committal fashion.

"I have to admit, I know it's small of me—but geez, she got under my skin," Brigid confided.

"Who, Fiona? Well, her bark is usually worse than her bite, but I admit, it does sound as if she treated you rather unkind," Maddie supplied.

"Well, he must see it, right? Oh, I doubt I'll ever understand men. Which is why I am so happy to have my education to focus on."

Connor waved a server over who promptly refilled their glasses.

"Brigid dear, it doesn't have to be all or nothing you know? You can have a career and your great love too," Maddie assured Brigid.

"Maybe you should set your cap on our young Michael, he's not that much older than you," Connor teased, wagging his finger at his granddaughter.

"Connor Mahoney, you're embarrassing the girl!" Maddie's eyes now took on a warning her husband knew too well.

"Women," Connor grumbled, scooting his chair back noisily.

Standing, and rubbing the small of his back gingerly, Connor gave a grandfatherly peck on the top of Brigid's head. "Well, he could do worse, and has, was all I was saying. Gonna go check and see how things are going in the kitchen," Connor mumbled, walking away as Maddie and Brigid finished the last of their dinner.

Later that night, Brigid sat cross-legged on her bed with her laptop resting comfortably in front of her. She was eager to hear all about Emma's first week and the power struggles she was trying to avoid with her well-meaning parents.

Emma wrote to Brigid about her adventures with Sam and the first week of school, reading like a short novel with twists and turns, highs and lows. She was filled with animated excitement, which seemed unfamiliar and new to Brigid.

Wanna hear something crazy?

What's up Em? Spill it.

Brigid waited impatiently for Emma's response.

I think Sam might propose at Christmas like you said!

The two girls fingers flew rapidly over the keys, deep in conversation as they lost track of time. Eventually, they typed their goodbyes, with promises to Skype over the weekend. Brigid fell into a deep sleep the minute her head hit the pillow.

She dreamed of curing cancer, accepting awards and smiling over at Michael MacShane, who stood off to the side holding a beautiful baby girl. Brigid woke the next morning, wishing she believed in fairy tales.

24

Three Years Later

Brigid parked her grandparents' car and turned off the engine. Looking up, she saw her grandmother waving to her from the kitchen window. God how Brigid missed her mom at that moment. She waved in return as she carefully removed a garment bag from the back seat and began walking up the cobbled path she had come to love so much over the years.

"Hey, there," she called out.

Connor raised his head from his task of sweeping the porch in a meticulous back and forth pattern. "Looks like the weather should hold for today."

"Sure looks like it. You want some help with that Grandpa?"

"No, no, this gives me something to do, and keeps me outta your grandmother's way."

Brigid chuckled at her grandfathers conspiring tone.

Connor began to whistle as he resumed the swish-swish pattern of his broom.

Hearing her grandmother on the phone, talking in a hushed voice prompted Brigid to change directions once inside, giving her grandmother privacy.

So much had happened in Brigid's life over the past few years. The memories began playing out as she walked down the hallway to her room. There were visits home to Oregon, as well as the trips her parents made over the holidays to Ireland, where they created many beautiful memories. All and all, Brigid's college years were more than she hoped for. Ashling rebounded in Brigid's second year at the university, prompting her to continue her accelerated courses in Ireland while

Ashling and Ethan decided it was time to do what they always dreamed about—travel.

"Your dad and I are finally going to do it, darlin'! I'm healthier now, and you need to concentrate on your last year of school. Tomas can easily take over for a while. Besides, your dad needs the break. I've put him through a lot."

"Don't say that, Mom. We're all so grateful that you're better now," Brigid remembered telling her mother a year earlier.

Unzipping the garment bag lying on her bed felt reminiscent of Brigid's high school graduation. Studying her reflection in front of an antique mirror, Brigid now stood in her cap and gown. There were a few notable differences from her previous graduation, besides the fact that Brigid had matured into a confident woman beyond her years.

She no longer wore a princess dress like the one from her high school prom. The woman in the mirror displayed attire suitable for the recognition and degree she would soon receive. Brigid scarcely recognized herself in the dark forest green robe, and gold stole adjusted over her neck and shoulders. She felt grown up in the gown, accented with gold piping. Soon Brigid would be seated in a large auditorium, one of the hundreds recognized for having earned various degrees, but for now, she stood in front of the full-length mirror, dabbing her favorite shade of pink on her lips that quivered ever so slightly.

Brigid thought about her parents and Malachi. Dear Mal, who visited her regularly in her dreams. Turlough would occasionally come to bring her news of Malachi and home which would make Brigid all the more homesick. "I wish you were here, mom," Brigid said to her reflection in the mirror.

As if on cue, her grandmother quietly entered the bedroom Brigid had called her own during her time at the university. Maddie did not pretend to conceal the emotion which coursed through her heart and veins. Brigid couldn't help but wonder what this moment must feel like for her grandmother.

"How do I look, Grandma?"

"Beautiful. More and more like your mom everyday dear."

Brigid turned slowly, making the few short steps to stand in front of the woman she had grown so close to. Maddie met Brigid's questioning stare with tumultuous unexpressed feelings and emotions. Both women understood this was a day of celebration mingled with sadness. Brigid knew her grandparents did their best to put on brave faces for her sake, just as she did for them, but this moment felt too big and what was not said, felt too heavy. Brigid blurted out in a soft, strangled voice, "I wish my mom were here. She should be here, you know?"

Brigid looked away quickly, embarrassed by her outburst.

Maddie's face softened into a sad smile.

"Yes, dear, she should. We are sorely missing her, especially today, aren't we?"

"Grandma, I don't mean to sound ungrateful. You and Grandpa have done and given me so much. I can never thank you enough. I just miss her." There was a painfully quiet pause, interrupted by the occasional cow mooing balefully outside.

"I mean, I'm happy they got the chance to travel, and I know they'd be here if they could. I'm just disappointed, and a little angry to be honest. We lost so much time together, and now on today of all days, when she could be here, she isn't."

"While it isn't your parent's fault a tornado sweeping through the east coast canceled their flight, I do understand, and you get to feel how you feel. That doesn't make you wrong. I'm disappointed too."

"I'm being childish."

"Brigid," her grandmother ventured tentatively.

"Yes," Brigid answered, equally cautious.

"I think it's time you go home, my precious granddaughter. Go back to Oregon, and leave no regrets behind. The graduate program will still be here in the fall if you want to come back."

Brigid merely nodded her head.

Connor, stood at the door with a bouquet of wildflowers mixed with heather and lavender, staring at an invisible spot on the wall, listening to his wife and granddaughter. His feet would not move. His voice did not work, and his mind raced with one lone thought.

Slowly he turned away from the bedroom door and with lead feet slowly made his way to the kitchen where he pulled out an old milk bottle, which would serve as a rustic vase—filling the glass jar halfway with water he carefully placed the flowers in the tepid water. Then he set the arrangement next to several cards that had arrived for Brigid. With great exertion, Connor lowered his weary body into a nearby chair.

"How is it that I am going to lose her too?" he said forlornly, rubbing the back of his neck. "How did the time slip away so fast?"

Back in the bedroom once belonging to Ashling, Maddie now spoke of the day's schedule, knowing it was time to embrace her granddaughter's accomplishments. She gave a nod of approval on Brigid's hairstyle. Next, they carefully laid out the rest of Brigid's outfit. With nothing left to chance, Brigid finally permitted herself to breathe.

Hours later, Maddie and Connor sat like proud peacocks while Brigid sat straight, looking prim, and quite frankly—bored, as she listened to the names drone out monotonously in alphabetical order. Brigid just happened to glance toward the auditorium doors as two people entered quietly. A look of surprise and recognition lit Brigid's face.

Just below the red exit sign, Emma and Sam entered the room, holding hands and beaming up at Brigid. Emma carried a large bouquet and Sam waved. Brigid took in the pair who stood with silly grins and forced herself to stay seated, smiling and shaking her head in disbelief at her friends. At that moment, a wave of awareness washed over Brigid. She fixed her glance on the exit sign above as if in a comic strip bubble over Emma and Sams heads. Brigid knew she had come to the right decision. The writing was on the wall quite literally. Her friends had come to bring her home. She thought her grandmother mentioned Emma's name on the phone earlier. It all made sense now.

"Brigid Ann Rafferty..." the Vice Chancellor called out her name. Brigid walked over and proudly accepted her diploma, quickly flashing it towards Emma, who continued clapping.

It was Brigid's time to exit this phase of her life and go back to Oregon to face whatever may be waiting there for her, and she felt at peace.

25

One Year Later

Brigid pushed the screen to the front door open and tested the porch with her bare feet. After welcoming the coolness, she stretched leisurely, much like the cat on the windowsill staring at her from inside the house.

Sensing she was not alone, she looked about her surroundings. A gentle smile rested on the man who sat motionless while he stared off into the distance from the old porch swing that Brigid had sat upon many times in her life. She studied his profile a moment, taking in the lines and dark circles under his eyes, and the way his fingers gripped the arm of the swing. His knuckles were an odd shade of white. He was lost in his memories again. Understandable, considering the day.

"Good morning to you, father of mine!" She tried for a bright and cheery greeting this morning.

"Hey, Sprite," Ethan said, looking startled.

"Got room for me on that swing for a minute?" Brigid asked, as she closed the screen door behind her.

Without waiting for an answer, Brigid scooted next to her father and rested her head against his shoulder. They rocked back and forth in silence, watching the day unfold before them. His flannel shirt smelled of wood, livestock, and coffee. She would never tire of the comfort and safety this childhood memory evoked. Ethan always made her feel safe, even though the roles had somewhat reversed since Ashling passed.

Her father was still himself, but just not as much so any more. When he smiled now, it never reached his eyes. He moved at a slower pace—that of an older man, not one who should still be exuding the energy of a healthy person in his prime. Sometimes it scared Brigid, and other times she understood it all too well.

"I was gonna go visit Malachi then maybe put some flowers by mom's marker. Would you like to join me?"

"No, Sprite, you go," he said, patting her knee.

Brigid knew her father never went to the place they chose for Ashling down by the edge of the old yew grove. Brigid rarely went there. It was Emma who regularly visited Ashling's memorial.

"Your mom would approve," Emma had said at the time they placed the memorial plaque.

Ethan still had yet to grieve his wife, who passed quietly in her sleep while she lay next to him, and Brigid knew that if he could mourn —even a little, her dad could begin to heal.

"That's okay Dad, we both know Mom isn't there anyway. She's always with us. I guess I like the option though, especially today. Anyway, I haven't been over there since that dream I told you about where she gave me a red ribbon. I still can't remember what she said. It bugs me," Brigid admitted, shrugging her shoulders.

They sat in silence, interrupted only by the occasional cow or goat that called out in the distance.

Ethan asked, almost as an afterthought, "Your residency still going well? Almost over with right?"

He was present now, and Brigid was grateful.

"Exhausting, but good. I've found a broom closet that doubles as my hideout."

Ethan shifted, studying his only child for a moment.

"You look tired. Are they pushing you too hard?"

Ethan had become increasingly overprotective of Brigid, and she was quick to reassure him. "No, I'm okay, Dad. It's the standard rite of passage, and it's important I to learn how to cope under pressure. I wanna be out there," she said passionately.

This time Ethan gave a genuine smile, one that tugged at her heart. Brigid craved to see the old Ethan, the laughing dad in his worn ball cap who would banter and make her giggle.

"Well, you had to try and break all the records out there didn't you, Sprite?" He said, referring to Brigid becoming a doctor at such an early age.

Brigid stood and leaned against the porch rail that was in desperate need of a fresh coat of paint.

"I'll be satisfied with finishing at the end of the year," she said, blowing a stray hair from her eyes.

She picked at a piece of cracked paint while assessing her father. Ethan seemed satisfied with Brigid's answer and slowly withdrew again into that place no one, not even Brigid, could reach. She knew it was pointless to continue to try to pull him back. When he got like this it was best to let him be. She pushed gently off the railing and kissed her fathers cheek.

Brigid needed to rid herself of the weight that sometimes came with being home. She wouldn't change a single day of being there, but seeing her dad despondent, on days such as today, made the loss of her mom all too real. Brigid realized there was only one place she wanted and needed to be to restore her sense of inner peace. Brigid needed Malachi.

"Your beauty never ceases to amaze me, Mal," Brigid said in greeting as she placed a loving hand on his weathered bark. A calming peaceful awareness tingled throughout her body. Brigid noticed how small her palm was next to Malachi's massive bulk.

"Have you come to sit awhile and talk with an old friend child? It has been a long while since we last met. Are you well?" Malachi asked in his deep comforting voice.

Brigid turned and walked the few steps to the nearby bench, brushing her fingers over initials carved a lifetime ago in the seat her father made for her and Ashling.

"Sometimes I think you are the only one in this world who understands me. You know more of my secrets than even Emma does." She sat lengthwise on the hand-carved bench to view Malachi and the sky above her fully, scrunching up her knees to fit more comfortably.

A sudden wind picked up, rustling the mighty oaks branches, but just as quickly it subsided. Brigid looked to see if Turlough had arrived, but not seeing him, she sighed in relief. The last few visits with the old crane were not happy occasions Brigid recalled. The last time she saw him, he came to tell her of Ashling's passing in her dream-state.

"I remember when you were just a girl and could stretch head to toe on that bench," Malachi said in a voice filled with melancholy.

"Oh no, not you too Mal. We can't all be in a gloomy mood today."

"Not gloomy child, just reminiscing."

He sounded like her Malachi again when he spoke next.

"Today is the earthly anniversary of your mother's transition. She resides in peace and grace, dear child. She is often by your side."

"How is it I can know what I know, do what I do, and still not feel her *here* with me today?"

"Tell me what you mean, child."

"For heaven's sake, I have talked to you since I was born. I communicate with birds, and when I was in Ireland, the Wee Folk spoke to me all the time. Today, of all days, why can I not hear my own mother?"

"Child, there is more than one way to communicate, you know that. Songs, nature, a memory..."

Brigid interrupted her friend.

"But she knows how much I miss her today. Sometimes I can't catch my breath. I feel like someone has punched me in the stomach. Today, when Dad and I need her the most, she's nowhere. She's left us all over again."

Malachi concentrated hard, trying to find the right words. "I'm sorry little one."

His branches drooped as if the weight was too much to bear. He slowly dipped a thin limb and brushed the top of Brigid's head. The gentle act of kindness from her friend was her undoing. She cried until there was nothing left to shed, then curled up on the bench and fell fast asleep.

Malachi never once complained that a part of his branch broke that day as he willed himself to lower his twigs even further to comfort the girl he loved more than life itself.

26

Malachi felt helpless that he could do no more than stand by and watch over Brigid who was caught up in a restless dream. Usually, the mighty oak enjoyed the security of his roots so firmly entrenched in the ground. He did the only thing he knew to do—he made sure his leaves rustled ever so slightly to create a soothing breeze upon her brow beaded with sweat. "What more can I do for you, child?"

He did not have long to ponder the situation. In the distance, the familiar reverberating heartbeat that Malachi knew sounded Turlough's arrival grew louder. He lowered a branch for his friend. Moments later, the giant bird swooped into sight.

"Greetings, Turlough. What brings you here today?"

The crane bobbed his graceful neck, tucked in his wings and murmured in his ever nasally voice.

"They called me here—the Priestess and Ashling Elizabeth." Turlough began to bugle, a sure sign important news was to follow, but Malachi gave his branch a solid thump.

Turlough ruffled his silk-like feathers but settled down quietly on his friend's outstretched arm high above the sleeping girl and snorted instead.

"You'll wake the poor child with that noise. See how she tosses?"

"Brigid Ann is restless because the Priestess and Ashling Elizabeth speak to her. She struggles with the message. The Priestess wants you to know what transpires with Brigid Ann and Ashling Elizabeth so you can assist Brigid Ann moving forward."

"The Priestess is kind indeed. Even knowing what I do about this family and their journey, any insights I am allowed is appreciated. Do tell me what you hear," Malachi insisted.

Turlough squawked, then pushed off Malachi's branch, gliding to the soft ground beside the bench where Brigid continued to toss and mumble in her sleep. He dipped his neck toward Brigid as if to hear more clearly. Ever so slowly, the crane's wings produced a hypnotic motion with each flutter of their large span.

The air around Malachi, Turlough and Brigid became electrically charged, then, with each pump of Turlough's wings, the ever soothing—*tun-tun, tun-tun, tun-tun*, created an air of calmness that reached Brigid's dream-state.

Even Malachi seemed to be more relaxed as he inquired, "Friend, what do they discuss that has our little Brigid so troubled?"

The beat continued. *Tun-tun, tun-tun, tun-tun.*

Turlough felt himself become immersed with the misty white clouds where three women stood and thought he was relaying what he heard to Malachi, but even he could no longer be sure.

Turlough stood motionless in a dark shadowed corner of what looked to be a tunnel, or perhaps the outside of a bubble of light around the women. He knew the Priestess called him here to be both witness and liaison. It was a trusted position given to him, and he did his job well over the centuries. Brigid, Ashling, and the Priestess, all appeared ethereal now, as Turlough listened in to their conversation.

"Mom, I can't do this anymore. It's too hard. Dad and I miss you so much," Brigid cried as Ashling held her daughter in her arms and stroked her hair.

"I want to stay here with you. It's peaceful. Please don't make me go back," Brigid pleaded.

"My sweet, sweet girl, I'm here now," Ashling spoke softly to Brigid as she did when she was a small frightened child.

"Mom, why is she here with you? I remember her, but I don't recall why," Brigid's voice trailed off in thought.

"This is your *namesake* Brigid."

Brigid set her attention on the lady in the sapphire gown with the primitive silver belt that hung low on her waist. She felt an instant connection. Looking into the woman's eyes, Brigid saw her own reflecting back. Upon closer inspection, she reminded Brigid of the good witch, Glenda, from one of her favorite childhood movies. The

Priestess smiled mischievously. Brigid wondered if the woman who shared her name read her mind.

"Yes, Brigid, my lineage is connected with you, your mother, and your grandmother. Ana and Ferax were also matriarchs and a vital part of your family legacy."

Brigid felt an instant bond as well with the white calf that stood by the Priestess's side. The calf casually began to amble towards her.

Tun-tun, tun-tun, tun-tun.

"Mom, do you hear a heartbeat too? I've heard it before, but I can't recall where or when."

Ashling merely smiled.

Tun-tun, tun-tun, tun-tun. Brigid slowly nodded her head. "Wait, I do remember. It was at Grandma and Grandpas. The day I told Emma about that crazy experience. She told me I was in shock hearing you had cancer," Brigid stated.

"Are you in shock, Brigid?" Ashling asked, laying her hand upon her daughter's cheek.

"No, Mom. I remember it all! How we all stood in a space together—the three of us. The Priestess gave us instructions of some sort and showed things. Right?"

"Yes, my sweet girl. There was such peace. It was the moment I knew I wanted to step into the role the Priestess showed me. It was a choice I understood to be the right one for me. It is now your time to see and learn more if you wish. Brigid, you have complete free will, and we will not interfere once we share the knowledge we have with you," Ashling said.

"Do I have cancer, too, Mom?"

"No, no, Brigid. You will live a long and happy life sweet girl, or else I would not have allowed this visit today."

"I want to learn more."

A sudden burst of color illuminated the space where Brigid stood. In a single pinpoint moment, various realities became apparent to her.

An image of a giant spiderweb dropped into Brigid's consciousness. Brigid's awareness heightened as she viewed a tangle of purposefully complex strings—a woven construction she interpreted as *here and there, alive and dead* fading like an *illusion.*

The web expanded, and Brigid was able to view it from all angles. She walked around studying the intricately engineered lines spun from seemingly erratic or aimless movements. Upon close examination, the systematically woven silk threads became one transparent yet solid masterpiece. Like an epiphany, Brigid had a moment of pure clarity.

"I'm ready. Tell me what it is that I need to know? What is it I am to do?"

"My child, we have waited a long time for this moment," the Priestess nodded.

"Mom, are you sure I'm not dead? Is this heaven?"

Ashling laughed, "Daughter of mine, you are very much alive and about to do a whole lot more living!" Her enthusiasm was contagious.

The Priestess said in what Brigid intuitively knew to be Gaelic, "We offer you the sacred knowledge of our people, with all its responsibilities, challenges and joys as the Legend has foretold. Will you accept it?" the Priestess asked.

Brigid nodded—yes.

The Priestess began a soft chant as she made a slow-moving circle around Brigid and the calf. As with her ancestors who came before her, Brigid soaked in the sacred downloads all at once, yet it felt as simple as remembering her name.

Brigid would later think, as her mother had done years earlier, of this time in the visit as watching an old-time movie reel playing out before her eyes. Some of the film advanced with mathematical equations, while others were laden with pictures of strange berries, herbs, and liquids, all laid out on a stone hearth. There was a rapid series of mish-mashed eastern and western medicinal principles that played out in slow motion.

The last download was fuzzy, almost as if purposefully edited. A tall form, a man Brigid sensed, held out his hand to her. She reached out to take it, but the figure faded from her sight.

"Brigid darlin', can you hear me?" Ashling called out from somewhere far away. "Come back to me now, sweet girl."

"Mom, I saw the veil and the illusion of death. That is how you were able to make your choice. Still, we all feel so separate from you *now*. We physically miss you."

Ashling's eyes grew misty until the familiar *tun-tun. tun-tun, tun-tun*, calmed her.

"I miss you all terribly. When we are together again, it will feel like the blink of an eye. Hold that thought, my daughter."

After a few moments of silence, Brigid asked, "What's it feel like Mom?"

"For me, it was like ice that finally thawed into a blissful body of tranquil turquoise water flowing freely without restraints. I was there, and then I was here. I have never felt such peace. Some I've met say it feels like rising into the pure white clouds. Others say it feels like rain finally being released from a dark, heavy cloud—to refresh and quench all of nature's thirst. I first understood it like that anyway. Some see a beautiful light or a golden cord. I know it's confusing."

As if reading Brigid's next question, Ashling supplied, "We are still us, only more so. We are unencumbered aspects of who we once were when we walked the earth. Although, some say they have unfinished work and remain in a place of quiet reflection. For them, it is a time of life review. Well, we all go through it, it's just some might take a wee bit longer than others to work things out. Regardless of our journey here, we all stay in a space that is supported by a loving presence which helps us and those we have left behind. It's different for each soul."

Brigid seemed to lose her focus as she watched a large exotic butterfly swish between the Priestess and her mom.

"Ferax? Oh, my. Is that her? Mom, in the story of Ana, Ferax came back as the most glorious butterfly and..."

Before Brigid could finish, the butterfly brushed gently along her left cheek. Brigid's eyes welled with tears. She whispered to the butterfly, "Hello Ferax. I see you in your dress of many colors, and I know you."

The calming *tun-tun, tun-tun, tun-tun*, softly floated in the air.

"Darlin'," Ashling said.

"Hmm?" Brigid replied as she watched the velvet butterfly rest on the calf's ear.

"Brigid, the time has come, and we need your help," Ashling told her daughter.

"The time has come? I don't understand, but tell me what to do." Brigid thought she should be more conflicted, but the energy insulated her in a haven of peace.

"Brigid, we will need you to wake up in a moment and go to your father," Ashling stated.

"No. *Please*, not yet! I know what we just said, but it's not like I get to see you every day, or pick up the phone to call you Mom..." Brigid's voice trailed off.

Tun-tun, tun-tun, tun-tun.

Brigid was calm once again.

"Turlough, please go now to Ethan," the Priestess kindly instructed Turlough who stood quietly off to the side.

The crane bowed his head in respect and faded from the bubble of light.

"When it gets too much, call for me darlin', I will come to you and make you hear my heart that beats with yours. I will come to you as a dragonfly," Ashling whispered.

Brigid nodded.

Ashling continued in a tone intended to alert Brigid. "Listen to me sweet girl. There is a man who is trying to take something which does not belong to him, and he feels your father is too weak to stop him. We need you to go to your dad, Brigid. Can you do that? Will you give him a message for us? He will only listen to you."

"I'll do whatever you ask, Mom."

Ashling downloaded her message as Brigid slowly nodded.

Suddenly, everything around Brigid faded away. Her eyes became heavy, and only the white calf remained—suddenly asleep at her feet. Feeling exhausted, Brigid laid down beside the calf and fell into a deep restorative slumber.

The next thing she knew, an onslaught of bugles woke her. "Stop playing that annoying trumpet," Brigid mumbled as she gingerly sat up and picked a twig from her hair as she watched Turlough fly above her head.

The trees began to blow in a sudden gust bringing Brigid fully awake. She sat for a few moments and processed all that had just taken place.

"I gotta go," she said, jumping to her feet. "I'll come back later Mal, and tell you all about it."

27

"Damn!"

Ethan swung his ax with more force than was needed as he replayed an earlier phone call in his mind. It was not the first time he had encounters with the caustic man. Ethan welcomed the distraction of the splintering wood caused by the force of the sharp metal blade. In moments like this, the diversion kept his heart from fragmenting into a million pieces as he often thought it might if he allowed even the slightest memory of Ashling to crash in on his tightly reined in emotions.

"If you were alive, vultures like that wouldn't be calling here acting like I wasn't capable of running the Double R on my own anymore." Ethan looked up hoping she'd be standing there, telling him he was acting like the old rooster, Angel. She felt so close sometimes— as if Ethan could reach out and touch her, but the reality that he couldn't ate away at his sanity more and more lately.

"Sell off the yew grove, like hell!" Ethan muttered to himself and took another whack at the piece of timber that lay before him like a sacrifice.

Ethan was sullen as he stared down at the severed trunk that once grew in the fertile ground. "You look like I feel," Ethan mused.

The life Ethan shared with Ashling was like the tree that lay before him. It too was once alive—thriving, and after Ashling left him, his world snapped in half. He died along with her and the diseased tree.

Ethan again cursed the man on the phone who made him a ridiculously insulting offer to sell off a portion of his family's prized acreage. "The nerve! Talking at me like he was doing me a favor. No, worse yet, as if I'm suddenly addle-minded."

Infuriated, Ethan continued his rant. "Those yews will always be yours, Ash," Ethan sacredly declared as he began to hack away on the pile of wood like the tormented man that he was.

Ethan wondered again why this so-called investor, Charles Thornbecker, wanted that particular piece his land. It wasn't common knowledge that the Rafferty yews were the ones used at the university. He didn't like or trust the voice on the phone and was sure his resounding no put an end to any more calls or questions that any parcel of Rafferty land was up for grabs. Ethan was sure Thornbecker would give up and go away as the others had over the past year.

Suddenly filled with rage, a mind-numbing pressure began to build in Ethan's head. His ears began to throb.

Then he heard it.

Tun-tun, tun-tun, tun-tun.

"What the heck?" Ethan dropped his ax and rubbed his ears. The steady constant drumming continued. Ethan's anger drained from him like a pressure valve that was slowly released. In its place was the sweet peace he often longed for but doubted he'd ever find again. He closed his eyes and sighed. Ethan refused to cry. He couldn't shed a tear after Ashling passed, making it easier to wall up that part of himself. He allowed only the softest piece of himself to remain available for his Sprite, and that cost him dearly.

Ethan walked around to the side of the house where Ashling's goats were munching away on alfalfa. He stood still and willed the heartbeat sound to get louder once again.

Peace. Such peace. It nearly brought Ethan to his knees.

Tun-tun, tun-tun, tun-tun.

With his eyes closed tightly, Ethan raised his face to the warmth of the sun high in the sky—smiling as his tense shoulders began to relax. It was then that Ethan felt a spark of something close to hope wash over him. Eventually, he dared to open his eyes, still afraid it would all disappear like a fragile, distant memory. Hearing a new sound he peeked over his shoulder to see his daughter coming towards him. She waved. He waved back.

"Dad, I've been looking everywhere for you," Brigid said in a breathless greeting.

"Hello Sprite, just taking in the sun. How was your visit with Malachi? Did you visit your mother's marker?" he asked, willing the peace and hope to remain a moment longer.

"Well, Dad, it's interesting that you ask. I didn't make it that far. I have a little story to tell you. Stay open, okay? Hear me out?"

Ethan actually laughed. Brigid grinned.

"I did live with your mother for quite some time Sprite. I personify what it means to keep an open mind!"

"Good." Brigid began to relay the events of the day.

A couple of times, Ethan would stop her, to ask a question or clarify a statement, but for the most part, he listened intently.

"Dad, there is one part that will tell us both for sure if I was only dreaming or if what I saw and heard is real."

"Go on, Sprite, what is it?" Ethan prompted his daughter as an orange dragonfly swished past Ethan's face.

"Mom told me I had to wake up. I had to get back to you and give you a message before it was too late. She and the Priestess said that there's a man who means you harm. He's been hanging around here —something to do with the yew trees."

The color drained from Ethan's face as he merely nodded.

"Mom said you needed to call the police and get to the grove Dad. I wasn't going to tell you that part, but she insisted I trust my gut. My gut tells me we need to get to the yews. Like now!"

Brigid suddenly felt panicked, but Ethan, who was already jogging across the yard, called out to Brigid, "Grab my cell phone off the counter, I'm getting the truck. We'll see what this is all about."

28

Ethan and Brigid were jostled in the cab of Old Blue as the wheels traversed the rocky lane. He was determined to make haste toward the trees on the farthest end of their property as his eyes burned with unshed tears. Ethan stared at the road in front of them, thinking back to the first time he brought his bride to the yew grove. Ashling was utterly enchanting as she laughed and ran barefoot in complete abandonment, as if one with the trees.

It was Ashling who brought attention to the all but forgotten yews on the Rafferty's property. They grew wild for many years, resting beneath the limbs of taller pines, yet when Ethan drove her out one day to the old orchard, he swore the once neglected acres appeared pristinely maintained and much more extensive than he remembered.

"The yew trees in Celtic lore are known to be a symbol of immortality and rebirth," Ashling told Ethan as she gently ran her hand along the trunk of one of the yews. The way in which Ashling spoke made it all sound quite mystical.

"Yews are also trees of protection. We'll need to be mindful and give special attention to them in the future. Ethan, did you know yews produce a substance used in chemotherapy protocols?"

"I know very little about the process, but I've heard that," he told her.

"There has to be a more organic and pure way to utilize the bark of the yew without causing the depletion of the earth's natural resources while minimizing the human body's turmoil. My mom would often tell me almost anything could be restored to health by the rich bounty the earth provided us."

Ethan prompted her to continue when she suddenly became shy.

"We've never had the need for any over the counter medications. My grandma's grandmother taught the rituals and traditions that were passed down to them. I guess it goes back many generations."

"Well, what do you do for headaches or broken bones?"

"Feverfew, butterbur, peppermint or lavender for headaches, and a physician for broken bones, silly!"

"Promise me you'll look at me like that forever, wife. And your laugh—well, it calls out to me in my sleep."

Ethan shook his head, "You're turning me into a hopeless romantic, woman."

Little did Ethan know on that brisk spring morning so long ago the impact these particular yews would have in the future, or how many events—past and present had slowly begun to intertwine like a web. Soon they would reveal a tapestry of ancient predictions and fulfill a Legacy established long ago.

The drive to the grove felt excruciatingly long, bringing with it painful and happy memories. It wasn't the first time Ethan caught himself feeling angry with Ashling for not opting for conventional treatments, and mainly why he rarely came on this side of the property. Forgetting Brigid sat beside him, he muttered, "She should have tried it!"

Brigid sat rigidly, biting her lower lip, and jumped at her father's harsh tone. "Tried what Dad? Who?"

Ethan hesitated briefly, then gripped the steering wheel tighter. There were no words to voice to his daughter about the rage he sometimes still felt over Ashling not wishing to go through chemo. Instead, he shook his head and drove on in silence. It was the best Ethan could do at the moment. Brigid knew her father all but forgot she sat next to him, as he drove closer to the edge of their property.

Ethan did indeed forget Brigid was by his side as he stared at a boulder near a tall sequoia. A slight smile touched his lips as he replayed the day when Ashling, still adjusting to Oregon and her new home, meandered through the grove. She glanced up from the root of a plant she held gingerly in her hands as she heard the crunch of tires rolling over loose gravel. She waved and called out to Ethan as he drove down the lane.

Ashling's eyes danced with pleasure, seeing her handsome new husband advance closer to her. He had that look that made her knees weak. She returned his spark with a knowing smile as he parked Old Blue, and not for the first time—Ethan froze, mesmerized by the sight of his mysterious redheaded wife.

Ashling would laugh when her husband got that particular look in his eyes, the one that said he had other things on his mind than talking about work, the weather or their bountiful herbs growing wild. Tossing her hair over her shoulder, Ashling turned and gave Ethan a saucy challenge. In her barefooted grace, she crooked a finger at her husband, who needed no further encouragement.

She took off in an encouraging saunter away from the truck, but Ethan, having already tossed his old ball cap on the hood of the pickup, dashed off in playful pursuit of his bewitching bride who made her way behind the large boulder.

It was much later as he plucked a stray leaf from her mussed hair that he promised to give it a gentle brushing when they returned home.

As they sat against the trunk of the lone sequoia standing tall amongst the yews, Ethan heard a fantastical story about his trees.

"I've told you I have a unique relationship with nature. I know you try to understand, even though it can be a challenge, Ethan. I get it. However, Leeza here," Ashling paused long enough to point to an unusually large yew, "She just told me that we could not deplete the bark from the yews here on Rafferty land. She says they grow in sacred soil."

Ashling went on to explain that the tree encouraged her to scrape a bit of its thin bark off the trunk and that it would not harm her or any of the other yew trees that grew on this protected space.

"Leeza says the trees have grown here for hundreds of years. They became depleted of their healing properties, but when you and your father perfected your soil, then spread it across the grove and ranch, they once again became able to absorb and produce their—gifts."

"What gifts Ash?"

It was then that Ashling showed her husband something he would question over and over throughout the years. She stood and walked over to the tree she called Leeza.

"Watch this, Ethan! May I?" Ashling asked the tree.

Satisfied with the answer, she carefully peeled a piece of bark away from the trunk and handed it to Ethan.

"Now watch the tree, darlin'," she said, pointing to the bare spot where the bark once wrapped protectively around the trunk of the tree.

"What on earth?"

Ethan swore his eyes played tricks on him as the bark slowly reappeared in the exact place Ashling had removed it just moments earlier. He thought it a quirk, but repeatedly his wife and the trees proved him wrong.

"They told me to do this. After I did, I was shocked too. Same thing happened with the berries. Ethan, it gets crazier. When I stood before Alfred here, it was as if he dropped all this information in my brain! I know that sounds crazy, but he did. He said to think of it as a recipe."

"A recipe?"

"Yes, that's it. They gave me parts of a recipe on how to cure illness in the human body using their bark and berries, and if I understand it correctly, it completely cures cancer."

Months of hushed conversations took place between Ashling and Ethan after that day before they finally decided to trust a friend of Ethan's who convinced them to bring samples to the university for testing. God, how the memories of Ashling crushed his soul. He pushed the scene from his mind—or tried to, as he often did.

They drove in pensive silence when suddenly Ethan's expression changed from grief to anger as he urged Brigid, "Call the fire department and say we need the sheriff too!"

Brigid saw what her father did. A beefy man dressed in black denim wiped his sweaty pocked face and blew his bulbous nose on a torn piece of cloth unaware that Old Blue approached. With a lit torch in his hand, he touched it to the dry wheat colored grass as a menacing flame hissed and crackled to life before her eyes.

The 911 representative picked up. After the aggravatingly calm request for the type of emergency, Brigid repeated what she saw—twice since the well-meaning operator seemed to need clarification.

"Yes, a man on our property, setting fire to our trees!"

After the location was confirmed, and the gate code repeated, Brigid hung up and tossed the phone aside. Ethan stomped on the accelerator as the startled man looked up. Dropping his still burning torch, the man began to run in the opposite direction of the oncoming truck.

At that moment, everything around Brigid became a slow-motion blur of events. Later she would try to analyze the serendipitous events and seeming coincidences that aligned to stop the devastating disaster. A chopper overhead arrived quite literally as she hung up the cell phone and dumped water on her mother's beloved yews engulfed in flames. Next, the police sirens which screamed repetitively pulled up near the Rafferty's truck.

Ethan wasted no time as he slammed the truck gear into park and hurled himself violently out of the vehicle. He began to run, leaving Brigid to stare after him as more emergency vehicles arrived. Ethan quickly caught up to the balding man who was no match for Ethan and his pent-up anger. The police officers, who were moments behind, had to drag Ethan off the arsonist who cried for Ethan to stop his crazed assault.

Brigid ran toward her father. Her voice stuck in her throat as she tried to scream for him to stop. Perhaps she did scream, for in that instant, Ethan halted the bludgeoning attack on the man lying in a fetal position. Ever so slowly, as if it had just started, it all ended.

It seemed even the gods were facilitating on the Rafferty's behalf. Just as the officer finished reading the Miranda rights to the pocked-faced man named Stanley, he quickly waived those rights and began confessing his crimes. Although he did not know the motive,

Stanley willingly gave up the name of the man who surely would have the answers.

"Thornbecker called in my loans. I had no choice. He'll take my fingers as repayment. He's had his goons do far worse. I've seen it with my own eyes," Stanley croaked.

This news produced a slew of oaths from Ethan.

"Thornbecker. As in Charles Thornbecker? I know that name. He's been calling me lately, trying to get me to sell off this part of our property that Stanley here just put a torch to."

"I wasn't trying to burn it all down. I was just told to burn enough to scare you a bit. You know, like a controlled fire," Stanley stammered, nodding his head like a bobblehead character.

"It's her fault! She scared me and made me drop my torch," he said, shoving a dirty finger towards Brigid who was nearby talking to an officer.

Stanley jutted out his double chin in Brigid's direction, then cowered away as Ethan took a menacing step forward.

"Ethan, let us handle this," the officer who appeared to know the Raffertys, stated sternly.

"Damn it, Phil, look what he tried to do."

Having completed her statement, Brigid returned to her father's side. Ethan hugged her fiercely.

"You okay Sprite?"

"Ya, just angry and confused. Those are my mother's trees. It's her legacy you pathetic excuse of a human! Her grave is not even ten feet from where you destroyed our land. What kind of creature does this?" Brigid ranted on as she thrust her finger towards the burned trees and the man walking in handcuffs to the squad car.

"It was yer fault, screaming at me like you did girl!"

"What are you talking about? He's deranged, Dad."

"You're the crazy one! Hollerin' like a Banshee at me made me drop my torch! It was just supposed to be a small fire," Stanley stammered as if trying to put a puzzle together.

"This mess ain't my fault. It's hers for freaking me out coming outta nowhere like she did." Stanley looked almost cartoon-like as he waited for Brigid to answer.

"What? I was in the truck with my father, you idiot! What woman? Whom did you see? Tell me!" Brigid ordered as her adrenaline-fueled her on.

"Impossible, my eyes had to a been playing tricks, or it was the smoke... I coulda' swore it was you. I saw a gal with crazy hair like yours come from outta thin air. Poof! Just like that, just yellin' like a hellcat for me to stop. I got spooked. Then you showed up, and she was gone. If it wasn't you girl, then who? Where is she?" Stanley babbled on as he peered out the squad car window.

Worrying her lower lip, Brigid turned and melted into her father's waiting arms.

"Get him outta here," Phil said to the driver of the police sedan.

Plumes of dust faded as the remaining emergency crews drove away from the Rafferty property. Wordlessly, as if they were both compelled, father and daughter were drawn to where Ashling's headstone laid, untouched by the flames that once burned inches from it.

"Thank you, Mom."

Brigid looked to the sky instead of down at the rose-colored marble that marked her final earthly resting place. Her mother wasn't there. Ashling's body was never laid to rest on the Rafferty land since Ethan ultimately honored his wife's fervent request to have her body released to a medical lab to be studied. There was something in the way in which Ashling had told Ethan, "Trust me, husband. You must do this. One day, you will understand."

Brigid had insisted on a marker near the yews, to honor her mother. Ethan understood Brigid's need and made sure it was placed precisely where both she and Ashling would have wanted it. Staring down at the cold stone, Ethan hung his head, jammed his hands into the front pockets of his jeans like a little boy, and soon his body trembled and shook with long-buried tears no longer able to be kept at bay.

Brigid could only watch as he dropped to his knees and cried. Silently, again, she thanked her mother for giving the man they cherished most in the world the opportunity to grieve. Time passed as both Ethan and Brigid gathered themselves. Ethan finally stood, wiping his eyes with the sleeve of his shirt, then took in a few calming breaths, and smiled over at his daughter.

"She came to you in your dream."

Brigid nodded.

"Your mom was here, trying to stop the creep until we could get here."

Brigid slowly, confidently nodded her head again with a twinkle in her turquoise eyes that locked with her father's in complete trust and comprehension of what had just taken place.

"Let's go home, Sprite."

Ethan looked tired but no longer tormented. He took his daughter's hand as they walked to the truck. Stopping as if he forgot something, he dropped Brigid's hand.

"Go on ahead. I'll be right behind you."

Ethan turned his head towards the singed yews. After a few minutes, he began to walk towards Brigid.

"You coming too, Ash?" he whispered into the wind.

Much later, when Ethan was alone in his bedroom—*their* bedroom, gripping her favorite hairbrush would he admit to himself he heard his Ashling laugh and say, "I'm right beside you darlin'."

29

Professor Albert Jones was preparing to deliver some essential news. What disturbed him, was that he had been unable to reach Ethan, even though he tried diligently throughout the morning. "Call me when you get this," Jones growled into the phone. After slamming the receiver down on his desk, he looked at his colleague and shook his head.

"Another news van just arrived," a co-worker informed him.

"Something's not right. Ethan always takes my call. We can't hold out much longer. Either I break the story, or this university will be a three-ring circus by the time the five o'clock news airs."

Albert Jones knew too many leaks had already surfaced regarding the Yew Bark Cocktail or the YBC as the research department referred to it. The whispers and jeers over the so-called all-natural cure turned into headline news overnight. Jones had to take control with or without Ethan's presence—the situation at hand was bigger than either one of them. The news vans parked in front of the school in hopes of an exclusive interview proved that. More were bound to follow. The time was now.

"Everyone's in the conference room, Professor—whenever you're ready," said a young woman poking her head in the door.

"Thanks, Kendal, we'll be right there. Well, let's do this. We'll give our team the run down and then speak with the press. Emma Daily was good enough to write up the press release," he said, taking one last look out the window.

Albert Jones gave the report highlighting the FDA's approval and requirements to begin large scale clinical studies using the YBC. It was a monumental task that was years in the making. He gave the crowd a few moments before silencing them to continue.

"For those of you who do not know, it will take a minimum of 2.56 Million dollars to get this out the door and into a clinic for further testing. It's still a long shot folks. I know it makes no sense when we're sitting on a formula that not only reverses but eradicates certain strains of cancer, but it's still too soon to celebrate. We know the YBC can do it with zero side effects, but the big pharmaceuticals are catching wind as well. No brainer to say they don't want this leaked to the public, so everyone, be aware moving forward. Oh, sorry to do this, but with the news vans and all, before you leave, an updated NDA needs to be signed by each of you if you wish to move forward on the project."

Emma remained as the group dispersed. "Are you still thinking the project should move overseas? I know Ethan mentioned a research group who was interested in investing."

"I am, but I need Rafferty to bless off on the deal, and I can't reach him. I was hoping I could hold the press off, but there's no way."

Before she could ask more, Emma's phone rang. "That's Brigid Rafferty. I'll find out where they are."

Albert Jones merely nodded as his attention was already shifting towards the Dean, who approached with a friendly smile.

"Brig, Where are you? Didn't you get the call from Professor Jones?"

"No, we've kind of had a situation here at the ranch we were taking care of. Why?"

"A lot's happened in the past few hours. Can you tell your dad, Jones needs to talk to him asap?"

"Sure. Everything okay?"

"It's good stuff. He wants to talk to your dad personally. What happened at the ranch?"

There was a long pause on the line.

"What's wrong Brig?"

"Hey, can you guys come over for dinner tonight? I'll tell you all about it when you get here, but first, there's a name that came up today, and it seems I've heard you mention it."

Emma pressed, "What name? This sounds ominous."

"Charles Thornbecker."

"Oh, you mean that sleazy lawyer? I've told you about him. That's the big case Sam's been working his tail off on the past few months. It's a big deal. I guess this guy is into all sorts of illegal stuff and so far, they haven't been able to make any charges stick to the weasel! Brig, Thornbecker is the shadiest lawyer in the state. Wait, why are you asking about him?"

Brigid's mind raced as the pieces fell into place. "Em, is he the lawyer for that big pharmaceutical giant, Greer & Slater?"

"Yep, that's the one."

"Listen, can you and Sam be here at six? It's important."

"We'll be there," Emma confirmed.

"Thanks. We appreciate this. I gotta go," Brigid said, hanging up the phone.

Two hours later, Ethan opened the door and greeted the couple in the customary friendship that had grown over the years. As he ushered them across the well-lit hall, Sam stopped as he pointed at a photo framed on the wall.

"Remember that night, babe?"

Sam's eyes twinkled as he looked at Emma, who smiled at the group of young high school students decked out in all their prom finery with no clue what the future would bring.

"How could I forget?"

She took a step closer to the photo as her face softened.

"Ashling stood behind you Ethan, and made funny faces to make us laugh right before you snapped this."

The hallway became silent with dormant memories.

"Right before Ash passed away, she asked me to hang this picture. When I asked her why this one was so important, she told me it's not only what the eyes see, it's what the heart remembers. Ashling was always after me to look at the big picture—the seen and unseen in years to come. I gotta admit it isn't easy."

Brigid called out a welcome that broke the aching sadness that hung in the air. Emma and Ethan shared a look of understanding as they all continued to the kitchen.

"Sam picked up a bottle of your favorite pinot," Emma said, as she pointed a finger toward Sam who waved it in the air like a prize.

Sam looked at Ethan and announced, "And I found this bottle of whiskey I thought we might try. You up for it?" he asked Ethan.

"Only if you make it a double after the day we've had around here."

Emma casually walked past Brigid to the old farmhouse table. She swung her leg over the vintage bench seat and laughed at Brigid, who was currently in a battle with a long string of melted cheese. Emma picked up her knife, and having mercy on her friend's plight, severed the stretchy hot mozzarella from the pan.

Sam popped the cork and poured a glass for Brigid and Emma, as Ethan worked the seal off the bottle of old Irish whiskey. Soon all four were settled down to a family-like a dinner. Ethan and Brigid began to share the events of the day. Sam peppered the Rafferty's with several questions now and then. When Ethan got to the part of where Stanley gave up Charles Thornbecker's name, Sam let out an expletive that got him a kick on the shin from Emma.

"Dad, this is why I wanted Sam here tonight."

"Sam, who's this guy, and what does he want from me?"

Sam gave Ethan the edited version of Charles Thornbecker, the longtime lawyer for, and most likely principal stockholder in Greer and Slater. It didn't take long for Brigid and Ethan to get a clear picture of how the Rafferty land came into play.

"Somebody's feeling threatened by the attention the YBC is getting. They must have heard something about our yews," Ethan stated.

"Not surprised. Thornbecker and Greer and Slater won't want anyone tapping into their trillion-dollar empire," Sam added.

"So, it seems if our yews don't exist, there's no new product, and Greer and Slater remain the monopoly they are," Ethan stated.

"Right. If they can keep you and the team from even starting a clinical trial, it's one less competitor for them to be concerned with.

There is likely more to be aware of now that the news is circulating," Emma added.

"They're afraid Ethan. Doesn't take much of a leap to see why Stanley was hired to set the trees on fire. They're sending you a pretty clear message," Sam warned.

"It was lucky you both were at the grove," Emma said.

Ethan gave a short laugh.

"Well if you call Sprite's dream—luck, then yes I guess it was." Ethan patted his daughter's hand.

"I fell asleep under Malachi and had the oddest dream. Mom was in it, and she told me to wake up and go get Dad."

"You know, I've heard about people that have those experiences. I never quite believed them, but coming from you Brig, I don't doubt it," Sam assured her.

"Well, I'll draw up an official-looking notice and send it to Thornbecker's office stating what we know. Should be enough to put him on alert. Hopefully, with everything else going on, he'll drop it. I doubt he'd risk the association with what happened in the grove today. Stanley is expendable. Thornbecker knows whatever Stanley confesses to won't stick to him."

"Do you think it's the last we've seen of Stanley?" Brigid asked, hating that she sounded fearful.

"Definitely, but I'll be paying him a visit at the jail tomorrow too. I think this was a petty scare tactic, and he blew it."

"Thanks, Sam. We appreciate your help," Ethan said.

"Oh, I almost forgot. Ethan, Professor Jones said he's been trying to reach you all day. Have you talked to him yet?"

"No, my battery died on my phone. It's been on the charger. I'll call him after dinner."

"You might want to get back to him sooner than later," Emma suggested with a small smile.

"Sounds mysterious, Em," Brigid added.

"It's almost a done deal, you guys. Ashling's vision for the yews —it's happening. There's more, but Jones wants you to hear it from him." Instead of the happy response she expected, Brigid and Ethan became quiet. It dawned on her, that while of course, this was a time to celebrate, the one person Ethan and Brigid wanted to celebrate with most was not physically with them. Emma became thoughtful as she wondered what to say or do. Sam, who may have felt the whiskey more than he realized, tried to lift the mood of the group. He gently nudged Emma and gave her a conspiring look.

"Tell them," he urged.

Emma glared at Sam, "I was going to surprise her tomorrow," Emma whispered.

"Tell us what?" Brigid insisted.

Emma reached into her sweater pocket and pulled out a shiny diamond ring. She couldn't stand it any longer. Her eyes danced with merriment as she did so.

"I had it all planned, I was going to walk in here tomorrow and flash this, but my fiancé here spoiled it. You idiot," Emma said, laughing as she rolled her eyes at Sam as he slid the ring back on Emma's finger.

"You guys did!" Brigid hugged her friends, as Ethan stood to shake hands with Sam and give Emma a fatherly hug. Emma wiped a tear as she hugged Ethan back.

"Well, congratulations to you both. It's a perfect match, and I know you'll be happy for many years to come," Ethan said with conviction.

"I thought you two had a plan? Isn't there still, what eleven months left before the official announcement?" Brigid said playfully.

"Well yes, but since we both want a baby like right away, we thought for my parent's mental health, we better do it sooner than later. We're eloping, at City Hall on Monday." Emma let the words hang.

Brigid and Emma looked at each other with saucer-like eyes before both women began jumping up and down like two giddy school girls.

"My parents are going to freak out!" Emma exclaimed.

"They'll go ballistic at first, but you're their only child. They'll work through it. They always do, Em. Let them throw you an outrageous party down the line," Brigid replied.

"Well, this calls for a toast," Ethan said as he splashed the amber liquid into his and Sam's glasses.

"Let's toast! To my best friends and two of the most loving and caring people we know!" Brigid said, raising her glass.

"Can we also toast Ashling? I feel like she's here with us," Emma said.

The atmosphere became like that of a chapel.

Ethan raised his glass. "To Ashling."

30

Brigid softly hummed one of her mother's favorite songs as she made her way toward Malachi. She observed the changes about her and savored the smells of the changing season.

"Fall was always our favorite time of year, Mom," she said, looking out over the kaleidoscope of colors bathing the property. The twigs and leaves crackling beneath her shoes reminded her of childhood memories when she and Ashling would collect only the most spectacular leaves to press in between waxed paper, making their version of stained glass to hang in the windows of their home.

Feeling chilled as a breeze whipped past her, Brigid pulled her oversized hood loosely atop her head, not caring that the wind played with her unrestrained mane of hair. She sunk her hands deep into the generous pockets that cradled her cold fingers.

Earlier in the morning, Ethan teased her, saying it was a good thing the hooded coat wasn't red or they might have to be on the lookout for the big bad wolf. Brigid secretly liked the idea of hanging out with the wolves.

She smiled and waved at the sight of her loyal friend as he came into view. A comfortable sense of peace washed over Brigid, filling her heart with a sudden need, mixed with relief, as she heard Malachi's rich baritone greeting.

"Ah, child, you've come to visit, and on such a chilly day." He sounded older, raspier than she remembered.

A wave of concern hit Brigid like the crisp cold breeze on her chilled face. She walked closer, laying her cheek to rest on the rough bark of Malachi's trunk. "I've never asked you this, but do you get cold when the weather turns, and you start to lose your leaves?"

Malachi took his time answering, as he often did. Brigid removed one warm hand from her pocket, patted the thick old trunk, then quickly dipped her fingers back into the warmth of the cashmere pocket.

"Well yes, I suppose, but I don't lose them all as you know, and after so many seasons I dare say, I welcome the change. I sleep a lot in the winter months. You know I'm an old man now, and it's not as easy as it once was to push out those leaves come spring!" He chuckled at his joke, but Brigid who was about to sit on the weathered and faded bench, turned instead, cocking her head to the side, examining every inch of the beautiful, sturdy oak tree she'd known all her life.

"Mal, are you well? I don't like all this talk about getting older. I couldn't bear it if anything ever happened to you. You're more than a friend. You know all my secrets, and, you know me better than I know myself," Brigid stated, working her lower lip.

"Child, please sit. I am well as you can see for yourself. I think the changes that come with each passing season are an ideal time to reflect, and I think I am a bit introspective today is all."

"Tell me what you've been thinking about Mal. Are you lonely? Do you need anything? I know I haven't been around as much the past few years. I'm sorry."

Malachi quickly answered, "No, no child, with all my friends out here I wish I had a little peace and quiet. Sometimes those squabbling crows get on my last nerve," he said with conviction. "It is not that I don't miss you, but if you are living a good life, then that is all that matters to me. Besides, you should know by now, you and I are a mere whisper in the wind away from each other."

Brigid sighed. Although she dutifully nodded her head, understanding there was not truly a separation, just a shift in perception of reality, sometimes her physical longings for those she could not be near tore at her physical existence.

"Are you well, child?"

Brigid's heart all but burst into tiny shards of glass with the sincerity of his question and the obvious love she knew Malachi felt for her. Brigid wanted to scream, *No—she wasn't well*! The ugly, bottomless black hole of sadness that came with missing her mom was about to pull her under like a deceptively calm river concealing a malignant undertow.

She wanted to cry and pound her fists at all the injustices life had thrown at her family while the rest of the world complacently accepted her illusions of well-being. Brigid was angry and sometimes felt it would eat away her last raw emotion, just as cancer ate away at her mother's fierce spirit, until all that remained was a listless skeleton, like the ones used in medical school labs.

Instead, she told her friend, "I'm a little tired these days Mal. My work schedule is grueling, but hey, on the upside, I'm going to be a full-fledged doctor soon. Can you believe it?"

"Of course I can believe it, child. You have always been meant to achieve great things. You are destined to be a great healer amongst healers, I dare say."

Brigid smiled at her friend. The way he spoke made her believe it might be true.

"You always support me Mal, no matter what. I feel like I've taken advantage of you over the years, always coming and dumping my problems…"

"Stop child, tell me you haven't forgotten all the good times?" It came out part command, part plea.

"One of my fondest memories is of you and your mother as you climbed to sit on my branch and you both passed the afternoon in laughter and daydreams while discussing all the things life had in store." Malachi went on to say, "You were very young, but I remember the time your father built you this swing here to be closer to me. Oh, and what about the songs you tried to teach me when you were just a teenager?" Malachi was no great singer. They both chuckled once again, at the memory.

"Let's not forget when you brought young Emma to meet me."

"Boy, do I remember that day. Mal, remember when Dad built this bench, and you told us we should all carve our initials here? Then, of course, there are the prom pictures."

Brigid and Malachi were silent as two bushy-tailed squirrels raced up then down Malachi's massive trunk. Brigid laughed.

"We have shared a lot, haven't we? I knew when I brought my pillow and suitcase out here that day so many years ago I'd never have a more treasured friend than you. I feel like I get to keep a piece of you with me always Malachi, but what about you? I mean, almost every family picture is taken out here with you. So there are photos in the house, on my phone, heck, there's even one of you and me on my grandparent's wall back in Ireland."

The sky had begun to turn heavy, weighted down by dark, ominous clouds which contrasted with a pale blue backdrop. The sky reflected Brigid's thoughts.

"Mal, what can I give to you of myself?" Brigid asked in a shaky whisper. It was becoming harder to keep her thin, frayed edges from unraveling.

"Your friendship has always given me a great sense of joy and happiness. What more could there be, child? I feel your heart beat with mine. It will always be, no matter our form."

"Even though I get that, it doesn't make it any easier."

The conversation had taken a very different turn from one that Brigid expected to have when she started on her walk to see her friend, and she suddenly felt fatigued. She was unreconciled with the notion that everyone and everything was connected.

After all, Brigid wanted to hug her mother physically, and to pick up a real phone, call an actual number and ask her mom if everything would be okay? Brigid knew she felt her mom, heard her whispers, and believed they visited each other in her dream-state. Brigid knew she should feel grateful, although sometimes these days— she just didn't.

Sitting in silence cross-legged on the bench, neither she nor Malachi spoke. Content to be in each other's presence, the tree and young woman quietly passed the hours. Together they watched the sunrise high above the mountains, as they soaked in the refreshing moments of the autumn day.

They listened to the approaching storm speak, and the trees echo back. For a long while, Brig sat suspended in time, eyes closed, face tilted towards the sky, never realizing the approaching storm clouds loomed overhead darkening the sky above them. Here, she was safe and protected by Malachi.

The afternoon sky rumbled and swished, fueling Brigid's soul. She felt fully alive as she held her reverent gaze to the heavens. She did not hear the vehicle that slowly rolled past her, nor did she see the bold stares coming from the passengers of the SUV as they passed by her on the way to the Rafferty home. Brigid, however, was hard not to notice. If one did not know better, they would swear they witnessed an apparition of fairytale magnitude.

The girl or woman on the bench had long golden-red hair waving like a welcoming hello. Her face, barely visible, all but begged for a closer inspection, the driver concluded. She shivered in the cold breeze, but her head remained in a private uplifted prayer. *She needs strong hands to warm her*, the driver mused. The primal and familiar urge jolted through him as he slammed on the brakes all but dislodging his two passengers.

Was she a waif, an apparition, or perhaps the goddess of his dreams who sat and worshiped the fickle sky above her? The driver needed more time to study her, to decipher who or what she was.

"What are you doing? Trying to break my neck?" the voice screeched like nails on a chalkboard.

The back seat window slowly rolled down. "Mate, leave me here if you would. I have research of my own to do if you know what I mean," a male voice filled with mirth told the driver.

Then to the female passenger, he added, "Careful, sweetheart, this one might turn more heads than even yours does," the man teased the passenger in the front seat.

The woman reached over putting her delicate hand on the driver's thigh, ever so slightly digging a well-manicured nail into his leg as she purred out, "Let's go, darling, we don't want to keep our host waiting now do we?"

The driver pointedly removed her hand from his thigh and placed it on the center console, then drove on without another word. The man in the backseat picked up on the tension and was more than happy to add fuel to the flame.

"When is it you are going back to France, or Scotland or hell, sweetheart?" he asked in a slow drawl.

The woman returned his remark with a glacial stare.

"Kids, could we please put on a professional front, if not for at least the next few hours, while we meet with Mr. Rafferty and enjoy what I hope to be an enlightening tour?" The driver shook his head, seemingly resigned to the banter.

There was no time to answer as the picturesque two-story log cabin came into sight. The driver whistled in appreciation at the long wrap around porch with oversized cushioned rocking chairs placed near each other. The scene called to him like a long-lost friend.

"Well if that's not something to see. Doesn't that look like a tree inside the house, or are my eyes playing tricks on me?" the man in the back asked his companions. The woman pressed her lips in a grim, disdainful line. The driver shook his head, unsure. They didn't have to wait long to find out. Ethan stood at the open door, offering a lazy wave to his guests who pulled to a stop in the sizable U-shaped driveway. The driver wasted no time as he strode up the steps to meet his host.

"Mr. Rafferty, I'm Michael MacShane. It's good to meet you finally." There was a slight pause, then Michael continued, "I was sorry to hear about Ashling. Even though our families were friends, I hadn't heard until I got hold of the articles Miss Daily wrote."

Michael stood and waited as his companions met up with him and introduced themselves.

"Sir, I'm Ewan Brodie, and this here is Fiona Stewart."

"Nice to finally meet you both. Fiona, thanks for making all the necessary schedule arrangements."

"My pleasure."

Ethan said to Michael, "Ash talked fondly of your grandparents and the friendship they shared with her parents. It's good to have you in the states finally, and at our home," Ethan added as he stepped back through the door offering a welcome again as the others followed him inside.

"Sorry, my daughter's not here to meet all of you. She'll be disappointed. This project is important her—well, to us all."

Ethan laughed, "But no pressure, you know?" Ethan said, giving a friendly pat on Michael's shoulder.

"We wouldn't have come all this way on a whim, Mr. Rafferty," Michael said in earnest.

"Call me, Ethan. Let's head to the kitchen. Can I get anyone coffee, ice tea, or something stronger?" Ethan asked as he led them through the house.

Ewan asked in a hopeful tone, "Gotta pint laying around, mate?"

Fiona's face turned an uncomplimentary shade of crimson.

"Dark or light?" Ethan reached behind him to the cabinet that displayed a variety of microbrews.

Fiona presented Ewan with a fixed look that would cause most men to wish the ground would swallow them whole. Ewan ignored her.

"I'm fine. Thank you," Fiona said in her most polished tone.

"I'll have whatever Ewan's having," Michael added as Ethan poured dark amber liquid in two beer glasses.

Ewan took great interest in questioning Ethan about the Oregon beers much to Fiona's not so subtle sighs.

"Ethan, I hate to sound unappreciative of your hospitality, but we only have about twenty-four hours before we catch the plane back to Scotland," Fiona stated by way of explanation.

Ethan jumped in, "Of course. You'll be wanting to see the trees. It's a short drive, but we should get on it before the rain hits hard. Do you want to follow me over in your vehicle so you can be back on the road before dark? There's a gate I can let you out by the trees. It'll save you time."

"Perfect. We haven't checked into the hotel yet. They said they'd only hold the room until seven pm. Some conference I guess has them overbooked," Fiona said.

Ethan grabbed the keys to Old Blue, and after Ewan had chugged the last of his beer, they followed Ethan back to the front door. As he took his leave, Ewan commented, "Hey, mate—you know you got a bloody *tree* growing in your living room, right?"

Ethan laughed, an honest to goodness laugh that felt foreign and needed all at the same moment. He smacked Ewan on the back and in a long forgotten playfulness remarked, "Tree? What tree?"

31

Oblivious to the visitors Ethan entertained, Brigid remained with Malachi.

"We lost about an acre of the yews. The squirrels and birds were all so frightened. We're lucky there wasn't more damage. Mal, what if it were you caught in the fire?"

"It's tragic and senseless child, yet I am well. Several hawks I know lost their homes. I've offered them shelter in my branches. Others are welcome if they wish. Child, we shall talk of happier things. Tell me your plans now that your education is complete," Malachi said as he guided the conversation towards Brigid's career and future.

"Obviously I've been giving it much thought. Since I want to go into research, I could be an intern or join Professor Jones and his team. But Mal, I'll let you in on a little secret. Someone is coming here tomorrow from Scotland. He's a representative for some big research team. It's all kinda secretive, so I'll learn more once he arrives, but he sounds very interested in partnering with us after reading Emma's articles. You know the ones I told you about a while back? Well, it makes me wish I could be a part of whatever comes next. I just feel like it's big, you know?"

Brigid laughed off the impossible dream she secretly fostered, but Malachi did not laugh.

"Anyway, there are a few realistic options open to me, but I know one thing for sure, I feel called to focus on cancer research."

Brigid looked towards Malachi, who remained silent.

"Do you think it's crazy that I want to honor Mom somehow through my work? Am I hanging on to the past? Maybe it's not all that healthy? However, maybe, just maybe, I can be a small part of one day preventing another family from experiencing what mine has gone through."

The tenderness in Malachi's voice touched Brigid's heart.

"You are certainly not crazy. Your desire is honorable. Have no regrets child. Whatever you decide to do, or not, promise me, you will have no regrets. Only walk your path. Never allow the whims of others to dictate how you move about this world. Ashling taught you that, did she not?"

"Yes, Mal, she made me believe anything was possible. You are wise to remind me of that. Thank you."

The day was fading quickly, and as much as she hated to leave her friend's company, she needed to be on her way. The incoming storm told her as much.

"Mal, I gotta go, but I'll be back for a visit soon. I promise."

Brigid gently rubbed one of Malachi's golden-brown veined leaves between her fingers.

"Thank you for always being here for me. I love you."

Ever so gently, Brigid hugged his thick trunk, placing one brief kiss on his scaly skin.

Before leaving, Brigid reached into her coat pocket.

"Mom always tied my hair up with red ribbons. This is the last one she gave me. There are stories I remember from my childhood— Mom called them Legends, that dated back centuries. Many had a symbolic meaning of the passing on of red ribbons throughout our ancestors time. It seems it was always from mother to daughter, but..." She let her thoughts trail off as if working some mystery out in her head.

"Malachi, I wonder if I might tie this particular ribbon on one of your branches. I want you to have it."

She could think of no better way to show her love for the old tree, which was the one real constant in her life. After all, the red ribbon was handed down to great healers, as she recalled. Hadn't Malachi healed all of her pain throughout the years? Even if it was a symbolic gesture, Brigid felt compelled.

"Mom would approve."

"It would be too great a gift child. The ribbon I believe is meant for you," Malachi humbly replied.

"No, it just makes sense." Brigid now stood close to Malachi straightening out the long strand of material.

"You and my mom were friends long before I came along, and it just seems, well, right for you to have a part of her and me with you." She smiled up at the stately tree.

"You would be doing me a favor Mal," Brigid assured her friend as she stretched up and tried to fasten the ribbon around a medium-sized limb. Malachi dipped his branch lower, to make the task easier for Brigid to complete her labor of love.

"There, now I will be with you every day, and Mom will be too," she whispered as her voice caught.

"Child, you do honor me. I shall wear the ribbon with pride and love." Malachi had to remind himself he was a mighty oak, not a flailing sapling. Still, his deep voice shook with emotions of his own.

"I'll see you soon, my dear friend," Brigid told him.

"Where are you off to now, child?" Malachi asked.

"Down to the yew grove. I want to pay a proper visit to mom's marker."

"The sun fades fast. The storm is near. It is destined to shake things up. Bundle up, child."

The human Malachi loved the most, raised her hood obediently, giving him a farewell wave. Brigid decided to take the shortcut she and Emma would often use as girls, allowing her time to get home before it became too dark. Soon she reached her destination and began walking about the area of burned trees. She felt a great sadness for the loss of the innocent tree life as well as for the dislodged hawks and countless other animals.

Looking around, Brigid realized it was not only people who had to reconstruct their lives after loss. She scolded herself for the melancholy mood hanging over her like the dark cloud above her.

She continued her assessment of the damage. "I thought more trees got burned. The firefighters said over an acre was affected. This can't be more than a quarter of an acre, at most."

She stopped to watch a fat robin with a twig in its mouth.

"Excuse me, do you live near here?" Brigid inquired.

"Yes, dear, the tree to the left of you, the tall, slightly singed one. See it there?"

"I do. Maybe its the lighting right now, but I could have sworn..."

"Your eyes don't deceive you. The fire's destruction was vast, but the caretakers are attending to the rebirth."

"The caretakers? Do you mean the Wee Folk?"

"Well, of course, dear, and the *other* caretaker, too. *She* waits for you! You better be on your way before the storm hits. I must finish building before nightfall."

As the bird took to flight, Brigid pondered the robin's words as she stopped in front of Ashling's plaque. Taking a plain handkerchief from her pocket, she knelt and began to wipe the soot from the cold marble stone. When she revealed the date of her mother's passing, she began to scrub with eyes blinded by tears, as if by doing so, she could erase the past and the anniversary of Ashling's death. Brigid let out a strangled cry, not unlike that of a caged or wounded animal. She had been strong for too long—trapped in a prison, not of her choosing.

Her muscles ached as she scrubbed the flat rectangle. Her hair fell in a wild tangle about her shoulders, and even though she bloodied a knuckle on the unforgiving stone slab, Brigid continued trying to remove the date she was powerless to put into remission just as she was her mother's cancer.

"*Why? Why? Why?*" she begged the etched writing to answer as her weary arms gave up their fight.

Brigid could take no more. She dropped the handkerchief and allowed her arms to fall to her sides.

"Brigid, darlin', stop! I'm not there. You know that my sweet girl."

Brigid hung her head and wiped her eyes with the back of her hand, leaving a streak of blood on her cheek. She rocked back on her heels and lifted her head, hoping to hear her mother's voice again. Listening intently, she watched the colors in the sky shift even darker. It reminded her of a sandscape she once had as a child. Brigid allowed her tears to fall freely now, lost in the thought of the novelty toy she would flip over and over to watch the millions of grains shift and flow, merging to create soft shapes of beautiful blues and grays within its two plates of flat glass.

"Perhaps this is what it feels like to lose one's mind," Brigid echoed in a hollow voice.

As a child, Brigid wanted to feel the sand inside the glass, imagining it to feel like sand between her toes—but it was always just beyond her reach, just like her mother was now. Ashling was beyond the glass veil, so it seemed.

As if on cue, the waning sun cast its light through the sandscape clouds, creating breathtaking crepuscular rays that soon began to shift and part. To Brigid, it looked like the shape of a portal. She now fully expected to hear the voice of God or the angels calling her to join them. She wanted to laugh but sobered quickly.

"Mom, is that you? I think I'm going crazy. Help me," she begged the angel rays in the sky.

"Brigid Ann Rafferty, enough of this. Listen to your heart. Do you hear me?"

Brigid did indeed hear her mother and smiled. She felt Ashling's essence close as if merging with hers to communicate.

"Oh, Mom, I miss you so much. I don't know what to make of everything happening."

"Darlin', the love I feel for you and your father, has magnified if you can believe it! I am here with you always. You don't have to make sense out of all this. You merely have to let yourself feel what you feel and do the best you can. Sweet girl, at times like these, you need to rest and be gentle with yourself. I know it's difficult, my darlin'. I know."

Ashling's soothing voice continued.

"I'm here, and you must believe we still communicate, just like I told you, even though it's different now."

Ashling went on to say, "Remember when you were a child and how you first learned that not everyone talked to trees and nature like you and I did?"

Brigid nodded, remembering her confusion and sadness for others who could not, for what they were missing out on, but also she remembered feeling different. Brigid could easily understand why people learned to turn down or close off this gift, to fit into what society expected.

"Tell me what to do? I'm so tired."

"Everything is unfolding as it is meant to be. You must go on with your life, and not just live—I want you to *thrive* and be all I know you are destined for! It is what I want for you. I know it may not make sense now, but one day it will. You still have dreams to accomplish. You will see, there is a purpose for everything—everything, darlin'."

With a mischievous giggle, Ashling said, "I promise you, great joy and happiness is just down the road!"

To that, Brigid replied, "Mom, what's so *funny* about my life right now?"

"Brigid darlin', you sound too much like your father these days. Never fear, I'm going to work on him next. It's time for him to move on too, but you first."

"Mom, what are you talking about?"

A dark thundercloud clapped loudly above Brigid's head and began to shake the sky, releasing random sprinkles. Brigid jumped, startled by the sudden roar crackling above her head.

"So it's a sign you need child of mine? Well, a sign you shall have, but you must go now—and run! This cloud is about to dump buckets, and I don't want you catching a cold when all the fun is about to start," Ashling told her daughter in a lilting voice that began to fade.

Just as Ashling predicted, the sky opened up and began a full force attack on Brigid's head.

"Hurry, run Brigid, but stay on the main road, it'll be less slippery. I love you! I'll see you in your dreams, darlin'."

As Ashling's voice faded into the wind, Brigid knew her mother was right. She needed to move quickly if she were to make it home before dark, and a hot shower was all Brigid could think of to clear her mind as she ran down the lane towards the house. Her sight was limited as the rain-soaked her hood, now partially covering her eyes. The sky turned a menacing black-gray, and intermittent bursts of thunder rang out in the air. Brigid never heard the SUV or saw it until it was too late.

Instinctively, seeing the oncoming headlights, Brigid braced her hands as if she could shield herself from the impact of the corner of the vehicle. Luckily, the driver saw her at the last minute and slammed on his brakes. Parking the SUV, Michael jumped from the car as did Ewan. Fiona remained seated, rubbing her neck from where the seatbelt seized up. Brigid stayed on the ground, sprawled unceremoniously at the feet of two men who stared down at her with grave concern.

"Shit! Shit! Shit!" Brigid repeated.

Ewan and Michael both knelt by Brigid, ushering commands at her to stay put and not move.

"I'm fine. You didn't hit me."

Brigid assured both men she jumped back before impact, although in truth, it felt as if a hand pulled her backward, and then she lost her balance. Michael allowed this information to settle in as the fear turned to anger.

"Are you daft girl!" Michael hurled at the muddied creature before him.

"You're frightening the lass, mate," Ewan said as he grabbed Michael's arm.

Michael never took his eyes from Brigid as he regained his composure. "Can you stand?"

She nodded, not trusting her voice. The men each took hold of the drenched woman's elbows, helping her up. Michael thought she looked like the most irresistible combination of a helpless kitten and ferocious hellcat all rolled into one. He sucked in his breath as he tried to remain aloof. He failed.

"What in the hell were you thinking running straight in front of a moving vehicle? Are you crazy, girl?" Michael barked out.

He was more shook than he knew and lashed out at the soaking, wet, muddy waif in front of him.

"Mate, you're behaving like an arse. She couldn't have seen you through the rain and hood covering her face, right lass?" Ewan prompted encouragingly.

"I'm so, so sorry!" Brigid answered through chattering teeth, mortified, and embarrassed as the stain of the earlier dried blood on her cheek slowly dripped like a tear to the ground.

"You're hurt! Get in the car. We'll get you help," Michael ordered.

"No," Brigid shook her head, not knowing if she should be afraid or grateful. She shot back, "You're on private property, and people are not allowed back on this part of the ranch! Yet, here you are, trespassing, trying to hit me with this beast of a vehicle, and now you want me to get in your car? Who's crazy now?" She countered, feeling the rush of adrenaline sweep through her body.

Ewan laughed as Michael and Brigid glared at each other.

Fiona rolled the window down.

"We're going to lose the Hotel, Michael! They said they'd only hold it another half hour. She's obviously homeless. Leave her be."

Fiona spat the last word out with disdain.

Seeing the three wet individuals turn towards her and the rented car, Fiona spewed, "Tell me you do not intend to allow her in here." Fiona cast a disparaging sneer towards Brigid.

Brigid sensed something vaguely familiar about the woman's distinct high pitched voice, but couldn't place it as the humiliation flooded over her. Before she could respond, Ewan taunted the woman in the front seat, "Fi, if you don't want to ride with her in the car, we can always call you an Uber."

Ewan took great care as he helped Brigid to the idling vehicle. After opening up the rear passenger door, he offered her a hand up. Brigid stared at the wildly handsome man with a deep dimple in his clean-shaven chin, who smelled of musk and soft leather, not sure once again if she should be afraid or laugh at this sudden turn of events.

Her mind raced back to the tree incident with Stanley. Was this another ambush on her family, she wondered? She was cold, soaked and afraid she'd catch pneumonia, so she took her chances, and climbed in, pulling her favorite ruined emerald green coat around her.

Michael also returned to the driver's side and slammed the door closed. He ran his fingers through his now dripping hair, and even in the darkness, Brigid thought she knew the man.

"What are you doing on our property?" Brigid asked as the vehicle began to pull forward at a slow pace.

"Your property? Priceless!" Fiona spat out.

Ewan and Michael became eerily quiet.

"Your property lass?" Ewan asked.

"Yes, you are on Rafferty land. Private property. How'd you get through the gate?" she asked the driver who peered intently at her through the rearview mirror.

Suddenly he began to chuckle.

Dancing eyes, crinkled with mirth, stared at her through the mirror—Brigid knew those eyes. They sometimes haunted her dreams.

Before she had time to react, they drove up to the U-shaped drive in front of the Rafferty's home. Michael quickly jumped from the car and jogged to the passenger side. Fiona, fully expecting him to open the door for her, sputtered as he walked past and opened the door for Brigid and offered her his hand. Willing herself to stop shaking, Brigid stared at his outstretched olive branch.

The laugh lines next to his eyes deepened—God, how Brigid wanted to trace those lines with her fingertips.

Brigid was sure, once she saw him in the light, that his eyes would be a magnificent color of deepest midnight blue.

She gave an audible gasp, knowing now, how and why he and the woman looked familiar—and wished the earth would swallow her up whole. With no such luck, and feeling a bit shaky, Brigid accepted the hand he held out to her and stepped down from the vehicle. Michael was feeling quite pleased—smug even, as he whispered in her ear, "Mo ghrá, how many more times are you going to fall at my feet? A fellow could get used to it, you know!"

Brigid's stomach flip-flopped. Oh, she knew what was coming. She held her breath, willing the woman inside her to push the childish flutters away. She braced herself in anticipation.

He did it. Unabashedly confident. Cocky. He wanted her. Brigid could feel it in the brief wink of his eye. And then, just as the moody skies above them floated by, the moment passed.

Ethan looked out the window from his chair in the living room. Seeing a vehicle pull up the drive, he strode to the front door and opened it as the headlights caught his oversized silhouette that filled the door frame. Within moments he realized Michael was helping Brigid from the car. Ethan, hurried down the steps. "Sprite, what happened? Are you all right? You're soaked." The shower of concerned questions continued.

Ewan casually walked around the vehicle to stand next to Ethan.

"Mate, the lass, is fine, just a little mishap, but with said mishap, we lost our hotel reservation, and we now find ourselves in need of hot showers and a place to lay our heads."

Ethan looked from Ewan's calm and amused face to Michael's unreadable one and finally settled on his daughter's.

"Sprite, are you hurt?"

She shook her head, no.

"There's blood on your face."

"Dad, it must be from earlier, I scraped my hand. I'm okay."

Then to Michael, he said, "I just left you guys. What the hell happened?"

"Wait, Dad, It's all my fault. I was with Malachi, then I went to see Mom, and she told me to hurry home, and my coat was drenched, and I didn't see the car." Brigid rambled on barely taking a breath. "Then I stupidly tried to throw myself on top of their vehicle," she said in an attempt at humor.

"I promise everything's fine. No one is hurt, and these nice people—brought me home."

32

"She must have hit her head. The mom's dead... right?" Fiona hissed in Ewan's ear as Ethan ushered everyone into the living room. Stunned by the remark, Brigid openly stared at the porcelain doll before her. Fiona had the good grace to look embarrassed. Over the years she had become accustomed to being brash, but even Fiona knew when she crossed the line.

Clearly embarrassed, she slowly began peeling her gloves off. "I've been told I have no filter, Mr. Rafferty. I think my nerves are a little more frayed than I imagined," she said, by way of an apology.

"This is my fault. Dad, I'm so sorry. I thought our guest—guests I mean, weren't coming until tomorrow. I guess I got confused. I put these people through a lot tonight, and I do apologize—to all of you."

"We're just happy you're okay lass," Ewan said trying to ease the tension in the room.

"Thanks, Ewan. Um, good to see you again, by the way. Although, I'm a bit embarrassed that I didn't realize *you* were the team interested in our yews."

"No need to be embarrassed, lass. We've been keeping this visit close to the vest, as they say," Ewan added kindly.

"Brigid here has had her hands full. Next week it'll be official. She'll become the youngest Doctor of Medicine in the state of Oregon. So, she hasn't quite been brought up to speed on all we have been discussing," Ethan supplied.

"Sounds like our ambitious friend here. I think he held the title for the youngest physician in Scotland," Ewan said hooking a finger towards Michael.

"I think I knew that. I went to listen to a lecture while I was in Ireland. It was a motivating speech," Brigid said, careful to avoid the piercing stare she felt upon her skin.

"Dad, the guest rooms upstairs are ready for company," Brigid prompted.

"Yes. Of course. We insist you stay here. Why don't you grab your bags, and I'll show you the way. We've got two bathrooms upstairs and plenty of rooms to choose from. I'm sure everyone would like to clean up a bit, then we'll eat," Ethan said.

"You too, Sprite. Go, before you catch pneumonia," Ethan instructed Brigid as if she were a child. Brigid nodded her head and ignored the faces peering back at her as she made her way towards the long hallway that led to her bedroom.

It felt like the walk of shame. Nonetheless, Brigid squared her shoulders and stood a bit taller. Michael smiled approvingly even as Brigid's wet socks noticeably squished between her toes on the hardwood floor while she made her way past him.

Once down the hallway, Brigid grumbled, "How on earth did I fall not once but twice at his feet? And, not only in one country but two!" She tugged off her wet coat and tossed it in a nearby laundry hamper, then kept walking.

She was miserable, cold, and tired as she stood on a thick rug next to an ornate claw style tub. With teeth that chattered, Brigid turned the hot water handle and ran her cold hands through the stream of warmth. She knew she should opt for a quick shower in her own bathroom and hurry back out to help her father with the guests, but she needed time to clear her head.

Taking her favorite bubble bath from a nearby shelf, Brigid twisted the lid of the glass jar, then poured in a heaping scoop of crystals. The calming aroma of lavender permeated the rustic bathroom as the tub filled with effervescent bubbles. She walked back to the sink to take off her earrings and bracelet, finally gleaning her first look in the mirror. What peered back at her was a wild-haired, muddy-faced creature she barely recognized. Brigid stared a full minute before she began laughing.

"Great! Just great," Brigid said as she began to scrub layers of muck from her face. After shedding the rest of her clothes, she turned off the blissfully hot water tap to the bathtub and walked to the nearby enclosed shower. She washed her hair, threw it up in a towel and quickly padded back to her readied bath and gingerly lowered herself with a sigh, grateful to be submerged in the clean, warm and relaxing bubbles.

Brigid played over the crazy events of the day, not even sure if she believed everything that happened. Sooner or later, she would have to face the group of guests in their home. *Just five more minutes*, she told herself resting her head on the tall back of the tub.

In the silence, with her eyes closed, Brigid allowed her mind to settle, only to be jolted by the squeaky hinge of the bathroom door opening. Once again, Michael and Brigid found themselves locked in a compromising situation. Brigid froze.

"Well, your father told me there was a bathroom down the hall, but he didn't tell me I'd get to share it with you."

Michael attempted a polite smile, but his wolfish appreciation danced with something not quite resembling a gentleman's demeanor, making the look in his eyes anything but innocent. It unsettled Brigid to her core, yet she could not bring herself to look away. It dawned on her that her father would have no way of knowing she chose the guest bathroom downstairs with the oversized tub.

Brigid's bedroom suite had a connecting bathroom with a smaller shower, but this bathroom had the irresistible nostalgic feel she craved from her childhood. It was her refuge when things became too much.

"I thought you were all upstairs," Brigid sounded almost too calm, even though she was sure Dr. MacShane could see her heart pounding through the frothy bubbles.

Leaning against the door frame as if it was a common occurrence for the man, he supplied, "Fiona and Ewan grabbed the two bathrooms upstairs, your father graciously offered me this one."

Silence followed.

The undeniable mutual attraction only added to the electrically charged air.

Somehow Brigid found her voice.

"Dr. MacShane,"

"Michael," he cut her off in a lazy tone that belied the desire he felt.

Brigid tried again, hoping the flush she suddenly felt on her cheeks didn't give her away.

"If you wouldn't mind, I'll finish up here, and you can have this bathroom all to yourself. I just assumed you and your companions would use the ones from the guest room, but of course, you'll want to get out of those wet clothes."

Michael seized the moment.

"Is that an invitation?" The wolfish grin was back.

Without waiting for an answer, Michael pushed away from the doorframe, as Brigid stifled the urge to jump out of the tub and run to her room.

In a far too casual and mischievous voice, Michael said, "Ewan and I are mates from childhood, but we'd never share a shower if we could help it."

"Oh, I assumed you and Fiona," she stopped herself from finishing the thought.

Michael knew what she thought. He was curiously pleased that she cared to think about it. He knew he should turn and go—yet his feet wouldn't move. Silently he cursed their betrayal as the enchantress in the tub held him spellbound. He was quickly losing himself in her unusual green eyes.

For the first time in many years, Michael realized he didn't want to be alone. More precisely, he no longer wanted to feel so lonely. He forced himself to calmly turn away from the woman in the tub as he quietly closed the door without so much as a backward glance, not trusting himself to speak another word. Brigid was left staring at the now vacant space, wondering what had just transpired between her and the elusive Michael MacShane. She allowed her eyes to close and process the latest events.

A half-hour later Ethan, Michael, and Ewan were seated in the Rafferty's kitchen, deep in an animated conversation. Soon after, Brigid came around the corner, barefoot with her hair in a ponytail, wearing sweats, a hoody, and carrying three large pizza boxes.

As a way of explanation, she shrugged her shoulders and smiled, "Thank goodness for late-night delivery service, huh? I bet you all are starving."

"You have no idea," Michael said casually.

Brigid would have sworn Michael's comment meant he was hungry for a little more than food. She suppressed a smile, thinking he intended for her to be the meal. She blushed thinking once again about Little Red Riding Hood and the big bad wolf.

"Whatcha got there, Sprite?" Ethan asked, halting her train of thought.

"After what I put everyone through I wanted to it make up. Food is the universal language of apologies, right? Besides, food's kinda our thing around here."

Pulling out dinner plates and napkins, Brigid breezed over to the table. Michael, having just taken in a breath of her earthy floral scent, fought the urge to pull Brigid to him when she leaned in close to set the table.

It took him months to get her out of his head after their first encounter years ago. Sitting at the Rafferty's kitchen table, Michael felt as if he had known her his entire life, instead of a few passing moments. Looking at Brigid now, she was no longer a girl, but a vibrant woman. Somehow though, still forbidden.

Brigid broke the silence. "Will Fiona be down to join us? She's gotta be hungry too?"

"Fiona asked us to make her apologies. She wanted to get some sleep. She has an early flight tomorrow," Michael explained though his voice sounded strained.

Realizing there was more to the story, but none of her business, Brigid tapped the pizza lids. "We've got cheese, pepperoni and that one has it all. Pick your poison, gentlemen." Brigid suddenly felt young and playful. It had been so long since the Rafferty home was alive with laughter and conversation.

"Got any parmesan, lass?" Ewan asked.

"Yep, right here. Catch," Brigid said as she tossed Ewan a package of processed cheese.

He laughed as he caught it. "Nice arm."

Michael felt a surge of something foreign. Jealousy? Envy? He needed another beer.

As if reading his mind, Brigid walked to the fridge and grabbed several bottles from a lower drawer. She closed the door with a swish of her hip and walked back to the table.

Ethan patted the bench next to him as Brigid sat down. "Let's eat."

The four adults set out to polish off the pizza Brigid ordered. Several empty beer bottles lined the table, as they fell into a comfortable conversation about work.

"So, what are your plans now Brigid since we're on the topic of you trying to beat my record?" Michael asked, feeling playful as well.

"How old were you Doctor MacShane, I mean when you got your first degree?"

"Call me Michael, please—and looking back, I was way too young." He sounded light-hearted as he held Brigid's questioning stare.

Brigid flushed thinking back to his request in the bathroom earlier. She felt shy, yet suddenly bold. It was Michaels turn to feel the heat on his face. He cleared his throat, in hopes to remain aloof. "So, you were about to tell us about your future plans."

"Well, I want to go back to..." Brigid caught herself. "I think I'm leaning towards an internship at the university in the lab. I want to stay connected to the YBC progress," she said with more confidence than she felt.

"Sprite, where do you want to go back to? Your mom said I was to encourage you to go back and finish. However, she never told me *what* or to *where*." Ethan set down his half-finished pilsner, giving Brigid his full attention.

Brigid took a deliberate bite of her pizza, trying to buy a moment to think, but she knew it was pointless to lie to her father.

"Oh, Dad, it's just childhood nostalgia—my silly daydreaming, you know? I think the events this week have gotten to me" she said with a dismissive wave of her hand. "Besides, I don't want to bore our guests with my whimsy about the Legend. We can talk about it later."

Ewan cut in, "Hey lass, what's this legend stuff? I got all night, and we Scots love a good tale," he laughed.

Brigid hesitated only a moment, as she peeled at the label of her beer absently.

"First, I want to clarify. I am not delusional. However, I did fall in love with the stories my mom would tell me as a child. She had a vivid imagination. Sometimes, It just makes me feel closer to her when I think about the way she would light up and talk about real or made up ancestors and events. Anyway, when I was studying in Ireland, there was this class I took. It was fascinating. It focused on our Celtic heritage, and it reminded me of my mom's Legends."

"The plot thickens! Do tell, lass" Ewan encouraged, while Michael's hooded stare never wavered from the face of the woman who sat across from him.

"Oh to heck with it," Brigid said, taking a deep breath.

"Well, you see boys," she said dramatically taking another drink of beer. The men chuckled showing encouragement for the storyteller in their midst. Brigid scooted to rest her back against the wall while tucking her feet underneath her on the bench. Clearly, Brigid was having fun.

"There's a Legend that has floated around my family for many generations. Think ancient Celtic era. It's about a boy and a girl from two opposing tribes that fall madly in love and are torn apart—forbidden to marry. Picture a Romeo and Juliet kinda thing. The sea separated them, yet they still knew they were destined to be together. They kept their love a secret, most likely because the girl was some sort of Priestess in training, and the boy was betrothed to a girl he did not love and one, not of his choosing. I think he was some sort of Clan

Chief. Anyway, I'm sure you can get the gist of it—the customs and all back then. Basically, his family put the brakes on the relationship."

Brigid stopped to take a bite of pizza. Chewing slowly, she made sure she commanded the room before continuing.

"So, love being what it is, the young couple dared to defy their respective families and came up with a plan."

"What kind of plan?" Michael asked.

"Well, they had a particular tree they'd meet beneath on the side of the water where the Priestess and her family resided. It was there that they decided to run away together. When the chosen day arrived, the young Priestess made it safely to their tree. Once there, she was to tie a red ribbon to the tallest branch she could reach. You know kinda like a flag, but smaller so nobody would take notice. The Clan Chief was to wait for the signal and go to her once he saw it was safe."

"A red ribbon, huh?" Michael asked.

"Yes. Mom said the red ribbon was sacred to our ancestors. It held special meaning for the healers of the villages and tribes back in those times. It was a symbolic ritual I guess you'd say," Brigid told Michael and Ewan.

"Anyway, before she could hang her ribbon so they could escape together, a devastating disease rocked the country, killing many people from all across the land. The girl, or Priestess in training—being a great healer, survived the deadly illness, but she feared for her true loves well being. She was desperate to find out if he survived the plague. One day, as soon as it was safe, she went to their tree and hung her ribbon again. The Priestess waited and waited. Months went by, but he never came. The young woman was devastated and rarely left the shade of the old tree. She lost her will to live and feared the worst."

"That the plague took the life of her intended," Ewan ventured.

"Exactly. She gave up hope and decided to end her life and join her beloved. It was then that he appeared and found her weeping under their tree."

"Well, what happened next lass?" Ewan asked, caught up in Brigid's tale.

"It's tragic. Unfortunately, as Legends go, there were those who didn't want to see the pair live happily ever after, and the Priestess was killed, but not before promising her love she'd wait for him on the other side of the veil."

"And that makes you want to follow in the footsteps of a Legend, why?" Ewan asked incredulously.

Brigid laughed. "No, I guess I should have led with the part where my mom's Legend states that the Priestess was the one who cured the deadly disease, but not before it wiped out most of her tribe. I want to cure diseases too. Lofty, I know. Anyway, the Legend kinda gets fuzzy after that part. Mom always told me she thought maybe she or I would play a part in curing some illness," Brigid added.

"Cancer," Michael said, looking into Brigid's eyes.

"It's why I decided to become a doctor. Go big or go home, right? But Mom and Dad believe in the yews and the YBC, and so do I. It became even more of a mission after my mom passed," Brigid said and gently squeezed her dad's hand as the room fell quiet.

"Well, the class I took not long after I bumped into you in the hallway that day, focused on the natural, Old World healing modalities, in particular, eliminating certain diseases and cancers. Something about it felt familiar, and I swear, I could finish the instructor's words before she could get the words out. It all felt like second nature to me."

"Wait, you two have met before?" Ethan asked.

"Dad, don't you remember me telling you about it? Doctor MacShane is the man I fell in front of at the university on my first day of classes. My coffee went flying all over the place. You and Mom tried so hard not to laugh."

"I guess I never put two and two together. That was a long time ago, Sprite."

Brigid looked at her father to make sure he was okay.

Michael became thoughtful for a moment.

"You hear about that berry in Australia that..."

Brigid cut Michael off—"That miraculously cured skin cancer? I watched a documentary on how by just rubbing the juice from it on patient's melanoma, it became non-detectable," Brigid said, snapping her fingers, "Just like that."

Then Ewan added, "The problem is getting something like that approved here in the states would be twenty, maybe thirty years down the line… if at all."

Ethan finally joined in. "Exactly! That's why your team being here to look at our data is crucial." Ethan shook his head, "Look, I don't mean to sound desperate, but the truth is we are. The university's about to cut the program."

"What?" Brigid demanded.

Michael thought she once again resembled an adorable hellcat—kitten. He smiled to himself.

"Look, Sprite, I was hoping I wouldn't have to mention it all to you."

"But Dad, if this deal doesn't go through, we don't have the means or the resource to carry on Mom's work. Your work! *We're so close*," she whispered, taking her father's hand in hers, forgetting anyone else was in the room.

Michael cleared his throat.

"Miss Rafferty," he said now in his most professional voice.

"Ewan and I planned to speak with you tomorrow, but as it is, we have *bumped* into each other sooner than expected."

Ewan laughed. "Funny mate—bumped into."

Michael went on.

"I've done some research on you," he said cautiously hoping he didn't sound like a stalker. "I know what it takes to get as far as you have so soon. Every one of us at this table knows we can eradicate cancer—naturally. Our team believes by combining our protocol with the Rafferty YBC we've found the solution," Michael reasoned.

"Oh my. Then your backing is essential, but what does all this have to do with me?" Brigid asked.

"Well, as I started to say, I told your father earlier today after we toured the grove, there was one condition upon my team taking on the extraordinarily large financial implications of moving this project overseas."

Brigid looked at her father's unreadable features.

"Which is? Because, I'm sure, within reason, we would have no problem accommodating whatever needs or concerns you have. Right, Dad?"

Ewan choked on his beer.

"The condition, Miss Rafferty, was on your agreement to join our team in Scotland. Your knowledge and understanding of the yews is essential, and the closest thing to having your father come with us. He declined. With your research background and credentials all but secured, it's only logical. We'll be needing a consultant. I won't move forward without your input on the project," Michael finished.

33

Brigid excused herself from the kitchen, satisfied that she maintained her composure long enough to calmly say goodnight to her dad, Ewan and Michael who remained seated at the table. So focused on getting out of the kitchen without making a scene, Brigid promptly stubbed her toe on the wall as she turned the corner, and bunny hopped a few steps to shake it off.

"Did I seriously just tell *the* Doctor Michael MacShane I'd consider his offer?" Brigid asked herself while she limped down the hall. She chuckled, relieved that she could find the humor in a situation like this.

Ewan and Michael had outlined the reasons they wanted her to accompany them to Scotland. Their rationale was logical enough, but the offer wasn't so much a request as an ultimatum. Brigid wasn't sure how she felt about that or the fact Ewan thought it humorous while Michael remained stoic.

She began to think about what it would be like to be part of the team in Scotland at the new cutting edge, state-of-the-art hospital. To be asked to sweep their floor would be an honor, and yet, two of the most prestigious men in their respective fields just invited—no, insisted she collaborate with their team.

"What on earth is there to think about?" Brigid asked herself. Her mood grew dark as she quietly shut her bedroom door, knowing it was her dad and his well-being that was holding her back.

"I gotta talk to Em," Brigid said, pulling her cell phone from her purse and dropping unceremoniously to a nearby chair.

Emma answered her phone and took it all in, inserting all the pertinent '*oh's*, *um's* and *ahh's* while assuring Brigid it was without a doubt what she should do.

"Being a part of Ashling's legacy and also doing what you love is your destiny," Emma said emphatically.

"Don't let this opportunity pass you by, Brig. As your mom would say, you have to follow your gut. You know it's the right thing to do. Besides, isn't that the cute doctor you had a crush on a few years back? Wait, before you answer that, I've wanted to talk to you about something for a while now. Something that might make your choice a little easier," Emma spoke tentatively into her cell phone.

"Are you okay?"

"Perfectly fine. No, this is a good thing. I've dreamt of something like this since we were kids. I only told Sam about it last month, and he said I should talk to you and Ethan."

"Em, what is it? You know my dad would do anything for you. You're family."

Emma gave a mirth-filled laugh on the other line.

"That's what Sam said. It's a rather brilliant plan if I do say so myself, and *when* you go to Scotland—my idea makes even more sense."

"You're killing me! Tell me."

"Well, for starters, I quit my job last week. Sam said the stress wasn't worth it. It's not like we need the money unless I lose my trust fund over this. To be honest, I've finally decided to do what's best for me."

"You quit your job?" Brigid's voice all but exploded through the phone as she fluffed a pillow, opting to get comfortable on her bed. "This is gonna be good," Brigid sighed dreamily, grateful to focus on someone else besides herself for a while.

Emma laughed, holding the phone away from her ear. The scene was one of many that had unfolded over the years; two girls, now grown women, talking for hours, and sorting out all of life's intricacies.

"Yep, I finally did it. Actually Brig, I've had a plan B for quite some time now. One day when we were teenagers, I sat on the bench by Malachi. I told him about it. He didn't laugh, so I took it as a sign. We both know I can't hear Mal speak, but still. So, ya—I told the senior partners in the firm last week. You should have seen their faces. Nobody, especially my age, walks away from the job I have, but I simply can't live my life trying to please Mother and Father anymore. It's exhausting."

"Em, you must feel so relieved, but what did your parents say?"

"Well, that's where I kinda wimped out. They're in Cambodia. One of Father's old partners will inform him I'm sure, but—" Emma went on, "Don't say it! I'm spineless when it comes to my parent's approval—even as an adult, I buckle under the pressure."

Brigid chimed in brightly, "I'm glad you did it. That job was sucking the life out of you. Tell me more."

Emma hesitated only a moment. "Well, you know I love the goats. The 4H experience is something I never forgot, and I miss Ashling dreadfully, Brig. I'm one of the few people who know and understand the steps in your mom's recipes. Heck, I helped make the cheeses almost as many times as you did with her."

"Probably more Em, when you count the years I was away at school."

"Maybe."

"You know I think of Ethan as a second dad. So hearing that you are hesitating about going to Scotland, I have to tell you all this now, because Brig, I have the perfect solution! Be truthful. You're afraid to leave your dad. On top of that, all the responsibilities have fallen on you and Ethan since your mom passed."

"I'm afraid he'll let everything my parents, and grandparents worked so hard for slide, and he'll just sit in his rocking chair on the porch all day. He's still young. He should get out and start living— really living again. Mom would want that."

Brigid and Emma quietly processed their emotions.

"Em, what have the goats got to do with anything?"

"I want to take over the manufacturing and running of Ashling's Company. There I've said it. I want to be the new CEO of *The Clever Goats*. Your mom and I had many discussions about how to turn her company into a non-profit. Sam could help with that. The profits, of course, would get funneled back into the cancer research. Brigid, you don't have time or the passion for it. It's an obligation to you, but not for me. I've watched you walking around like a zombie, trying to be all things to everyone. You know your mom would approve of this. I love the company as if it were my own. Plus, it would allow me time for my writing. Brig, I'm good! I have things to say, and I think I can express my thoughts in a way that will draw people in. I think I can combine my love of writing, having a career working with the goats, and honoring Ashling with this idea."

Brigid was quiet. Too quiet. "Brig, are you still there?"

Silence followed.

"Oh, Gosh! I swear I thought you'd be somewhat happy, or relieved. Forget I said anything, okay? I didn't mean to upset you." Emma tried to take back her words while Brigid sniffed on the other end of the line.

"Brig, say something. Anything!"

Suddenly, laughter filled the space between Brigid and Emma's cell phones. "Say something, huh? How about, when can you start? I'm so relieved! You have no idea how I've been struggling to make it all work."

Emma let out an audible sigh, and both women instantly began talking over each other at once. They agreed to speak with Ethan the next day, already knowing that he'd welcome the addition of Emma at the ranch, and in business.

The two friends chatted a little longer, with Emma ending the call by instructing Brigid to inform the esteemed Doctor MacShane that she would accept his offer. "Oh, will I now? Bossy much?" Brigid tried to sound irritated, but she was secretly beginning to get excited about the prospect of a new beginning.

After Brigid hung up the phone, she connected it to the charger. Needing time to reflect, she tiptoed through the dark house, stopping in front of the old oak tree. Wide awake with a mind full of thoughts, she circled the room until she stood facing a large window overlooking the Cascade Mountains, then settled herself on the chaise lounge near the back of the tree and fell into a peaceful slumber.

The sound of a man and woman talking in hushed tones woke her. Soon she realized they sat on the opposite side of the broad oak trunk without knowing they had company. Brigid wondered how long they had been there, and what she should do now? Should she pop out and say hello, startling the pair, or stay snuggled, hidden in her secret spot? Brigid felt like she was spying in her own home.

She thought to make a ridiculous yawn or some animated gesture to alert the couple of her presence—after all, Brigid thought to herself, how much more awkward could this situation get? However, she didn't inform them. She remained planted quietly on the chaise.

Realizing the couple on the other side of the tree was Michael and Fiona, Brigid frantically rattled off in her mind all the reasons why she shouldn't remain quiet. Instead, she stifled a sigh. By the tone coming from both Fiona and Michael, she might as well add listening into to his private lover's quarrel to the list of embarrassing moments since meeting Michael MacShane.

Brigid heard her name and froze. She couldn't possibly move now. She hated herself for doing it, but Brigid inched closer to try and understand the conversation more clearly.

"Tell me, Michael, is this because of that Rafferty woman?" Fiona sounded petulant.

Michael answered in a soothing, reassuring voice that one would use with a small child. "Fi, you know there was never an us, in the sense you hoped. You know you don't love me the way you should, and I love you like a *sister*."

Fiona sounded desperate, "But we could have something if you would just allow it!"

Michael stopped her.

"Fiona, you are in love with someone else, and it's time you came out and admitted it. Quit throwing this back on me."

Fiona made a squeak that made Brigid either want to hug the other woman or roll her eyes. Instead, Brigid scooted another inch forward, trying not to miss a single word.

Michael merely ignored Fiona and continued. "Tell him, Fi. You might be surprised to hear that he feels the same way."

Michaels words came out more like an order than a request, and Brigid had a feeling he was a man not accustomed to being told, no.

The petulant tone was back in Fiona's voice when she said, "He hates me. Always has, and you know it!" she spat out. "You know as well as I do, he thinks I'm only after his money."

Michael chuckled. "You've given him good reason over the years now, haven't you, Fi? We've talked about this, and I know you've behaved as you have to protect yourself, afraid you'll get hurt again. So, instead, you've transferred all those feelings on to me because you knew I was safe, but we were never meant to be."

It sounded as if he had recited this more than once, and prepared himself for Fiona's rebuttal. "Then if it's not because of her, it's because of your ridiculous Legends. Oh, grow up, Michael!"

Fiona goaded him now, but Brigid was curious about the reference. Fiona, realizing she was not getting the reaction she wanted, tried another approach.

"What can I do? What happens next?"

Brigid heard the fear in the other woman's voice.

"Fiona, go tell Ewan how you feel. Be honest and just lay it all out there. You might find he has been putting up his own walls for fear of rejection or subjecting himself to that slicing tongue of yours." Brigid heard Michael's tone soften as he teased and encouraged his companion.

"You tell him for me," Fiona begged.

Brigid wanted to laugh. She felt like she was spying on two schoolyard kids. She imagined Fiona passing a note to Michael, but instead, she heard Fiona raising her walls.

"Never mind! I'm out of here in the morning anyway. Forget this conversation ever took place. I'll ready the labs, make the calls, and be sure everything happens so you can shine—as usual. Ewan can puff his chest out at the money he's going to throw at this ridiculously overpriced project that won't dent his pockets or amount to shit, and I'll do what I do, play the cast aside victim. I'll leave the rest up to you."

"Oh good god, Fi. Quit being a martyr. What do you have to lose? Put it all on the table for once in your life and stop running. You are not an orphan on the street any longer. You are not the waif you think yourself to be. You are not Ewan's biological sister even. Hell, you weren't even raised together after his parents split. The truth is, you both were pawns in a selfish game his parents played. Fi, it's time for you to come to terms with who you are and who you are not. Screw what you think society dictates. Go after what you desire. What you deserve."

Holding her breath, Brigid prayed that Fiona would proclaim her love for Ewan, who was the apparent subject of the beautiful woman's heart. Instead, it sounded like Fiona stood. Brigid peeked around the tree.

"My flight leaves at nine in the morning. Mr. Rafferty said he'd drive me. Goodnight, Michael."

With that, Fiona strode from the room leaving both Michael and Brigid, who continued to peer from around the tree, to watch her go.

Brigid wanted to master that exit, she thought to herself. Fiona didn't stub her toe, trip or embarrass herself. Complete poise and restraint.

Michael exhaled slowly, running his hands through his hair, rubbing his aching neck. He was concerned for Fiona. Having lost his parents too, he innately understood the struggles Fiona experienced and her struggle with self-worth, although she masked it well enough over the years. Michael also lived with the ache he knew Fiona was experiencing. It was a void that neither of them believed could be filled. The emptiness could drive a person to insanity—or at the very least, to a place where they no longer knew themselves.

Brigid sat opposite of Michael with her back against the tree, her knees pulled up, as she quietly wrapped her arms around them, resting her chin on the soft material of her leggings. She thought of all she heard Fiona and Michael share in confidence. A new understanding and respect replaced the misconceived conceptions she made of the porcelain doll, Fiona.

Porcelain was delicate. So fragile, that the slightest stress could crack its beauty, that much was true, although, the process of becoming porcelain meant it came under firing not once, but twice, to become so beautiful. Perhaps humans were created the same way. Brigid made a mental note, knowing what she must do come morning. She rested her back against the tree as she made her plan.

Michael, exhausted from all the day's drama, took a long drink from the beer he held and leaned back against the matching chaise opposite Brigid. A peaceful silence filled the room. Brigid and Michael were at ease with their solitude as they each basked in the warm space bathed in starlight.

"Why does Ethan call you Sprite?"

Brigid's eyes grew big with surprise. She inhaled deeply, shaking her head, wondering how Michael knew she was there.

She smiled. Michael smiled too, thinking of the *hellcat*-kitten who was hidden opposite of him, already having surmised it just another innocent accident, when it came to the enchanting Brigid Rafferty.

"I fell asleep on the chaise. I didn't know what to do."

Michael prompted again, "Why does he call you, Sprite?"

"I tried to tell you both I was here," Brigid sounded distressed.

Michael chuckled.

"Why does he call you Sprite?" Michael pressed.

"Fiona needs you Doctor MacShane."

"Michael," was all he said.

"I could tell Fiona feels lost and scared. I could hear it in her voice. I know that plea."

"Isn't Sprite an American drink?"

Brigid laughed.

"I suppose it is."

It was refreshing to hear the mysterious whimsy of this woman's laugh. Michael wanted more of this light-hearted banter to continue. "Why does Ethan call you Sprite?"

"Fine. I'll tell you. When I was little, I would run barefoot through the property. You see, I've always hated shoes. Feeling the connection with earth under my feet was a love my mom and I shared. Anyway, Dad would always try to make me wear shoes."

"And having to wear shoes upset you?" Michael teased.

"No, not shoes so much, but the thought of harming another soul," Brigid said almost reverently.

"Do tell, how does wearing shoes hurt others?"

Brigid could almost see his eyes twinkle from the other side of the oak.

She went on more confidently, "You see, the Wee Folk run through our land, and they live and play all around our house and fields, but near the pond mostly. Ever since I was a small girl, we've been friends. They take care of our home, yews, and property," Brigid said in a lilting tone.

"So, even as a young girl, I knew if I had shoes on my feet, I could step on one of them without knowing it. They move with lightning speed, but of course, I didn't know that at the time," Brigid said as if it were obvious.

"Of course," Michael murmured.

"So, one day, Dad saw me racing through the meadow. I was quite tiny back then, my hair much redder than it is now," Brigid added as if this were important.

"Mmm, I see," Michael interjected.

"Well, when I saw my dad, I ran to him and threw myself into his arms, as I would back then. He said I ran so fast, he could barely see me, and that I reminded him of one of the free-spirited Sprites my mom would describe back in Ireland. The name stuck, I guess."

For some reason, Brigid didn't feel strange or uncomfortable. It felt natural to tell Michael something personal about herself.

"You know, there is another explanation of Sprites. Would you like to hear mine?" Michael asked.

Her heart pounded wildly in her chest.

"Sure," she said a little too breathy.

"Well, Sprites were once believed to be the figment of the imagination. Red streaks of light, flashing ever so briefly in the sky, and then—gone. Leaving the beholder to question if what they witnessed was real, or if the magic they experienced when seeing the flash, was ever even there," Michael revealed to Brigid in his intoxicatingly slow cadence.

The air filled with innuendos and unspoken words.

Brigid silently pleaded with the man on the other side of the tree to continue to talk to her in his soft, lazy, Scottish brogue.

"Once the red flash was gone, a person could drive themselves crazy, looking for it, and thinking about the momentary beauty they witnessed."

Brigid whispered, "Are the Sprites you talk about real?"

"Oh, it seems, they are very real, very magical, and very elusive. I wouldn't have believed it myself until I had proof," Michael said in a way that had Brigid instantly asking, "Proof, Doctor MacShane?"

"Michael," he said a bit too intimately for someone she barely knew. Brigid ignored the fact that her head called her a liar when in her heart, it felt like she was coming home.

She concluded, she must have hit her head just as Fiona had suggested earlier. It was the only explanation as to why she let her emotions sweep her away in this seeming fantasy. Brigid wanted to stay right here, with this man, locked in their private conversation forever.

"You see, I realized today, Sprites are real—not just the flashes of light in the sky, one wonders if they truly saw," Michael added intimately. He murmured, almost as if he spoke to himself, "One literally sprang up before my eyes today, and I'm not about to pretend any longer that what I saw and felt was imagined—as I did years ago."

Brigid was sure there was a double meaning here too, but what it was, she could not be entirely sure.

Maybe a minute, or perhaps five had passed, when Brigid heard the floorboards creak. He was leaving.

Brigid felt an ache she couldn't explain if she tried. Clenching her arms tighter around her knees, she attempted to keep the tears at bay and her emotions buried.

"I'll see you in Scotland, *mo ghrá*."

With that, he left.

34

"What has you up and out before the birds child?" Malachi's baritone voice rung out as Brigid waved hello.

"Couldn't sleep."

It was strange, Brigid thought, how much could happen seemingly overnight.

"I needed to talk with you."

"Sit, let's visit," Malachi said, as he invited Brigid over to the tree swing.

She lowered herself and began to sway slowly back and forth.

Brigid jumped right in. "Well, the last twenty-four hours have been eventful. I was offered a job in Scotland—for a year. Oh, and I think I'm head over heels in love with a man I barely know who could potentially become my boss. The worst part about this is that I want to take the position in Scotland, but I feel guilty for even thinking about leaving Dad alone. Mal, I don't know if I could say goodbye to you again, either."

"Well, that is a lot happening all at once. Tell me about Scotland, child," he urged.

Brigid began to share the story from start to finish of the circumstances in which she met Michael. Malachi listened intently. Soon, she was telling him about sitting under the tree in the living room the night before and how her heart ached when Michael left the room.

"He said something as he turned to go Mal, in Scottish or Gaelic, but I don't know what it meant, I almost felt like it was some private joke or something," Brigid told her friend.

"This young man sounds like he came a long way to find you, child, I doubt there was a joke at your expense. Do you recall what he said? Maybe I can help you," Malachi offered.

"I wish I could. He said it so softly, almost like maybe he hadn't meant for me to hear."

"Time has a way of sorting everything out child, but the one thing I know for certain is that your father would never want, nor need your pity. He and your mother have always given you wings to fly, have they not? He would not clip those wings at such a pivotal time in your life."

In a softer tone, Malachi added, "You know in your heart, I feel the same way."

Brigid knew her friend spoke the truth.

"I had a dream about Mom last night."

"Was it a dream?"

"I'm not sure, that's the other reason I wanted to talk to you. To ask your opinion."

"Tell me about it child."

"Well, we were back in Ireland. It's where I had my first encounter with the Priestess. It was the day Mom told us she had cancer. I forgot most of it, but last night, I remembered parts of what happened. I distinctly remember Mom saying she was willing to go ahead and help me and Dad get the YBC ready. There was more—something about Dad and his destiny, but I can't recall the words again. I do remember her saying, *This is where the fun really starts.* It's not the first time I heard her say that in the last forty-eight hours, so I kinda feel like it was my subconscious working stuff out," Brigid reasoned.

"Or?" Malachi challenged.

"My gut tells me it was her confirming what she whispered in the wind the other night. In the dream, all these images passed before my eyes. It was like watching an old film reel in black and white. I feel like I saw some kind of instructions or equations, but I got frustrated and woke up because I couldn't figure it all out," Brigid finished.

"Maybe it is not the right time to have all the answers. Maybe you were offered an invitation, and more shall be revealed. Perhaps you are merely to ask for the next best step and then proceed accordingly," Malachi replied.

"Maybe. Do you think it has to do with me staying in Oregon or going to Scotland?"

"Perhaps, child, but promise me whatever you decide, you will not make choices based out of fear. Your father will be fine, and so will I. It is our greatest joy knowing you are happy," Malachi assured her.

Brigid nodded her head. An alarm on her phone began to ping.

"Oh no, it's almost seven. I gotta go!" She jumped up and brushed herself off.

Out of the corner of her eye, she saw Turlough.

"When did you get here?"

"Just arrived for a little visit with my dear friend Malachi just a few moments ago Brigid Ann. It's good to see you are well," the crane said as he bobbed his head.

"I wish I had time to sort this out fellas, but I gotta get back to the house." She waved goodbye and was off at a steady jog.

As if on cue, she saw Ewan up ahead, in black running shorts and a plain white tee shirt jogging at a leisurely pace. It was easy for Brigid to catch up to him, as she was already in her running shoes.

"Ewan, wait up," she called.

Seeing Brigid approach, he waved and gave her a friendly nod. Soon the two set steady pace side by side as they headed towards the house.

"Lucky I ran into you. No pun intended! I have a favor, Ewan," she smiled brightly glancing towards him.

"A favor, huh? Well, sure, if a can lass. What'll it be?"

"Dad and I have a meeting at nine a.m that he forgot about, and I was wondering if you wouldn't mind driving Fiona to the airport? Dad was supposed to take her, but we can't miss this meeting. The airport isn't far from here, and you could take one of our cars if you wanted. I feel terrible for asking." Brigid tried to sound sincere.

"You're asking a lot, lass," he said in mock horror. It'll cost you one day," Ewan said with a chuckle.

Brigid nodded her head and laughed, "Ah Ewan, you may be owing me," she said with a wink as she ran off ahead of him.

35

Michael spent a restless night, dreaming about a woman with long flowing hair, whose open and calm gaze reminded him of the water off the island of Taransay. He slept through his alarm the next morning, something that would greatly surprise anyone who knew him. He willed the visions to continue while he kayaked through the chain of islands in search of a woman who called out to him. Michael paddled towards the sound of her urgent plea—to rescue her from some unknown danger, but he woke drenched in sweat before he could take hold of her reaching hand.

Michael was grateful that he alone knew how the night's events shook him to his core, especially when he realized the face of the woman he was searching for, was that of Brigid Rafferty.

"Oh God," he groaned.

At that moment, Michael knew he was in trouble. The night before he called Brigid *my love*. He silently prayed she didn't understand his term of endearment that somehow spilled from his lips. Chills ran down his spine. It was not the first time he had the dream or vision of the woman with turquoise eyes. Walking into the bathroom, Michael turned on the faucet, filled his hands with cold water, and splashed it on his face. He stared at his reflection in the mirror.

"Good lord MacShane, you're going mad," he scolded the image staring back at him.

"*Wee Folk*? She thinks that's something unusual? I could tell Brigid Rafferty a story or two," he grumbled.

Michael's brows slowly knit together, as a soft skeptical grin replaced the scowl. "You could tell her man. She'd get it. She wouldn't doubt you," he tried to convince the silent figure who stood opposite of him.

Michael dried his face and brushed his teeth. Finding his mood improving, he began to whistle as he dressed in faded jeans and a simple button-up shirt which he left untucked.

Thinking he could finally share his story with someone else, Michael felt as if a lifelong weight was suddenly lifting off his shoulders. Since his childhood, he carried a memory or whatever one would call it, of himself as a Scottish Highlander. If he was completely honest, Michael *remembered* his life as a Clan Chief.

He had never questioned it as a child. His parents and later his grandparents never doubted or told him otherwise. So, for many years he naturally assumed it to be true that once in a long-ago lifetime he was a revered leader of a powerful clan.

As Michael grew older, he learned, not everyone believed as he did. His innocence was shattered the day a group of classmates teased him mercilessly. It was then that Michael began using his fists and silently began to bury the Highlander in the dark recess of his mind. Not long after, Helen and Alistair took Michael out of his traditional school and helped him accelerate his education. Eventually, he forgot everything his memories told him to be true.

That was until he saw Brigid Rafferty sprawled out before him on a university hallway floor in Ireland. Michael clearly remembered his intake of breath as the young woman looked up in embarrassment at him with her strange colored eyes. Michael remembered being aware of Fiona's hold on his arm, but it was Brigid's eyes that he felt grip his soul. She was utterly transparent in her vulnerability, and at that moment, Michael saw flashbacks from his life as a Highlander.

His mood turned somber again, remembering the pain of a lifetime ago. He pictured Gillian, his beloved—savagely killed before his eyes. Michael easily recalled his life as a powerful MacDonell, yet was powerless in her death, and how his sworn enemy, Lars, had plunged an arrow into her heart. The once free-spirited woman who ran laughing barefoot through the hills, lay crumpled in a heap on the earth she loved.

As a small boy, Michael would sometimes wake in a cold sweat from the nightmare, calling for his mother. The dream always ended the same. Gillian lay in MacDonnell's arms, slipping away—with a solemn promise to find him, someday, somehow, and they would have the life they dreamed of.

"Look for my ribbon, my love. I promise I will find you."

Trapped in the last, fitful sleeping memories, Michael would hear Gillian's final, haunting gasp of air.

"I command you to live, Gillian. You must!" MacDonnell whispered as he ordered her to take another breath.

She refused him that request and died with her turquoise eyes fixed upon him. Gillian was gone. He was helpless to save her. With all his rage and grief and one last battle cry, MacDonnell lunged at his enemy.

The coward who had taken his beloved's life died before he could ready another arrow. MacDonell's spike hit its mark as his enemy perished in a heap at Gillian's feet. MacDonnell disfigured what was left of Lars and left him for the animals. Then he carried his love several miles to his fortress. He held her lifeless body close as he trudged along in pain. A guttural cry escaped his lips as he kissed her face. It was then that Michael, in his youth, would wake with a startled shout.

Staring now at his trembling hands, Michael tried to shake the memory which felt as fresh as the day it happened lifetimes ago. "Get a grip MacShane," but his memories continued to flood his mind. He thought about the previous night as Brigid appeared in front of his SUV. In the darkness, he mistook her muddied face and tangled hair as bloodied. In that moment she was not Brigid— but his Gillian.

Michael remembered every detail. The pain as real as if it happened only moments ago. He forced himself to shake the images from his mind inhaled the strong aroma of coffee drifting down the hall. He could spend no more energy reliving a past from a lifetime ago. His feet led him to the kitchen, where he saw Brigid sitting on the island swinging her feet back and forth with a bowl of oatmeal in her hands.

His pulse raced, seeing her with her hair tied up in a messy ponytail. It was apparent from her attire and face that still slightly glowed that she had just come in from a run.

"Good morning son, hope you slept well," Ethan said as he walked over to to the cupboard, reaching for a mug and handing it to Michael.

Some foreign emotion tugged at Michael. *Son.*

Brigid dipped her head and took a bite of her cereal as she peeked up to steal a glance at the man she had such an intimate talk with just hours before.

"Hungry?" Ethan asked.

A wicked grin flashed briefly across his face. Brigid blushed deeply. However, before Michael could answer, there was a tap on the kitchen door. Emma walked in without waiting for a reply, calling out a cheery hello. She stopped short of bumping into Michael as he stood close to where she entered.

"Dang," Emma gushed at the striking figure of a man before her. Her blush rivaled Brigid's.

"I mean, excuse me. I didn't expect..." Emma tried again, looking to Brigid for help, but Brigid looked to her friend and mouthed, "*See, I told you so.*"

Michael offered Emma a friendly handshake.

"Michael MacShane," he said.

"Oh pleasure to finally meet you face to face Doctor, I'm Emma Daily," she shuffled her messenger bag from one arm to the other and grasped his hand in return.

"Please call me Michael," he said, stepping aside to allow Emma to enter.

"It's good to put a face to what prompted this incredibly exciting endeavor, Miss Daily."

"Call me, Emma, Please. It's an honor to meet you, and I know we are all so very thrilled the Rafferty's work caught your attention. I'm sure you're already finding out this is truly an amazing family!" Emma's words exuded love and protectiveness for the Raffertys.

"I thought we had an appointment later today at the University, Emma?"

"Oh, we do. I didn't expect to see you here," Emma said, looking pointedly at Brigid.

"That's my fault, so much going on all at once. Sorry Em. Um, Dad, I asked Emma to stop by, and I asked Ewan to take Fiona to the airport for you because Emma only has a small window of time this week, and we both wanted to talk to you about something."

Michael leaned towards Brigid casually. "Clever ruse. You just wanted to give Ewan and Fi time," he said under his breath. Brigid shrugged her shoulders noncommittally.

Emma raised a curious eyebrow in her friend's direction, then seeing a perfect opening, began to prod Brigid into making her next move. "Well Michael, as it seems, your timing is probably just as perfect as can be. Besides, my proposal for Ethan can wait."

"Sounds intriguing, but then this whole visit has been unlike any other," he said to no one in particular.

"I do believe Brigid here has some news of her own you might want to hear first, Ethan."

Brigid all but dropped her bowl on the island as she jumped down. "Emma," she scolded her friend.

Emma set her bag down, ignoring Brigid's indignant stance and tone.

"Any coffee left Ethan?" Emma asked sweetly.

"Yep, just brewed a fresh pot," he said, as Emma meandered over to the coffee maker pouring herself a steaming cup.

Ethan casually went to stand by Brigid's side.

"You know Sprite, your mom used to do that," he said as he leaned down and quietly spoke into her ear.

Brigid's head sprang up. "Do what Dad?"

Placing his hands on her shoulders, he replied, "Your mom would bite her lip, and wring her hands, just as you're doing when she had something difficult she had to tell me."

Brigid closed her eyes, willing herself not to cry.

Ethan continued in a steady and assured voice, "Sprite, I am going to make this easy for us all." He spoke just a little louder, knowing all in the room would hear.

"I want you to go to Scotland, Brigid. The truth is, I'd be disappointed if you didn't. Raffertys have never cowered away from their dreams or responsibilities. I expect no less from my only child. This is what your mother would want too."

With that, he kissed her cheek.

"Emma, why don't you walk with me to the goat pen, and you can tell me what's on your mind," Ethan said to Emma who promptly followed him to the door.

He gave a long and considering look at Doctor Michael MacShane as if sizing him up. Having made up his mind, Ethan gave a nod of approval to Michael and walked out the door with Emma.

"Brig?" Emma asked with concern.

"I got it from here, Em."

"I know you do, and you're going to do great things in the world, my friend," she said, leaving with Ethan.

The air hung full of possibilities. Michael hoped Brigid didn't read his thoughts as he locked eyes in such a personal way. His heart was pounding so loud he was afraid if Brigid spoke just yet he wouldn't be able to hear her. He said a silent prayer. Please, *mo ghrá* come home with me.

As if to answer the unspoken invocation, Brigid smiled an innocent, trusting, and confident smile at the man who made her stomach flutter. "Doctor MacShane…"

"Michael," he challenged her.

She nodded her concession. "Michael, I would be honored to join your team if the offer is still on the table."

Michael stood, in what he hoped would appear to be a casual non-affected manner and walked to the sink to buy himself some time. He rinsed his cup and placed it in the dishwasher as he'd seen Emma and Ethan do. Brigid watched with keen interest as Michael turned to face her briefly, then walked to the door. Her heart felt like a drum.

Opening the door, Michael was grateful for the burst of fresh air that greeted him. With his back now to hers, Brigid thought he might leave without saying a word.

Michael knew he must leave, and quickly, knowing if he stayed a moment longer, he couldn't be responsible for what would happen next. "I asked Fiona to book you a ticket before she left. Your flight leaves tomorrow morning. Pack warm clothes," he threw over his shoulder as he quietly closed the door behind him. Finally outside, he exhaled, then began to whistle as he sauntered toward the rented car, allowing his smile to widen.

Inside the Rafferty's cozy kitchen, Brigid stood on a braided rug from Ireland, peering after Michael from the window above the sink as he walked to his vehicle.

"This could be fun mom," Brigid said to the woman she felt by her side.

36

"Sprite, I don't want you to be worrying about me. It's time I start living life again, and I mean it. This project, our project, in Scotland, is part of this Legacy you and your mom talk about. You need to grab this opportunity."

"I know, and I'm excited, but Dad, I'm just as happy to hear you're ready to start rebuilding too. It's what Mom wants for us both."

"And that is what we will do. You'll leave in the morning, and I will get back to the business of running this ranch. Emma will become the new CEO of your mom's company, and come the holidays I'll travel to Scotland and Ireland to see you, Maddie and Connor. It's just a blink of the eye, Sprite."

"And I'll be back the following spring for Emma and Sam's wedding. I know they wanted to elope, but I'm glad the Daily's convinced them otherwise. Emma and Sam deserve to celebrate their big day in style."

"So, it's settled."

"Yes. It's settled. Except I still need to go tell Mal goodbye."

"I know that's never easy for you, Sprite. Why don't you go see him now, and later I'll take you to dinner to celebrate your new job. Call Emma and Sam. Ask them to join us."

"What would I do without you, Dad?"

Ethan kissed Brigid's head as she hugged him fiercely.

"Go, before I start getting all sappy."

Putting on a brave smile, Brigid swallowed the lump in her throat as she greeted Malachi and told him of her plans.

"I'll await your safe return, and for you to share all your joyous news with me. As you know, Turlough will bring me updates, and we can still communicate through him. It will be as if we were never apart, dear child."

Even Malachi had a way of renewing Brigid's confidence that she was making the right choice and that goodbye was not forever. "I like knowing that. Plus, it'll make Turlough feel even more important, won't it? I think he secretly wants your approval. Maybe in some way, we all do. I will miss you, dearly."

She hugged her friend tightly around his trunk. He dipped and swished his leaves gently in return, brushing softly against Brigid's back.

"I'll be home soon, but I will think of you every day. Don't let the squirrels get on your last nerve, and Mal, don't forget I love you."

"And I love you, dear child."

With a final pat on the deeply wrinkled creases of Malachi's trunk, and a sanguine heart, Brigid left her treasured friend, ready for whatever the next year would bring.

37

Scotland

"Once again, we thank you for flying with us," a chirpy attendant announced.

Brigid was eager to stand on solid ground after her long flight, but she quickly found her jet lag would have to wait. Seeing a sign with her name in bold letters being held up, Brigid walked towards the woman holding it. She tried to ignore the disappointment of not being met by Michael, but by Lena, a tall, and rather pale looking woman.

"It's nice to meet you, Lena, but I thought Doctor MacShane would be picking me up," Brigid said a little too quickly.

"He's been detained. Is this a problem, ma'am?"

"No, of course not," Brigid assured the thirty-something-year-old woman.

Lena thrust her glasses up on her crinkled nose—far too close to her eyes. Brigid wanted to gently reach out and pull them back to a natural position but smiled warmly all the same.

"I see you have your luggage. Shall we?" Lena asked, pointing towards a waiting car that whisked the two women off to Brigid's new flat where Lena gave her a quick tour of the tiny space.

"The driver will be back to pick you up at seven in the morning for your first day. Then after that, you can decide if you'd like to take the local transit or walk. The hospital isn't far from here at all. I've taken the liberty of stocking your fridge. Let me know if you'll be needing anything."

"Thank you, Lena. I've never had an assistant before. Also, thanks for making me feel welcome."

And, so Brigid's journey began.

There was much to learn, and on most nights Brigid would fall into bed exhausted, yet pleased that her contributions seemed to be genuinely appreciated. A month had come and gone, and still, there was no word from the elusive Michael MacShane. Brigid all but gave up on seeing him or Ewan until the day she walked into her office and was greeted by a tornado of energy Lena unleashed.

"Good, you're here! You'll be on time for his visit," Lena said by way of greeting as she rushed to a long metal table and scrunched her glasses up high on her nose while shuffling papers from one pile to another unnecessarily.

Brigid fixed a practiced look of neutrality to cover up the excitement she could feel swelling up. It was about time, yet she wasn't sure how she felt at that moment. Nervous? Happy?

Her assistant quickly dashed Brigid's hope, by saying, "I haven't seen Ewan or the chemist—whom I believe you've met a time or two? Anyway, they plan to review the data gathered to date. They'll both be here throughout the week," Lena replied.

"Oh," Brigid replied lamely. "When do they arrive?"

"Today—anytime now. Should prove invaluable moving forward," Lena blinked rapidly, making her glasses bob up and down.

Brigid walked to a microscope, dipped her head, and studied whatever was before her in the petri dish with intense concentration. Lena continued to rearrange files at her already pristine desk.

"Is everything all right, Brigid? You look a little pale."

"Yes, everything's fine. Nervous, I guess. I hope they like what we've been doing."

It was late in the afternoon when Lena announced Ewan was on his way. Moments later there was a light tap on the door, and without preamble, Fiona appeared, followed by Ewan. Fiona gave Brigid an unexpected smile. It was bright, warm, and if Brigid was not mistaken, friendly.

"You're a chemist, Fiona?" Brigid blurted out by way of greeting. She was instantly ashamed, and it showed on her face. Fiona waved her off as if it were nothing.

"Don't worry. I deserved that. However, I received my doctorate in chemistry a little over a year ago. Michael and Ewan aren't the only overachievers in the group—and now we've added you to our little list," she stated without the edge Brigid would have expected.

Brigid bit the inside of her cheek to refrain from another lapse in etiquette. Ewan stood behind Fiona, bigger than life, and beaming with a fullness and contentment of a man in love. Brigid's assumptions were soon confirmed when Ewan looked at Fiona and she at him.

"Hey lass," Ewan boomed as he plopped down on a nearby chair. "How's my favorite redhead?"

"Hello, Ewan. It's so good to see some familiar faces finally," Brigid beamed.

Ewan cocked his head to the side as if he was confused by her greeting. "What do you mean? Is our old MacShane behaving poorly towards you since you came to our bonnie country?" he asked in a lazy drawl.

Brigid gave him an owl-eyed blink that said she did not understand his meaning. "Ewan, I've yet to see Doctor MacShane. I assumed there was a delay, or he was with you. Am I mistaken?" Brigid sounded genuinely baffled.

"You mean today," Fiona slowly added, as if talking to an addled child.

Both Fiona and Ewan took notice of Brigid's perplexed expression.

"He's in Scotland?" Brigid strained to keep her voice natural.

"In his office. At least that's where we left him earlier," Ewan said sounding just as confused as Brigid felt.

"How long has he been here?" Brigid inquired trying to appear reasonable but failed.

"Well, I don't know about today, but a little over two months— just like you."

Fiona and Ewan exchanged puzzled looks.

"He's been here, working in the hospital the whole time?" Brigid implored, one octave too high.

"For heaven's sake, the man's office is just down and around the corner from yours. How is it you have not yet seen him? You should be working side by side," Ewan sounded exasperated.

"Dr. MacShane corresponds through emails," Lena added politely.

"Lena, why have you not informed me Doctor MacShane has been working here?"

Lena turned away, not wanting to meet Brigid's questioning stare. An eery silence came over the room. Brigid's head became dizzy. Lena remained with her back to Brigid.

Ewan was the first to recover as a slow grin began to wash across his face. Fiona was soon to follow. Brigid's eyes narrowed to cat-eyed slits.

"Where is he? Where *exactly* is his office?" Brigid asked a bit too calmly.

Fiona spoke first, with a knowing gleam in her eyes.

"Michael's office is to the right, then down the hall. It's the second door on the left and looks oddly like a broom closet. I would imagine you will find him in quite a foul mood at his desk," Fiona supplied with a Cheshire Cat grin.

"That explains a lot," Ewan said to Fiona while sending a wicked grin Brigid's way.

"Would you like us to walk you there lass? We wouldn't mind a bit, would we, Fi?" Ewan asked quite solicitously.

"I think I can manage, thank you," Brigid said slowly.

Oh, she'd find him all right, Brigid thought, suddenly fueled with a wave of slow-burning anger. She took a deep breath as she tightly secured a lid on the petri dish she was feigning interest in.

"I'm forgetting myself. After all, you are here to see the lab results to date, yes? Let me grab my laptop, and I'll let you both have a peek. It's all quite promising if you ask me," Brigid's professional facade was neatly in place, but both Ewan and Fiona knew Brigid was not as calm as she appeared.

Fiona gave Brigid a respectful look of approval with a decided nod of her head. "I like you, Brigid Rafferty. I hope we'll take the time to get to know each better in the coming months."

Brigid assessed Fiona in much the same way.

"Thank you, Fiona..." Then, Brigid laughed, searching her memory for Fiona's last name. "I confess, I don't know your last name."

"Oh well that's quite all right, I'm just getting used to it as well," Fiona said mysteriously.

"Excuse me?" Brigid blurted out.

"Oh," she said as she held up her dainty left hand which showed off a simple diamond ring. "We just got married. Last week."

Ewan stood and placed a possessive arm around his new bride's waist.

Fiona glowed. "You're the first to hear our news. Michael was too sour, and I didn't want him to spoil all the fun for me. I couldn't wait to tell someone. I'm sure this comes as no surprise as our brief encounters have been less than cordial—but, I have a short list of friends." Fiona mocked herself without a trace of self-pity.

"Well, congratulations! I guess I didn't realize you two were—close," Brigid said in a casual tone looking at the happy couple.

"Let's just say, someone gave us a little shove in the right direction," Ewan added.

Brigid smiled, handing Fiona her laptop and Ewan the printed financials accounts he asked for.

"I'll leave you to look things over for a bit. If you two will excuse me, I have a quick errand," Brigid announced as she retrieved a file from her desk.

"Mmm," Fiona replied lost in the data, but Ewan chimed in, "Second door on the left." His wicked smile was back, but Brigid ignored it as she opened the door.

Fiona reached over and playfully smacked his arm.

"What?" he asked innocently, "I'm returning the favor!"

Brigid blushed at Ewan's unnerving smugness but continued down the hall stopping at the unmarked office.

"It does look like a broom closet," Brigid muttered as she tapped on the door.

"Come in," a deep male voice called from inside.

Brigid knew the owner of that voice. She stood tall and took a deep, steadying breath. With her brightest smile, Brigid swooshed cheerfully in the room catching the surprised look on Michael's face. Without waiting, she strolled purposefully up to his desk as if she had done so a hundred times, then placed a thick file down in front of him.

She smiled sweetly and said, "Doctor MacShane, I need your original signature on pages thirty-two and forty-seven, and I think you'll agree with the findings on the last page. If you do, initial here. The YBC results from last week are particularly exciting. That's on pages fifty-seven and fifty-eight, I believe."

Brigid turned, hoping to match the exit she once watched Fiona make. Giving Michael no chance to respond, she casually strolled out of his office, quietly closing the door.

Doctor Michael MacShane was as intrigued yet pricked by Brigid's dismissal of him. He closed his eyes and replayed the thirty-second interaction. Then, thinking back to the conversation he and Brigid had regarding Sprites, he laughed. "This could be fun, *mo ghrá*."

38

"Brigid!" Fiona called out, as she breezed down the hospital corridor. Brigid waited patiently for Fiona to catch up.

"What happened with you and Michael?" Fiona asked, seeing no reason to be coy.

"Let's just say Dr. MacShane, and I have a new understanding."

"I see. Well, I was waiting for you because Ewan and I wanted to invite you to dinner tonight."

"Oh, I doubt I'd be outstanding company after today's fiasco," Brigid said, but Fiona merely scoffed.

"Well, we did hope to go over some of your findings, but I suppose I could make an appointment with your assistant, if you prefer."

"I'm sorry, Fiona. I'm behaving poorly. I would like to have dinner with you and Ewan. I've wanted to talk about the clinical trial, but also to get to know you both better. Admittedly, you and I got off on the wrong foot. I don't have any friends over here—I better not alienate myself from the two people who do want to hang out with me." Brigid said, giving a self-deprecating laugh.

Fiona gifted Brigid a bright smile.

"Meet us at seven-thirty. I left the restaurant information with the woman in desperate need of a stylist, just in case you were available to make it."

"You mean, Lena?"

Fiona smiled, pleased with herself. She had no doubt Brigid would be joining them.

"Seven-thirty," Brigid parroted back, nodding her head.

"Oh, and Brigid, it might not hurt if you admitted you're in love with Michael. The in-between stuff is a waste of time. Trust me on this one!" Having nothing else to say, Fiona sashayed away, leaving Brigid's ears to ring with her parting words.

"Could this day get any stranger?" Brigid sighed as she reentered her office where the rest of the day went on without any more surprises or interruptions. It was after five when Brigid finally looked at the clock.

"Oh geez, I'm gonna be late. I wanted to go home and clean up first," she said to Lena, who was clicking away on her laptop.

"Go, I'll finish here. I can lock up. If you leave now, you'll make it in plenty of time," Lena assured her boss.

"Thanks, Lena," Brigid said as she grabbed her purse and sweater, hurrying off with a quick goodbye. She rushed to get ready, surprised at how much she was looking forward to some adult company —not that Brigid minded hearing Lena chat about her cats and their daily antics, but for the most part, Brigid remained an unintentional loner since arriving in Scotland. She dearly missed Malachi, and it was days like today Brigid became the most homesick. She pushed her melancholy thoughts away as she brushed her hair.

The restaurant was a short walk away from her home, and she arrived promptly at seven-thirty. Looking around at the upscale establishment. It wasn't difficult to spot Ewan and Fiona. The restaurant had less than ten tables, and Fiona quickly caught Brigid's eye, waving her over with a gesture Brigid thought to be a Queen receiving her subject.

Waving back, she headed towards the couple, stopping short, seeing a third person seated with his back to her, and a single empty chair directly across from him. Brigid knew that wavy head of hair. She dreamt of running her fingers through it way too many times. It was too late to turn tail and run—besides Brigid didn't want to. She knew she looked good in her blush-colored dress that hit just above her knees.

She was suddenly feeling *sassy*, as her mother would say as she greeted the table with her brightest smile. It was clear Michael had not expected her either from the look on his face, but he quickly recovered and followed Ewan's suit, standing to greet Brigid.

"Nice dress Brigid," Fiona said approvingly, although Brigid was sure Fiona was surprised that she hadn't shown up in a flour sack.

"I didn't know you'd be here," the words fell out of Michael's mouth, and he instantly regretted his tone.

"Nor I—you," she smiled sweetly.

Ewan added, with his now predictable wicked grin, "Oh, I thought we mentioned it. Didn't you mention it, Fi?"

"Hmmm, must have slipped my mind," Fiona remarked, sounding bored.

Michael held the chair while Brigid sat down.

Fiona crooked a finger to call over a nearby waiter.

"Champagne all around please," she told the man.

"I feel like celebrating," she told her companions.

"And what might we be celebrating Fi," Michael asked with droll interest.

"Love. I feel like celebrating love."

She flashed her wedding band at Michael, whose face instantly softened into something resembling brotherly love.

"Oh Fi, good girl lass," he said as he reached over the table, taking her left palm in both of his, and warmly kissed her hand.

"Hey mate, I'll thank you to be leaving the kissin' of my bride to me," Ewan elbowed his oldest and closest friend.

"It's about time you two wised up. Congratulations," Michael said and meant it.

Ewan's phone rang. He made a show of sounding interested, concerned, and dismissive all at the same time. The champagne arrived and was poured before the foursome just as Ewan clicked off the call.

"Perfect timing," he said as he downed his drink in a single toss of the fluted glass.

"Fi, that thing I thought might happen, just happened. We need to go."

Fiona, taking a slow, delicate sip of her imported golden bubbles, pondered Ewan's statement. She all but purred while drinking the last of her champagne. Slowly rising, she dabbed the sides of her cherry red lipstick with her linen napkin, then after dropping the cloth on the table, she walked away.

Brigid openly gaped at the woman who as she left. No goodbye. No apologies. She merely stood, turned, and walked away.

"Dang, she's good!" Brigid uttered to herself.

Michael muttered as he glared straight at Ewan, "Bloody hell."

Much to Michael's disapproval, Ewan laughed, as he also stood, tossing his napkin on the foodless table.

"Brigid, lass—we're even, and now the rest is up to you," he grinned broadly. To Michael, he added, "Carry on, mate, and quit being such an arse."

Michael stared at Brigid, and Brigid stared at her champagne flute.

"Bloody hell," Michael said again, downing the glass in his hand.

As if on cue, a waiter appeared. "Two fingers—whiskey, top shelf, neat, make it quick," Michael requested.

The server nodded as he hurried off to do his customer's bidding.

"Well Miss Rafferty, it appears we have been set up."

"Brigid," she said, looking directly at him, with a gleam in her eyes.

"I do believe you are right, Doctor MacShane, but why?"

"Michael," he responded, with the start of a twinkle in his eyes.

The waiter handed Michael the drink, and he made quick work of downing the dark liquid.

Brigid winced.

"Liquid courage, Michael? I wouldn't have thought it about you —until today that is."

The barb stung, and Michael was quiet for a moment. "I know I shouldn't feel like I owe you an explanation, but we both know I do."

Brigid gave him a nod that confirmed she thought so too, although, he did not notice any trace of judgment or disdain.

"Is it too soon to order another double?" Michael asked, somewhat playfully.

"I think you should order me dinner first. I was promised food, and I'm starving!"

Michael had the good graces to look embarrassed.

"Forgive me," he started to say, but the waiter interrupted.

"Shall I give you a little more time?"

"No, we'll order now," Michael replied.

There was only a moments pause after the waiter left the table. "Why'd you avoid me?" Brigid didn't see any point softening the question.

"Because, you scare the hell out of me, and I have a lot riding on this project. Ewan's sunk a lot of his personal capital into this study because he knows what it means to me. Fi can work anywhere, but she decided to stick with us. Brigid, quite honestly, I can't afford the distraction." He tried to read Brigid's reaction to no avail.

"Well, we have a problem, then don't we Michael," she said his name slowly.

"Because you scare the hell out of me too. You know we all have a lot riding on this project. So what do you propose we do?"

Several moments passed. Michael studied Brigid with deep interest, almost as if seeing her for the first time. Brigid didn't shy away and did her fair share of memorizing Michael's features.

The waiter arrived and placed their food before them.

"What does *moe graw* mean," she tested the words on her lips.

"Ah, you heard that, did you? Mo ghrá means *my love*, Brigid."

Much to Michael's surprise, the woman across from him gave little other reaction. He wondered if he should speak. Then, as if coming to a decision, Brigid broke the silently charged air.

"I use to have strange dreams when I was a child. There would be nights when I'd call out in the middle of the night, and my mom or dad would come racing into my room and find me soaked in sweat. They thought I was ill, but when I woke up, I would tell them how I was just killed. Of course, I was just a child, but in my dreams, it felt very real. You know?"

Michael nodded slowly. He knew very well what she meant.

"I was too young to know anything about romantic love, but I can still remember the physical ache in my heart as I would try to reach out and grab this wild warrior by his hand, but I couldn't." Brigid tried to keep her voice in check, but it caught all the same.

Michael reached out across the table, taking her hand that lay before him like an offering.

"Did the dream end there?"

"Sometimes. I remember waking up hearing the warrior call to me, like from inside a tunnel. I didn't understand the language, but in my dream, I remember promising him we'd find our way back to each other. I was too young to have such a vivid dream. It was rather traumatic. My friend, Malachi, always told me not to be afraid, as sometimes dream visits have different meanings. As the years went by, the dream faded. I hadn't thought about it for many years. Back at our house when you left the room, and you said mo ghrá, I knew I had heard those words before. When I fell asleep that night, I had the dream. The one I had as a child."

Brigid and Michael found themselves locked in a time and space of their own, where only the two of them existed. Brigid was afraid to move, yet quietly asked the man across from her, "Has the warrior in my dreams found me?"

Michael knew that once he spoke the words and all they implied, there could be no taking them back. He looked tenderly at Brigid and gave an almost imperceptible nod. With that nod of his head, he chose his future. "Aye, mo ghrá, it seems we have kept our promise to find each other."

Dinner was all but forgotten as the evening progressed.

"Michael, you were right to think this could become a distraction, but, what do you say, we merely put us on hold until we save the world?" she laughed.

"You're right of course, but if we make this pact, there's something I must do first before I can concentrate on anything else."

Without warning, Michael pulled Brigid to him in a slow exploring kiss that lingered and intensified. The connection between them had undeniable promise. Michael was the first to break away, knowing if he didn't do so now, he couldn't.

"Now do you see why I hid like a scared schoolboy?"

The connection Brigid was feeling with Michael was more potent than any word she could put her emotion to.

"Let's go, mo ghrá. We'll figure all this out later. Tomorrow I want you to meet some of the people who are participating in our study. I want you to see and hear their stories, and understand the Legacy you and your parents have set in motion. I want you to see it for yourself."

She took Michael's hand and followed him to his parked car. "I'm grateful for the opportunity. I haven't talked to anyone who has taken the YBC."

"One of the perks of testing off U.S soil."

Electric silence filled the car as they drove the short distance. So much had been revealed and there was still so much that lay before them. They both knew there was much to process, but their obligation to clinical study came first. Parking the car in front of Brownstone, Michael began to open his door.

Brigid stopped him.

"Please stay here. If you get out of this car, I can't be held responsible for what happens next."

She tried to sound playful, but Michael could not deny the intimacy he heard in her voice, understanding it was meant all for him. He leaned his head back on the headrest and closed his eyes.

"You better go now—and hurry," he said without opening his eyes.

Brigid smiled, quickly leaning over to kiss Michael's cheek. Just as quickly, she was gone.

39

"I heard you had quite an interesting conversation with some of the people in the study group. They all loved you, of course," Michael said as he walked down the hospital corridor with Brigid.

"Oh, Michael, these people are amazing and so brave. I don't know that I could go through what they have—hope I never have to find out. It was hard enough with my mom."

Michael nodded in understanding.

"They were fascinating people, and they all had a different reason for committing to the study. One man was there because of a promise he made to his wife of forty-six years. There was a daughter who was there because her parents begged her to be. So she's doing it for them. Kelsey, the one that has that engaging laugh, she told me her husband barely spoke to her because she chose to join the YBC trial instead of going the traditional route. I can see she doubts if she's made the right decision. One of the most fascinating stories is the man who blew everyone's socks off in the states by beating his cancer. He came here to reboot his body, as he says it."

"Ah, Brad? Yes, he's a remarkable success story. Hearing the patients perspectives, and journeys is one the reasons I wanted you to be here. I knew you'd get it, especially after your mother's unique experiences and choices. It's such a personal thing," Michael added.

"I have to admit, it brought up some stuff for me," Brigid confided.

"What kind of stuff?"

"Well, when I was still in Med School, I did a rotation in Oncology. There was this one particular patient that made quite an impression on me. Her name was Donna. She never came to treatments with anyone. No family, no friend, and I always wondered why. She was always pleasant yet quiet. I overheard her tell a patient in the next chair that God was her reason, and when the time came, she prayed her parents would be waiting to take her home to heaven. I admired her faith greatly, but there was a deep sadness about her. One day I saw her leaving the radiation room. She walked slowly—as if resigned. I asked her if she needed anything, but she just smiled, you know, one of the kinds that don't reach the eyes. As I was looking at her, I realized she wanted to *go home*, as she put it, and it wasn't sadness so much but peace with a choice."

Brigid looked at Michael.

"Go on. I want to hear this."

"Donna's eyes, they reminded me of someone today. They were a very intriguing bluish-gray. I remember Donna telling me she finished her last radiation treatment. I wished her well, and that was it. Later I found out she was only halfway through her treatment plan and refused further treatments. The burns from the radiation were more than she could take. She knew it was time to leave it in someone else's hands greater than her own. Watching her walk away that day, I knew I would devote myself to the YBC research and finding a cure for cancer that didn't ravage the body, mind, and spirit."

"Brigid, not that I disagree with you, but in my career, I have seen cancer patients and their families and loved ones become so much stronger, insightful, brave and more committed to life after undergoing surgeries, chemo, radiation, whatever we throw at them."

"I agree, but I believe we have the answer to taking away all the fear and pain that comes from traditional medicine. Isn't that what you've worked for too?"

"Of course, we just never want to discount the good—the miracles modern-day medicines and treatments currently provide."

"Of course you're right, it's just when I lost my mom, I was angry. I kept that part of my grief hidden for quite some time, and I guess I forget sometimes there is another side to the coin," Brigid confided.

"It's a sad reality that so many cancer patients deal with such insurmountable pain," Michael added.

"I agree. So, to circle back to today, when we were in visiting with our patients, there was this woman whom I was simply drawn to. Her name was Carin, and she has the most beautiful bluish-gray eyes I've ever seen. She was telling me about her family. She has a big family, Michael! She was inspired by them to do whatever she had to do. More than that, she had an inner light. I can't explain it, she shined from the inside out, if that makes sense. She did chemo and a round of brutal radiation. She stayed positive the whole time, telling me that she would do anything to rid her body, and her life, of the cancer invading her. She told me she has a lot of living yet to do. I don't know. It just made me think about how different the journey is for each person." Brigid became quiet.

"Brigid?" Michael questioned as they stopped walking.

"Sometimes, I still feel like my mom gave up, even though logically, I know she didn't. I know she did it her way because of her beliefs. Seriously, whose reasons and motivations matter more than the person diagnosed with cancer?" Brigid sounded frustrated.

"Do you think your mom made the wrong choice?"

"In separating degrees, my dad and I feel that mom didn't exhaust every possibility open to her, while Carin did. It just got me to thinking, what if my mom had been more like Carin? Doesn't that sound horrible?" she asked, wanting to look away.

Holding her gaze, Michael responded without hesitation.

"You're asking that of a highly educated, *prodigy* who still wants to kick his father's arse for a series of *stupid* mistakes. I'm certainly not one to judge how you're processing," he told her gently.

"There are so many ways to look at our situations with our parents. In the end, though, they all made choices based on what they knew or were feeling at the time."

"That's all any of us can do. Sometimes, when I miss my mom, like today, it just makes me all un-rational," Brigid shrugged.

Michael desperately wished he could take Brigid in his arms, right in the middle of the hospital. He could see by the vulnerable look on her face she would welcome the comfort. Taking a deep breath, Brigid was first to break the unspoken intimacy building between them.

"It's late, and you have that early morning consult, and I promised my dad I would Skype with him about some family business, so I guess we should call it a day."

"And what a day it's been mo ghrá."

Michael walked Brigid to the door where he briefly allowed his hand to rest upon hers, knowing this was the start of their new life together. There was no rush, only curiosity mixed with the excitement new love brings.

Leaning against the inside of the now closed apartment door, Brigid began to feel an intense clarity wash over her. "I understand now, Mom. None of this would be possible if you didn't make the choices you did. You lived your way, and are still here, helping us all forge our way into this beautiful and messy life. Thank you for leading me to Michael," Brigid said, wiping a stray tear from her cheek.

40

Ten months later

Brigid walked into her lab to see Lena waving loose sheets of paper in the air. "I thought you'd like to see these reports first thing."

"Good news or bad?" Brigid asked taking the pages from Lena who stared expectantly at her boss.

"Oh, my," Brigid said, slowly scanning the documents.

"Lena, Where's Doctor MacShane? Has he seen this?"

Lena shrugged her shoulders. "I'm not sure."

"Well, don't you have anything to say?"

"I have to find Michael," Brigid responded as she rushed past Lena.

"That's what I thought you'd say," Lena grumbled.

Brigid began to walk, then jog towards Michael's office. She slowed her pace just enough to turn the corner—and collide with the man she sought.

"Ah, mo ghrá, promise me you'll never stop doing this," he said intimately.

"Did you hear? Did you see the results?" Brigid asked breathlessly.

Reluctantly, Michael put Brigid at arm's length although his hand still lay possessively around her waist." I was coming to ask you the same thing, but I'm happy you ran into me first."

He gave her a quick wink.

Months of built-up tension hung between them. The results were now in, and in Brigid's mind, all bets were off. Feeling the possessive yet gentle hold of Michael's hand, she knew he felt the same way.

"Come with me."

Brigid laughed as she tried to keep up with his long strides.

"Where are we going?"

Michael said nothing as he led her to the parking lot. Opening his passenger car door for her, she stared up at him.

"You've snapped, haven't you?" Brigid playfully challenged.

Michael concluded he had no choice—leaning down he kissed Brigid before he shut the door.

Neither of them spoke as he easily navigated the Glasgow streets. It wasn't long before they reached their destination.

"Oh, what a lovely park," Brigid exclaimed.

"We walk from here. The road is closed ahead to vehicles."

Brigid contemplated Michael as he moved towards the passenger side, gallantly opening her door. She bestowed him a radiant, trusting smile in return. He reached his hand out to her. She happily accepted it.

"This place has special meaning to me. I've never brought anyone here before today," Michael told Brigid.

"There's something I want you to see," he said, steering Brigid onto a path she would never have seen if Michael hadn't pointed it out.

"Back home, I'd be taking off my shoes through here, but I'll just walk gently," Brigid murmured reverently, as she stared at the ground.

Michael didn't question her, merely slowed his pace. As they walked deeper into the park, the sounds of dogs barking, children laughing and couples strolling faded from sight. They found themselves alone, deep within the expansive wilderness.

"What's that over there? The colors are so extraordinary."

"That's what I want you to see."

"Well come on, it's calling us! Can't you hear it?"

She began to jog ahead of Michael, still cautious as to where her feet landed on the soft ground. Michael watched Brigid for a moment taking in the magic of the moment, then quickly caught up with the woman who was unaware of the powerful pull she had on him. Brigid stopped short, seeing a prickly bush at the trail's end. Michael bumped into her, but Brigid merely laughed.

"Can't we get any closer, Michael?" Brigid asked, anxiously.

Brigid needed to see whatever was beyond the thick barrier.

Michael gave a throaty laugh. "How much closer do you want to get mo ghrá?" he whispered in her ear.

She swatted playfully at him but treated him to a lingering, promising gaze before growing serious again.

"It's beautiful. Please tell me we can get to it," she whispered.

"We can, but we have to go through there."

He pointed at a small opening about two feet from the ground. "You afraid of a little dirt?"

She responded with an unladylike snort.

"How'd that get there?"

"I carved it out years ago."

"Come on, let's go," she said, tugging on his hand with childlike excitement.

Crawling through a small thicket on their hands and knees, Brigid felt alive. It seemed forever since her heart felt so light. Once through, she stood staring at a small, contained meadow with patches of emerald grass splattered as if by an artist's hand. In the middle grew a yew tree. The trunk equaled Malachi's in size and stood tall and healthy with its gnarled branches that twisted and turned downward then up again.

"Oh, my," Brigid glanced at Michael whose hooded stare took in every movement Brigid made. He wondered if she would see what he did the first time he stumbled upon his secret garden. He hoped she'd feel it course through her veins as it did him, and speak to her in the gentle whispers he always believed were reserved just for him. It was the first time since his parent's death, Michael wanted, no—needed, someone to understand him. He prayed that someone was Brigid.

"This tree," Brigid breathed, mesmerized by the ancient beauty before her. It looked to have multiple trunks intertwined over hundreds of years and braided into one, creating a solid fortress. Layers of soft moss blanketed the majestic tree like a cloak. Brigid struggled with her emotions, remembering in her youth when children teased her. Could she trust Michael with all she was feeling and with all she heard this stately, soulful tree whisper to her? This place was sacred ground, much like the Rafferty yew grove, and Brigid wondered if Michael knew it. He was standing so close behind her. She could feel his breath on her. The heat of his body all but merged with Brigid's.

"I saw you under that oak tree the day your dad gave us a tour of the yew grove. At the time, I didn't know it was you. I thought my eyes were playing a bloody trick on me, having seen some spirit in a hooded cloak. Then I saw a red ribbon blowing in the breeze, tied to a branch. I shouldn't have been able to see it. It was a stormy sky, but the ribbon, it was illuminated. I can't explain it, but I knew that when I saw the ribbon something major was going to change my life."

"Change your life? What do you mean," Brigid knew his answer would change her life as well.

"You put the ribbon on that oak tree in Oregon?"

"I did," she whispered.

He took Brigid's hand and walked to the opposite side of the yew. He didn't say anything as she stared at the faded and frayed red ribbon that fluttered in the breeze like an old friend waving hello.

"Michael, did you tie this ribbon here?"

"Sounds crazy, but my mom came to me in a dream when I was in my teens. It was It was a low point in my life. I felt I'd never find someone who would truly understand me—or I, them. I doubted everything, especially following through with my medical internship. I was so young. Anyway, she came to me and told me to find the old family ribbon."

Michael glanced at Brigid, feeling the need to explain. "It's a family thing with the ribbon. Family lore, but I'll tell you about it another time. However, Mom instructed me to tie the ribbon to my favorite branch. That way, my true love would know how to find me— and I, her. I remember climbing as high as I could, trying to find the perfect branch." He smiled at the memory. "Ha, I didn't want her to miss it out here."

"It's a perfect branch and a perfect ribbon," Brigid assured Michael.

"In the *dream*, I asked her how we'd find each other. She said something about this white bird with a crimson mask that would find my mate, and he would bring her to me. I figure it's a metaphor or something," Michael laughed.

"Turlough!" Brigid's eyes grew wide.

"That is the name my mom said in the dream. I have never told another living soul that name."

"Michael, tell me more!"

"Brigid, my mother promised me I would fall in love and marry a Great Healer from the New World, and I would know her by the red ribbon and her hair like a sunset."

Michael took a strand of Brigid's hair in his fingers and stroked it gently.

"Then, Mom laughed! I swear, her exact words were, *Don't worry Mikey dear, this is where the fun begins! I will help align everything and make it so simple, your young woman will fall at your feet, and you will never again feel alone!* Then, years ago, when you showed up the first time," Brigid cut in, "You mean when you literally found me in the hallway at your feet?" she quipped.

Michael turned towards Brigid. He stopped inches from her, lazily resting one muscular arm above her head on the corded yew trunk, then slowly leaned in, closing the gap between them.

"Mo ghrá, I've waited my whole life to find you. Tell me you are not a dream or some sprite that will disappear?"

Brigid tried to think of a witty response, but words weren't needed. She reached up and pulled Michael in for a sweet lingering kiss that left no doubt they were not dreaming.

"I talk to trees, Michael."

"Mmm, tell me more," he replied as he kissed her again.

Brigid told Michael all about her childhood. Although he stopped her occasionally to ask a question or two, she left nothing out.

Michael, in turn, entrusted Brigid with details on how he once almost took his life as a young boy.

"The world would be much darker without you, Michael MacShane," Brigid whispered as she stroked his cheek and placed a gentle kiss where her hand once laid.

"Mo ghrá," he sighed.

"Speaking of darker, it's getting late. Much as I hate to leave here we should get going." He took Brigid's hand and began leading her back through the meadow. "Promise me we can come back here again soon," Brigid said as they walked hand in hand, each processing the serendipitous events of their lives.

"So, the results!" Brigid blurted out, finally remembering the reason they were brought together. "Aye, the results. More than we hoped for." Michael stated.

"Incredible, right?"

"It's the proof we needed. We've got ourselves a cure for cancer." Michael affirmed.

"Just imagine, a world with no more fear, pain, and suffering," Brigid murmured.

"We have a ways to go, but it's a start," Michael confirmed.

41

The old house was empty and quiet as Ethan stood looking out the window at the massive oak, with the tire swing swaying in the breeze. He was missing Ashling and the life they once shared. It was a dark and dangerous road he was allowing himself to tread. Slowly Ethan walked to the minibar and poured himself a generous shot, then opted for a double. Before he could down the liquid that sometimes helped to take the edge off his pain, his cell phone pinged, alerting him to a text from Brigid.

Hey Dad! Be on the lookout for an email I'll be sending. We did it—You, Mom, all of us! Just wait until you read through it. It's extraordinary. We found a natural way to treat cancer without side effects. It's still top secret, so you can't tell anyone, but I couldn't keep it even a minute from you.

Ethan didn't care that a tear slid down his face while he read Brigid's text. Setting the alcohol aside, he grabbed his ball cap and proceeded outside. Looking out now over his property, he smiled thinking back to the day when Ashling told him how their yews were magical as she danced barefoot through the grove of trees. He wondered, as he had done many times over the years, just how long had Ashling known she had cancer, and that by harvesting the herbs that lay beneath the yews, and then brewing them into a tea with the bark from their trunks, that it would fuse within her body and aide it with the antibodies needed to find the cure?

She must have also known at some point the tea would stop working, yet still she allowed herself to be a vessel. Of course, Ashling would find a way around allowing cancer to define her life, just as others with a diagnosis do. She trusted her family lore about great healers—believing her body was a part of the Legacy and that MacShane's team needed it to conduct the final phase of experiments that led the way to legitimize the YBC. Of course, she would have kept the news that she donated her body to science from him until it was too late to stop her.

Because of Ashling's choices, real individuals experiencing remission, restored health and well-being, was not only possible now, but a reality.

"Ashling," Ethan ground out. "God forgive me, but I don't know if knowing all this now helps or not without you here to see our lifelong dream—decades of work, coming to fruition."

Without thinking, Ethan headed towards the oak. Twice he stopped to turn around, sure someone was following close on his heels. Both times all Ethan saw was his shadow.

"I'm losin' it," he mumbled.

Reaching Malachi, Ethan took his time walking around the broad base, then absently pushed the empty swing, feeling a gut-wrenching sadness. He shielded his eyes as he looked up at the red ribbon tied to a branch, then settled on the bench he remembered making as if it were just yesterday. He sat down like a weary old man, resting his head in his hands.

The wind picked up from out of nowhere, and Malachi's branches swished as loudly as the ocean waves crashing against large rocks.

"Hello?" Ethan lifted his head and looked around.

"Who's there," he called out.

No one answered.

Ethan grunted.

Amid the sudden windstorm, Ethan swore he heard Ashling. He knew it was just wishful thinking.

The gusts blew harder.

"It's time, darlin'! It's time for the fun to begin again."

Ethan stood, grabbing ahold of his hat so the burst of wind wouldn't sweep it away. As suddenly as it began, it stopped. The air became still. Malachi's branches now merely fluttered ever so lightly. A soft vibration hummed in the air.

Tun-tun, tun-tun, tun-tun.

Ethan stood and faced Malachi with a perplexed look on his face.

"Did you hear that," he asked the oak.

Silence.

Ethan willed the tree to talk to him.

Nothing.

He knew it was futile. He never could hear the tree.

"Dad, you out here?"

"Holy shit! I've lost my mind."

Again, "Dad?"

This time it was louder and closer.

Then he heard Brigid laugh.

"There you are. Surprise!" Brigid blurted out as she ran towards her father whose open arms were waiting as she flung herself into them.

"Sprite!"

"So, after all these years, I finally catch you and Mal having a heart to heart, huh?" Brigid beamed as Ethan held her at arm's length to get a better look.

"It was rather one-sided conversation," Ethan added wryly.

Brigid, who had been staring at Malachi, looked at her father now with a bittersweet expression.

Brigid walked to her beloved friend, resting her cheek on his gnarled trunk, and loving the feeling of her old friend's essence once again.

"Mal said, it wasn't him but Mom, you heard. Was she here with you. Did you hear her?"

Before Ethan had the chance to answer another, more profound, hello rang out.

"You hear that, right? If you don't, I think I'm going to need to see a different kind of doctor," Ethan said, not sure he was joking.

"I just happen to have brought one along with me," she laughed.

"We're over here," she called out as Michael MacShane appeared on the gravel path.

Brigid whispered, "I hope you don't mind. I brought a special friend home."

Ethan caught the look of love on his daughter's face. He saw the same look reflecting on Michael's. At that moment he swore he heard Ashling telling him to behave.

"Ethan, happy to see you again. Hope you don't mind me dropping in too. Brigid wanted to surprise you," he said in the way of a greeting as the two men shook hands.

Having recovered his wits, Ethan replied, "Don't mind it one bit. Hope you'll be staying a while this time?"

Ethan knew he sounded hopeful, but having Brigid home was something he had thought about more often lately.

"That's the plan if you'll have me. I came here to see you personally, sir. Her too, of course," Michael added with a quick wink as he inclined his head towards Brigid.

Brigid leaned a bit closer to Malachi and nodded her head. "Hey, why don't you two go bond for a few, I want to say hello to Mal for a minute. I think Michael wants to talk to you about something anyway, Dad."

Michael looked momentarily panicked but recovered quickly. "Still fond of those microbrews Ethan? It's been a long flight. We came here straight away from the airport, and I could sure use a drink about now."

Ethan nodded, somehow, aware of what Michael MacShane was nervous about, but it was a father's duty to make him squirm a little. He turned to lead the way back towards the house and whispered under his breath, "I could use your input about now, Ash."

Once again, the *tun-tun, tun-tun, tun-tun,* settled in his heart as a gust of wind brushed past Ethan.

Brigid turned and hugged her friend.

"Oh, Mal, I've really missed you! I have so much to tell you."

She settled on the old wooden swing, pushing back and forth with natural ease and began to tell her old friend all about her adventures. Malachi could feel the new leaves burst forth from his branches as he shaded his favorite human. He stretched his roots out as far as he could, relaxing into the comfort of the warm earth, feeling more alive than he had in years.

Epilogue

Ethan's laughter rang out as he sat on his front porch making silly faces at the toddler who was attempting to mimic the older man's expression. Sam joined in, causing Emma and Brigid to turn their heads and smile at the two men clearly enamored with the little boy.

"Here they come," Brigid said, turning her attention back to their driveway where three black SUV's came to a stop at the roundabout in front of the house. Michael emerged from the first vehicle and waved, winking at his wife who beamed with a radiant smile.

"Here, let me take him, Ethan. They'll be wanting your attention, and we know this little guy doesn't like to share you."

Ethan patted the blond-haired boy on the head as he handed him to his father.

"I don't know about this, Sprite. Is it too late to back out?" Ethan asked, coming to stand next to her on the porch.

"Way too late," Brigid laughed as she waved to the people walking towards them.

Ethan gave one last half-hearted attempt to turn away the attention about to take up the next couple months of their lives.

"Still think we are documentary worthy material?"

"These people certainly think so," Michael answered for Brigid, as he inclined his head towards the group walking towards Ethan on the porch.

The first person to walk up the steps with Michael looked like a breath of fresh air. She was a forty-something woman who exuded friendly energy as she bound up the steps.

"Sloane, this is Ethan Rafferty and my wife, Brigid."

The woman by Michael's side reached her hand out to Brigid first, "Sloane Collin's, great to finally see you face to face."

"We're excited to have you here," Brigid assured the woman who was staring now at Ethan with undisguised interest. Brigid thought it wasn't entirely professional interest she saw in the friendly woman's expression. A third person casually stepped off to the side of the wrap around porch and quietly began filming, trying his best to fade into the woodwork.

Ethan seemed momentarily flustered as he reached a hand out to the woman with fawn brown eyes and short-cropped hair.

"Nice to meet you, Sloane. Welcome to the Double R."

It wasn't lost on Brigid that both Ethan and Sloane may have lingered over their clasped handshake or that the confident-looking woman may have blushed ever so slightly. It was, however, the toddler who broke the spark of chemistry between the two newly acquainted pair.

"Me—me," the little boy called out stretching and reaching for Ethan.

"Asher wants to meet the pretty lady too, Dad," Brigid teased.

Sloane walked the few steps and stood next to Emma, Sam, and the engaging child with wiggling arms. "So, this must be the one and only Asher Bolden I have heard about," Sloane said as she cast a warm look Ethan's way.

"Yep. Emma and Sam here named the little bugger in honor of my wife, Ashling."

Then Ethan addressed Asher's parent's, "Sloane, these are the brains behind this operation, Emma, and Sam Bolden. I hold them responsible for all the excitement here today."

Both Sam and Emma chimed in their greetings. "Pleased to finally meet you, Ms. Collins. Your documentaries are legendary around these parts," Emma added.

"Ah, call me Sloane, please. I can't express how grateful I am that you both contacted me. I can't tell you all what an honor it is that you've chosen us to tell this amazing story."

Sloane gently held out her hand to Asher, who took it and squeezed her finger tightly.

"What a legacy of a name you have, little man. I have heard great things about your namesake. Ashling was a true visionary."

Heads nodded in agreement.

The rest of the film crew casually climbed out of the vehicles, stretching their legs and looking about the property. Camera operators began recording Sloane, who was both producer and director of the documentary series about the Rafferty's yews, their vision and finally the long road to finding a noninvasive cure for several types of cancer.

In the beginning, Ethan shied away from the idea, but his reservations were quickly soothed and overturned by Brigid, Michael, and the Bolden's assurance that the documentary would bring awareness regarding the effectiveness of the YBC Protocol, and hopefully open doors to its usage in the states. Eventually, Ethan blessed off on the project, and as he noticed Sloane, he was glad he did.

"There's a friggin' tree in the house! Dude, get your cameras and the sound-men in position, I want to get everyone's reaction to this," a focused crew member called out.

Ethan chuckled.

"Sloane, I hope the flight and drive were easy?" Ethan asked.

"I have family here, close by actually, so I've been staying in Oregon these past few weeks wondering why I've been away so long."

"Nothing compares to our Pacific Northwest, that's for sure," Ethan added holding the door for her.

Brigid elbowed Michael, who smiled at the instant connection Sloane and Ethan were sharing.

Ethan was attentive as he ushered Sloane into the kitchen where trays of food were laid out in a bountiful buffet.

"I hope everyone came with appetites. We've got a big lunch ready," Emma announced to the group. "I have a special treat for you.

Over here we have all of Ashling's famous cheeses. I'm shamelessly hoping your camera crew gets a few good shots! We never turn down good publicity," Emma teased.

Both Michael and Brigid's heads turned as they heard a cry from a baby monitor sitting on the island.

"God I've missed her sweetness," Michael crooned.

"Lizzy's missed her daddy something fierce," Brigid responded.

"She's too young to miss me, don't you think?"

Brigid turned toward her husband and taking his face in both her hands assured him, "Lizzy knows you, and you'll see the minute you walk into the room."

"Sloane, please excuse us for just a few. Dad, would you mind getting the line started so everyone can eat? We need to check on the baby."

Brigid kissed her father's cheek and smiled at Sloane.

"Keep an eye on this one for me, will you? If I know him, he's headed for dessert first."

Sloane gifted Brigid with a conspiring smile, "Since I always go for dessert first, you might have just asked the wrong woman!"

Ethan laughed, the rare laugh, that told Brigid her dad was still in there, waiting to come alive again.

As Michael pushed open the door to the room that once belonged to his wife, the most beautiful site caught his eyes. His turquoise-eyed infant connected with him and wiggled in a way that meant she knew her daddy was there. Without hesitation, Michael went to the fair-skinned child holding her arms out to him, as he gently picked her up, "I can't get enough of her, mo ghrá," he said as his voice caught.

Brigid stood next to her world and confirmed, "Neither can I."

Michael turned towards Brigid as he held his daughter in his arms, "Look, they're going to be busy the next hour or so with lunch. I want to go sit by Malachi with just you and Lizzie. I've got something for Little Miss here. Just feels right that I give it to her underneath Malachi's ever-watchful eyes."

Brigid was intrigued, "Really, husband? Do tell."

"Grab her blanket, let's go," was all Michael gave away.

Leaving through the back door, the new family headed down the old and well-worn path towards Malachi, laughing and chatting with their perfect little daughter all the way.

"Hello Mal, look who's here," Brigid said, then paused as she tilted her head.

"You think so?" Brigid asked the old oak.

"What'd he say?"

Brigid beamed, "He told me Lizzy looks like me more every day, only with your dark hair."

Michael kissed Brigid's forehead then led her to the bench. They sat in comfortable silence as they enjoyed the peacefulness that surrounded them. Brigid slipped off her sandals and squished her toes in the grass.

"Your dad and Sloane seemed to make a connection. Did you notice?"

"I did! I think it's great. Dad's been alone too long, and if he finds someone—well, I know Mom would be happy. I'd be happy."

"Are you happy Brigid MacShane?"

"More so than I ever dreamt I'd be."

Brigid became serious. "Michael, I have never known such peace or completeness as I have since I met you. We were meant to be, and our people made sure we would find each other. I am beyond blessed and happy."

Michael kissed the top of Lizzy's head and said, "While I was back in Scotland, giving my interviews to Sloane and the crew at the hospital, an old woman gave me an interesting gift. I'd never seen her before. It was rather surreal. She came up outta nowhere."

"Michael, tell me more."

"Well for a minute she just stood there and stared at me. I mean she was really old, and the whole thing was unsettling. She walked up to me and held out her hand. She must have motioned for me to open mine, and well, I did."

"What did she give you? What'd she say?"

"She said, *This belongs to Elizabeth Faith MacShane. When you return home, you must give it to her, and it will protect her always.*"

Brigid cocked her head to the side with a definite look of skepticism.

"I'm not joking, mo ghrá! Then she put this in my hand and walked away, singing a melody I used to hear in my dreams as a boy after my mom died."

"Show me," Brigid whispered.

He opened his clenched fist to reveal a crimson strip of faded cloth.

"Oh my, it has a single strand of *gold*," she said as if that explained it all.

"Gold?"

"It's the Legend of The Priestess, Michael. I assumed that it ended with me and you, but only once in all the history of this tale being retold, has there been mention of the ribbon with the single gold strand and that was when the Priestess predicted the Healer in the New World would one day eradicate the dark disease that overtook the land."

She went on, "I know it sounds crazy, but the Legend states, *The red ribbon with the gold thread, was said to be as old as the Moon Goddess.* None of the red ribbons before this one have had the gold thread!"

Lizzy looked at Brigid and cooed, as if in agreement with her mother.

"Well then, Little Miss, let's just put this around your wrist for the day, and when you are older, you shall keep it as a talisman. If you choose to save the world, your mom and I will be right by your side."

Lizzy cooed once again. Keeping her eyes focused on Malachi, she babbled as if carrying on the most interesting of conversations.

"Don't tell me," Michael shook his head in resignation.

"Are you sure you don't want to know?" Brigid asked with a twinkle in her eyes.

"I don't need to. I'm fairly sure you're about to tell me that Malachi just said something extraordinary to and about our daughter."

Brigid nodded her head.

Michael gently took Lizzy from Brigid. He walked closer to Malachi. Brigid stood, dusted herself off and went to sit on the old tree swing. She smiled at Michael who now held Lizzy up towards Malachi.

Tears filled her eyes as Malachi dropped a branch ever so gently, allowing one of his soft leaves to brush Lizzy's cheek. Michael appeared just as moved by Malachi's gesture.

"Dear child, Lizzy has your mother's essence within her. Michael's mother, Faith's, as well. Did you know that?"

"I feel them around Lizzy. It's comforting."

"What's Malachi saying mo ghrá?"

"That our moms are like her guardian angels."

"I wish they were physically here to watch her grow up," he said, looking at Malachi.

"Together we'll make sure she knows the role our moms played in not only our lives but the lives of so many others through their strength and courage," Brigid added.

"Come on, we better get back before we're missed," Michael said, taking Brigid's hand.

Brigid lay her cheek against Malachi's warm trunk. "I'll see you tomorrow." Then she added, hearing the loud whirring of Turlough's wings, "Looks like you've got more company. Tell him we said hello, Mal," and with a final pat on the burly oak's scales, Brigid wrapped Lizzy in her arms and turned for home as she heard Turlough break through the veil.

"Where is she off to old friend?" the crane asked as he dipped his neck in Brigid's direction.

"Home, to start the next adventure."

Does she know yet the role Elizabeth Faith is to play in the coming years?"

"No, not yet."

"There is much needed to rid the human's planet from the darkness that sometimes settles in their hearts. Greed, fear, the lost art of listening to each other. It is more disruptive than a cancer cell."

"Oh, but they now know how to reverse the disease in the body, and besides, it is not all doom and gloom old friend," Malachi said as a bright orb the size of golfball appeared and floated between the crane and oak tree.

Turlough began bobbing his head up and down in agreement with something the orb that they knew to be Ashling conveyed.

"I agree, child, this is where the fun begins again. Humans are far more capable of healing this planet than we once gave them credit for," Malachi affirmed.

The orb spoke again.

Turlough responded, "I suppose I agree, Ashling Elizabeth. More and more people are listening to their intuition and following their gut."

"What's most important is we will all be watching over them and guiding little Lizzy as she grows and explores her world. We will stand alongside her as she experiences times of the darkness of the soul, and celebrate her many achievements along the way," Malachi stated.

"And will she live a rich and full life, Mal?" Ashling questioned.

"Indeed, she will! We shall all nurture and protect her, dear child. Lizzy is greatly loved indeed. She will live a charmed life, and like you, will be the one who talks with trees."

As Ashling, Turlough and Malachi watched Brigid and her family walk away, the ever comforting, *tun-tun, tun-tun, tun-tun,* drifted softy in the air.

The End

Made in the USA
Monee, IL
11 January 2024

50819827R00177